THE SIREN

Also by Alison Bruce

Cambridge Blue

THE SIREN

Alison Bruce

Constable • London

Constable & Robinson Ltd
3 The Lanchesters
162 Fulham Palace Road
London W6 9ER
www.constablerobinson.com

First published in the UK by Constable,
an imprint of Constable & Robinson, 2010

First US edition published by SohoConstable,
an imprint of Soho Press, 2010

Soho Press, Inc.
853 Broadway
New York, NY 10003
www.sohopress.com

A copy of the British Library Cataloguing in Publication Data
is available from the British Library

UK ISBN: 978-1-84901-023-8

US ISBN: 978-1-56947-605-5
US Library of Congress number: 2010012916

Typeset by TW Typesetting, Plymouth, Devon
Printed and bound in the EU

1 3 5 7 9 10 8 6 4 2

Mixed Sources
Product group from well-managed
forests and other controlled sources
www.fsc.org Cert no. SA-COC-1565
© 1996 Forest Stewardship Council

To Jacen with love.

No More Blue Moon to Sing

– your lyrics say it all.

This book is dedicated to you.

ACKNOWLEDGEMENTS

This is the moment when I can show appreciation to the people who have helped me. Top of the list are Broo Doherty and Krystyna Green who have been wonderfully supportive throughout the writing of *The Siren*.

Thank you to Peter Lavery for his enthusiasm and thoroughness and to Richard Reynolds, Rob Nichols and Georgie Askew for their expertise.

For helping me research interesting injuries to live bodies I'd like to thank Dr TV Liew and for help with equally interesting dead bodies, thank you Dr William Holstein.

To Lisa Williams, Cher Simmons and Kat from Cherry Bomb Rock Photography – cheers, I had a great time.

And for both personal and creative reasons I'd like to publicly say a big thank you to the following:

Kimberly Jackson, Martin, Sam and Emily Jerram, Eve Seymour, Kelly Kelday, Claire and Chris, Stewart and Rosie Evans, Elaine McBride, Julia Hartley-Hawes, Dominique and Simon, Stella and David, Martin and Lesley, Tim and Diane, Laura, Laura and Charlotte, Genevieve Pease, Michelle White, Jo and James, Brett and Renee, Nicky and Alex, Neil Constable, Rob and Elaine, Gillian Hall, Shaun Gammage, Rob and Jo, Gloria and Martin, Barbara Martino and Alison Hilborne.

And last, but certainly not least, my totally brilliant step-daughter Natalie Bainbridge.

ONE

It was the red of the match heads that caught her eye.

Staring into the kitchen drawer, Kimberly Guyver had no doubt that the matchbook had been there since the day she moved in, and she didn't see how she could have overlooked it.

Its cover was bent back, so she picked it up and folded it shut. Its once familiar design consisted of nothing more than two words printed in gold on black, in a font that she happened to know was called Harquil.

It said: Rita Club.

She folded both hands around the matchbook, cupping it out of sight. She could feel the high-gloss card smooth against her palms. It reminded her how long it had been since her hands had been that silky, her nails as polished. It reminded her of Calvin Klein perfume. Of impractical shoes. Of sweat and vodka shots. And the pounding bass that had drowned out any attempt to reflect on the mess she was currently in.

Maybe the matchbook hadn't been hiding, because maybe she hadn't been ready to notice it until now.

She leant an elbow on the draining board, then plucked a match from one end of the row. It lit at the second attempt. She held it to the corner nearest the 'R' for 'Rita'. The card curled before succumbing to a lazy green flame. She wondered if it was toxic, and realized the irony if it was. It burnt slowly until the flame reached the match heads, which then ignited with a sharp bright burst.

She dropped the remnants of the matchbook into the sink, and kept watching it, determined to witness the moment when it finally

1

burnt itself to nothing. It was down to merely ash and a thin plume of smoke when the voice from the doorway startled her.

'Mummy.'

She took a moment to wipe her face and hands – long enough for him to speak to her again. This time his voice was slightly more insistent. 'Mummy.' He looked at her with a gaze that implied he knew far more than he was capable of knowing at two and a half, and she immediately felt guilty.

'Riley,' she answered, using the same urgent intonation. She held out her hand. 'Come and watch Thomas while I take a shower.'

She paused by the window, noting the afternoon sun was now low over Cambridge's Mill Road Cemetery, its glow picking out the wording on the south- and west-facing headstones, casting the others in deep shadow. It was hot for June, and any areas where the ankle-high grass grew without shade had already taken on the appearance of a hay meadow.

The burial ground was shared between thirteen parishes. She knew this because she knew the cemetery better than anywhere else, better than any other part of town, better than any of the many places she had briefly called home, even the one that had lasted for six years, or this current one where she'd lived for three. She knew the curve of each footpath, and she had favourite headstones. Plenty marked with 'wife of the above', but none, she noticed, marked 'husband of the below'. Lots, too, who 'fell asleep'. And if marriage carried kudos, so did age: in some cases a mark of achievement and in others a measure of loss.

She loved some stones for their ornate craftsmanship, others for their humble simplicity. She taught herself to draw by copying their geometry and scripts and fallen angels. The school claimed she had a natural aptitude for art but she knew it was the cemetery that taught her balance and perspective, light and shade and the importance of solitude.

In isolated moments, when her feelings of abandonment became all but overwhelming, she'd return to certain memorials that had stayed in her awareness after her previous visits. Like that of Alicia Anne Campion, one of the many who had *fallen asleep*. She'd gone in 1876 at the age of 51, and had been given a low sandstone grave topped with white marble, shaped like a roof with a gable at each end and one off-centre. The elaborate carving was still unweathered. Kimberly knew how to find it at night-time and had often sat there in the dark, with her back against this grave and the pattern close to her cheek, her fingers tracing the crisp lines that the stonemason had chiselled.

Mill Road Cemetery was also the place she'd hidden when, at fourteen, she'd tried her first cigarette, and where, at fifteen, she'd lost her virginity to a boy called Mitch. She never found out whether Mitch was part of his first name or his last, or no part of his real name at all. He'd smoked a joint afterwards, and she tried it for the first and only time. He then told her to fuck off. The smoke made her feel queasy and giddy, so she stumbled and caught her knuckle on the sharp edge of a broken stone urn, and went home with blood smears on her hands and a new anger ignited in her heart.

But no bad choice was going to come between her and the way she felt for that place, and she later exorcized the memory of it with a succession of equally forgettable boys, until nothing but Mitch's name and a vague recollection of smoking pot stayed in her head.

People walked through all the time, taking shortcuts, taking lunch. People actually tending graves were few, and she guessed that the number of people who knew the place as well as she did was even less. Most visitors didn't know about the thirteen parishes; even fewer knew that the curved paths and apparently shambolic layout of trees and graves formed a perfect guitar shape. She'd sketched a plan of it one day, then in disbelief double-checked a map and, sure enough, found this huge guitar hidden in the centre of the city.

The guitar's neck belonged to the parish of St Andrew the Less and, although level with the rest of the cemetery, it stood a storey higher than the houses backing on to its west side. They were Victorian terraces, originally two-up, two-down workers' houses, but almost all of them had since been extended.

One of these was Kimberly's. It had a single-storey extension that stretched to within a few feet of the cemetery's perimeter wall. When she first moved in, she'd seen that as providing a good fire escape: an easy climb through her sash window, then across the flat roof to safety. But, almost as soon as he had been big enough to stand, she'd realized Riley's fascination with the large open space that lay just over their garden wall.

For now, though, Thomas the Tank Engine was enough to hold his interest, so she left him sitting on one of her pillows, hypnotized by the TV at the foot of her bed. Just this one time, she hoped he would leave her to shower in peace, enjoying the water close to scalding and the jets needling her skin.

She reached for a towel, realizing that she'd stayed in the shower for much longer than she had planned to. She could hear the Fat Controller having a few issues with one of the less useful engines, and knew the DVD had been on for over half an hour.

'Riley?' she called. With no response, she guessed he was probably just too engrossed to hear her, and she called him again.

She took another towel and wrapped her wet hair in it, then returned to the bedroom just as the theme song began. Thomas the Tank Engine was chuffing along the track with the credits flying up the screen, but Riley had climbed under the covers and was sleeping too deeply to care. Kimberly curled up beside him, wrapping her arms around him, and he shifted a little, resettling with his head closer to hers. His hair tickled her cheek. He smelt of baby wipes and jacket potato, and his proximity soothed her more than any amount of showering could have done.

It was a tranquil moment, broken only by the main-menu loop on the DVD, then a few seconds of cheery music that had already been repeated too many times. Kimberly stretched herself towards the remote, aiming to scoop it near enough to reach the mute button. She touched one of the channel buttons instead, and the image that flickered on to the screen seemed as familiar as Thomas the Tank Engine.

She recognized that skyline, the rocky outcrop, the barren coastline. But she took a second or two to understand this was no DVD, no fictional footage. It was the news.

A fragment of her life was appearing on the television and, as sure as the carving on Alicia Campion's grave, its details were now set in stone.

She felt realization burn through her chest, dropping like a molten leaden weight into the pit of her stomach. She saw the winch, and the wreck of Nick's car that now hung from its hook. The car that she'd last seen when that same stretch of the Mediterranean sea had swallowed it.

The reporter's voice began to penetrate her shock. 'The vehicle was recovered last week after some divers reported that it appeared to contain human remains. It wasn't until today that the Spanish authorities have been able to confirm the identity of the occupant. The victim is named as former Cambridge man Nicholas Lewton, who had been living and working in Cartagena until his disappearance almost three years ago. Police are now appealing for information, and a spokesman has confirmed that this death is being treated as suspicious.'

The phone sat on the bedside table nearest to the window. It rang just as she was reaching for it. She looked out across the cemetery, towards the rear of another row of houses. Because they were built on higher ground, her bedroom directly faced the rear windows of their ground floors. One of them had been sandblasted, leaving its brickwork paler than that of its neighbours. Trees rose in-between, but she could see its upper floor catch the last of the sunshine and glow a fireball orange.

The ground floor of the same house was partly obscured in summer, but Kimberly knew that her caller was standing just inside its patio door. Probably squinting into the sun, staring over at Kimberly's house, waiting for her to answer the phone.

Kimberly pressed the 'answer' button. 'I saw it,' she said. 'Let me get dressed. I'll meet you outside.'

TWO

Kimberly grabbed some clean knickers and a bra from her chest of drawers, then pulled a dress from her wardrobe. Tugging them on quickly, she scooped up Riley, draping him over her shoulder, hoping he wouldn't stir, then managed to transfer him into his push-chair without waking him. She left her house by the front door, and hurried to the nearest entrance leading into the cemetery, a narrow gateway at the top of the guitar's neck. The path ran in an arc that curved like a broken string towards the other side of the green enclosure. She and Rachel always met at the midpoint, a circle that had once been the site of the chapel of St Mary the Less.

Kimberly arrived first. There were four benches, spaced around the outside of the circle, and she chose the one which would give her the best view of Rachel's approach.

It was a few minutes later before she saw Rachel's figure appear briefly, then disappear, between the trees and shrubs further along.

She could easily have cut across and made it in half the time, since Rachel knew her way round here almost as well as Kimberly did. This was a good sign, Kimberly decided: a sign that Rachel didn't feel the same panic as she herself felt.

She watched Rachel reappear from behind a yew tree and disappear behind an overgrown buddleia, noticing that her friend's stride, though brisk, was not rushed. *Measured*, that was the word. Rachel was always the calm one, weighing up the options, measuring her response. It was a joke between them: Kimberly gets them both into trouble, Rachel gets them out.

The sun was at the back of her neck, reaching its still warm fingers around on to one cheek. It was a slow, burning heat that made her feel impatient to get out of it.

When Rachel emerged into view again, she was still about a hundred feet away, but Kimberly sensed there had been a change in her friend. In the few seconds she'd been out of sight, she'd been overtaken by a shadow. There was now a slowing of her usually lively stride, a new gravity dragging at her limbs, like hesitancy and indecision were both pulling at her hem. There was maybe eighty feet between them now, and Rachel's features appeared as nothing more than shadows and indistinct shapes, but they were composed differently today.

Riley moved one arm out into the sun, and Kimberly used this movement as a reason to turn her attention to him and fold it back inside the shade of the canopy. She knew she was kidding herself; in truth she felt like she'd been staring at Rachel, in some kind of bad way. She waited until Rachel was about twenty feet away before looking up at her again, hoping to find comfort there.

Rachel's toe caught in a small ruck in the grass and, momentarily, she stumbled. It was nothing, just a tiny break in her stride, but it seemed to be a further sign of the way her previously graceful gait had become self-conscious and unsure. She stopped ten feet off, and managed a small smile: one that flickered on to her face and was gone in the next instant. Kimberly had painted Rachel's portrait many times, but never like this. Not ever. Something fragile but significant had deserted her friend.

Kimberly felt her stomach lurch.

She glanced around her, taking in everything as if it was the first time they'd come back to this spot in ten years. If the grass that lay between them looked the same as it ever had, it was the only thing that did. The graves were older, some had crumbled, others had toppled. The surrounding houses were filled with new families. The drugs were harder, and year on year the rain fell ever heavier. And neither of them were children anymore.

Kimberly stood up and stepped a little closer.

Rachel frowned. 'I was as quick as possible,' she said. And spoke as if answering a question. Making a defence.

'I know. It's OK.'

'Is it?'

'Shit, Rach, it's got to be.' Kimberly heard the tautness in her own voice.

In response, Rachel closed her eyes and pressed her hands over her ears. Kimberly had never noticed the frown lines on Rachel's forehead until now.

'Rach, what is it?'

'We should go.'

Kimberly glanced around.

'No, Kim, I mean *go* go,' Rachel corrected her, 'leave the area until it's sorted.'

'We already did that, remember?' Kimberly's thoughts were suddenly overtaken by the idea that she'd seen some fundamental part of the picture through the wrong lens, or from the wrong angle. She couldn't decide what exactly, just that her view had somehow become distorted.

Rachel shook her head and turned away, but not before Kimberly had spotted the tears welling in her friend's eyes.

She found herself at Rachel's side, wrapping her arm around her shoulder. 'This isn't like you at all. I'm relying on you to bail me out.' Kimberly gently turned Rachel's face towards her. 'Tell me what's wrong.'

Kimberly guessed she knew Rachel better than anyone, and she could only remember Rachel crying twice before, once at her mother's funeral and once at school on the day they'd met. Kimberly was the emotional, volatile one, while Rachel was the thinker, the planner. Never the crying type.

Rachel blinked and tears fell from both eyes, making identical trails down each side of her symmetrical face. She didn't meet Kimberly's gaze, but instead stared past her and into the pushchair. She tried to speak but the sentence churned into a sob. There was definitely something odd about the way Rachel stared at Riley, and the unease twisted tighter in Kimberly's gut.

Rachel's breathing steadied for a moment. 'I didn't know you'd have Riley,' she blurted.

'I wasn't going to leave him indoors, was I?'

'I don't mean now. I meant . . .' Rachel held out her hands in an expansive gesture, a gesture that said *Think bigger*.

'You meant what?' Kimberly demanded, but she could already see she'd been naïve. She felt a familiar anger rising, and she tried to restrain it, grabbing at its tail and willing it to go quietly back into its cage.

Kimberly asked her again, knowing that her voice sounded hard and unforgiving. 'What was it you meant?'

This was the wrong tactic with Rachel, and Kimberly knew it. Rachel stiffened, then pulled away and began walking the more direct route back to her house.

By the time Kimberly had manoeuvred the pram across the bumps and heavy clumps of grass, Rachel had almost reached the low wall before her back garden.

Kimberly spoke again as soon as she thought she was close enough to be heard. 'Please, Rachel, I don't understand.' Parking the pushchair, she caught up with her finally and reached out for the woman's arm. 'What's scaring you, Rach?'

The next moment Rachel was hugging her, constantly repeating her name. Kimberly held her close at first, gripping her as tight as she was being gripped. Then the seconds began to stretch on too long. This wasn't just an expression of close friendship, and Kimberly didn't understand it. It began to feel claustrophobic. She needed to know what Rachel was now feeling, needed to catch her breath and assess this new pitch of emotion. *Is this love or fear, or something else? Regret perhaps?*

But, in their relationship, Kimberly believed she was the sole custodian of all the regret. She'd held on to it for so long now.

She eased herself free.

'I know how much I owe you. I'll never forget that, and I'd never want you in any danger because of me.'

Rachel turned to her, her eyes already puffy and her nose running. Her words sounded thick and heavy. 'Everything's scaring me. You, Stefan . . . the whole fucking, miserable mess.'

Then, Rachel began backing up as she continued, 'Go away. Take Riley and go. I'm not going to tell you anything you don't already know, so don't ask me any more. Just get away from Cambridge.'

'I don't know *everything*, do I? What's it got to do with Riley?'

'Kim, there's nothing else I can say.'

'There is. Just tell me what's happened.'

Rachel hesitated and, when she finally spoke, her voice was barely audible: 'You saw the news?'

Kimberly couldn't let it go so easily and followed her right up to the low wall. 'Spain's a thousand miles away, probably more. It has nothing to do with Cambridge.'

Rachel shook her head and stepped right over the wall. They were only thirty feet from the pushchair but Kimberly wasn't prepared to be any further from her son. She hurried back to collect it, and pushed the buggy towards Rachel. 'Wait, there's something else, isn't there?'

'You really must go away from here.'

'I can't just vanish.'

'You have to. I'm going early tomorrow.'

'Without Stefan?'

'No.' It was Rachel's instant answer, then she checked herself. 'Maybe. Look, the less you know the better.'

'You've had it all planned.'

Rachel shrugged, but seemed increasingly uncomfortable.

'Why didn't you warn me earlier?'

Rachel shook her head. 'It was an old plan – one we never thought we'd need.' Again her gaze alighted on Riley.

'Is he in danger, too?' Kimberly whispered.

She guessed Rachel wished she could deny it, but instead she gave her a small nod. It did nothing to soften the sense of betrayal: Rachel had let her down but more than that she'd let Riley down.

The truth of the situation seemed to strike Rachel only then. She paused, then said, 'OK, how long do you need?'

Kimberly couldn't help the sarcasm. 'To arrange a new life?' she snorted.

Rachel didn't visibly react. 'To collect some cash and a car and go,' she said quietly.

That sobered Kimberly. 'I don't know.'

'I'm all ready. Why don't I take Riley for a few hours? Pick him up when you're sorted.'

'I don't know . . .'

'It's all I can offer.'

And Kimberly could tell then that there was no half-truth or selfishness in the suggestion. 'Help me get the pram over the wall.'

Rachel nodded reassuringly. 'You know I'll look after him. I've always tried, you realize. And, Kim, please don't tell anyone else what I'm doing.'

Kimberly nodded silently, then hung back until both of them were out of sight. She finally made her decision and turned – but not towards home. Instead she left the cemetery at the south-west exit, then broke into a run.

Change was in the air, and it smelt sour. Maybe there was something bad coming, or perhaps it was already blowing in and opening up gangrenous wounds in her current life. One thing was certain; it was stirring up the one memory that she never wanted to revisit: hot pavements and the sound of her own footsteps echoing on them as she ran for help.

THREE

Rachel was in the habit of deliberately studying her own house each time she approached it, no matter how short a time she'd been away or which elevation she was facing. It was a habit she had developed as a form of motivation, a reminder of how far their hard work had brought them and what they could accomplish when they remembered to work together. She had finally realized that such achievements had been brought about by nothing but her own determination. And, although her motivations subsequently changed, her habit of staring at the house remained.

It was a mid-terrace residence with a small passage that led from the back garden straight through to the street at the front. Including this in its overall ground plan made the house several feet wider than the neighbouring properties. It had allowed Rachel and Stefan space for an upstairs bathroom and an en-suite extension to their bedroom. The house was one hundred and seven years old and had spent the entire post-war period mostly in the hands of the same family.

The first thing they had done was hire a skip. Apart from three brief trips to the landfill site near Milton, it remained outside for a full week as layers of the house's history were stripped away and discarded. The thick brown and cream lounge carpet, the wood cladding from the chimney breast along with the two-bar electric fire with the fake coals. A free-standing kitchen unit and a Belling cooker. The twin tub with its flaking paint, rusting from the bottom up. A double bed with velour headboard and the plastic laundry basket printed with orange and yellow flowers all over its lid. Interior doors, strips of old skirting, the sink, the bath, the immersion heater, and on and on until all that remained had been a windowless, featureless shell.

They'd then extended outwards at the back and upwards into the loft. And the builders had used the narrow side passage each time new building materials were delivered. Everything from wiring and plaster to shelves and cushions was replaced.

But the passage itself stayed, too convenient to be deprived of it for the sake of a few extra square feet of floor space. They'd never worked out how to give the place a more contemporary feel, and so this passageway and the one surviving plum tree stayed as relics of the house's original guise as a cramped and unfashionable Edwardian family home.

Although Rachel always studied her own home in this way, she rarely thought about it in any depth. For some reason today was different, and by the time she'd manoeuvred Riley's pushchair in through the patio doors, she was preoccupied with the idea that she was leaving the one place they'd truly made their own.

She corrected herself: the one place *she'd* truly made *her* own.

Rachel drew a deep breath and wondered if living alone somewhere new would really be any better.

It was her exchange with Kimberly that had brought about this occasional sentimentality, Kimberly whose pregnancy had brought her a sense of purpose as well as a beautiful baby boy. Rachel loved this house but it was just a house, a means to an end. Her next steps were all about getting herself to a point where she could afford to be sentimental. The chance to become as lucky as Kimberly.

She lifted Riley on to the settee, and he opened his eyes. 'Hi, Riley. It's Rachel.'

'Where's mummy?'

'Gone shopping.'

That satisfied him clearly. He was still drowsy and turned his head to one side.

'Sleepy boy,' she murmured and stroked his hair. He seemed oblivious to her and a minute later she was in the kitchen with the hob alight and a deep pan of cold water sitting over it. She was sure he would come to find her when he wanted attention. And, even though she couldn't see him, she'd hear him if he called out.

13

She went back to thinking about the house, trying to imagine locking the door for the last time, then telling herself that there was no point in getting emotional when the decision had already been made.

She was far too deep in thought to notice the lengthening of the shadows outside the kitchen window, or the TV burbling in the front room. It was the key in the latch that made her start, and notice that the water in the saucepan was now boiling. The tiles behind the cooker were moist with steam.

She glanced at her watch but didn't bother looking out into the hall. 'You're early,' she called.

There was no reply, so she tried again. 'Stefan, I'm in the kitchen.'

She listened for a reply but, if he had bothered speaking at all, he'd only mumbled one, merely grunting back at her some dutiful greeting. 'Sulky git,' she muttered, slowly drying her hands on the nearest tea towel, feeling acutely aware of how stale the air became when they shared it. She knew she should go to welcome him, though, and make the effort for one last meal.

She straightened up, determined to seem caring, relaxed, content and display every other positive aspect of being happily married that it was appropriate for him to see.

That lasted all the way along the hallway and as far as the front room, where he stood in the doorway with his back to her.

'When d'you want dinner?' she asked, her smile fading as he turned and she could see the darkness in his expression. She glared instead, knowing that the words would come out of her mouth sounding sharp and indifferent. 'What's up now?'

She looked inside the room and the answer was all too obvious. While she'd been distracted by a saucepan of boiling water, Riley had gone out of the lounge and found the CD racks in the front room. There were at least thirty cases, now separated from their disks and booklets. She knew immediately that most of them were hers, but she doubted that would change the outcome.

'What the fuck's he doing here?'

Rachel lowered her voice, hoping he would take the hint and do the same. 'That's not why you're back?'

He kept his voice at the same pitch, not exactly loud considering it came from a six-foot-two wall of a man. But it was loud enough. 'Answer the fucking question.'

'You're back because you saw the news?'

'I said answer the fucking question.'

For the first time Riley glanced over at them. He grinned and shook another loose CD on to the floor.

'Shhh,' Rachel said, 'I *am* answering.' She backed away from the door, jerking her head to persuade him to follow her to the kitchen. Thankfully he did.

'No, you're not.'

'Shut up, let me finish, and you'll see that I'm actually answering the fucking question.'

She paused, wondering whether she'd already pushed her luck too far. He looked angry, pissed off even, but was yet to tip into the *dangerous* mood. She knew she now had to try to keep things smooth.

'Go on, then.'

'You saw the news, and Kim's seen it too. I've taken Riley while she sorts some stuff out. She's going to leave town for a while.'

'Like we don't have our own shit?'

'It won't hurt for us to stick together.'

She saw him change then, a tiny twist in his expression, more tension evident round the mouth and a narrowing of the eyes. His voice took on another tone, a kind of one-wrong-step-and-you're-out type vibe.

'You mean loyalty? That's new.'

'What?'

'All this faithful crap doesn't include me, does it?'

'I haven't a . . .' She could see where this was going but had no idea why they were heading there. She tried to remember anything she might have said or done to trigger this jealousy. She kept returning to the idea that somehow he'd discovered the only thing that couldn't be explained away. He was standing about six feet from her but his fury seemed to fill her entire field of vision.

'I kept my mouth shut. I put up with your coldness, always avoiding me touching you, but don't you think it's always on my mind, Rachel? I don't need you telling me how you're going to stand by her, when you won't stand by me. Rubbing my face in the shit like that. Do you see what I'm saying? Do you? You have pushed me until all I want to do now is snap. I'm not keeping my mouth shut any longer. So tell me . . .'

'What?' He waited for just a few seconds before he spoke, but to Rachel it felt like several long minutes, and in that time she was no closer to finding anything to say to save her situation.

When he finally whispered the words, she wanted to sob with relief. 'Who are you shagging?'

Who are you shagging?

She shook her head and kept her response low-key. 'No one.'

'Liar.' He stepped closer, and in response she stepped backwards. The wall behind her was nearer than she expected, so she found herself pressed up against it. Stefan leant towards her, one broad hand pressed to the wall on either side of her face.

She tried to turn away, but those big hands were quick and she found herself slapped back against the wall. 'This is stupid,' she breathed.

He just shook his head. 'I have to know,' he said finally.

'There's no one.'

He grabbed her face, cupping it in his hands, pressing his thumbs into her cheekbones. 'Tell me.'

Out of the corner of her eye she saw Riley appear in the hallway. He remained silent, with an intent expression on his face. Stefan gripped her just as tightly as she tried to smile despite the pain.

She knew he would let her go soon, and until then there was nothing else to say.

FOUR

It was approaching 8 p.m. and the afternoon had faded. Inside Parkside Pool the artificial lighting maintained the illusion of daylight, but the restaurant had already closed and the children's swimming class had finished. Only a few adult swimmers remained to wind down the day.

The man at the very back of the viewing gallery sat low in his seat. He held open a copy of *The Times* but wasn't reading anything on the page in front of him. Below him, Gary Goodhew swam the last of his hundred lengths with the same swift but unrushed front crawl that he'd used on the first. He cut a clean line through the pool, with a technique close to textbook perfect and timing that was damn near metronomic.

Goodhew left the water then. He didn't use the steps, just made the sort of easy exit rarely accomplished by the unfit or overweight. Judging by the female lifeguard's intent expression, she'd already spotted that he was neither. He tugged his towel from the back of a chair and rubbed his hair a couple of times, enough to leave it looking about as tidy as it ever appeared. He headed towards the men's changing rooms, as lithe and almost as fluid when he walked as when he was swimming.

The spectator slipped away then, similarly fluid and equally focused, the evening having proved more than satisfactory. It had taken Goodhew forty minutes to swim just over a mile and a half, and in that time he had demonstrated discipline, fitness and an undoubted capacity for patience. Perhaps patience was the wrong term for it, more like a determination to play the long game. All of

17

these were attributes that Goodhew normally hid behind a mask of quiet diffidence.

Not that this was news to the spectator, who had drawn several conclusions before today, and was only present here to confirm them. DC Gary Goodhew, the youngest detective serving at Cambridge's Parkside Station, wasn't the only one capable of silently observing the truth.

From leaving the water to exiting the building Goodhew took less than ten minutes. It wasn't a hot summer yet, but more than warm enough to lift the remaining dampness from his short and slightly unkempt hair. He ran his fingers just once through the front, as if that would salvage something. There wasn't any particular style to salvage, so the result was pretty irrelevant.

As he turned right from the pool, the Parkside Station fell within his line of sight, and he wondered what would be waiting for him on his return. But then, as he turned right yet again into Mill Road, he forced his thoughts away from matters of work.

In fact the coming fortnight would hold nothing more taxing for him than meeting a light-hearted challenge set by his grandmother. Just returned from two weeks in Cuba, she had flown back bursting with stories of jazz and salsa clubs. She reckoned that his choice of spending his two weeks' holiday in Cambridge couldn't touch that, especially when the place was already his home town.

He'd grinned and said, 'You'll see,' despite having virtually no plans yet for his time off.

Now he walked alongside the clog of traffic that inched slowly in each direction, first overtaking then being overtaken by cars that were heading away from the city centre. In recent years Mill Road had become an end-to-end traffic queue, but it was far more than just a commuter route. The shops ranged from a tattooist and a traditional toyshop to antiquarian books and an oriental supermarket, with newsagents and kebab shops in between. Some had unlocked their doors at 6 a.m., while others would stay open until two the following morning. No other part of Cambridge was so diverse or vibrant.

Goodhew took the next side street, and from there it was just a short walk to the former bus garage that housed the car-repair workshop of O'Brien and Sons. In fact there was only one son but apparently Vincent O'Brien had always been inclined to exaggerate. The old man was semi-retired now and mostly Bryn worked alone, grumbling that he was tempted to amend the sign to read 'O'Brien's Son'.

Their paths had crossed a few weeks earlier, and maybe if they hadn't been at the same primary school they wouldn't have bothered maintaining any contact. But that small patch of common ground had proved enough of a link for them to forge the early part of what might potentially grow into a firm friendship.

Or potentially amount to nothing.

Gary was still taking stock and as cautious of becoming close friends with the bad boy and joker of the class as Bryn himself was undoubtedly cautious about becoming mates with the class loner. Old reputations could prove stubborn ones to shake.

For now, though, Goodhew was more than happy to take the suggestion of an evening spent visiting a few local pubs entirely at face value. This was his fortnight off, after all.

So far, he'd found Bryn easy company, almost like they'd been friends all along rather than just acquaintances with a fifteen-year gap in their joint history.

There were no cars parked outside but the concertina doors were still open, and Bryn's turquoise and white Zodiac was parked in the centre of the workshop beyond. Bryn had changed out of his overalls but still had a spanner in one hand, which he raised in greeting when he spotted Goodhew.

'What do you think?'

The car had just been repaired and resprayed. 'It's good.'

Bryn stood at the back of the car and surveyed the repair from an acute angle. 'It's more than good.'

'Have you been admiring that car all afternoon?'

'Absolutely.' Bryn shrugged happily. 'And how did you get here?'

'Walked, why?'

'What is it with you and cars? You're in the middle of a two-week holiday, so I thought the first thing you'd do is sort yourself out with a vehicle.'

'I don't really need one.'

Bryn possessed a habitually open expression, with big eyes under eyebrows that always seemed slightly raised. He raised them a little further. 'You should still get one. People like to know about your car; it tells them something.'

'I'm not getting a car just to tell people which pigeon-hole I belong in.'

'Yeah, but the no-car pigeon-hole is for pensioners, misfits, eco warriors and the really skint. Oh, yeah, and the losers who've lost their licence and have no hope of getting it back, ever. If you had a car, it would be easier for people to weigh you up.'

'And I suppose you're going for quirky, retro, in a kind of James Dean way?'

Bryn grinned. 'No, I'm going for *He looks like fun and isn't that car cute with its roomy interior and leather upholstery.*'

'And that works?'

'Yeah, girls love it. We could take it out tonight.'

'To go two hundred yards?'

'Trust me, we'll park it outside, then sit at a table right next to it.'

'If you say so,' said Goodhew and he smiled, mostly to himself. Bryn was a natural flirt and it was this and his laid-back charm which drew women, not his beloved car. In fact, Bryn possessed a natural lack of inhibition, a quality that Goodhew could recognize but never himself own.

Bryn lobbed the spanner so it landed in the top tray of his tool chest. 'Let's go.'

The Zodiac turned out of the yard, its engine burbling and the chrome glinting under the orange glow of the street lights, and somehow Goodhew couldn't help feeling that they were driving towards far more than just another night at the pub.

FIVE

By 9 p.m. most of the through traffic had gone and Mill Road was now occupied meeting the demands of the local populace, news-agents and convenience stores seeing a steady stream of customers while the pubs and takeaways geared up for the Friday-evening rush. The air had cooled but the pavements still radiated a lazy warmth, and there was no urgency to the general busy-ness.

One figure moved a little faster than the rest. The boy was about seventeen years old, eighteen at most. He wore a hooded sweatshirt and baggy jeans, with hefty trainers that looked as though they really belonged to someone several inches broader and taller. He walked quickly with loping strides, concentrating his weight on the balls of his feet like he needed to fill out his gait as well as his clothes. His eyes stayed on the path, a few feet ahead of him, only glancing up every thirty seconds or so to take in a new snapshot confirming his route towards the cemetery.

He heard his name being called, and stopped briefly to join a group of five other teenagers hanging around outside an off-licence. He stopped for as long as it took to blag a cigarette and roll it and light it. 'Cheers,' he nodded, unsmiling, then added, 'Later.'

He was slightly built and wiry, with an arrogance in the way he walked, like a boxer, though he wasn't.

Just before he reached the Locomotive pub, he crossed over the road in a diagonal line, ignoring the traffic and slapping the roof of a small red Fiat which refused to slow for him to pass.

He turned immediately right, heading down a long straight avenue of sixty-feet-high trees, and through the gateway at the south-west corner of Mill Road Cemetery. The area was unlit, but enough grey daylight remained to show him the way.

The path split and he followed it to the left, along the rear perimeter fence of Anglia Ruskin University, until it curved again. He slowed, checking that he was still alone, then slipped through a gap in the shrubbery.

Eight minutes later he reappeared, a little less cocky but still as alert, and began to give the area one more 360-degree scan. He had made it through less than ninety degrees before something caught his eye. He stood stock-still, adjusting his vision to the strange flickering, and confirming that his orientation was correct. Then he took off. He ran, keeping to the centre of the pale gravel path, and glancing regularly from the fire to the track and then back to the fire.

He already realized that a Gwydir Street house was burning, but now needed to know which one. There would be other people moving across the cemetery, shadowy figures, drawn to the hypnotic dancing light at the upstairs windows. He had to get there faster. He sprinted, finally leaving the path and stumbling over unlit and uneven clumps of grass.

As he reached the property's low rear-garden wall, he gasped. 'Oh, fuck.'

He scrambled over the wall and ran to the patio door. It was locked. He cupped his hands to the glass, and peered inside, but found the curtains drawn. Behind him someone shouted, 'Get back!' but he barely heard it over the sound of the house whispering and crackling in his ear.

He banged on the glass with his fist. 'Open the door.'

He ran along the passage to the front of the house, and banged on the door there too. He then looked through the letterbox, found the hallway was empty. He turned his head to one side and tried to peer up the stairs. The top step was just in view, lit by a slow strobing of heavy light interrupted by thick smoke curling downwards.

He shouted through the gap, 'Rachel? Rachel!' then threw his whole body at the front door. It held too solidly.

There were other people out in the street by now, alerted by his shouting and then seeing the first signs of fire appearing in the upstairs windows at the front. He was oblivious to them as he dialled 999 on his mobile. 'Fire!' he shouted into the phone, then repeated the address when he spoke too quickly.

A hand tugged at his arm and he turned round to see a middle-aged man.

'You need to get back, son.'

'I can't.'

'Is someone in there?'

They both looked towards the front door.

'I dunno, but I need to find out, don't I? We gotta break in. We can smash that panel then unlock it.'

'No, that could cause a fireball.'

'She could be trapped.'

'I called the fire brigade, too. Just wait.'

'No, I can't.' He was no more than six feet away from the door, but he already knew that trying to force the lock was a mistake. The weak point was the thin pane, so he jumped at it, kicking out with his oversized trainers. He thought at first that the double glazing had shattered but, although the exterior glass broke, the interior pane had only crazed. He fell back on to the pavement, still staring at the stubborn door, just as the upstairs windows blew out. As glass rained down on him, he bent his head, stunned and defeated. Knowing that he couldn't yet grasp all the implications.

He staggered to his feet, aware for the first time of the drama that he and the middle-aged man had played out in front of a larger audience.

In the distance sirens wailed. They would be coming from the left, so he turned right and ran for it, bursting through the thin barrier of voyeurs and towards the safety of Mill Road.

SIX

Bryn knew that taking the Zodiac was an inconvenience, since he'd have to drive it back to the garage after his second pint. No way was he going to leave it parked outside overnight, or let it be out of his sight. But he also wanted to find out whether Gary had ever experienced the buzz of just hanging out in a car this cool, and whether it was possible to inject a little harmless irresponsibility into their evening.

After the first fifteen minutes, he realized such effort was wasted. Gary calmly pointed out that they were doing little more than a walking pace, and besides there was not anywhere to park.

Bryn cast him a sideways glance. 'Cars really aren't your thing, are they?'

'Only in a practical way – on a par with a microwave or washing machine.'

'Right.'

Bryn swung the car into a side street; never mind the availability of decent beer, he knew that the Six Bells offered the perfect combination of two pavement tables and some roadside parking. And today their luck was in: not only was there an empty parking bay but two empty seats almost next to it. Shame they'd have to share the table with two girls.

He pretended to ignore them as he reversed his car into the available space, but in truth he'd already noticed that they were both blonde, nicely tanned and about his and Gary's age.

Within five minutes of sharing the same table they discovered that the girls were called Becky and Trina. Trina was tall and quiet, while

24

Becky was attractively plump and wore black shorts and high heels. Bryn loved shorts and high heels.

Bryn chose to ignore the fact that neither Gary nor Trina had much to say to each other.

After one drink together, Bryn offered to buy another round. Gary stood up abruptly. 'No, my turn. What would you like?'

Becky apologized. 'Actually, we need to make a move.'

'Already?' Bryn sounded surprised.

Trina nodded. 'Yep, Becky's right.'

Bryn passed his empty glass to Gary. 'Same again for me, thanks.'

Becky and Trina had left by the time Gary returned from the bar. 'You're looking pretty cheerful considering they've just abandoned you.'

Bryn shrugged. 'She's going to ring me.'

'But she went?'

'It was a prior arrangement.'

'Or so she said.'

Bryn studied Gary for a moment, realizing that neither understood the other's irritating logic. 'Look, I can either think she was making an excuse just to get away, or assume she was telling the truth. Neither's going to kill me, whether she rings or not, so I might as well enjoy waiting to find out.'

Gary looked sceptical. 'Now, that's what I call a positive way to look at it.'

'Don't take the piss. I just get out there, put the odds in my favour, and hope for the best. How was her mate?'

'She's a trainee accountant.'

'Not what I meant, at all. She was attractive, smart, and plenty going on. You went off to the bar and d'you know how she described you?'

'No.'

'Wholly unavailable. Probably because you give out this I'm-not-interested thing. You could make the effort at least.'

Gary shrugged. 'Maybe.'

Bryn didn't push it any further. He saw that Gary had stopped listening, in any case. He was staring ahead towards the junction with Mill Road, and he'd obviously noticed something.

'Let's go,' Gary said suddenly.

'Where?'

'Different pub if you like.'

'I haven't finished my pint.'

But Goodhew had already left the table and was heading towards the junction with Mill Road.

'And I need to take my car back to the garage.'

'Catch me up after you've done it,' Gary called over his shoulder.

Whatever was drawing Gary away now also held more interest for Bryn than finishing his last half pint. He shouted, 'Hang on.'

They turned right on to the main road, where Gary seemed to begin following a small pack of six or seven students. He was only walking still, but his stride remained swift and assured until he drew closer to them, then it faltered.

'What's wrong?' Bryn asked.

'I thought she was with them.'

'Who?'

'This girl . . . Claire. We used to go out together. I'm sure I just saw her.'

'And?'

'Nothing. It would have been good to catch up, I guess. But then again, maybe it would have been a bit weird.'

Bryn looked at him for a long moment, pulled Gary towards the kerb and then across the roadway. 'We'll go down Gwydir Street.'

'I didn't know she was back, that's all.'

'Keep walking. Next pub does great food.'

'You need to go back for your car?'

'I'll do it later.'

Bryn never believed that he was much of a thinker, but he'd been doing a lot more of that since he'd met Gary again. Right now Gary seemed to have withdrawn into his own thoughts, walking no faster than Bryn but two strides ahead. The guy definitely kept his cards close to his chest, and Bryn wondered if Gary ever played Texas Hold 'Em. There was something about him that made Bryn's own life now more complicated, yet he still had no idea what really made Gary tick. It wasn't Bryn's own staple diet of cars, pubs and casual sex, that was for sure.

26

In the distance two sirens started up, out of time with each other and creating a wave of sound that lapped repeatedly towards them. After a few seconds a third joined in, and with it the tone of their evening perceptibly altered. Bryn noticed this primarily because he saw a change in Gary, like a sudden awareness: first a tilting of his head to pick out the sounds coming from the city centre, then looking back towards the main thoroughfare as his eyes surveyed the entire street, then turning back to observe a mother pushing an empty buggy . . . then the pedestrian who ran towards them, and finally, at the furthest visible point, the group of people silhouetted in the open doorways of the houses at the bend in Gwydir Street.

Gary and Bryn never made it to the next pub. Without warning, Gary broke into a run. Bryn said nothing. He could tell that his friend's senses were now concentrated elsewhere, and it was all he could do to jog in Gary's wake and watch him accelerate, turning the short distance between them into a gulf.

Gary vanished around the bend in the road, and was soon out of view. Bryn picked up speed, and behind him the sirens grew louder.

SEVEN

Goodhew smelt the fire before he saw it. It wasn't unpleasant at first, merely a hint of bonfire night or the modest incinerators which burn waste at allotments. Then the house itself came into view and he realized there was nothing modest about this fire: it was devouring the building from the inside out. As the air began to taste bitter, he knew the smoke was infected with layers of partially combusted chemicals like varnish and paint, producing toxins that would make the flames gutter in sinister shades of blue and green.

Most of the people in the street stood immobile and silent behind an imaginary cordon, curiosity taking them only so far down the intrusive path of not minding their own business.

One man stood closer than the rest, a fifty-year-old with a ruddy complexion and an all-over look of solidity. He had his feet squarely planted and his hands on his hips, clearly assuming that he'd taken ownership of the situation. Goodhew addressed him first, having to raise his voice over the sound of cracking timbers. 'I'm an off-duty police officer. Is anyone inside?'

'We don't know.'

'Whose house is it?'

'A man and a woman – foreign-sounding surname.'

'And there's been no sign of them?'

'Nothing.'

Goodhew pointed at the passage. 'Is that the quickest way to the rear?'

'Only way there, apart from going through someone else's house.'

'Have the neighbours been evacuated?'

'Yes.'

As Goodhew sprinted through the passage, the heat searing through the brickwork could be felt against one side of his face. In his heart he knew that there was little to be done: the fire at the back of the property would be as intense as it was at the front. There would be no chance of entering, nor any chance of anyone coming out, but he still needed to check for himself. For a few strides his feet seemed to find nothing but a constant shingle of broken glass, but he kept running until he was clear of it and well into the centre of the garden, then turned to face the house. Bloody Hell. The windows were gone and the roof was alight: all that was visible of the inside were brief outlines of rafters and walls, glowing brightly before melting into the cavern of fire.

He walked to the very rear of the garden and could, over the wall, see that there were also people dotted around the cemetery, watching as keenly as those at the front of the house. A single figure moved, and she had just reached the wall when he first spotted her. She half climbed, half fell over it. He stepped forward to help her, but she waved him way,

'What's happening?' she gasped.

'Do you live here?' he asked.

She shook her head, but didn't answer. Instead she pushed past him as if taking in the full extent of the blaze for the very first time. 'Is there anyone round the front?'

'Is this your house?' Goodhew wasn't sure if she'd heard, because she never took her eyes from the upstairs window. 'I'm a police officer,' he explained, then repeated, 'Is this your house?'

She darted forward, but instinctively he grabbed her arm.

'There's someone inside,' she yelled, and fought to free herself.

'How do you know?'

'I saw someone move. I saw them,' she screamed. 'Up there, look.' She pointed to the left one of the pair of upstairs windows.

'No, no.' He held on to her. 'It's just how the flames look.'

'Someone walked past that window. I saw them.'

He paused, eyes fixed on the void that had once been a bedroom window, then he saw it too. But it wasn't a person, just a ghost, created from smoke and shadow and flame, that calmly stepped through the inferno. That was no longer a bedroom, or the place for any living creature. The building's only remaining role was to burn.

'There's no one,' he shouted.

She stopped struggling to escape him, and he then knew that she believed him. 'I need to find my son,' she gasped. 'Have you seen a little boy?'

'No, I haven't. Where should he be?'

'He was here . . .' She averted her eyes from the house. 'He must be out at the front,' she replied decisively.

Goodhew understood how she was more than aware of the alternative statement but wasn't willing to consider it. Smoke hung round the passageway, a faint but regular flash of blue light penetrating it from the far end. He now held on to the hope that they would find her child safe and probably in the care of the emergency services. 'I'll walk round to the front with you, but we'll never get through here.'

They started to climb over the wall together, but by the time he'd managed just a few steps over the uneven ground, she had covered twice the distance. As he scrambled after her, only the pale gravestones were visible, yet she wove her way between them with surefooted ease. He knew that somewhere along this perimeter wall there was a gate that would lead through the car park of some small business units, and back out on to Gwydir Street. He only knew its approximate location, but she found it at once, and was halfway over the adjoining wall when he finally caught up with her.

'The gate's locked,' she explained, then swung her other leg over and dropped to the ground behind.

He followed, inquiring, 'How old is he?'

'Two,' she replied, but didn't wait for him.

He caught her again as she turned through the car park, towards the street. The houses facing them were ominously well lit by the colours of emergency.

'His name's Riley,' she added.

'And who's he supposed to be with?'

'My friend, Rachel . . .' Perhaps she might have added a surname, perhaps not, but at that moment she turned the corner and saw the full chaos of firemen, residents, smoke, water and devastation. She stopped in her tracks. 'Oh fuck,' she whispered, then began shouting to the people standing closest. 'Have you seen a little boy? I'm looking for my little boy, Riley. He's with my friend, Rachel. I'm looking for Rachel and Riley.'

A few people shook their heads, while a few others just turned away.

Goodhew grabbed her arm and guided her through the crowd. 'What's your friend's last name?' he asked quickly.

'Golinski.'

'And your name?'

'Kimberly Guyver.'

'Stay right there,' he instructed her.

The fire officer gestured for him to stay back. 'Behind the cordon. It isn't safe here.'

Goodhew quickly explained the situation. The fire officer shook his head and instinctively they both glanced back towards Kimberly Guyver.

She, too, ducked under the tape. 'They can't be in there. Why wouldn't they have just got out? Oh, shit. Shit. Riley, Riley!'

Goodhew reached her first. 'They're doing everything they can.' He hated the words even as he said them. They sounded so ineffectual but they were all he had.

'And they're searching the house, aren't they? Who's gone inside?'

'They can't go in,' he replied quietly.

Kimberly drew a long breath, and then fell silent.

EIGHT

The fire blazed ferociously, and for a time it seemed that the fire brigade's attempts to quench it would not put it out far ahead of its natural end.

Kimberly waited.

Four police cars soon arrived, the first bringing a man she guessed must be a more senior officer. She watched as he spoke to various people. He glanced over at her once, but she read nothing in his expression.

She felt the urge to approach him, to ask him for news, but she gave in to a greater urge that told her to stay where she was. Keep still and quiet like that would fool fate into moving on and leaving herself and Riley untouched. Like those plane-crash victims she'd read about, dead in the wreckage but with their fingers still crossed in hope.

She didn't notice who came with the other three vehicles; she studied each as it arrived, but only to see whether a small boy might be staring back at her. Everything else seemed a silent and timeless blur. She had no idea how long she'd stood there before she was gently led over to one of the cars. Nor had she any idea how long she sat in the car before the flames and smoke cleared enough to reveal the dead features that had once been her friend's home. Someone had put a cup of tea in her hands; her fingers were woven together to cradle the cup. It looked full still, but felt almost cold.

Mr Senior Officer was talking on his mobile. He looked like a serious type, a man obliged to deliver bad news many times in the past. She studied him, wondering what he would say to her. He tilted his head slightly to one side or he was listening, but apart from that seemed contained and neat, not one to waste time or energy on any unnecessary movements. Someone who could keep his feelings to himself. She guessed that's how it had to be, in a job like that.

Her brain created a half-formed picture: his face remaining expressionless as his words dragged her down into darkness and loss. She stopped herself from taking that thought further, since it was disloyal to Riley. It felt like she'd lost faith in him, even though nothing that was happening could have been within his control.

For the first time she realized that she wasn't alone in the vehicle. A WPC sat in front of her, in the driver's seat. She must have become aware that Kimberly was now watching her, for they suddenly made eye contact via the rear-view mirror.

The policewoman turned. She had large dark eyes which seemed to assess Kimberly's face before she spoke: 'Are you warm enough?'

'Yes.' Realizing, as she replied, that she was shivering. 'Tired, I think,' Kimberly added.

'Sure. But this isn't necessarily the best place to wait. I can arrange for us to be inside somewhere nearby. 'Somewhere warmer, more private?'

Kimberly shook her head. 'How long before they can carry out a search?'

'I don't know – but not yet. I'll ask them in a minute.' She reached over the back of her seat to the one next to Kimberly. 'Put this round yourself, at least.' It was a thermal blanket.

'Is that clock correct?'

'Yes.' It read five minutes past midnight.

'And I've been here all this time?' Kimberly wondered how those vital hours had slipped past, unnoticed.

'It's the shock, but don't worry. When you said you wanted to stay, we asked one of the paramedics to check you over.'

Kimberly remembered then, the green uniform, a firm voice, and her shaky replies. 'And you're my babysitter?'

'I'm new, so I don't know my way round well enough to be anywhere else right now.' The young woman hesitated, then reddened slightly; clearly the words hadn't come out quite the way she'd intended. Not that it mattered. 'Constable Sue Gully,' she added.

'You already introduced yourself, didn't you?'

'Yes, sorry. I wasn't sure if you remembered.'

'Only when you said it.'

PC Gully looked awkward for a moment. 'I'll get that update, then.'

Kimberly watched her climb out of the vehicle and approach Mr Senior Officer. They seemed to continue speaking for several minutes, though it could have been less, then they headed back together.

Kimberly hoped fate wasn't paying attention. She crossed her fingers, in any case.

Gully opened the door. 'This is DI Marks, and he needs to talk to you.'

He'd stopped about six feet back from the car. 'How are you feeling?' he asked.

'I'm OK.'

'Good. I need to check some more details. All right if I sit in the car with you?' He didn't wait for her to answer. Gully returned to her seat in the front, while Marks walked round the car and joined Kimberly in the rear. 'You said that your friend Rachel was looking after Riley?'

'Did I?'

'You did. And is that correct?'

'Yes, since late this afternoon.'

'Yesterday afternoon,' Marks corrected, his expression remaining impenetrable. 'And you've had no contact with her since?'

'Nothing.'

'Did she often look after the child for you?'

'Sometimes, yes. She's very fond of him.'

'And her husband, Stefan Golinski, what else can you tell me about him?'

Kimberly wondered what else she'd already revealed. Gully was meant to be taking the notes, but instead she looked questioningly at Marks.

'The people we've already asked think he does some kind of night shift and, based on that information, I'm working on the assumption that he was probably not at home at the time of the fire. If you can tell me where he works, I'll send a couple of officers over to speak to him, being Mrs Golinski's next of kin.'

Mrs Golinski. Kimberly never thought of Rachel by her married name, just as Rachel – or sometimes as Rachel Hurley. Eleven years old still, with white school socks, and the shape of her AA cup bra showing through the thin cotton of her white school shirt. How had they travelled so many miles through the eleven years since?

I've known Rachel exactly half my life. Rachel Hurley, not Mrs Golinski.

She felt suddenly and inexplicably defensive. Like making her think of her best friend in such a formal and unfamiliar way was merely his attempt to pull them apart. Unless it was those other unwelcome words – *next of kin* – that she was reacting to.

'He's a doorman at the Celeste. It's a nightclub down Market Passage, just off Sidney Street.'

'Yes, we know it.' He opened his car door again. 'I have to speak to a couple of my officers. It will only take a few minutes, then we'll be leaving for Parkside Station –'

Kimberly interrupted him even before she discovered whether this was the end of his sentence. 'I need to stay *here*,' she insisted.

'The fire brigade will be on hand to make sure the fire is fully extinguished, but they won't be able to start making the building safe enough to search until dawn at the earliest. There's nothing else that can be done at present. PC Sue Gully is going to stay with you.'

His tone was firm but empathetic. He broke off eye contact, then moved on to his next task, before she could engage him in any argument.

She saw him go and talk to an officer wearing plain-clothes. He had jet-black hair and listened carefully to Marks, nodding agreement frequently. He'd now been joined by the young officer who had first helped her, he wore jeans and a casual shirt, and spent more time watching the fire crew than paying attention to his superior. The one with the black hair was older, therefore probably more senior, and it certainly looked like he had far more to say.

'That's DC Goodhew and DC Kincaide,' Gully informed her. 'Kincaide's the smart one.'

Kimberly didn't inquire whether she meant smart by nature as well as appearance. Instead, she preferred to assume they were all going to be equally astute, and that she and Riley were in safe hands. She vowed to set aside her ingrained distrust of the police.

'I haven't met Goodhew yet, he was on holiday when I started,' Gully added.

The two DCs turned away, and DI Marks headed back towards her. He took a keyring from his pocket and pointed the car key at the saloon parked in front of them. It beeped and its lights flashed twice as it unlocked itself. She knew it was time to leave.

Kimberly looked at the devastated facade of Rachel's house once more, and silently prayed that it was as vacant as it appeared.

Gully started the car, and they followed Marks' vehicle out of the road.

Kimberly didn't and couldn't blame the DI for the interviews and paperwork that were now taking her away from her vigil. She realized she'd been loaded on to a conveyor belt, had just felt the lurch as it clunked forward. She didn't blame the process, but it still made her want to vomit.

NINE

As soon as the police cars began to arrive, Goodhew knew his presence was probably redundant. His boss, DI Marks, had already instructed him to take a holiday, and he'd been emphatic: two weeks, no excuses. He'd delivered this instruction with a *don't call us, we'll call you* diatribe that had started with a few compliments on Goodhew's work and ended with a rant about what happens to detectives who have no social life and burn out before they're thirty.

Marks acknowledged his presence with a single nod, then turned away, busy with more pressing tasks. The fact that Marks knew he was still hanging about and still didn't invite him back on duty seemed pretty conclusive.

Bryn was waiting further down the street and Goodhew headed over to him.

'Didn't want to stand around gawping,' Bryn explained.

'Yeah, I know what you mean.'

'Didn't think I should just go and leave you, though.'

'Thanks.'

'Was anyone inside there?'

Goodhew shrugged. 'They don't know yet.' He sensed Bryn was uncomfortable at the prospect. 'Take your car home, and I'll catch you tomorrow or something.'

Bryn nodded. 'You're off, then?'

'Yeah, I think I need to.'

Perhaps Bryn assumed he'd head home then. Goodhew wasn't officially on duty, but leaving the scene was also out of the question, and for the next half hour he joined the ranks of the bystanders.

Like them, he spent most of the time gazing at the fire, fascinated by its terrible beauty. But, unlike them, he also watched, so far unsuccessfully, for the arrival of a woman with a small boy, and periodically he glanced over at Kimberly as she sat in the back of one of the patrol cars.

Goodhew began to feel restless. It was a feeling he knew well, and it ticked away in an inaccessible corner of his brain: quiet at first, but increasing in volume and frequency. Thoughts and adrenaline now racing, he needed to be engaged, physically and mentally

This need to be on the other side of the cordon grew rapidly. He decided to wait for the right moment when he could ask to be given something to do, but soon realized that Marks was altogether too busy. In fact the only person who looked under-utilized was DC Kincaide. A few minutes earlier Kincaide had finished a call on his mobile, and Goodhew hadn't noticed him do anything since.

For the weeks leading up to his current holiday he and Kincaide had been working together, since Marks seemed to think there was something beneficial in it for both of them. Neither of them shared his opinion, and that was probably the only thing they did agree on. Goodhew had hoped that two weeks away from him would allow him to approach Kincaide differently, but here he was at the halfway mark and automatically assuming that Kincaide was slacking. In truth he had absolutely no reason to consider Kincaide at fault; it was just something about his body language and that over-manicured appearance that hinted at a sense of self-importance. Equally, Goodhew didn't want to admit to himself that Kincaide was irritating him just as much as ever.

He knew how ridiculous this seemed; he didn't need to like someone to have a professional relationship with them, and it shouldn't be so difficult to set aside personal differences when there were so many more important things at stake. Like helping Kimberly Guyver find her son. He didn't need to glance at Kimberly's expression to confirm how small-minded he was being. He felt ashamed; it really was pathetic.

He walked over to Kincaide. 'How's it going?'

'I hate fires.' Kincaide scowled. 'What are we supposed to do here until it's put out?'

'It's frustrating,' Goodhew agreed, then paused, using this one second of silence as a comma between one subject and the next. 'If Marks puts us together again, we should make more effort to co-operate.'

'We should, should we?' Kincaide replied, continuing to scowl.

'Look, I don't want ever to screw up because my attention's being diverted by a bad atmosphere between us. And I can't imagine that's what you want, either. It doesn't achieve anything, does it?'

Kincaide stared at Goodhew as if searching for a hint of insincerity. Finally the last remnant of the frown left his face. 'No, it doesn't.' He slipped the mobile into his breast pocket and held out his hand for Goodhew to shake.

Shortly afterwards, Kincaide returned to his vehicle, claiming he had something to do, leaving Goodhew standing where he was. That handshake had been too firm, and it had felt both fake and forced. Goodhew could have tried to convince himself that this assessment was still being petty, but he didn't.

A few minutes later, DI Marks approached Kincaide, and Goodhew walked over to join them. Marks' face was lit by the street lamps that cast light at an unflattering angle, adding several years to his actual forty-three. Goodhew's boss had a fifteen-year-old daughter called Emily, and maybe parenthood could provide an additional perspective to a situation like this one. Marks looked tired, weighed down by the night, and perhaps he wasn't joking when he claimed that Emily had caused so many of the grey flecks in his once glossy black hair.

'The fire crew is in no hurry to go in, and there'll be several hours of damping down needed before they can assess whether it is structurally sound to enter. At the moment, the fire officer reckons that there is still a strong chance of the roof collapsing.'

Kincaide was the first to comment. 'And what about the cause?'

'Again, they're not committing themselves, but at this stage are happy to label it "suspicious". And until we know otherwise we need to proceed on the basis that both Rachel Golinski and Riley Guyver are still alive.' Marks glanced at each of his subordinates in turn. 'I'm sure I don't need to emphasize to you the damage false hope can cause, so please remain cautious until we receive some definitive answers.' He continued speaking for several more minutes, but Goodhew heard very little of it above the tick-tick-tick of his own restlessness. He cared about what Marks was saying, and certainly had great respect for him, but felt the time for standing on the sidelines was almost over.

It *needed* to be over.

Marks then switched to his *in conclusion* tone: 'So speak to the husband, find out whether there's anywhere else the wife might be, especially anywhere she could have taken the youngster. Be tactful, but also pin down his own whereabouts in the last twenty-four hours.'

Marks turned to Goodhew. 'And *you'll* need to make a statement. I'm happy for you to do that now, or . . .'

Kincaide interrupted, 'He's still on holiday.'

Marks raised his eyebrows very slightly, like he was just considering the concept of being surprised. 'Are you, Gary?'

'Hopefully not any longer, sir.'

'I thought not, so I'd like you to go along with Kincaide.'

'To see the husband?'

'Yes.' Marks looked at Kincaide, then at Goodhew, and again at Kincaide. 'Get on with it, then.'

Kincaide straightened. 'Absolutely, sir.'

Goodhew didn't comment, as he turned towards Kincaide's car. They could drive away from the scene of disaster, but he knew that the ghosts of flames and the stink of bitter smoke would be coming along for the ride. His eyes made one last sweep of the situation, taking in the fear, shock and confusion, the mess and chaos, activity and exhaustion. But nothing stood out more distinctly than the huge question mark that now hung in the air between Kimberly Guyver and her best friend's burning home.

TEN

The building which housed the Celeste had been a nightclub for more years than Goodhew could remember. Its entrance was in Market Passage, one of several narrow pedestrianized short cuts that connected one central shopping street to another.

As a small boy, his parents had often taken him and his sister to the cafe in the Eaden Lilley department store. They always used the Market Passage entrance, where the Blag Club displayed glossy, two-colour posters promoting events that were consistently 'unmissable' and 'the best in Cambridge'. He'd been about seven at the time, and just realizing how much more he could learn now he could digest the more difficult words. Those posters hinted at the existence of a more dangerous and adult, after-dark world, certainly far more interesting than teacakes and a glass of Ribena in the coffee shop. He had looked forward to the posters like waiting for a favourite page in a weekly comic.

The venue had undergone several name changes, and he'd moved on by another nine or ten years, before he got to discover that the reality was an anticlimax: a hot and deafening few hours that served only to remind him how little he understood most people of his own age. As far as he knew, the Celeste was just another such incarnation.

Market Passage was L-shaped, with the Celeste at the bend. Kincaide now parked the car across the entrance to the short side of the L, with all four wheels up on the pavement. It was impossible to get closer.

There were a few people walking around or loitering, always in small groups, and Goodhew knew they'd been immediately pegged

41

as police. On this occasion it didn't matter, but he wished that Kincaide could learn to be a little more subtle. It wasn't feeling alienated that bothered him but the risk of alienating other people. And such unnecessary pavement hogging, especially in a pedestrian zone, undeniably smacked of self-importance.

A group of twenty-somethings glanced over as they passed by. The tallest male in the group kept his eyes on Kincaide for longest, then continued glancing back over his shoulder. Kincaide made a big show of locking the car, and brushing down his suit, returning the guy's stare the entire time.

Goodhew sighed to himself and headed towards the Celeste, muttering, 'What's the point?'

'Point of what?' Kincaide was suddenly almost alongside him.

Goodhew hadn't realized that Kincaide had caught up with him, or that he himself had even spoken out loud. 'All that macho posturing crap.'

Kincaide shrugged. 'They don't know any better. They're ignorant, that's all.'

Goodhew smiled to himself, making sure he didn't reveal his next thought out loud.

The club door was heavy, artificially aged and adorned with rough-cast ironwork to resemble the entrance to some building from the middle ages. Like a church, or a castle. The doormen matched the door, standing beside it in an identical pair.

They simultaneously gave a sideways tip of the head, nodding the pair of visitors through to the woman on the desk. She wore a name badge which read 'Jodi' and a T-shirt which identified her as *Your Celeste Hostess*.

Muffled music sneaked down to them from somewhere overhead.

Goodhew spoke first. 'We need to speak to one of your staff called Stefan Golinski.'

She gave each of them a shrewd once-over. 'Blimey, I didn't ever think he'd really do it.'

'Sorry, do what?'

'Mule called you, right?' She waited for them to answer, looking like she was trying to decide whether they weren't responding because it was none of her business, or because they were too dim to unravel a four-word question. She must have then decided it was the name that was throwing them. 'I don't know what he's really called,' she added, smiling hopefully.

Kincaide's tone remained deliberately patient. 'We just need to speak to Mr Golinski.'

'Well, he didn't come back.' She raised her henna-ed eyebrows. 'Like anyone thought he *would*. Went off like a rocket.'

'OK, so where's this Mule guy?' Goodhew asked.

'Go through.' She'd been taught that same slight tip of the head as used by the bouncers. 'Up the stairs, then straight to the back. I guess he's in the kitchen – they'd've wanted him out of sight, eh?'

'Thanks.'

Lights shaped like lilac rock crystals lit the stairs, and the same theme continued through the building, with the same mellow illumination cast on a variety of coffee tables positioned around the perimeter of the room. As clubs went, it was pretty small, even low-key, but it had one thing that many other local nightspots were missing – plenty of customers.

They headed on into the heart of the club, its dark walls throbbing ever louder with the pulse of the bass. Peering across the dance floor, Goodhew spotted the door to the kitchen.

Kincaide's focus fell about twenty feet short of target. 'Pity my wife doesn't wear underwear that shows off that degree of flesh.'

Goodhew didn't even look. Maybe it was just him, but there was something about standing in front of a burning house which had now taken away the appeal of bare skin glistening under the hot and distorted beams of light.

The kitchen was just a brightly lit cupboard, measuring about eight feet by ten. It contained a sink and a fridge and a microwave, but something about the lack of any other cooking equipment told Goodhew it was more about securing permission to use the premises as a nightclub rather than a venue for fine dining.

The only occupant was slicing hot-dog rolls with a large bread knife. He looked up, blade in hand, and nodded warily. The man's hair was shoulder-length and beach-bum blond, but his tanned face was marred by a swollen lip and large welt that ran from his right cheekbone up to his eyebrow. His right eye was red and almost closed, contrasting with the left one, which was wide with surprise. The overall effect was demonic.

'You're Mule?'

'Yeah, and you're the police, right?' He had a distinct New Zealand accent. 'I *told* him not to bother.'

'Who?'

'Our boss, Craig.' Mule's right eye looked like it hadn't finished swelling.

'Craig what?' Kincaide had his notebook out already.

'Tennison.'

'And your full name?'

'Mule.'

Kincaide was about to demand more details, but Goodhew cut in, 'You should get it looked at.'

'No point.'

'Well, an ice pack at least.'

'Gary,' Kincaide spoke in a voice that he might save for a small and annoying nephew, 'if he needs medical help, I'm sure he can get a lift to Addenbrooke's.' Then back to Mule. 'Stefan Golinski did this?' he asked.

Mule nodded. Goodhew kept quiet.

'Why did he hit you?'

'Jealous – thought I was shagging his wife.'

'Were you?'

'No, not this time.'

'So, you previously had a sexual relationship with Mrs Golinski?'

'No, I mean this time it wasn't *his* wife. I'm seeing someone who's married, and the bloke doesn't know. Point is, I'm not seeing Rachel Golinski – never was, never would. Rachel and I are friends, but Stefan just doesn't get it. He thinks she should just look into his eyes and need nothing else from life, if you know what I mean.'

'So where is he now?'

'How should I know? He's not here in the building, that's for sure. Took off in a rage. Ask Craig – he knows what Stefan's like, and might know where he goes to cool off. I didn't touch her, though, but Stefan couldn't accept that, it was like he'd already decided what the truth was, and wouldn't listen to anything else.' Mule tried to make some kind of facial expression of resignation, but it ended in a wince. 'Look, why not just talk to Craig.'

They left Mule in his kitchen, clutching the bread knife and resolutely slicing open more hot-dogs rolls. Following his directions, they located a plain door set in the wall opposite the bar.

It had a code-operated lock but no buzzer, then again, no one could have been expected to hear it over the constant, pumping music. Goodhew scanned the room for assistance, but he needn't have bothered. Kincaide dug him in the arm and he turned to see the door had already been opened by a man he immediately took to be another doorman. This one was slightly less imposing than the first two, if only because he actually smiled.

'We're looking for Stefan Golinski.'

'Come on through.'

There was nothing plush about the area they entered beyond the door. Overhead the ceiling was bare concrete, with air-conditioning pipes running along each RSJ, and a single naked bulb hanging from a wire cord in the centre of the room. The furnishing was equally sparse, just a few stacking chairs deposited around a moulded plastic table, and he quickly led them past these towards the rear of the room, where a lightweight wall partitioned off a small area that housed a desk, a PC and a couple more chairs. It was only then that they realized they'd just met the manager.

'Plush, eh?' he said.

They introduced themselves.

'Craig Tennison,' he announced, and shook hands with each of them in turn. He was aged around the forty mark, with the look of a man who was still too fit to turn to fat but also too laid-back now to keep it all as toned as it had once been. 'Solid' would be a fair description.

He perched on the edge of the desk and offered them the chairs. 'Did Mule call you? I know he's a bit knocked around, but I'd be happier if he dealt with it outside working hours. It doesn't help the business to have the police turning up every five minutes.'

'Every five minutes?' Kincaide queried.

'Just a figure of speech. We don't have much trouble but we don't want it either.'

'Tell me, did anyone witness this assault on Mule?'

'I caught the tail end of it.'

'And what time was that?'

'About eight, I guess.' He paused to think. 'Yeah, that must be about right.'

'Then what?'

'Stefan stormed out.'

From where he sat, Goodhew could only see the back of the PC, but he could hear it whirring quietly and was prompted to speak for the first time. 'You have CCTV here?'

'That's right.'

'Digital?'

'Yes, of course. There's no risk of forgetting to put a fresh tape in these days, so it's all there. I think you'll see Stefan storming out, but not the fight itself. That kicked off once Mule went in the storeroom.'

'And then you walked in on it?'

'Yeah, I'd been looking for Stefan, wanted to know why he wasn't manning either of the doors. He seemed wound up when he started work – has a knack of creating this kind of tension in the atmosphere. So, anyway, I pushed open the storeroom door just as a load of boxes came crashing down on top of Mule. Then Stefan barged past me . . . and I shouted after him, warned him that if he disappeared this time, his job wouldn't be waiting for him when he got back.'

'Is he usually so volatile?'

'Not really. For as long as I've known him he's had a temper, but today was in a whole different league. I went as far as running after him, caught up with him, but he wouldn't tell me where he was going . . . which brings me back to my original question – did Mule call you?'

'No, he didn't. He might be in need of medical attention, by the way.'

Kincaide smirked. 'Excuse my DC, but he seems to want to play doctors and nurses today. But we're not here in relation to that incident. There's been a serious fire at Golinski's home address, and we need to discover the whereabouts of both him and his wife Rachel.'

Tennison looked startled. 'But they're not there, right?'

Goodhew had shut his mouth after his colleague's latest sarcasm, and intended to let Kincaide do the rest of the talking. For now anyway.

'At present we don't know precisely where they are.'

Tennison seemed to take a few seconds to grasp the implication. 'Did Stefan raise the alarm?'

'Why would you think that?'

'I don't actually think anything. If he had raised the alarm, then it would prove that he'd been home. But chances are he's letting off steam somewhere. So why did you ask all those other questions?'

'Because understanding his current frame of mind may prove crucial.'

Tennison stared at the floor, concentrating. 'I'll tell you what,' he said finally, as he looked up again, his expression more determined. 'Stefan's a hard bloke. He can be a nutter, a bastard even – but never to her. When she was around, he was as soft as shit. If you're thinking that he's lost it with her, well . . .' He drew a breath and wagged his index finger. 'I can't see him hurting her, no matter what the provocation. But that's just my opinion, of course – just my own opinion.'

ELEVEN

Back out in the street, Goodhew noticed their joint reflections in a window. He could identify the pair of them like they were part of an old snapshot: familiar faces but made easier to read given the opportunity to view them in detachment. Perhaps that was all hindsight really was: the chance to see clearly what was originally clouded by the emotion of the moment, rather than anything to do with the passage of time. He still felt his irritation at Kincaide: it kept crawling under his skin and it was hard not to scratch it. But in the window he saw the visual confirmation of his own tenseness and Kincaide's insouciance, the latter too self-aware to be genuine.

What was the point of pretending that Kincaide wasn't deliberately pushing his buttons, when they both knew the score? 'I'm not your DC,' he said flatly.

'In theory, but who would ever guess?' Kincaide grinned lazily. 'We got off on the wrong foot, right?'

'And I was trying to –'

'I haven't finished. I know what you were trying to do – find some way we can have a –' he paused to make the quote signs in the air '– healthy working relationship. There's nothing in that for me, Gary. Watching you flail around isn't weighing on my conscience, and the last thing I want is you getting chummy with me and starting to think that you can poke your nose into my private life, too.'

'Your home life has nothing to do with me.'

'Yeah, right, so when I have a crack at the new WPC, you're not going to automatically run to the nearest patch of moral high ground? I don't think so.'

'I'm sure she can take care of herself.'

'And Mel couldn't?' Kincaide spat out Mel's name so it hit Goodhew like a slap in the face.

They'd stopped beside their car, standing square on to each other, neither of them even aware of who might have been passing by.

'So this is what it's really about? You latched on to Mel when she was having a bad time with Toby, and you convinced her you were going to leave Jan.'

'And what are you, some kind of umpire? How's this clearing the air?'

The conversation had skewed off the narrow path marked 'civilized', and it was now threatening to skid out of control. But Goodhew could still see that there was some truth in Kincaide's point, and hit the brake. He wondered how much of his dislike for the man was fuelled by his latent feelings for Mel. He had no immediate answer. 'Fair enough,' he said finally. 'I guess it wasn't any of my business.'

'I don't give a shit what *you* do outside work.'

It was another very good point.

'What's funny?' snapped Kincaide.

Goodhew turned away. 'Let's just go.'

The anger had left him, and Kincaide seemed to sense this. They headed back to Parkside Station, and would have made the journey in complete silence if Kincaide's mobile hadn't rung. He switched it to hands-free and they were both greeted by the voice of DI Marks.

'Any progress, Michael?'

'Nothing yet, sir.'

'Goodhew with you?'

'Yes, sir.'

'No news here either,' Marks continued. I'm leaving Kimberly Guyver's house now, and PC Gully will stay with her. I want you two to knock it on the head for tonight and meet me back at the station at 8 a.m. All of us will be better for a fresh start.'

Goodhew was glad he wasn't driving, as he didn't want to have to keep his eyes at road level. Instead he stared up above the rooftops towards the tangerine glow that bled from the streetlamps, staining the indigo background of the sky. He then looked in the direction of Mill Road, but was unable to distinguish any difference in the light visible from that part of the city. He wondered whether the blaze was finally over.

Their car journey was short but claustrophobic; the city seemed huge by comparison. It always held the answers for him, so it was inevitable that he chose not to make the short walk home but instead found himself walking in the opposite direction at 3 a.m.

Every irrelevant thought regarding Kincaide was left behind in the dusty car park of Parkside Station. He knew he would end up at the Golinski house but didn't hurry; he wanted to enjoy the company of his thoughts along the way. They came tentatively at first, too fleeting to grasp or analyse.

A breath of unease.

The shadow of loss.

The distraction of sirens blotting out every other sound, demanding to be observed and obeyed.

A taste of fear. Not a taste for it. The pedestrian who had run towards him earlier had manifested more of it than any of the idle bystanders had displayed. And Kimberly Guyver also, before he'd known her name. In his mind's eye she appeared paper-thin with it. Distressed. Taut. Beautiful and brittle.

He pulled himself up short before he stepped off the kerb.

What was it that jarred?

A taxi was the only vehicle in sight, and he had plenty of time to cross the road before it reached him, but he was aware of it only in the abstract, he had no sense of its speed or distance from him. Its headlights shone steadily and ever closer. He watched it intently, like it was delivering the answer.

A light went on, but it was nothing to do with the taxi.

Yes, Kimberly Guyver was beautiful, but with relief he realized that this adjective hadn't come to him in the distorted glow of the fire. He'd seen her before sometime, when her black hair had shone in the sunlight and her bare skin was tanned and radiant. Her dark and petulant features had turned many heads, including his own. But the memory was translucent, dissolving into nothing as soon as he tried to identify it. Tonight he'd only seen her desperation, but without doubt he recognized her from somewhere else. For now he just couldn't remember where.

This shifted his priorities so that he never turned into Gwydir Street, instead following his new thoughts until they took him in a full circle back to Parker's Piece, and towards the empty building that stood on the far side. The first three floors were in darkness but a single light shone from his attic window. No one else lived in any part of the building, and the light worked on a timer, set to switch on from 7 p.m. until whenever he eventually made it home and turned it off.

Weariness caught up with him as he climbed the silent flights of stairs to his front door. He turned off the light in the window, then sat down in the nearest chair, feeling strangely reluctant to cast off his smoke-impregnated clothes. He only meant to stay there for a minute or two, but was still in the same place when he fell into an exhausted sleep.

The television set had a seven-inch screen, and a small aerial like a tilted halo. The picture was poor, but as long as Stefan didn't move the sound remained clear. Stefan didn't move at all.

A reporter was at the scene, using a lot of words, a lot of meaningless spiel best interpreted as 'We know nothing'.

She stood to one side of the camera shot, and over her shoulder was his house. He watched the smoke, then her mouth move, then the smoke again. Smoke, mouth, smoke, his gaze flicking back and forth across the screen until it got boring.

He knew what they'd find there: a lesson in what happened when betrayal overstepped the point of possible forgiveness.

Sometimes it wasn't enough for people to suffer pain; sometimes it was more important to show everyone else the price that must be paid. Those were the unwritten rules. The unfair part was the notion that not everyone would be made to pay.

But, as he thought it over, he was sure that would not be allowed to happen here.

Mouth, smoke, mouth. Not so boring, after all.

* * *

Riley's bowl tipped over and the contents hit the floor, splashing outwards like vomit. He didn't look at all concerned. In the whole of his short life, he'd never had to feel fear.

TWELVE

At 5 a.m. Kimberly slid open the sash window. She felt like she'd been holding her breath for hours, but now, with her lungs tight with anxiety and the house feeling stale, she admitted to herself that she needed air. There was no breeze but clean air soon filled the room by replacing the warmth which slipped outside.

Night had almost passed, streetlamps were glowing and lights had come on in a few of the houses bordering the cemetery, but the brightest by far shone from Rachel's house: a floodlight that was directed on the front elevation, but glowing above the remains of the collapsed roof like an unnatural, clinical-white sun about to rise and shine on her life.

Kimberly was neither a church-goer nor a hypocrite but her brain repeated two words: *Please God. Please God.*

Over the last hours, her hopes and ambitions had withered, her sense of independence become frail. Riley had become her every reason to live, and he was out there somewhere she couldn't see, couldn't reach.

Please God. Please God.

She closed her eyes and tried to feel her child's spirit; she believed her love for him was strong enough to know whether he was safe. Whether he was alive. Whether he was waiting for her – bewildered, crying, feeling abandoned.

I'm sorry. Please, God, help me.

She knew that gnawing emptiness too well. The futile search for love and safe harbour painted her every single childhood memory, a pattern of false hope and abandonment and finally anger.

53

Producing a fury that had smothered all her vulnerabilities, and still rode on her shoulder.

That rage wouldn't do anything for her now except choke her ability to think clearly. Tears slipped from her tightly closed eyes and the fresh air seemed to calcify within her body, gripping her chest, burning her lungs. She fought to wrench in a breath and whispered to the open window, 'I love you, Riley.'

Goodhew left his flat at 6 a.m., and was in the water by ten-past. He was the only swimmer present; in fact the pool was officially still closed but the lifeguards knew him well enough to let him in and trust him not to drown. He swam for forty minutes, and on several occasions swam a full length on a single breath, eyes open and watching for the blur of the end wall as it came into reach.

He'd long since learnt that starting the day this way mitigated the effects of his perpetual sleeplessness. A distant clock chimed seven as he pushed open the outer door of Parkside Station, and the first person he saw there was Mel.

She'd changed her hair; it was shorter and a little less spiky, more Titian than red now. It suited her.

In that first second they both instinctively smiled – open and spontaneous – before settling on expressions that were a little more guarded.

'Why are you here this early?' he asked.

She screwed up her nose. 'Stuff to sort out.'

He immediately searched her face for any sign of upset. 'Everything OK?' he asked.

She understood and a small thank-you of a smile reappeared in one corner of her mouth. 'Yeah, yeah. I mean stuff here, just work things. Don't worry.'

He nodded and the silence between them turned into one of those unnaturally long gaps. Mel salvaged the moment by flourishing one of her almost legendary Post-it notes.

'By the way, the Guyver woman's gone back to the house in Gwydir Street.'

'What's happened now?' he asked in surprise.

'Nothing – she just wants to be there. It makes sense, I guess. She'd want to be the first to know, right?'

54

'And Marks took her?'

'No, Gully. You know, the new woman?'

'But Marks was OK with that?'

'Upstairs couldn't get Marks on his mobile so she left a message with me, knowing that I'd see him as soon as he came in.'

'So he's definitely coming here first?'

'How should I know? I get here early to catch up on some admin and suddenly I've been promoted to station oracle. He's back at eight, that's all I know.' She slapped the Post-it note on Goodhew's sleeve. 'This is what I get for having the desk nearest the entrance, isn't it?'

Goodhew balled the paper and dropped it into the bin. 'No need to mention this to Marks, I'll explain when I see him.'

'No problem,' she said.

He turned for the door and she turned back to her PC. Their conversation had ended a little abruptly but for now, at least, that was the best way.

Gully had parked as close to the Golinski house as possible. In this street it was impossible to be more than a few feet from someone's front door, or someone else's net curtains. Gully's patrol car was now at the side of the road and within fifty yards of the Golinski house. A little too close to everything for comfort. She sat in the driver's seat, Kimberly Guyver right behind her, thus easily visible in the rear-view mirror if she chose to look. For now, though, Gully was slightly relieved that she had the choice.

The task of staying with Kimberly had sounded deceptively simple. Kimberly had called it baby-sitting, and Gully had really thought it might be that straightforward: a few hours spent with a restless but exhausted charge. Gully knew that she was only a junior officer, that she carried no weight in any part of the investigation, and that her relationship with each of her new colleagues was just beginning.

She'd immediately picked up on Kimberly's discomfort whenever around the police, and Gully's instincts told her this extended to all kinds of authority figures – including those who pushed bureaucracy, or anyone who colluded with them. It was logical then that Gully's own inexperience and unfamiliarity with the official process were the very reasons that Kimberly had made her the channel for all her hopes.

Gully never intentionally shirked anything but this particular responsibility rested heavily on her. She could have argued that it wasn't hers to carry but, more than that, she felt it wasn't hers to avoid.

It was when she and Kimberly conversed that she sensed it most. Therefore Gully feared showing the wrong emotions, and similarly that she might show either too much or too little of the acceptable ones: sympathy, promise, faith and even strength. Gully felt under pressure not to make any mistakes in her interaction with Kimberly. Therefore a few minutes with no eye contact or conversation was unlikely to harm either of them.

She now absorbed the mess outside: same event, different aftermath.

The fire had left Gwydir Street looking hung-over and dishevelled, like it had awoken to face cleaning up the last traces of some rowdy carnival that had pushed its way through the narrow thoroughfare. Where cars were still allowed to park, they'd been jammed into too few spaces, standing non-parallel and untidy. Many curtains were still rucked from people peering out and some front doors gaped open and probably had been since first light.

The road was wet, the pavements strewn with cigarette ends and partly burnt paper. When a man stooped to pick up a piece, she recognized him at once as Goodhew, the detective she'd heard about but hadn't yet met. The piece of paper was white and narrow, maybe out of a notepad or similar. He turned it over, and back again, then he put it in his pocket. The other pieces would soon be trodden into the pavement, but for now they fluttered in tiny ticker-tape-like shreds.

He looked about her own age, though she guessed he had to be a couple of years older, but twenty-five maximum. She didn't even know if it was possible to be a detective sooner than that. So, assuming there was no such thing as a buy-it-yourself detective badge, he had to be sharp; probably a bit of a nerd as well as a high-flyer. She thought that he was probably here because he'd decided to interfere with her morning and it grated on her.

56

He tapped on the driver's window and gestured for her to get out of the car. She removed her seatbelt and climbed out, each movement as clipped as her tone. 'What?'

He held out his hand. 'I'm DC Goodhew. Gary.'

They shook hands but she didn't smile, and forgot to introduce herself. 'I know who you are.' She tried to look confident but was aware how her eyebrows had drawn together, locking her forehead in an involuntary scowl. 'I left a message for DI Marks, so he knows we're both down here.'

'He's not in, so he doesn't know yet. Mel passed your note to me, and it seemed odd, so I just want to make sure that everything's OK.'

'She wanted to come back here. I think she's been awake for most of the night, and of course she's desperate for news.' Gully heard herself making too many excuses, talking away any illusion of assertiveness, but she was finding it hard to stop. 'She wanted to stay here last night but, of course, that wouldn't have been sensible . . .'

'And this *is*?'

'Why not? She's not under arrest and she's had no news yet of her son or her best mate.' Gully managed to stop herself talking before she was interrupted, and challenged him with a look of determination.

'Because . . .' A deep irritation filled the word; he must have heard it too because he paused for breath. 'Look, if they suddenly find a body in that wreckage, you're going to have the locals right in your face. Not to mention the press. You've spent some time with her, so do you think that's fair?'

Maybe if she'd held his steady gaze, and had the courage of her own convictions, it would have been different. She could have answered that, *yes, it was the right decision*, and only realized the flaw in her judgment at a later and more humiliating moment. Instead, though, she glanced at Kimberly and understood how much more vulnerable she'd now made her.

Gully's cheeks flushed. She wished there was some dignified way out of this, but he was just standing there while she squirmed, and this smart-arse detective was looking on like it was the first time he'd ever seen someone screw up.

And she was blushing again – just the thought that she was at risk of blushing made it happen, the medical term being 'idiopathic craniofacial erythema'. It was virtually untreatable, and according to various family members, boyfriends and acquaintances it was either cute or funny. Ha-bloody-ha. She knew that any attempt to keep her feelings private would trigger it automatically.

She shook her head, then reddened further. 'Shit.' She turned her face away. *Shit, shit, shit.*

'You've been up all night, so you're bound to be really tired . . .' He stopped as soon as he saw her anger now turning on him.

'Hang on, I can see exactly where you're going with this. I can see I ballsed up, but don't patronize me, please.' She phrased the *please* more like an insult than a request.

'I wasn't.'

'Not much.' She poked a finger in his direction. 'Why don't you put it down to hormones as well as tiredness?'

'No,' he said flatly, 'I'm not going down that road. And if you want to, that's up to you. But not here, not now.' He took one step back, as if he'd done his bit of damage and now he was ready to walk away.

Her bad temper evaporated as quickly as it had arrived. 'Just back off,' she said more quietly, 'I don't need favours. I appreciate your advice, but I'll see Marks and put my hand up to it.'

'You'd better get over to Parkside or back to Miss Guyver's house, then, Marks is due to get in at eight.' Goodhew started reaching forward to open the car door for her, but stopped abruptly. 'Too late,' he observed.

Activity outside the Golinski house had suddenly ceased, the fire crew now gathered in a fatigued and dirty group. They were being briefed by the fire officer.

One of them was skinny and squatted on the balls of his feet, leaning his elbows on his knees, his body taking the shape of a question mark. He wiped his face a couple of times, taking several attempts to clear the worst of the grime from his eyes. He didn't look in the direction of the patrol car, but to Gully it was still obvious that what he was feeling was pity, and all of it directed at Kimberly.

Goodhew knew that one of them should go over before the fire officer approached to take them to one side. 'Do you want me to speak to him?' he asked Gully.

'No, *I'll* go, thank you. I can handle it.'

It seemed like her automatic response was to reject anything that could be construed as a favour, no matter how minor. As she strode towards the fire crew assembled outside the shell of the house, any trepidation she was experiencing was well hidden. First impressions had shown she possessed resolve, and he guessed that she was determined not to make a second error too quickly.

Goodhew climbed into the car along with Kimberly, sitting at the other end of the rear seat.

'Have they found something?' Her voice contained a heavy burr of emotion, but the delivery was unflinching.

'PC Gully's just gone to find out.'

'I see. This'll be it, then.'

It was as if she spoke more to herself than to him, but he queried her in any case. 'It?'

'Yes, the final crank and tip.' She pushed her hair away from her face, and he noticed that her hands were shaking even though her voice was not.

'You'll have to explain.'

'It's like a rollercoaster: it starts moving and you know you can't get off. You meant to get on, but at the same time you don't really know what you're letting yourself in for. It climbs slowly, seems to take forever, and then when you reach the top . . .'

'You get the final crank and tip?'

'Yeah, and that's when you really know what's coming. Rachel and I used to say that.'

'About what?'

'You name it: work, people, going out, staying in.' She half-smiled; it was a private and cynical reaction. 'What did you expect? Some big insight, I suppose. Right now I'm looking down and wondering how far I'm going to fall. But it shouldn't need a detective to work that out, right?'

He nodded. 'If there's still no news of your son at this time, I'm going to take you back to the station.'

She smoothed two or three imaginary tangles from the ends of her hair. 'Riley will be fine, I know it. And Rachel, she's my best friend – I can't lose her.'

'And there's her husband.'

'Stefan?' She looked perplexed, as though she'd forgotten his existence until that moment. 'Where is he?'

'We don't know – can't find him. He could be inside.'

Kimberly didn't reply but looked back to the house, and it was as if she could see something different there now.

He looked back, too, but all he saw was the fire officer stepping away from Gully, leaving her white-faced and hesitant. She possessed new information, that was obvious; she might as well have advertised it with an audible alarm emitting an insistent, multi-decibel screech. He wasn't the only one who tuned into it, and more front doors had begun to open by the time she was back in the driver's seat.

She faced Kimberly briefly, before turning back to slide the key into the ignition. 'I think we should go back to Parkside Station.'

Kimberly adopted the same resolute tone. 'What have they found?'

'There's been a development.' Falling back on stock answers was not going to work, and Gully seemed aware of this, but Goodhew could also tell that she didn't know how to handle the situation. He stayed where he was and kept quiet, but caught her eye in the rear-view mirror and willed her to give Kimberly some information.

'I don't want to leave until you tell me,' Kimberly said firmly.

Gully turned her head to face them both. 'As I said, there's been a development.'

'Is it a body?' Kimberly straightened, bracing herself for the impending drop.

Goodhew gave up trying brainwaves as a method of communication. 'I think the basic details would be appropriate, now that we've come this far.'

Gully nodded and he saw the apples of her cheeks brighten with two small thumbprint-sized patches of red. 'They found a body.' She raised her hand in a calming motion. 'They believe it's adult.'

'*Believe?*'

'It's not your son.'

Nothing in Kimberly's expression changed, but the fingers of her right hand curled around the internal door handle and Goodhew noticed how the first two fingers of her left hand were already crossed. 'Is it female?' she asked.

'It's too soon to tell.'

'Too burnt?'

'We'll let you have as much information as we can, as it becomes available, but meanwhile, until formal identification takes place, nothing else can be confirmed.' Gully seemed to know that this was the moment to close the conversation and leave Gwydir Street. She glanced at Goodhew. 'Am I dropping you at Parkside?'

He nodded and Gully turned away to start the engine.

And, maybe for no other reason than that Kimberly now had a clear view of his face only, she asked him the final question. 'Will they have finished searching?'

He shook his head. 'No, not yet. I'm sorry.'

The patrol car pulled away from the kerb, but not before two firemen appeared from the house. They carried a stretcher between them, and a sealed body bag lay on it, its burden barely large enough to rise higher than the sides. It looked like something that had been full of air and had deflated, collapsed in on itself, leaving just pockets of nothing. It seemed impossible that there was enough inside there to be anything resembling a person.

Kimberly's voice was now quieter, but as firm as before. 'Actually, I want to go home.'

THIRTEEN

Marks was in and out of Parkside Station in a matter of minutes; long enough to hear that a body had been recovered from the Golinski house and to discover that Kimberly Guyver had been there in the street to witness its removal.

Some days, DI Marks felt like he woke up tired. Today was one of those: he had known it from the moment his alarm sounded and he double-checked the time, momentarily convinced that it had malfunctioned. He felt like he'd just dozed off, but somehow he had obtained his full quota of sleep, and work was calling.

A deep irritation niggled at him on days like this, and he resented each little rut that jolted his progress. He felt annoyed with his own slowness, annoyed at the minutes wasted before he even left his bed, then increasingly irked with every other small setback he encountered.

He hadn't made any comment when he'd been informed, but there was plenty he planned to say. Plenty.

And each phrase would include the name Goodhew.

But then what did he expect? For all Goodhew's capabilities, the results came with a price: a lack of conformity – 'random' as his daughter would say. Right now Marks preferred other words like 'naïve' and 'undermining'. What did Goodhew think he would achieve by taking Kimberly Guyver back to the scene of the fire?

Marks pressed the 'unlock' button on his car keys. He would take Gully aside and ask her how she'd been led into it. Her experience as a chaperone was limited but at least she had some; that's why he had picked her . . . Maybe he himself was to blame: too much too soon, especially for a new arrival.

Marks recognized the man leaning against a car parked two doors away from Kimberly Guyver's house. It was Ollie Baker, photographer with a local news agency. As soon as Marks swung into the same road, Ollie raised his over-large camera and rattled off a few shots. This did Marks a favour, since it restored him to a state of outward calm; always the most productive state, he reckoned. If the world was fair he would have thanked Ollie, but instead he blanked him.

Gully opened the front door and he blanked her too. She followed him into the room by a couple of steps, and found herself a perch on a dining chair in the corner, directly behind Kimberly. He sent Goodhew to make hot drinks then turned his full attention to Kimberly Guyver.

'How are you?'

She shrugged. 'What d'you expect?'

He nodded, taking his time, watching her watching him. She was trying to read his expression, guessing whether he brought news or just questions. It was the usual response.

'We don't have any news of your son yet, but I can tell you that the body recovered from the fire was adult and female.' He paused to let her speak but she said nothing, so he continued, 'Searches are now under way, initially in the grounds of the cemetery and Anglia Ruskin University. We have to pursue all the possibilities, just in case Riley is on his own and hiding somewhere.'

'Because that body is Rachel's?'

'We start with the most likely options, and since she was the only female occupant . . .'

'I understand.'

'We need some more details on Riley. We've checked his birth details and notice you registered his father as Jay Andrews. Is that correct?'

'Of course.'

'And does Mr Andrews still have contact with his son?'

Kimberly nodded and shrugged at the same time. 'Yes.'

'You didn't look too certain. Are you still in a relationship with Mr Andrews?'

'He's in a nursing home.'

63

'He's unwell?'

Kimberly looked down at her hands, massaged the little finger of her left hand for a few seconds, like it was a talisman.

'He was in an accident.'

'When?'

'Before Riley was born.'

She looked at him and he suddenly wondered if this was the first time she'd made proper eye contact with anyone, not masked with fear or grief, or blinkered by her obvious disdain for authority.

Her dark eyes still challenged, but her voice had become quiet and sure. 'Jay was my first serious boyfriend . . . though I don't mean the first one I slept with. But I didn't think you could stay with your first boyfriend forever, so we split up – and Rachel and I went off to work in Spain. She . . . Rachel and I have been friends since our first week of senior school. Jay and Rachel never got on, but that's how it goes, isn't it? You see your mate less in order to be with your boyfriend, and you turn your boyfriend down sometimes so you can hang around with your friend. Anyway, Rachel was kind of pleased when we cleared off to Spain, but after a few months she grabbed me one day and said she thought that I ought to make it up with Jay.'

She fell silent, as if reliving the moment, then continued, 'I was stunned. I had no idea they'd even been in touch. It was more than that, though. She'd arranged for Jay to visit and, as soon as I saw him . . .' She paused and, though she was still looking at him, Marks felt as if she'd left the room. And then her remaining words arrived via a burst of warm Spanish sunshine. 'They say you know . . . you know when it's right? That's how it was, and I promised I'd follow him home as soon as I'd worked out my notice.'

'And?'

'He got attacked later that night . . . wrong place at the wrong time, or whatever the saying is. I didn't hear anything about it, as there were always British tourists getting into trouble one way or another, so it was a couple of days before I was told . . . And another month before I found out I was pregnant.' She leant back in her chair. 'Happy?' she asked.

That caught Marks off guard. 'I'm sorry?'

'Do I pass?'

'There's no test here. We're just gathering facts.'

'Well, Jay's at the Hinton Avenue nursing home. He has a brain injury and he's paralysed, can't walk or talk. Apparently that's how he'll stay. Check it out.'

Marks nodded. He understood. 'We also need contact details for your family. Anyone in the immediate area?'

'No one.'

'Sure? Further afield then?'

'No.'

'So no one who's going to be distressed if they read about it in the paper first?'

'How soon will that happen?'

'The next edition.'

'You mean lunchtime, then? Well, there's a woman, my friend. She's like my Mum. Better than.' The words seemed to knot in her throat, so it took her a few seconds to be able to speak again. 'I hoped he'd be back soon. I don't want her upset. She doesn't deserve it.'

'What's her name?'

'Anita McVey, but can we just wait? Not for long . . . but 'til the last moment possible, just in case.'

'We can be careful about any details we release, but we also need to stem any press speculation and make sure that what they print helps us as far as possible. Our press officer has released an initial statement which simply explains that we are conducting an urgent search of the area in order to locate a missing two-year-old. We'll ask people in the neighbourhood to check their outbuildings. We also need to ask . . .'

'Whether you can search here?'

'Yes, it's standard procedure.'

He caught another flash of defiance in her expression. 'I'm sure it is.'

He chose not to pursue it. 'The other thing we'll need from you is a recent photograph of Riley. A clear snapshot – anything that shows his face clearly.'

'I know the type of thing. I'll go and see what I've got.'

She rose and Gully pointed to herself, to ask if she should follow. He shook his head and mouthed *Not yet.*' He glanced at the walls and mantelpiece, noticing there were no photographs on display. He then leant forward and discovered that the mantelpiece had been wiped clean, but the top of the television had not.

No sounds from upstairs, no opening of drawers, or clattering of photo frames. The kitchen was quiet, too. 'Seems like Goodhew may need help operating the kettle.'

'Do you want me to go?'

'No, wait here. The hot water's *my* department!'

From the moment Marks told her they were searching the cemetery, Kimberly knew she needed to see for herself, lay to rest any worry that Riley was lying in the deep grass or in one of the sunken hollows left by collapsing soil. An uninvited image had burst into her mind: a huddle of people crowding round something on the ground and looking back towards her with pity. And as hard as she tried to reach them, the harder she was dragged away.

So she understood the need to produce a photograph, but the need to check out the rear window had grown more urgent still.

In the window frame Rachel's house appeared just off-centre, like Mona Lisa's eye. As much as it commanded attention, all the activity was further in the foreground, as police and volunteers poked through every private corner of the graveyard. Kimberly pressed her hands to the smooth glass. Then she heard the voices drift upstairs from below. They spoke in low tones that were never meant to reach her, but the house had thin walls. At night she could hear the pumping of mattress springs and the subsequent flushing of the toilet which came from next-door, so picking out words spoken in her own home was never going to be a challenge. And she'd expected close scrutiny, since that was the police all over.

They would be assessing the situation, seeing her and Riley merely as a set of statistics. That DI had already said it: 'most likely options'. What did that mean in her case? To look for traces of blood that had been wiped from her walls? To contact Social Services and ask what they knew about her? Had they ever been in contact? Were they in any way concerned?

She could almost see the woman answering their questions: a functional woman, with functional clothes, functional shoes, and with thin pink fingers that tap-tap-tapped efficiently through the child-welfare database.

'Yes, we have her here. Kimberley Guyver, date of birth 27 November 1987? Let me see . . .' The woman would smile, tight-lipped and disapproving. 'Nothing recent, but we've had her in the system since the early nineties . . .'

In the system.

Well, the photo they wanted was gone, along with a small selection of her other favourites. And they'd only get it if she was forced to tell them everything. She rapped the window frame hard with the back of her hand, making her knuckles sting.

Was that the answer? Was there anything in it that would help Riley? She didn't know, couldn't think through all the ramifications. Her head felt jammed with too many thoughts, each tangled with the last, and the next. None of them finding room to breathe.

She was about to turn away from the window. Afterwards she would wonder whether she had been on the verge of telling the police everything, and whether the outcome would have been better if she had. But at that moment she spotted a figure staring across the cemetery towards her.

He saw her spot him, and he dropped the hood of his sweatshirt long enough for her to see his face clearly. He made the 'phone me' gesture.

She shook her head and stepped back from the glass.

He mouthed two words.

She read them at once, but it was a few more seconds before she understood what they might signify.

And, to be quite certain, she'd spend as long as possible in the bathroom . . . then stall like crazy.

Goodhew had no objection to making the hot drinks but on this occasion knew it translated as 'get out of my sight'. As a precaution he'd also brewed a pot of tea *and a* pot of coffee. But such chores often presented opportunity: in this case a chance to look through the kitchen cupboards.

67

Marks entered in time to see Goodhew dropping a handful of potato peelings back into the composting bin. Goodhew had washed and dried his hands before Marks inquired, 'Finished?'

'Yes, sir.'

'Find anything useful in there?'

'No, sir.'

'You should think about where you direct your energies, Gary. For example, taking Kimberly Guyver to the fire site this morning . . .'

'I know, sir.'

Marks scowled. 'You know what? That it was foolhardy? That it's lucky the repercussions weren't worse? What exactly were you thinking?'

Goodhew did his best to look contrite, and lowered his voice so PC Gully wouldn't hear. She might not welcome any favours, but he couldn't bring himself to drop her in it either. 'I don't know. I didn't think it through. Sorry.'

In response Marks lowered his voice, but managed to sound both louder and angrier. 'I didn't have you pegged as someone so easily led astray by the charms of the opposite sex.'

'It wasn't like that.'

'Tell me, how much of that conversation in there did you hear?'

'All of it.'

'Thought so.' Marks had clearly moved on. 'I'd like you to check out the Jay Andrews story.'

'I already did. There's someone of that name who's resident at Hinton Avenue nursing home. They also confirmed that Kimberly and Riley Guyver are regular visitors.'

'Someone's going to need to tell him about his son.'

'*I* can go.'

'Did they say anything about his condition?'

'No, I kept it really brief.'

'Didn't want to miss anything from the other room?' Marks managed a wry smile. 'So what else have you found?'

'Two boxes by the back door: personal papers in one, groceries in the other.'

'No photos?'

'No, sir, but it looks like something was standing on the mantelpiece until recently, so maybe she removed a photograph for some reason.'

'That crossed my mind, too.' Marks tilted his head to one side and frowned as he thought. 'Let's see what she brings us,' he said finally, but he continued to frown.

'Everything OK, sir?'

Before he could reply, Gully opened the kitchen door. 'There's a woman here to see Kimberly Guyver. Says she's Anita McVey.'

FOURTEEN

Anita McVey was in her fifties, with a boyish figure dressed in purple and black; more shades of purple than Goodhew knew names for although he definitely spotted magenta, indigo, mauve and what looked like the colour his mum had once tried on their front door, described on the tin as 'Racy Rubine'. The hair escaping from her baker's-boy hat was the same shade as Kimberly's, but beyond that he could see no resemblance. Anita's appearance was one of deliberate chaos: over-accessorized and curly-permed, primary school teacher with a twist of Marc Bolan.

She looked neither surprised nor fazed by the police presence in the house. 'Is she upstairs?' Gully nodded and Anita dropped her rucksack-sized handbag on to the settee, then plonked herself down next to it. 'Does she know I'm here?'

Once more Gully nodded. 'I can call her again.'

'No, she'll come down when she's ready, I'm quite sure.' Anita looked directly at Marks and seemed to be assessing him in some way. He excused himself and disappeared back into the kitchen; as if on cue, Gully followed.

Neither Anita nor Goodhew spoke. He was aware that Kimberly had been upstairs for some time, although probably less time than it seemed. On days like this, minutes ran at a different rate. He decided to go and look.

Goodhew was halfway between floors when he heard the bathroom door unlock. He waited where he was until she reappeared, and she passed him on the stairs without comment, but there was no mistaking the heaviness as her feet struck each tread, or the exhaustion which blanked her expression. Kimberly stumbled onwards, sagging only as the older woman's arms wrapped themselves around her. She buried her face in Anita's shoulder and they hung on to one another. Kimberly was taller and of stronger build, yet Anita was now the anchor, or maybe the tugboat guiding her to somewhere calmer.

Anita was the first to speak: 'Why didn't you call?'

'I don't know.' Kimberly began to sob. 'I thought he would turn up. I didn't want to upset you.'

'You silly girl.' Anita closed her eyes momentarily. Goodhew felt like an intruder but not guilty – they were beyond thinking about him. Instead they shared words: small sentences passing back and forth, sometimes coherent, sometimes cracked apart.

'They don't know where he is,' Kimberly said at last, and Anita stared at him then, and he felt the responsibility of being the face of *They*. 'What if he was in the fire?' Kimberly added.

'And you really don't know?'

'They think maybe Stefan . . .'

'And why would he?'

'Maybe you know his aggression towards Rachel . . . What if he didn't know Riley was there? I never guessed . . .'

'How could you?'

'I knew he hit her once. She kept it quiet, but I knew.'

Anita shook her head. 'Riley can't just vanish.'

'What if I never see him again?'

'Oh, Kim, that won't happen. It won't.'

Anita pulled her even closer, murmuring quiet words of comfort.

At least she didn't say the words 'I promise'. Why did they so often slip out when people were not in a position to use them? To Goodhew's relief she stopped short of that; and to his greater relief his mobile rang before he needed to consider whether Anita was taking Kimberly too far down the road of false hope.

It was the fire officer, too exhausted to deliver more than the bare facts. 'No other bodies . . . Probable arson . . . Awaiting tests.'

Goodhew ended the call. It was ironic that he was probably about to deliver a greater dose of false hope. Kimberly had already caught the positive note in his voice, and now looked at him expectantly. Relief already swelling inside her.

'Riley's not in the house,' he confirmed and, despite doing his best to keep the news low-key, she now looked as though her son was within touching distance.

'They're positive?' she gasped.

'Absolutely,' he replied, and in part he couldn't help but feel touched by the moment, but that feeling was quickly overtaken and swallowed up. It was too fleeting, too fragile, and he found it impossible to believe it held any real substance.

He needed to leave the building, get outside, get moving. And keep moving, probably.

This doing nothing always got to him – even if it only felt like doing nothing. He couldn't stand the way it pressed the air from his lungs, and clawed his muscles up into tight knots.

Stefan was out there somewhere, and if Riley was with him, he had to be in danger. Even if Riley was elsewhere, he still had to be in danger.

The kitchen door was slightly ajar, and Goodhew pushed it wide. Gully had been watching the front room through the chink. Marks was on the phone.

Goodhew took his own phone out of his pocket, and his call to the station connected almost immediately. He asked to be put through to the local intelligence officer, and had reached the top of the stairs by the time Sergeant Sheen picked up.

'Once I heard they'd not found another body, I took a bet I'd be getting a call from you. Regarding Mr Golinski, am I right?'

'What have you got on him?'

'Not much, but here we go. Stefan Golinski, born in Birmingham 25th October 1977. Couple of minor offences, then given community service for an assault back in '95, when he was . . .'

'Seventeen.'

'Yep. Then he moved to Cambridge, where his name pops up two or three times in relation to a spate of drunken brawls, but no charges. Seems like the same culprits were rounded up each time, and he was one of them. Then nothing . . . grew up, maybe.'

'Maybe.'

'Or he got better at not getting caught. Here's one titbit you might like. Seems that on each occasion the same type of injuries were inflicted, and the only person confirmed as being present at every incident was Stefan Golinski.'

'But still no prosecution?'

'CPS dropped it, because of no witnesses, no CCTV, no forensics.' Through the open door of Riley's room, Goodhew spotted a small pair of slippers. He went through and picked one up, and balanced it on the palm of his hand. 'What injuries?'

'Broken ribs and fingers. The fingers crushed, the ribs kicked in.'

Goodhew placed the slipper back alongside its mate. 'Got to go,' he said, his thoughts no longer with Sergeant Sheen.

Kimberly was standing in the doorway. She'd frozen as soon as she saw him there, her eyes wide and her lips parted, as though caught in mid-thought. 'I've come to find a photograph of Riley.'

'You look better,' he remarked.

'I'm doing OK . . . you know, comparatively. What's the police view at present? Cautiously optimistic, maybe?' Her tone was bitter.

'Maybe. You don't like the police much, do you?'

'Maybe you'll give me some reason to . . . but it seems like the world's packed out with *maybes*, doesn't it?'

As she opened the wardrobe door, he realized that there were no clothes inside. Instead he was looking at the inside of a compact art gallery.

'That's where I've seen you.'

'Pardon?'

'You sell paintings at the craft market – the Sunday one on Market Hill.'

'Sometimes.'

'I nearly bought one.'

'Yeah, you and a hundred others.' She seemed curious, though. 'Which one?' she asked.

'The girl falling from the punt.'

'This one?' She reached into the wardrobe and lifted a canvas out towards the light.

It was bigger than the print he had fancied, and showed a young woman in rolled-up jeans and a short-sleeved red shirt. Her feet were bare, the shirt riding up to expose the bare skin of her lower back. She clung on to the punting pole, laughing as she tried to keep her balance. She was a redhead but it didn't disguise the resemblance to Kimberly herself; the same bold features, large almond eyes, full lips and look of open defiance. She was painted in acrylics, using heady saturated colours. Behind her, in pen and ink, rose the stern facade of St John's College, solid, disciplined and unamused at being nothing but a prop.

He could easily have said 'She's beautiful', and it wouldn't have been anything but a statement of bald fact. But he knew that would be inappropriate, so he just nodded and said, 'That's the one.'

'Why didn't you, then?'

'Why didn't I what?'

'Buy it?'

She had a way of making the simplest questions direct and personal. He shrugged, unable to explain why the picture had seemed too bold, too energetic for his wall. He had left the print because, though it had provided an attractive moment in his day, it was just a bit too frivolous to take home.

'I don't think I had anywhere suitable to hang it.'

'I see.' She took it from him, put it back in the cupboard. 'At least you've the decency to keep words like 'juxtapose' and 'Vettriano' to yourself.'

'Closer to Al Moore's pin-up art than to Vettriano, I think.'

She didn't comment but passed him a small, square canvas. There was the pen-and-ink background again, but glasses suspended by their stems and bottles of wine this time. In the foreground a woman of about twenty held her glass aloft and smiled, her eyes a little unfocused, perhaps from the effects of her first glass.

Kimberly cleared her throat. 'Rachel,' she announced.

'How long ago?'

'Four years, give or take.'

Goodhew had developed a small but persistent habit of late. He found himself wondering whether there was anything different to be seen in a person pictured shortly before their untimely death. Some hint that they subconsciously knew that they were sitting for an image that would soon be part of a police appeal or a news bulletin, or just a page-filler to evoke a sympathetic mutter and a shake of the head before the reader flipped over to the celebrity gossip printed on the following pages. The idea was illogical, but he still looked.

He now drew no conclusions about Rachel's personality: it did not jump from the canvas the way it seemed to from Kimberly's portrait. Who Rachel was – or maybe who Kimberly thought she was – wasn't on display. But the moment seemed real enough, not an imaginary scene like the one on the punt.

'And did you paint this from a photograph?'

'No, sort of from memory. I started it that same night.' She could tell that puzzled him. 'I mean the night we were in that bar. She was drinking but I was sober, so I saw her at various stages during the evening. There was this moment' – she tapped the canvas – 'that moment in fact, when she seemed to be in the perfect place. We shared a flat then, and I stayed up 'til dawn making sketches. I went into her room and copied her nose and mouth while she was asleep. Those were the bits I couldn't do properly from memory.'

She took the canvas from him before he'd finished looking.

'Was that in Cambridge?' he asked. 'I don't recognize the background.'

'Artistic licence,' she replied, and said it quickly and lightly. And immediately he wondered if she was being sarcastic or telling a lie. She obviously heard it in her own voice, too, and corrected herself. 'We were in Spain for a while.'

'Working?'

'Yeah, it started as a holiday, then we decided to stay on.' Kimberly paused then put more emphasis on the start of the next sentence. 'I painted Rachel quite often.' It seemed a clumsy change of subject.

Kimberly's front door was fitted with a bell but no knocker, so the only alternative to ringing was to push the hinged letterbox open and let it spring shut again, with an abrupt snap-snap-snap. That was the sound which now carried up the stairs, providing Kimberly with a more convincing way to avoid discussing Spain.

Inside the cupboard was a shoebox sitting on a shelf. She pushed the lid to one side. 'You go and answer the door. I'll find you that photo.'

'The others are down there.'

'Just PC Gully. Anita's left and your boss has gone to hurry up the search outside. I thought they would have finished by now.'

'They decided to concentrate on the cemetery and university grounds first.'

As he said this, he heard the front door being opened. They both tried to listen to the conversation, but could only catch a word or two.

'Who is it?' he asked her.

'I can't tell,' Kimberly replied. 'But it sounds a bit like Tamsin.'

'Who's Tamsin?'

'Her dad owns the Celeste.'

'And you know her?'

'Unfortunately.'

Kimberly slid her hand further back into the shoebox and flicked through several more snapshots, finally picking out one which was posed more formally than the rest. She stared at the toddler in the photo and Goodhew could see that the distraction of the previous few minutes was gone. As the little boy grinned at her with a lopsided expression full of unbridled mischief, she touched his face and drew in a long slow breath.

'Just then when we were talking . . .' she began, but the words wouldn't come.

'I know – you hadn't forgotten him.'

She nodded, then managed to say, 'Stefan has no reason to hurt him.' There was no sign that she was going to cry, but that didn't mean she relished being confronted by an unwanted visitor.

'You can stay here while I find out what she wants?'

'No,' her grip on the photograph tightened, 'I'm not going to hide from her.'

FIFTEEN

Kimberly had long since chosen to forget the occasions when she'd socialized with Tamsin Lewton. The idea that there'd been anything approaching warmth between them served only to deepen the hostility she felt now.

She doubted that Tamsin had changed much: still youthful yet mature, blonde but intelligent, tanned but never trashy. She had the look of a woman who planned to do nothing but marry well and age gracefully. To live off family money, yet claim to be her own person.

Kimberly knew she was being judgemental, a bigot, a bitch even: and for all she repelled the idea of any charitable thoughts towards Tamsin she still knew that only two events had made her shut her heart against her. One betrayal apiece. She couldn't find enough compassion to care that Tamsin's eyes were welling with tears, or accept that maybe Rachel's death might be a blow to both of them.

Tamsin reached out her hand as if she thought Kimberly would want to embrace her. Kimberly didn't.

'How are you?' she asked quietly.

Tamsin withdrew her hand. 'Poor Rachel.'

'They haven't identified her yet.' It was an illogical thing to say. Who else was it going to be?

'Who else could it be?' Tamsin echoed the thought.

'Well, I don't know,' Kimberly snapped. 'At the moment I'm not sitting round playing guessing games. Why are you here?'

'It's about Nick.'

At any other time, Kimberly would have braced herself for those words. She was expert at controlling her expressions, seeming maybe a little too calm to be natural, but at any other time she would certainly not have gasped or blinked, or floundered for words in the seconds that followed.

'Nick?' she repeated, and she silently cursed herself for being caught off guard. *So* fucking off guard. 'Now is not really the time to be telling me about Nick, is it, Tam?' She tried to sound genuinely indignant. 'Do you think I care?'

Tamsin reddened. 'He's dead.'

This time Kimberly was ready. She shook her head in disbelief. 'When?'

'The whole time. They found his car. Divers found his car. There was an accident . . .'

'He crashed?'

'No, someone else had an accident, went off the road into the sea ten miles from Cartagena. Divers went to recover the body, and found Nick's car.'

Kimberly imagined the scene: the Merc being winched clear of the water, the police, the body bag, Nick's parents. She stopped then, unable to think beyond them: Trudy and Dougie. 'How is she?'

'Who?'

'Trudy?'

'I think you know. Is it Riley that's missing?'

Kimberly looked down at the photo still in her hand. At the wonky smile and the innocent eyes. She handed it to Tamsin. 'The police said they need one.'

Tamsin studied it, then gave it back. 'He looks a lot like Jay.'

'Rachel thought he was more like me.'

Tamsin didn't stay much longer. Kimberly's habitual animosity towards her was temporarily displaced by feelings of sympathy, some kind of shared grief perhaps. But she knew it wouldn't last. At the front door, Tamsin hesitated before stepping outside. 'By the way, the police are now investigating Nick's death. We believe he was murdered.'

Goodhew reached the door before Kimberly had had the chance to close it fully. 'I just want a word with her,' he explained, 'then Marks wants us all back at Parkside.'

PC Gully was already halfway across the room after him. 'Marks said you weren't to run off.'

Goodhew glanced back. 'Like I said, I won't be a minute.'

He left, and Gully turned to Kimberly. 'He'll catch us up.' Gully looked uncomfortable.

Kimberly had noticed her blushing earlier, too, each time over very minor incidents. She wondered whether the policewoman could be even younger than she looked. Or maybe out of her depth?

Kimberly nodded towards the door. 'I'm ready.'

The police car was the closest vehicle to the house. Goodhew was further down the street, already too deep in conversation with Tamsin to acknowledge their departure. As Gully drove them out of the road, Kimberly's last glance backwards registered Goodhew making notes and Tamsin talking, probably far too freely. She knew Tamsin's agenda – and Anita's, and maybe even Stefan's. She wondered about Goodhew's, though; she found it hard to believe that he really had remembered her and her painting. Why would a police detective have been hanging around the street market? Without opening herself up to paranoia, no viable answer came to her. No, she didn't understand his agenda, but her own was more straightforward.

At 5 a.m. every day, Riley would wake up and climb into her bed. He slept again then, with his head on her shoulder and one hand on her stomach. It was peaceful and perfect.

Her own agenda was therefore clear: get Riley safely home, no matter what the cost.

SIXTEEN

The walk from Blossom Street to Parkside Station took him no more than five minutes. Goodhew used every second to inhale fresh air: it enlivened him, it took his thoughts away from the inertia of that house, from the smothering wait and the distorted clock that was ticking unpleasantly in the corner of Riley Guyver's life. Wait, hope, wait, hope . . .

He turned on to East Road, where the air was less clean; bursting instead with street fumes, the smell of petrol, a kebab shop, bus diesel and dust.

It smelt great.

His head was full of his various conversations with Kimberly, the things she'd said and the things she hadn't. He knew far less about her now than he'd thought he'd already learnt during the few minutes they'd spent watching the blaze.

She had been just one entity then: a mother terrified for her child, a woman fearing the future, a human being in need of help. He knew that there was far more to her than that, like there was far more to everyone than how they might be perceived in one traumatic moment. But he could not shake the feeling that the woman he'd tried to talk to today was different from the one yesterday. Walls had appeared, mirrors, shades, and somewhere amongst them he'd lost sight of her. She had reappeared in kaleidoscopic fragments: a moment of distrust, a flash of openness, a breath of fear and a millisecond of hate. She'd been holding back at the one time no parent could afford to do so. He didn't yet understand her motivations, didn't like the possibilities either, but equally couldn't erase the memory of the first moment he'd seen her at the fire, nor could he shake the instinct that told him *that* had been the real face of Kimberly Guyver.

He wanted to keep walking – past the police station and on to wherever Stefan was hiding, there to find Riley and bring him home. He recognized a metaphor as he thought one.

He didn't relish trading the inside of one building for the inside of another, but he knew that Parkside had to be his next stop, and hoped he could make some independent progress before Marks caught him and reeled him back in.

Goodhew switched his mobile to silent and slipped in through the main entrance, past the desk sergeant.

The first stop was Sergeant Sheen. Sheen shared his office with two other officers, but neither of the pair would have dared to call it theirs. In fact Goodhew found it difficult to keep tabs on who was the current incumbent of each of the other chairs. The rule for that room seemed simple: if you weren't Sheen, you had merely a desk and chair, and no licence for any overspill. If you were Sheen, however, every other square inch was yours for the taking.

The room was small and crammed with box files and ring binders; it had two card-indexing systems, one that was alphabetical and religiously but grudgingly replicated on to his computer, and a second one which only Sheen ever touched. 'My red box,' Sheen described it in his strong Fen accent. Since it had now spilled over into six overflow boxes of various colours, its loose title was a fair cautionary hint as to the state of the contents.

Only Sheen ever touched it because only Sheen was half capable of finding or deciphering anything it contained. Mostly it held pages of his own notes: sheets of A4 smothered with the entangled scrawlings of four different colours of ballpoint pen. Here he wrote down thoughts and ideas and random facts, none of which could be considered admissible evidence, but all of which might have had a *slight chance* of being crucial at some point.

Goodhew had only to mention the name 'Nick Lewton' for Sheen to start flipping through those layers of crinkled paper.

'Now, I know that name. I can see exactly what the page looks like. I'll find you the official bits in a mo', but you'll be wanting this too . . . once I find it.'

After nothing appeared from the first three boxes, Goodhew was starting to fidget. 'If you like, I could start with the information on file . . .'

'No, no, here she is. Start with this one. It's got all the vital notes.' Sheen held it up, but stopped short of letting Goodhew actually take hold of it. 'Green notes are mostly cross references, tells me what items might be linked, no matter how tenuous. Here's your Spanish disappearance.'

The page was written in landscape format, and he tapped the top right corner. 'There's young Nick doing his vanishing act.'

Goodhew took the sheet by the opposite corner and, with a combination of earnest interest and firm tug, was successful in extracting it from Sheen's right hand. He was surprised to discover that it wasn't actually dedicated to Nick Lewton's disappearance; instead it was headed 'Dougie Lewton and Family'.

'Don't tell me you've never heard of them?' Sheen had noticed Goodhew's expression, and grinned. 'Don't take offence at this but that's because you've only been here five minutes. You're hardly going to know about a family that moved away about the time you were probably doing your GCSEs.'

Goodhew suspected that he was about to learn enough information to pass an exam. He pulled up a chair.

'The dad, that's Dougie, he's a real London boy. He moved out here in the early seventies with enough cash to buy himself into a couple of pubs. Our cousins in the Met told us he was into booze, bets, boxing and boobs. He described himself as a promoter, which just meant he had fingers in lots of pies. They didn't have anything on him, claiming he could pull his finger out of any one of them pies and it'd be clean. He married Trudy – she was the daughter of a boxer named Noel Dowd. Dougie didn't want to do anything to upset Dowd, so vowed to keep a low profile with the ladies after that.'

'And then he had his kids?'

'Nearly there, nearly, but first he set about making money here in Cambridge. He was smart, built up the pubs, leased them out, bought student accommodation and rented it out, too. He bought property at the right price and sold it at the right price, and all through this there were rumours – stories of competitors going under and students getting shafted.

'Then came the kids, two of them, Nick and Tamsin. They were in their teens before I first saw either of them. I was patrolling the centre one night after the student clubs had shut. Nick was fifteen, and I caught him shagging a girl in the doorway of the chemist's down King Street. Cocky he was, told me they were queuing for condoms but couldn't seem to wait for opening time. I took both their names and told them to clear off. There was something in the way he looked, though, and I thought there's one to watch.' Sheen nodded like he was wholeheartedly agreeing with himself.

The pause offered an opportunity for Goodhew to query another name on the sheet. 'So who was Rita?'

'Now you're going back to the eighties, and it's not who, but what. Cambridge used to have a club called the Dorothy, so Dougie opened a rival one and christened it the Rita Club. Then in about '85 he moved into the Rose and Crown – used to be on Newmarket Road, a real drinkers' pub, but shut down after the smoking ban came in a couple of years ago.'

Goodhew leaned forward in his chair, willing Sheen to move on. 'And he sold the Rita Club?'

'You have to remember those were the days when people packed the pubs in the evenings. Come a Thursday or Friday night they were wall-to-wall with customers. Dougie Lewton didn't sell it, he just kept buying, opened the Rita, bought two or three more pubs . . . then the Smoke and Light Club. He never off-loaded any of them until the late eighties when he got shot of the lot just before the property crash. The only one he kept was the Celeste.'

'The Celeste in Market Passage?'

'That's right,' Sheen raised his hand, 'but back to Nick first. Just as I'd suspected, he turned out to be a troublemaker. What I'd seen wasn't the start of it, and in fairness to Dougie he did try to keep a rein on him, but then there were a couple of nasty fights, and Dougie packed up his wife and kids and left for Spain. Seemed like it happened overnight.' Sheen clicked his fingers. 'Just like that, it was.'

'So he sold the Celeste?'

Sheen paused and bent across until his face was close to Goodhew's. 'My youngest boy is just like you: no pause button, just fast-forward. Now, if you don't want to be bored with a long story about my son James, I suggest you let me finish this one at my own pace.'

Goodhew nodded. 'Sorry.'

''Parently he sat on the money until he had the chance to buy a club in Spain. Called it the Rita Club, too, and it's one of them hot sweaty places, full of boobs and booze, just like Dougie likes it. Funny way to keep your kids out of trouble, if you ask me, but when I heard that Nick was managing the club, I thought maybe he'd come straight. At least until I heard he'd disappeared.'

Goodhew wondered how Sheen knew all of this.

'And the reason I know all of this?' Sheen continued. 'Because of the Celeste. I keep my ear to the ground when someone still owns a venue like that. Now I'll go and find you all the official details on file.'

Goodhew turned his attention back to Sheen's sheet of paper, and realized that all the seemingly random names and arrows now made sense. He suddenly hoped that Sheen wasn't planning early retirement.

SEVENTEEN

In the end, Sheen sent Goodhew away with just the promise that whatever other documents he had would follow later. 'I bet your DI's lookin' for you,' he added sagely.

Goodhew felt his conscience poke at him: he knew he was playing the odds by risking being unavailable when Marks needed him most. He assured himself that nothing urgent could have taken place over the last hour, but when he retrieved his silenced phone from his pocket and saw that there were six missed calls, his pulse quickened. He headed for Marks' office, ringing the voicemail because, if he was being honest, he was too much of a coward to phone Marks direct.

Message one was Mel who, in a hushed voice, hissed, 'Just to let you know, you're wanted.'

Message two was Marks himself: 'Goodhew, phone me.'

Goodhew was skipping straight to number six when Mel announced her presence by thumping his arm. 'Marks has started a briefing. You'd better get along there, fast.'

He thanked her and nipped along the corridor, picking up the indistinct sound of Marks' voice reverberating through the thin walls of the large office allocated as the incident room. Goodhew eased the door open, slipped through and slid into the nearest available seat. The room was stuffy and slightly stale, like the air was just on the turn. There were nearly a dozen people there already, and not one of them seemed to notice his arrival. Several held coffee cups as if they had paused just before taking a swig. He hoped this was because the coffee was unpalatable, and not a reaction to the update.

Marks was standing in front of the wipe board, next to which an easel displayed a single oversize photographic print of Riley Guyver. The child wore stonewashed jeans and a royal-blue and red striped T-shirt; he had looked straight into the camera, so now his gaze seemed locked on to Goodhew's.

'This picture is the most up-to-date available,' Marks continued, 'and therefore the image that our press officer, Liz Bradley, has issued to the press and television. It will appear in the later edition of this evening's newspaper, on the TV news and on most of tomorrow's nationals.'

Riley's eyes were darker than Kimberly's, but Goodhew could see that the child had inherited some of her air of defiance. Maybe the gaze was a little less angry, and a little more determined, but it was there.

'Next we have our main suspect, Stefan Golinski.' Marks remained silent as he spent a few seconds pinning a ten-by-eight enlargement next to the image of Riley. 'Just to add to what we already know about him, I can confirm that Golinski has no previous for any offences against children, but he's not exactly in anyone's baby-sitting circle either. So we're looking at two scenarios, one where two people have disappeared in separate circumstances and the other, more likely, scenario where those disappearances are related. As far as we know, there have been no sightings of either individual. In Stefan's case his bank account remains untouched, his known email accounts and mobile phone totally unused.'

DC Charles raised his hand. 'What about his car?'

'The car is a little more complicated. For whatever reason, it seems he was not in the habit of correctly registering vehicles and therefore didn't bother with insignificant detail such as insurance. All we know is that he's recently been driving a dark-coloured Toyota saloon. Nothing of that description was left at the Park Street multi-storey last night, but he's known to have used it from time to time. The car park has handed over the footage, so a couple of people here are going to have the unenviable job of watching through it until he's spotted. Once we have the registration number, we can get the ANPR system to flag up any recent activity.'

Inwardly, Goodhew groaned. ANPR stood for automated number plate recognition, which was efficient at producing data but the task of analysing it could be mind-numbing, and because of his late arrival he felt sure the job was heading his way. He glanced around at the others, and willed it to fall into someone else's lap, Kincaide's for first choice but, beyond that, anybody's lap except his own.

Marks pinned up the next photograph, announcing, 'Kimberly Guyver.' It was a recent snapshot and definitely not a police photo. The shot was cropped tightly to her face but it looked like she was somewhere outside, since the light seemed natural and there were patches of green in the background which could be shrubbery. She wore a blue shirt unbuttoned at the neck and maybe was sitting on the grass, because she was smiling up at the camera, her eyes bright and her teeth looking very white against her tanned skin. The camera had been smiling back down at her, making good friends with the curve of her cheek and the deeper curves of her cleavage.

There were a few grunts of interest, a couple of muttered comments and one stifled laugh. The collective response was primal, pack-like: that stale smell had to indicate a surfeit of testosterone. Goodhew noticed the stiffening of Marks' spine and the beady-eyed look that he cast around the group. Most of them were still too focused on Kimberly's cleavage to pick up the warning signals, and still the room didn't settle.

Marks clapped his hands together twice. 'Yes, as several of you have already noted, she is an extremely attractive woman. Good powers of observation are certainly part of the job, but far better directed elsewhere in this case. DC Charles?'

'Sir?'

'What exactly is amusing you?'

'Nothing, sir.'

'And you, Young?'

'Nothing, sir.'

'I disagree, you're both letching down a young woman's top and giggling like a couple of fourteen-year-olds. I chose this photograph for a reason: to demonstrate the unpleasantness this young woman will be put through if this investigation is not resolved quickly and she is shown to be anything but the most saintly of mothers.' He poked his finger at each of them in turn, 'That prurient attitude will just be the tip of the iceberg. Remember, Kimberly Guyver is Riley Guyver's mother, and Rachel Golinski was her best friend. She, too, has feelings, and do not forget that. Until evidence tells us otherwise, she is first and foremost a victim in this case. Is that clear?'

There were various nods and grunts of assent. Goodhew half expected Marks to repeat his question in pursuit of a more enthusiastic response; but he didn't. As for becoming the prime candidate for endless hours of viewing CCTV footage, Goodhew guessed he was now completely off the hook.

It took Marks another ten minutes to conclude, while pressing home the status of the case. 'Finally, Rachel Golinski's autopsy report will be with us at any minute. Remember, this is a murder enquiry until I tell you otherwise.' Only then did he start allocating tasks. Kincaide and Goodhew were left until last.

'Kincaide, take yourself down to Hinton Avenue nursing home and find out the extent of Jay Andrews' incapacitation . . . Does he know his son is missing? Does he even know he has a son? When did Kimberly Guyver last visit? So on and so forth. If he can't answer, find out what you can from the staff.'

Which left only Goodhew.

Everyone else was still in the room, ostensibly waiting until the completion of business, but Goodhew knew it was more about making sure everyone got what they deserved. And for this reason he wanted them to witness whatever Marks was about to dish out.

'And last we have our new boy, DC Goodhew, left there on the bench as the team was selected. Why would that be?'

'Sir, it's –' he began, but Marks cut him short.

'Rhetorical, Goodhew, rhetorical. I don't actually want to know why. Once again, you felt the need to go off on your own sweet way. I have now just demonstrated how it puts you outside the team.

'As you know, the Fire Service received an emergency call alerting us to the fire, while eyewitnesses seemed pretty certain that a teenager who had been trying to access the property had also rung 999. Perhaps they are one and the same individual, perhaps not. It's a pay-as-you-go mobile, and I want you to locate it.'

With that, Marks dismissed the team.

PC Wilkes was waiting to enter the briefing room just as they were all leaving. She carried an A3 manila envelope. Goodhew looked back once as he reached the end of the corridor, to see his boss heading in the opposite direction, same envelope in hand, back to his own office.

By the time Goodhew turned the corner, the other detectives had already reached the top of the main stairs, and he followed them without attempting to catch up. He didn't feel as though he was being ostracized in any way; he hadn't been in the department long enough to be *in*, never mind being back out again. Goodhew kept an expression of downcast humility all the way to the bottom of the stairs while, moving as one, his colleagues headed out the back entrance towards their various vehicles.

Goodhew himself left by the front door, and set off on foot. And, step by step, his serious expression transformed slowly into a grin. He had little to go on, that was true: just a voice recording, a mobile-phone number and a couple of witnesses. But he'd just realized that the teenager he and Bryn had crossed paths with on the night of the fire was the one he now sought. That made Goodhew one of those eyewitnesses mentioned and, more importantly, he now had some idea which direction the anonymous caller had taken, and what the caller looked like.

And, to cap it all, Marks had left him alone and unsupervised. This was a chance to prove something to his boss, and Goodhew had no intention of wasting the opportunity.

It had been two hours earlier when Gully arrived at the station with Kimberly Guyver. The policewoman had pulled back out of Blossom Street just as a local news crew pulled in, and then returned to Parkside with a young man on a small but overly loud moped in pursuit. She suspected him of being another media man, maybe a photographer, and kept checking her rear-view mirror anxiously, not liking the way he kept so close to her back bumper. He remained on her tail until the final junction, when she turned right but he headed straight on, slaloming through the queue of morning traffic and out of sight.

Gully felt a mix of relief and foolishness. Surplus adrenalin had begun pumping through her veins; fully charged, with no release now but to carry on pointlessly circulating until it burnt out. She made it into the car park with a faultless imitation of composure, then delivered Kimberly to the first interview room, where press officer Bradley and another PC were already waiting.

Gully didn't hang around for any further formalities, as the first signs of a headache were gathering around her temples. Instead she sat quietly in the staff kitchen and sipped from a mug of hot water.

She was reboiling the kettle when DI Marks peered in. 'Everything all right?'

She nodded. 'Bit of a headache, nothing really.'

'How's your second week going?'

'Fine, I think, sir. Kimberly Guyver's waiting for you in the first interview room. If it's all right, I'll take a break, and get something to eat.'

'You look like you could do with a couple of hours off. Any case like this has the potential of turning into more of a marathon than a sprint. No point in making yourself ill on day one.'

Gully flushed. 'No, it's nothing like that. I'll be fine.' That wasn't true: pressure was mounting behind her right eye, and it throbbed with every word she spoke. If it didn't subside quickly, she'd be facing a full-blown migraine – the hereditary Achilles heel embedded in the DNA of all her father's blood relatives. 'I'll be pleased to stay with Kimberly if she decides to go back home.'

'We'll review that a little later.' He opened the door and half-turned as if about to leave, then stopped. 'Bear in mind the possibility that the mother's somehow involved.'

'No. She's distraught.'

'Word of warning, don't get too close.' He held up a hand before she could object. 'You shouldn't have taken her to the fire scene earlier.'

'I'm sorry, I realize I made a mistake.'

'Second week, so you're bound to make them. Just don't be too accommodating. I don't only mean with the public, but with our detectives too.'

She couldn't work out if this last part was a caution for the future or admonishment for other errors that she wasn't even aware she had made. She couldn't now trust herself to ask him what he meant, since she could imagine the question coming out with a hostile edge to it, or maybe his answer exposing her in some horribly inexperienced light.

As it was, she wished the floor would open up and swallow her.

This time he did leave, making a parting comment that he could manage without her until she felt up to it. Perhaps it was said out of sympathy, but if it was supposed to make her feel better, it failed.

She wished she'd been honest with Marks about taking Kimberly to the fire scene before he'd heard it from Goodhew. Gully stayed in the kitchen, nursing both her head and her dented confidence, until the second dose of paracetamol kicked in. By then she'd already made her decision: get back to Kimberly and stick with her; she'd then show Marks that she was more than capable of staying detached.

She was in the corridor heading towards the interview room, when Mel Lake caught up with her.

'Did you notice anyone hanging round the cemetery?' Mel asked.

Gully kept walking. 'Who wants to know?'

Mel passed her a Post-it note, which Gully glanced at. 'No, I didn't, but when you next speak to DC Goodhew, make sure he understands that I didn't spend all my time at that house staring out of the bedroom window.'

Mel looked amused. 'No problem,' she said, and took back the piece of paper.

She might not know Mel properly yet, but that fact that she was a chirpy little cheerleader for 'Team Goodhew' stood out a mile. Gully had nothing else to add, and found herself returning her own version of a superficial smile, before stepping forward to knock on the interview-room door.

EIGHTEEN

The mobile phone that had made the 999 call had been topped up on four occasions in the last two months, and the top-ups had been purchased at three different newsagents: WH Smith in the city centre, and the Star off-licence and Lally's both in Mill Road. At least the service provider had supplied that much information, but the calls sent and received were unavailable until the morning.

Goodhew left off visiting the city centre until last, since it seemed far more likely the lad he was seeking was local to the Mill Road area. And infinitely more likely that one of the family-run shops might be able to identify one of their regular customers.

Two top-ups had been sold at the off-licence, but the woman at the cash desk couldn't remember arranging either.

'I would have been here, though; if the shop's open I'm in it, simple as that.' Her name badge read 'Jill' and he quickly realized that this seemed to be the most complex piece of information that she was prepared to divulge. 'We get loads of people through that door, love, all sorts.'

He tried rewording his enquiry and she came right back with, 'Like I said, love, we get all sorts in here.'

He made one final attempt. 'He's quite lightly built, mid to late teens, might have been wearing a baggy grey sweatshirt?'

Jill behind the till shook her head. 'Wouldn't know, darling. The ones like that all look the same.'

He prayed that Lally's would prove more fruitful or, more precisely, that a visit to Smith's wouldn't be necessary; though that chain probably had some fancy sales system that would pinpoint exactly when the sale went through, and at which of the tills, from which information they'd be able to identify where to search for the customer's image on their security tape. It would be a long job and too many hours had slipped away already.

Lally's was a long narrow shop with the counter situated near the rear wall. No name-badge this time but the owner, a forty-five-year-old man with a quiff and a London accent, introduced himself as Raj. 'Yeh, I know who you mean.'

Goodhew asked for a name, but Raj shook his head and grinned broadly. 'It's not that easy, I'm afraid. He comes in all the time, but I don't know if I've ever seen him here with anyone else, so I've never heard him being called by name.'

'Any idea where he lives? Which way he goes from here, or from which direction he comes in?'

'Somewhere towards the centre . . . I don't know. I've seen him down towards the cemetery entrance. Mill Road Cemetery, if you know where that is? Is it drugs, then?'

'No, why d'you ask that?'

'Dunno, but he seems the type, I s'pose. I guess he could live over that way, but then why come all the way up here when Norfolk Street or maybe even East Road's shops are closer?'

The description Raj gave clashed with Goodhew's own memory of the youth. Raj thought he was a couple of inches taller, maybe five-foot-eleven, only about fifteen years old, and never remembered seeing him without his black baseball cap, *ever*. Goodhew began to wonder whether they were thinking of the same lad; and, even if they were, he asked himself if he could genuinely recognize him again. He guessed there were many such things you'd never know until the moment came, and this was probably one of them.

The sky was overcast but the air was warm and static. Goodhew started at a brisk walk but soon broke into a jog, and by the time he reached Mill Road Cemetery he was breathing more quickly and his shirt was feeling heavy against his skin.

He walked through to the centre where a circular footpath ran round the site where the chapel had once stood, and sat down at the bench giving him the best view of the cemetery's southern end. It meant he could cover both the main entrances. Goodhew didn't have a newspaper to hide behind, so he sat forward, elbows on knees, mobile in hand, and did his best impression of a man deciding what to include in a vital text message. He stayed like that for almost an hour, swapped seats, then did the same, this time facing the north end. The afternoon drew to a close with no progress.

The number of people passing through began to increase as school ended and offices began to close. He decided to patrol the perimeter and check if there was any other obvious reason that the teenager may have been in the cemetery.

He didn't know the graveyard too well but was well aware that one of the more derelict corners was a hang-out for drug users. Dense and neglected shrubbery had turned that area into a green tunnel ending in a cave. He picked his way through a depressing litter of syringes, discarded lager cans and rusting aerosols. Ivy and bramble had swallowed most of the memorials. Next to one stood a moss-covered statue of what appeared to be a headless chorister, one of its hands holding a broken tablet of stone. By its feet the faces of flat gravestones stared up at a canopy of ivy-choked trees, most of the carefully incised words obliterated by time. Mute monuments and the dispossessed; it struck Goodhew that this corner was a place for people who didn't have much of a voice in the world at large. Debris was strewn deep into the brambles, and he felt it a pity that the people who cared for the grounds never ventured this far, but a greater pity that so many other people needed somewhere like this. He felt heavy with the heat, and with his lack of progress.

Then he saw it.

He'd begun to turn away when a spark of recognition flooded his brain. Black cloth amid the tangle of undergrowth. He dropped to his hands and knees and tried to reach into the bushes. He was about a foot short, though he leant into the brambles and felt them snagging on his shirt. He shuffled forwards an inch, then another, ignoring the thorns grazing the back of his outstretched hand. Finally his first two fingers were within touching distance, and with a pincer action he used them to catch hold of it. He tugged it towards him until it was finally free. With his other hand he reached into his front pocket for a clear plastic bag; he shook it open and dropped his find into it.

Only then did he take a closer look at the baseball cap that he hoped would bring him a step closer to their elusive caller.

Marks had laughed on seeing Goodhew, at which point Gary realized that his jeans were streaked with dirt and grass stains, burrs were in his hair, and some sort of cobweb was clinging on to his shirt.

'I'd have had an apoplectic Kincaide on my hands if I'd sent him instead. That or no cap.' Marks had then muttered in afterthought, 'Take a break, a couple of hours, get cleaned up, have something to eat, then come back. I need everyone pushing this one – it's taking too long to make headway.'

On this occasion Goodhew had done just what he was told, in essence at any rate. He showered, changed into fresh jeans and his much loved dark-blue shirt, then hurried across Parker's Piece to the gym adjoining Parkside Pool. It was now a few minutes after seven and he'd promised to do his grandmother a favour.

'We have a man shortage,' she'd informed him, following that announcement with a low, husky laugh. 'The ladies will love you.'

Evidently that was supposed to sound like a good thing.

He'd made one, albeit feeble, attempt at making an escape. 'I can't dance.'

'Of course you can. You just can't salsa yet, and that's the entire purpose of the lesson.'

That conversation was haunting him now as he climbed the stairs and caught the first strains of an upbeat number which sounded like it might be titled 'Torture with Gusto'. As his grandmother was by far the fittest pensioner he knew, he wondered if any of her elderly friends would have expired by the end of this class. He was surprised when he opened the door and saw that 80 per cent were his age, and about 90 per cent of those were women.

That equated to an attractive 72 per cent young women, though that was nowhere near being the most attractive figure in the room. His heart sank and he took a step backwards; the best route would be a quick retreat. He heard his grandmother's voice before he could escape any further.

'Gary, come on in!'

And, for the second time in less than an hour, he did exactly what he was told. He considered this further as he found himself stumbling round the floor with Connie, a bossy but gorgeous doubly left-footed Italian who snapped at him every time she herself made a mistake, and again when he shared about thirty seconds of perfect synchronicity with the very toned Nicole. By the end of the class he figured that following orders once in a while could provide some pleasant side effects.

He walked to the pool's café with his grandmother, and bought her a pot of tea and a portion of chips for himself, which he doused in salad cream just because he felt like it. 'I reckon I've burnt this off already.'

'You enjoyed it, then?' his grandmother asked.

'It was OK,' he conceded.

'Liar, you loved it.'

'It was OK,' he repeated, but broke into a grin. 'Fair enough, it was fun.' But his enjoyment was just a burst of sunshine between the clouds. 'I will have to go in a few minutes, though.'

'So you're working on the Riley Guyver case?'

'You don't miss much.'

Outside, the grey evening light was fading, leaving their surroundings looking increasingly melancholy.

'Gary, I really want to say something, but I don't want you to think I'm turning into some manipulative busybody in my late middle age. On second thoughts, however, I think you know your own mind very well.'

'Blimey, this is sounding rather deep already.'

'I can continue?'

'Well, you have to now. That's too much like only half a story.'

She wiped a smudge of her red lipstick from her mug and placed it back on the tray, then spread her manicured hands palms-down on the table. 'Sometimes I can detect a certain expression on your face.' She held his gaze steadily in hers. 'Why do some cases make you feel so individually responsible? Like when you get a bee in your bonnet, and start running your own parallel investigations.'

'I haven't done that for a while.'

'Only because Marks is keeping you so busy. I can completely understand the general urgency of finding this little boy, but has it ever occurred to you that the cases that motivate you to go one step further are the ones that strike a chord with you in some personal way?'

'No, you've lost me.'

'You pick out people who need help, because they don't quite fit – because you don't quite fit.'

It was a remark that stung more than he might have expected. 'So how does that apply in this case?'

'Describe Kimberly Guyver's looks.'

'Better than average?'

She gave a short laugh, 'Yes, and Cambridge dabbles in adult education!' She shook her head. 'Like it or not, in today's world looks like hers could open doors all over, and what does she do with them but sit at home and paint pictures? She actually wants people to look at her paintings, not at her.'

'And you reckon I want to help her just because she's good-looking?'

'Don't be stupid.' The irascibility in her tone was uncharacteristic. 'I know very well that's not the way your brain works.'

His corresponding moment of irritation was replaced by a sense of curiosity. 'So . . .?'

She stared at him thoughtfully. 'I'm struggling to find the right words, Gary.'

'I'm sorry, I didn't mean to sound annoyed.'

'No, no, I think I explained it in the wrong way. Forget I said anything.' She reached forward and squeezed his arm. 'Oh, and before you go I have a letter for you.' She passed him an envelope.

He folded it in half and slid it into his pocket. 'Thanks.'

'You could actually read this one.'

'What does it say?'

'It's confirming the final transfer of all assets left to you by your grandfather.'

'OK,' he said, 'I'll have a look.'

'Gary, I understand. Now that it's all in your name, there's no need for me to know any more. I'd rather we stayed friends than have this cause a rift between us.'

That was the moment when he knew conclusively that she truly understood him. 'Me too,' he said. He leant across and kissed her cheek. 'I'll see you soon.'

As he returned to work, the envelope in his pocket weighed surprisingly little, but her earlier words kept bothering him. What was it about Kimberly Guyver that was drawing him in? And how would his grandmother know?

Michael Kincaide had driven away from Parkside Police Station preoccupied by the suspicion that he'd ended up with the short straw somehow, while Goodhew had been handed a comparative gem. He decided to skip lunch, thinking that perhaps if he got back promptly, Marks would give him something more challenging to tackle.

Hinton bloody Avenue nursing home?

It was less than a mile from Kincaide's home and he'd often seen their minibus driving through the area. It had wheelchair-lifting gear on the back and as many staff as patients inside, and he didn't know why but something about it made him feel uncomfortable. No doubt the whole community-care initiative had a lot going for it, but that did seem like a whole lot on running around when it was basically a hospital ward in all but name.

Hinton Avenue was a wide road of 1930s bay-fronted houses, of which the nursing home was the most impressive and sat on a plot easily twice as large as its neighbours. He parked up, and showed his badge to a young Filipino nurse. She asked him to wait but didn't hurry off to fetch anyone. The reception area was nothing more than a couple of wing chairs placed in a wider part of the corridor.

Standing at one end gave him a view of the patients' lounge. 'Which one is Jay Andrews?' he inquired.

'Over in the corner.'

Jay sat in a high, padded hospital chair that tilted back at a 45-degree angle. His body slumped over to one side and his head tipped back further still. He was grinning, slack-jawed and vacant.

'He can't speak, then?'

'Oh, no.' She looked apologetic. 'You can chat to him, though.

Go over and introduce yourself. He's always pleased to have a visitor. Would you like me to find the manager for you now?'

'Thank you.'

Kincaide moved closer and watched Jay Andrews for the next few minutes, realizing there was little point in attempting an introduction. Kincaide wouldn't have known what to say anyway, and he wasn't going to risk the embarrassment of being seen talking to himself. One thing was clear: Kimberly Guyver had been telling the truth. Eventually he retreated towards the door.

'Detective?' he turned to see a stocky woman with a man's haircut. She held out her hand. 'Amanda Tebbutt. You're here about Jay's missing son?'

'That's right. Was he a regular visitor?'

'Of course. Kimberly used to visit when she was pregnant, then she brought the baby in after he was born, and at least once a week ever since.'

Kimberly Guyver's story clearly checked out: the dates, her visits, all of it. He double-checked some of the detail, and finally Amanda Tebbutt invited him to go through. 'You can talk to him,' she confirmed.

'But he can't talk to me?'

'That's right, but Jay has some eye movement.'

Kincaide declined, deciding he'd seen enough.

DI Marks had spent the rest of his working day in the morgue at Addenbrooke's Hospital.

If Sykes had been anything but a pathologist, his precise and deliberate way of enunciating words and constructing sentences wouldn't have held Marks' attention quite so readily. But somehow when Sykes was ready to speak, Marks was always ready to listen.

As Marks entered the laboratory, Sykes was opening a drawer in the mortuary refrigerator. He was short and of dainty build, and nodded Marks a greeting from the other side of an obese male cadaver. 'Clearly it's not this one you're after,' he said, coming as close to making a joke as Marks could remember. Sykes slid the drawer closed, and gripped the handle of one two columns back, then one row down. 'Do you need to look?'

'*You* tell me?'

'Only if you're interested. My report will be sufficient.'

'Fine by me.'

Sykes had a thick folder ready waiting on one end of the stainless-steel slab. He let the contents slide out into his hands, then set them neatly in a square pile. 'I suppose you're going to want the usual concise version?' He didn't wait for a reply. 'The fire didn't kill her – no burning to the throat, no smoke evident in the lungs.'

He extracted the first photograph, Marks narrowed his eyes, trying to blur the image enough to pick out the basic shape of her features. After a moment, he gave up and concentrated on an area of skin that Sykes was pointing out. 'On television this damage is always exaggerated: the skin trauma is rarely more severe than this here, unless of course there's an accelerant involved. If the aim was to disguise the cause of death, it was a bad tactic; particularly in a case such as this. A person with good muscle tone burns far less readily than one with a high percentage of body fat.'

'But you know the cause of death?'

'Let's start with the time of death. The fire investigators will be able to give you a better idea of how long it would have taken the building to burn, but off the record I think it's almost certain that accelerants were used, so it may have been on fire for a relatively short time before the alarm was raised. Here's the bad news: the time of death was sometime before then, and sometime shortly after Rachel Golinski was last seen alive.'

'That's it?'

'Pretty much. I can't make estimates about the degree the body has cooled, but if you can be sure of what and when she last ate, I may be able to calculate something from the progress of the food through her digestive tract. Sykes reached for another photograph. 'This may interest you more.'

It was a skull X-ray.

'She has two teeth missing from the lower left side of her jaw. Look at the same area in the photograph and you can spot a small cut on her lip.'

Marks peered at the photograph again, and thought he could pick it out.

'She wasn't alive for long enough after that for a swelling to appear. Now look again at the X-ray.' Sykes drew his pointing finger across the base of the skull. 'From here to here there is a large cavity at the back of the head, so it appears likely that she was shot in the head, and this is the exit wound. As far as I can see there are no other injuries.'

'You've run toxicology tests?'

Sykes tapped the pile of pages. 'It's all in there: not many results in yet but a full list of every test I ran, and why. The teeth were dislodged by a single blow, the angle of which was slightly upwards, its momentum and force sufficient to knock her to the floor or stun her. It's consistent with a punch. She then suffered the second injury.'

'Why in that order?' Marks realized the stupidity of his question as he said it.

Sykes rewarded him with raised eyebrows and an extremely patient reply. 'For two reasons. Firstly, a shot to the face that leaves a saucer-sized hole in the back of the head is very likely to be fatal. Secondly, unless she somehow remained standing for several seconds after her demise, I'm sure delivering an upwards punch would have been a very tricky feat.'

Sykes tapped the X-rays and photographs into a neat stack, and slid them back into a buff folder which he dropped loudly on to the dissection table.

Marks put his hand on the file. 'This is for me?'

'Absolutely.'

'And you'll let me know as soon as anything else shows up?'

Sykes nodded. 'Two prints and an enlargement?' Today he was being positively hilarious.

NINETEEN

Marks wasn't at Parkside: in fact everyone seemed to be out of the building. Goodhew decided to follow suit, phoned Bryn, and ten minutes later arrived at his workshop. Bryn's Zodiac was parked between the open doors, there were no other cars around and Bryn had the look of someone who'd started winding down several hours earlier.

He was sitting astride a Harley Softtail, while pretending to rev the engine and steer.

'You're not ten, Bryn.'

Bryn ginned and sat back in the leather seat. 'My dad's banned me from even sitting on it.'

'You *are* ten! Does this mean the end of your love affair with the Zodiac?'

'No, it's just a quick fling. It belongs to my dad's mate, Kevin. We're keeping it safe here while he's on holiday.'

'Are you up for that pint we missed the other night? I thought we could walk down Gwydir Street.'

'Pick up where we left off?' Bryn dismounted the bike. 'Sure.'

Less than ten minutes later they sat in the beer garden of the Cambridge Blue. Gary had bought the first round, a pint for Bryn and a Coke for himself.

The table stood at a ninety-degree angle to the rear wall. Gary wasn't saying much so far, and at first Bryn wondered whether the burnt-out house nearby was preying on his friend's mind.

Then Bryn noticed Gary's untouched glass. 'Of all the pubs to choose, funny how we end up in the only one that overlooks the cemetery.'

Gary dragged his attention away from the deepening shadows on the other side of the wall. 'Of all the pubs in all the world . . .'

'Yeah, yeah. Who are you looking out for?'

'No one,' Gary replied.

'Bullshit,' Bryn whispered. 'I know you're on duty, and you know I know – and there's no one else here to convince. So is this *no one* male or female?'

'Why?'

'Just making conversation.'

That was the last sentence spoken for several more minutes, though they both turned their chairs so they were positioned at a better angle to see the cemetery.'

'Male actually,' Gary said finally.

'Young, old?'

'Teenage.'

'Junkie?'

'Possibly, no idea. Why d'you suggest that?'

'Couple of lads presently heading for Crack Corner, over there.'

'No, not them.'

'So you know who you're looking for?'

'That's what I'm hoping. Actually,' Gary turned so he could watch Bryn's expression as he spoke, in case his words resonated, 'I think we both saw him. When we were running down Gwydir Street the other night, you know, towards the fire, there was a teenager coming the other way.'

Bryn's mind was blank, and he guessed his expression matched, because Gary now tried describing the precise moment in several different ways. He wondered how anyone could ever remember this kind of detail. 'Doesn't ring a bell,' he confessed at last. 'Sorry.'

'Don't worry about it. It was a long shot.'

Bryn was about to add some quip about his own lack of observation, but instead he blurted out, 'Riley Guyver's mum is climbing over her own back wall.'

Gary was on his feet in a moment. 'Funny how *you* can spot the women every time,' he muttered. By the time Bryn decided to follow, Gary was already over the nearby wall.

Kimberly had tied her hair into a ponytail. As disguises went it wasn't anything much, but she had noticed how the media only seemed to be using photographs where her hair hung loose. Her plan for avoiding detection involved slipping out of her bedroom window, across the flat roof and over the wall into the cemetery, then making it as far as the nearest exit, without being spotted. Once she was safely in the city, she doubted anyone would look twice.

East Road was ever busy, so she hung back until there was a decent gap in the traffic, then sprinted across and kept running. Up the pedestrianized Burleigh Street and through Fitzroy Street, slowing only to catch her breath as she passed along the deserted New Square footpath that took her towards the open greens of Christ's Pieces. She wore jogging bottoms and a T-shirt, making her look like just another runner. As soon as she thought she could make it the rest of the way without taking another breather, she bolted again, her strides lengthening across the close-cropped lawns, and it seemed just a matter of seconds before she was dashing over the cobbles of St Andrew's Street.

It was good that she'd kept fit. Normally running just made her feel liberated but today that training would also allow her to arrive at the Celeste without feeling dishevelled or burnt out.

As she strode through the entrance, the doormen stepped quickly aside. Jodi glanced up in surprise, but Kimberly didn't even slow. 'Tell Craig I'm coming up,' she ordered. She took the stairs at a run.

Her employment at the Celeste had been brief but the familiar smell of spilt alcohol and stale bodies hit her hard. But, then, what was the Celeste but an extension of her time out in Spain? The Celeste had brought her home, and had seen the last days of a role she'd briefly played.

Outside Craig's office, she raised her fist to bang on the door but it opened straight away. She followed him through to the back. He still had the plastic table and chairs.

He offered her one. 'Classy, I know.' He didn't smile.

'I'm fine.' She looked at him and wondered what she'd been expecting, and why he thought she'd come here.

'I'm sorry about Rache.'

She dipped her head in agreement. 'Me too.'

'And Riley.'

Without any warning, Kimberly found herself fighting tears. She didn't want to cry any more, but for a moment there was an awkward pause.

Craig pulled one of the chairs closer to them. 'If you sit, I'll sit.'

She managed to thank him.

'You know me, ever the practical one.' He looked too big for his chair, like the average adult on a kid-size seat. 'Which is why I finally threatened to call the police. I'd had enough of Stefan.'

'So why didn't you?' she asked.

'One last chance, I suppose. You know how it is.'

She ignored the comment. 'Tamsin came.'

'To see you?'

'You didn't know?'

'No, not on club business, then? I guess it was about Nick.'

'So you saw the news?'

'I didn't need to. Dougie rang when they first found the sunken car. It was long odds that it was going to be anyone else.'

'Guess so.'

'I'm glad they found him. It's better for everyone, especially his family, but you too, Kim. It ends all that speculation. It was unhealthy.'

'I know. I'm sure it's been really tough for them.'

Talking to Craig made Nick seem real again. She didn't know why, maybe it was because she'd seen Craig and Nick together every day she'd worked at the Rita Club, so just talking to Craig made it seem as though Nick could come walking through the door at any moment. Complaining about the staff, or the customers, or his family, or the money. 'You're right, it is the not knowing.' Kimberly knew she was ready to say what she'd come to say. 'In fact that's why I've come, sort of. I don't want anything hanging over me.'

He looked wary. 'Like?'

'I want you to help me. I've left Spain behind. I've changed a lot.'

Craig leant back in his chair, as if observing her from a few extra inches away would give him better perspective. 'I don't know.'

'I don't think I deserve . . .'

'No need to explain. Look, I see girls here night after night, and I'm sure that I'm often seeing them at their most . . .' he waited for the right word to arrive '. . . irresponsible. But it doesn't mean I assume they're going to live their whole lives like that, does it?'

She shrugged. 'I hope not.'

'Only you know what took you to Spain – and what brought you home.'

'Right, and I don't want it following me forever.'

Craig sighed. 'And you want me to do what, exactly?'

Her hands lay in her lap, her fingers woven together. If she pressed her palms together, it would look as if she was praying. 'Talk to Dougie for me. Ask him to get Tamsin to leave us alone.'

'Us?'

'When Riley comes home, I want to know I can just have a proper life with him. That's all.'

Chasing after Kimberly took a combination of luck and judgement and, as Goodhew quickly discovered, a fair amount of speed. By the time he reached the cemetery exit leading on to Norfolk Street, she was just disappearing out of sight, heading towards the town centre. He ran after her, using his mobile to ring Bryn. 'Town centre,' he instructed. 'Go via Burleigh Street towards the bus station.'

Goodhew took a longer route, through the terraces named for the market garden that had once extended where they stood: Adam and Eve, Prospect, Orchard. By the time he broke out on to Emmanuel Road, facing Christ's Pieces, he was panting hard. He stopped and drew a couple of deep breaths. Damn, where was she? Then he saw her dart out of New Square and towards the centre. He kept her in his sights this time, and when he saw her running past the closed shops he guessed exactly where she was heading.

Before the last corner, he stopped and waited for Bryn. And when Bryn finally caught up, he had to wait for him to be able to speak. Bryn leant against the nearest wall, first with one hand, then with both, then he sank to the pavement. Finally he gasped, 'I'm not very fit.'

'She's in the Celeste.'

'And?'

'They've all seen me before. I thought you could go in, have a drink, see what she's up to.'

'You're kidding?'

'No. Just pretend to be a punter.'

Bryn clambered to his feet. 'How has this happened to me? I'm the mechanic, you're the policeman, and I don't want to get involved.'

'You didn't have to run all the way here. And if you really don't want to go in, that's fine.'

Bryn glared at Goodhew. 'Don't wait for me, then. If I find out anything, I'll phone you. If there's nothing to say, then I won't.'

'Thanks.'

Bryn checked the state of his hair in the closest window. 'Now piss off,' he hissed and disappeared round the nearest corner. Goodhew smiled to himself: he had a strong feeling that Bryn wouldn't go anywhere he didn't want to.

Goodhew wandered across to the other side of Sidney Street and sat down in the doorway of Oxfam. It afforded him a good view of both of Kimberly's most likely routes away from the Celeste, so he decided that the best thing he could do was to sit and wait there for as long as it took.

TWENTY

Riley's hand was small but, when he chose to hold on to hers, his grip was determined.

There were many things about Riley that were proportionately very big for someone barely three feet high. Sometimes it was the additional work he created, the mess and chaos, or the days lost to colds and sickness and teething. More often it was the way that his presence alone had made her suddenly care about a wider orbit, about the other side of the world and the future beyond her own lifetime.

Most of all it was the way he anchored her: the way one tiny five-pound baby had possessed the strength to end her desire for self-destruction with his very first breath. In fleeting moments, she still saw that baby. The toddler that had replaced him had continued to keep her moving forward even when such progress frightened her.

She understood her role; to walk alongside him along the road to his independence, to know when to hold his hand, and when to hold back, and when to eventually stop and let him go ahead. She wasn't ready to let go of Riley. Not now. Only one day when he was ready. When the baby, and the toddler and the child would exist only in her memories, and the young man was ready to glance over his shoulder and wave her goodbye.

The tears flooded her eyes and she stumbled on to the pavement outside the Celeste.

She pulled the hairband out of her hair and hung her head, protecting her face from curious onlookers by covering much of it with one hand positioned like a visor. She could no longer run now; the resolve had left her muscles, they wanted nothing but to fold.

The path beneath her feet seemed blurred. Only the diffused lights from the bright shopfronts marked her route.

She walked on, blinded by crying, her anguish fuelled by the realization that she was sinking, that the tears filling her eyes were no different from seeing through the eyes of a drowning man.

She normally shut most people out, yet those she trusted she trusted absolutely. But they could be counted on one hand, and, of those few, Rachel was dead and Jay was only just clinging on. Which left three, including Riley. Now she needed to protect them, not the other way around; she'd swum too far out of her depth and she was in danger of taking everyone down with her.

Somehow she needed help; asking Craig for assistance had been hard enough, and it had done nothing to assuage her fears. She guessed the Lewtons would never forgive her, and maybe they were the only ones able to contain Stefan.

There were a few people nearby: she could hear their footsteps as they overtook her or passed in another direction. It took her the length of Sidney Street, and half of St Andrew's Street, to realize there was someone walking in the same direction and at pretty much the same pace. Someone who was walking just a few steps behind her.

She wondered where Stefan was, and what he was doing. And who or what was driving him. And, in an irrational moment, she wondered whether it was he who was following her. And in the next moment she knew: who else would it be but a reporter? Some piece of shit, no doubt, a no-conscience hack just looking for an opportunity to screw her over. Or, worse still, a grimy little photographer with his finger on the trigger ready to shoot holes in her life. She felt her strength return. She knew what they would do: just push and push until she cracked, then use this as proof that she was an animal, a social group F piece of trash, and not a fit mother for the innocent little boy. She also knew what she *should* do: keep her eyes cast to the ground and remain tear-stained and dignified.

She slowed.

Well, fuck it. She wasn't some reality-show asset ready to be wheeled out at every photo op. Or a criminal. Or even a victim.

She swiped her hair away from her face. She'd slap the fucking camera out of his hand before he had a chance to fire off the first shot. It wasn't exactly a plan, more a thought and action so closely coupled that the first wasn't complete when the second was initiated. She spun round and lunged at him, her arms flailing as they sought out the non-existent equipment. From close range, she shouted something into his face, spitting the words at him – at that moment feeling like she was capable of killing.

He was fast, though, and caught her hand as she swung at his face. 'No,' he said, that was all, just the one simple word but it was enough to make her look at him properly. She hesitated, then shrank back, but he still hadn't let go. 'Walk with me,' he said and, the entire time, his voice remained calm and even.

She found herself turning back towards home and he fell into step beside her. 'We can go the long way back,' he suggested. 'Then we can talk.'

'Why?'

'Good for both of us?'

She nodded and knew she'd gone beyond the point of battling with him. 'Do you prefer Goodhew or Gary or Detective?'

'Whatever suits you.'

'Is this an official conversation?'

He gave a sheepish smile. 'No, and I'm not supposed to be here either.'

'I see,' she said and they spent the next few minutes in silence.

'I can tell you're not a great fan of the police,' he said finally. 'Since I was about eleven it's all I wanted to do.'

'Why?'

'Don't know, actually. Maybe it started before that, but my grandparents lived across from Parkside Police Station, and I just remember staring out of the window one day and deciding.'

'And you stuck with it?'

'Stubbornness; it's a character flaw.'

'And now, in return, you want me to tell you why I started hating the police?'

'Not if you don't want to.'

A scowl flashed across her face: this conversation was already feeling cathartic, and that alone should have made her question her own judgement. But her mouth was carrying on, with no intervention from her brain, and she decided to let it go. 'Who likes the police, anyhow?'

He didn't comment.

She pressed him. 'Aren't you going to ask what I was doing?'

'No.'

'But you'll sneak round behind my back and try to find out anyway?'

'Of course, I want to know what's going on, we all do, and the number-one priority is finding Riley.' His gaze was steady. 'But I was there at the fire with you. I don't doubt you for a second.'

She stopped herself from making some sceptical reply like 'Oh, really?' or 'So you say'. All along, there'd remained an edge to her voice, but now she didn't want to kill the conversation.

And so they continued: a volley of sentences, silence, then words again. Somewhere along the way, the conversation's self-conscious-ness dissolved, her preconceptions were forgotten, and they were just two people.

'Tell me about Jay,' he said.

'You met Anita? She was my foster mum. Bet you knew that already?' She didn't wait for a reply, it didn't matter. 'She was my third foster home, because I couldn't settle at the others, and I didn't want anything to do with her either. Not at first. I was twelve when I went to her, and I think it's a vulnerable age ... maybe every age is, but for me it was like I had one foot in childhood and one in adolescence, and I seemed to step forward with the wrong one every time. She understood, she always does.'

Hearing her use of the present tense jarred but Goodhew didn't question it.

'Sometimes I think you meet people you can't help but like. D'you know that feeling?'

'Yeah,' he nodded. 'And I don't know why but they're usually the ones that turn out to be really good for you – or really bad.'

'Because, once you know you like them, you can't stay dispassion-ate like you could at the start of any other relationship?'

'Or maybe it's the other way around, and you're drawn to them because instincts tell you that they have the ability to evoke emotion?'

111

'I see, so you're one of those people that looks for the alternative answer?'

'I know it's never good to jump to conclusions, if that's what you mean.'

Her throat tightened, so she nodded and took several deep breaths until she felt it was safe to speak again. 'I was telling you about Jay.'

'Go on.'

'Anita fostered him, too. He left before I arrived, then came back again when I was fifteen. When Anita and I spent time together she expected respect and decent manners, but she didn't ever get that from me. Even so she was always there to go back to whenever I needed her. She believes in all this hippy stuff, you know, free the spirit and it will return to you. And I was angry when she got charge of me, and I stayed angry, and did all the things angry teenagers do. Were you like that?'

'No, I was sent away to school . . .'

'Boarding or Borstal?'

'Boarding, thanks, and I hated it. I didn't fit in. I suppose I could have got angry, instead . . . I don't know . . .'

'You must know. Sex? Drugs?'

He gave a funny half-smile and shrugged. 'Old films, actually. Black-and-white ones. Robert Mitchum and Humphrey Bogart. And Veronica Lake. I was in love with Veronica Lake.'

There was no answer to that. 'Anita's love is unconditional, she's just there for you, and I woke one day and saw that, if only I stopped tilting the wrong way, my life wasn't really so bad. And when I saw that, I also saw Jay like it was the first time. We were together for eighteen months.' Kimberly paused. She saw the flaw in telling the story, chapters she wasn't prepared to share. She jumped forward: 'After Jay and I split up, Rachel and I decided to go to Spain, just like I told your boss . . .'

'And Jay came to Spain and was injured somehow?'

'In a bar fight.'

'Was he the fighting type?'

'No.' The first time she'd ever heard that type of question, it had stung. Jay had never provoked anything in his life. 'No,' she repeated, 'he was stronger than that.'

She knew Goodhew didn't know Jay, so she was the only one who could have detected that there were similarities between the two men. Goodhew's eyes, too, held the kind of expression that was built on truth. Only Jay had ever looked at her like that: simple honesty, no agenda.

It shouldn't be so rare in life, she concluded. They were close to the cemetery already, and she wondered at how most of the journey home had just vanished. 'Jay can't remember the attack. Or at least he's never told me about it.'

'He spoke?'

'He has something called Cerebromedullospinal Disconnection.'

'Locked-in syndrome?'

'That's right, so he can't talk but he can move his eyes. We learnt Morse code together: we dot with the right and dash with the left. We're quicker now, though it was funny the first few weeks we tried it – my co-ordination's not all that. He said I had a Morse code impediment.'

'He can hear you, right? So why don't you just talk to him?'

'I do but it was good to learn something together. I suppose it's our thing now, and we can have private conversations. He can express emotion with words, before it was just yes, no, yes, no. Now he can ask me proper questions and I can tell him everything that's been happening. We've always talked a lot, and he's just the same person, people can't get their heads round it.'

She thought Goodhew was about to say something.

'What?' she asked, noticing a strange look in his eyes. She wondered who or what he could see when he stared at her.

'Are you going back in through your bedroom window?'

'How did you know?'

He shrugged. 'We have to walk our own path, don't we?'

That's when she knew she could ask. 'If I needed it, would you help me?'

He nodded. 'In any way I can.'

TWENTY-ONE

It was just after 9 p.m. and Gully was alone in Kimberly's sitting room. Kimberly had gone to bed and there was one other PC on duty but he was posted out on the doorstep.

She didn't want to put on the TV; it would be too tempting to become mesmerized by the 'breaking news' banner scrolling along the bottom of the screen. In theory it wasn't going to tell her anything vital that she wouldn't find out first via phone or a visit, but there was always the chance that an apparently unrelated item would turn out to be linked: *Man commits suicide, two dead after fatal crash, man holds child hostage, child's body found in the Cam.*

Even though she told herself that the idea was far-fetched, that she was merely the victim of her own overblown imagination, she knew that if she switched the TV on she wouldn't be able to resist flicking back and forth between the news and whatever programme she might kid herself she was really watching.

Luckily she'd had enough foresight to raid her own small collection of books. It was split roughly into two categories, cookery books and crime novels, neither of which would do now. That left only one candidate, a battered copy of *Jane Eyre* which she'd started once but never completed. In fact she'd only read the first few pages. She didn't remember actually disliking it, so maybe it was the inevitable conclusion she couldn't face: downtrodden woman saved by dashing hero, feeble female falling into macho arms, forever thankful at fulfilling her life's ambition of becoming a wife.

Gully reopened the novel despite feeling sure that her relationship with the 'heroine' was going to descend through many degrees of increasing distaste. She frowned as she read it, and she'd finished almost twenty pages when there was a knock at the door.

It was Kincaide with a carton of tea bags, two pints of milk and a packet of digestive biscuits. Gully wasn't a big fan of men bearing gifts but this offering was more practical than flattering.

'Are you OK?' Kincaide asked her.

'Why?'

'You look pissed off. Is she hard work?'

'No, she's gone to lie down. I think the last couple of days must be catching up with her. She's been prescribed some sedatives, too. What are you doing here?'

'I was hoping to catch Gary, as he said he might finish off here. And, as I was coming anyway I thought you might need these.'

'Thanks. I'm not expecting him.'

Kincaide tipped his head in the direction of the stairs. 'I think he's got a thing for her.'

'No, that's rubbish.'

'Come on, you know Gary . . .'

All she knew about Gary Goodhew was that he'd warned her about taking Kimberly to the fire scene one minute, then dropped her in it with Marks the next. The point that was even more evident was that she didn't really know *anyone* at Parkside. Marks had told her to avoid being 'too accommodating' with the detectives, and she had no idea whether that was a standard warning dished out to all new PCs, or just the female ones. And she certainly wasn't about to ask. 'Phone his mobile. I haven't seen him.'

'I tried. Don't worry about it. I won't wait around for him.' Kincaide flipped the packet of biscuits over in a half somersault, 'Where do you want these?'

She took them into the kitchen. He followed her through and she guessed she wouldn't be getting the whole packet to herself. 'Tea?' she offered.

'I won't say no.'

By the time she'd boiled the kettle she'd relaxed a little, and realized that this was an opportunity to find out a little more about Kincaide and maybe also find out how she might integrate herself into the department a little more quickly. They took their second mug of tea back into the sitting room, where Kincaide moved her book aside so he could sit down.

'My wife's into all these, too. Something to do with Colin Firth and a wet shirt apparently.'

That made her smile; she liked a man who could poke fun at himself. 'This is the first proper conversation I've had with a colleague since I started.'

'It always takes a few weeks to break the ice.'

'I know, but I've already had a slap on the wrist from Marks.'

'About taking the princess to the fire?'

'How did you know that?'

'Mel told me.'

'Mel?' *How the hell did she know?* 'Great, that means everyone knows.'

'Not necessarily.'

'Well, I never told her. She doesn't even speak to me unless she has to.'

Kincaide took a fresh biscuit and snapped it in two. 'Did she know you'd gone down there?'

'Yes.'

'Then you saw Goodhew down there, too?'

'Yes.'

'Well, there you go.' Kincaide looked at her as though he'd just spelt it out in words of one syllable. Which, when she thought about it, he had, but it still wasn't clear enough. Kincaide raised an eyebrow. 'Mel and Gary?'

'Really?'

'I'll be straight with you. Gary and I often work together, but we don't totally see eye to eye. Sometimes it's OK, but sometimes we grate. I'm married, a bit older, more settled. I'm not judging him . . . well, I try not to.'

Gully didn't know whether she wanted Kincaide to say any more, but he continued.

'I don't want to bad-mouth anyone I work with but, now the subject's come up, maybe it would be fairer for you to know the background.' He passed her the digestives. 'Or would you prefer it if I didn't?'

'No, it's fine,' she replied.

116

'They split up a few weeks ago. The problem is Gary doesn't keep his affairs out of the work place. Mel was gutted and kept trailing after him; now it's impossible to work out whether they're back together or if he's moved on to someone else.' Kincaide shook his head. 'At some point Marks will probably warn you off him – he's already got a file on Gary in his office. It's about this thick.' Kincaide made a gap of about ten centimetres between his palms. 'Maybe I'm a bit straight-laced, but I'd hate you to be caught out.' He gave her an easy smile populated with beautifully straight white teeth. 'On the other hand, a quick fling with Gary will give you plenty in common with quite a few ladies at Parkside.'

Gully wasn't sure what to think, but this explained quite a few points, like Marks' comments and Mel's cheerleading, and Goodhew's attentiveness to herself and Kimberly that morning at the fire.

They shared one more cup of tea. 'Looks like Gary's not coming.'

'He does have a habit of getting sidetracked, but I ought to get home anyway.' He glanced at his watch. 'My wife's been away on a course, and I'd like to be in when she arrives back.'

'Of course.'

After he'd gone, she went up to check on Kimberly. Her bedroom door was still firmly closed and her breathing obviously too quiet to carry through the walls. She was glad that Kimberly was finally managing to sleep.

Gully sat herself down on the stairs, because she sat on the stairs at home when she needed to think.

She didn't entirely believe Kincaide, but all that weighed against what he had said was a belief in her own ability to judge character. There was nothing about Goodhew that struck her as being anything but ordinary, so she couldn't imagine him romancing half the station, somehow.

Then, again, there was definitely something about the way Mel looked at him.

In the end Gully decided the real question was whether it was any of her business, and that depended on two things: whether it had an impact on her work or on the reputation of the police. That sounded a bit self-righteous. No wonder she didn't have any mates yet.

Time for another biscuit.

As she stood up, she heard a sound, and for a second thought it might have been caused by pressure on a stair tread. She froze, taking care not to alter her balance and risk causing another creak. Then it came again, and this time she could tell it originated from Kimberly's room.

Gully moved up to the next step.

The third creak was more distinctive, and this time she identified it as the sash window being eased up inside its snug-fitting frame.

If Kimberly was too hot to sleep and needed the window open, why was she trying so hard to keep it silent?

Gully guessed there might be a rational explanation, but decided she wouldn't wait to think of one. Kimberly could be out of the window and away by then.

Gully crept two or three steps closer, until she had a firm grip on the handle, then burst the door open wide. The only light in the room came in along with her from the landing. She saw a dim figure start, and her hand groped around until she found the switch. As she flicked it on, the first thing she saw was a fully clothed Kimberly, her face flushed and very wide awake.

Gully pushed past her, reaching the window in time to see a second figure retreating back over the high garden wall.

'Who's that?' she demanded.

Kimberly stripped down to her underwear before she replied. 'None of your business,' she said, glaring. 'I don't like being spied on.'

Gully felt her cheeks redden to a hot, dark shade. 'Are you going to bed now?'

'No,' Kimberly snapped, 'I don't think I can sleep.' She took her dressing gown from the end of the bed and slipped it on.

Gully turned away and stomped back down the stairs. Kimberly followed, no doubt moving like some sultry lingerie advert; hot, silent – and hiding something. The last hour had revealed far more than Kimberly's 36DD lace bra.

Gully recognized Kimberly's 'caught out' expression. The sexy underwear. Skin aglow with the sheen of perspiration. The mystery man scuttling away.

This wasn't the behaviour of a worried mother.

Except the man was no mystery. Gully had positively identified him.

And his wasn't the behaviour of a trustworthy DC.

Goodhew had just affected her job, and her employer, and she didn't care whether that judgement seemed sanctimonious or not.

She called in to the station and explained that she needed a break, asking for someone to replace her until morning. Bottom line, it was now her business. No doubt she'd be in trouble over this, too, but sometimes simply doing the right thing outweighed the consequences.

Goodhew returned to Parkside just long enough to discover that there was no new information waiting for him. No emails, telephone messages, or notes from Marks. No clues to anyone else's progress either.

Nothing.

He walked home, then drew a chair up close to his window. A small but powerful telescope mounted on a tripod was already pointing at Parkside Police Station. It gave him a clear view of the all the windows facing on to Parker's Piece, and a partial view of the nearest adjacent side. He could see his own desk, Marks' office and anyone who came or left via the main entrance. He watched the building for several minutes, hoping for the visit of inspiration.

There was nothing to see.

He'd spent an afternoon merely chasing a potential witness, a task which came with the unspoken message that Marks was keeping Goodhew on the periphery. Goodhew wanted to phone him; he didn't believe for one second that his boss was at home and asleep. But first he knew he had some threads that needed to be mentally tied down. There were too many of them flapping around, and they needed tethering before they started wrapping round his brain like a tourniquet.

It had been a little over twenty-four hours since the fire, and, if Stefan had a little luck on his side, Goodhew could imagine that it wouldn't be too difficult for him to conceal Riley for that period. Trickier once the child's photo hit the national press and the public turned hungry for every last detail. Trickier still if Stefan didn't intend for either of them to be found.

Goodhew had only a small window into the investigation but he knew that public tip-offs had resulted in police divers searching the Cam out towards Grantchester, and that the police helicopter had been circling over the farmland backing on to the chalky slopes of the Gog Magog hills.

Other strands of the investigation were less easy to pinpoint. He suspected Kimberly was hiding something. Not to do with Riley's disappearance – but what then? Rachel, Jay, Anita, the Celeste, the Lewtons: every other strand was connected to her and it was impossible to guess which of them had any relevance at all.

His attention was drawn away from the station to encompass the whole vista; the darkness was a great leveller, unlit windows were indistinguishable and the lit ones were just glowing geometric shapes. In the dark there was little identifiable architecture: the buildings constructed of glass and prefabricated slab jarred less than usual against their more traditional neighbours. The cars were just headlights, tail lights and, once in a while, a glint of chrome. And people were just smudged dots. It was the composite of all these that made up the city.

It wasn't a question of what elements to include in the picture. It took each house and school and office to make Cambridge. It made sense that it took everything, from the Grand Arcade and the curve of the Cam right through to the rising bollards and abandoned bikes. Start to remove those things and gradually it would become the wrong Cambridge, or maybe not even Cambridge at all.

When he'd returned to his flat, it had been with little expectation of going to bed. Sleep never came easily to him and he'd drifted into the bad habit of either flaking out on his battered leather settee and waking up again in the small hours, when the pre-dawn chill took hold of him, or else lying in bed reading until the small hours and then passing out. Either way he rarely enjoyed more than five hours' sleep each night. Just because he couldn't rest didn't mean he wasn't tired. And now he could see how this new thought of his related to the investigation, but was just too fatigued to translate it into action.

He plugged in his jukebox and let the Bel Ami warm up before leaving it to run on the random free-play setting. He knew he needed to go to bed, but made coffee instead, opening his last two days' post as the kettle boiled. Three bills and two offers of credit cards. At the bottom of the pile was the envelope his grandmother had passed to him. He took all the correspondence and the coffee back to the window seat. The envelope was A4 size and made of an off-white vellum with a woven texture more than strong enough to hold its weighty contents. It was the kind of envelope only ever used for documents connected to death or property or family provenance. Or in this case all three.

His grandmother called him money-phobic. He was sure he wasn't, but just holding the envelope left him slightly nauseous. He drank half his coffee before looking inside.

What his grandmother had called 'a letter' consisted of a quarter-inch-thick sheaf of papers each bearing the letterhead of his grandparents' solicitors, Mason, Willis and Wollaston. Just as she'd said, it did confirm the final transfer of assets from his grandfather's estate into his own name.

News of that inheritance had been a recent and complete shock; until then he'd believed that everything had passed to his parents when he was eleven; that it had long since been spent on everything from his unhappy private education to the social-climbing stint that had eventually wrecked their marriage. In fact their inheritance had been only a fraction of his, and the idea that he'd inherited far more than it had taken to destroy his childhood was now proving too much for him to assimilate.

He flicked through the pages: the items ranged from a box of 'sundry books' held in storage to his flat and the entire building beneath it. All he wanted was some clue that might explain the origins of it all. There was nothing which seemed remotely personal until he reached the bottom of the pile. Pinned to the final sheet was a square, white notecard, and he knew, before he detached it, that it was one of his grandmother's. He turned it over. There was just one sentence written in her artistic hand: *Don't worry about where it came from, it's nothing bad, just enjoy.*

It wasn't long before his thoughts were drawn back to Rachel

Golinski. He then wondered who else might still be awake and what tomorrow would bring. Behind him the jukebox hummed, and in front of him Cambridge slept. He closed his eyes and let the day fade away. His post slid from his lap to the floor, but he didn't stir.

Sleep was finally reaching Stefan Golinski.

He spat and the result hit the floor like a dead jellyfish. He thought of Rachel's expression. At least Mule had shown fear, but she had just looked insolent. His anger was slipping away but he still believed she was a bitch. A treacherous, deceitful slag.

He'd loved her like she was a goddess, set her on a pedestal so high that falling from it was bound to be fatal. And, when that pedestal was constructed of nothing but a teetering pile of filthy banknotes the collapse was inevitable.

And from this he understood one thing: life was about money, always about money. No one was above it or immune from it.

Right now he regretted the day he'd met her.

And her fuck-up of a mate.

But right now was all he had, and his anger extended far beyond Rachel and Kimberly. His head hurt; it thumped and felt heavy. He wanted to sleep.

He didn't know whether there was enough time left to settle every score.

He tried to think what he'd achieved, and which bits he regretted. Only time would tell. It just might not tell him. Inside his own head he grinned at himself. Hadn't he always known it would end like this? Not exactly like this, but in this way – like Butch Cassidy, like Harrelson's Mickey Know, like Vincent Vega.

He wanted to go out fighting, to see death reflected on the faces of those that betrayed him. And it didn't matter whether his own death followed instantly.

He closed his eyes and slept, with his teeth gritted into an expression that merely resembled a smile.

DC Michael Kincaide was asleep in front of the TV when Jan Kincaide arrived home. She sat on the other settee and used the remote to silently catch up on the news headlines via Teletext. A couple of times she glanced across at her husband, as if expecting to see there the answer to a question she hadn't yet put into words. There was no revelation, though; just that same old niggle of discontent and the ongoing puzzle of whether he was part of the problem or part of the solution.

She turned off the TV by kicking the wall switch with the toe of her boot.

She considered waking him and urging him to go to bed, but in the end she threw the spare duvet over him, killed the lights and left him there.

Once Kimberly was certain that PC Gully's replacement was asleep, she dialled the numbers, pressing each digit firmly and without haste.

Anita answered straight away. 'You shouldn't be calling.'

'It doesn't matter, we've made a mistake.'

'What mistake?'

'The whole thing. We should have trusted them.'

'We can't change things now.'

'Listen to me. We *have* to.'

'You'll never keep him. They'll take him away from you, I know they will.'

'But you never thought of how we were going to end it. We don't have a plan.'

'I told you, I'll go forward when it's safe.'

'It won't work.'

'Go to sleep, Kim. You'll feel differently tomorrow.'

Riley Guyver lay on his blanket. His earlier ill-temper had long since subsided into a broken pattern of sobs and sniffs. Once every few minutes he had repeated his order, 'I want Mummy.'

But the once robust demand had faded, and was now no more than a whisper, the last gasp of rebellion: 'I want Mummy. I want Mummy. I want Mummy . . .' Until the whisper faded into nothing, and anyone listening would have thought he'd already gone to sleep.

TWENTY-TWO

Goodhew woke with a start, the only sound was the amplified scrape of the stylus on the run-out of whatever the last track had been. He rose quickly and turned the jukebox off, before it could select the next single, then returned to the window and stooped to collect the scattering of post which lay on the floor.

He put the pages in the right order then checked there were none missing before sliding them back into the vellum envelope. Stupid, really, since they couldn't have gone anywhere while he slept; but he knew that checking and rechecking was part of his MO.

Like now glancing down the lens of the telescope and making a quick survey of Marks' office.

He frowned and pulled back, then looked over towards the station with his naked eye. He peered back through the sight, shut one eye and nudged the scope around by a couple of degrees.

Yes, he had seen it right: Gully was there in Marks' office. And he knew, from her swift and purposeful moves, that whatever she was up to wasn't happening with her boss's consent. She'd switched on the overhead lights. That was a sensible move; far quicker and less suspicious than fumbling around in the gloom.

She tried the filing cabinet first, found it was locked. She spun round and he guessed she was looking for the key. For once, the tension had drained her face of all colour, no hint of blushing. Her lips were pressed together in determination.

And his instincts told Goodhew that this scenario added up to very bad news.

* * *

DI Marks had a single filing cabinet and Gully guessed that if there were any personal files in Marks' office, that's where she'd find them.

She'd pulled at the handle but wasn't surprised to find it locked, even so, she didn't hesitate. Though drawn to the idea of stepping back out into the corridor and shutting the door quietly behind her, she'd made a rational decision to do this and backing out wasn't now an option.

She could picture Marks' car key, which hung on a ring along with a lone house key, so if he didn't carry the one for the filing cabinet with him, she figured there were high odds of finding it here in his office. It wasn't lying on top of the cabinet itself, so she turned to the desk and immediately found it hanging by an elastic band from the desk key which still sat in its lock.

Obviously DI Marks was not the head of crime prevention.

Gully's heart began to thump. She wondered why nature generated such a distracting noise at the moment she needed to concentrate and hear clearly.

She slid the key from the desk and turned back to the filing cabinet. Her trembling fingers fumbled to grip the other key, and her heart beat harder as she stabbed it into the lock.

The drawer rattled open, creaking and groaning along its ten-inch journey to the front of the runner. She glanced over her shoulder at the door then dragged her gaze back to the files. No one would come in.

She found Goodhew's file in the third drawer down; it hung at the front of about ten others. His file was the fattest: not quite the encyclopaedia that Kincaide had hinted at, but very large, especially for a DC of only a few months' standing.

Afterwards she would wonder why she hadn't just left it there, why this proof of its existence wasn't enough to convince her that Kincaide was telling the truth. Perhaps it was human nature or a kind of Pandora instinct that made her pull it out.

She held it with the spine resting in the palm of one hand, then opened the front cover so she could see the first page. It was a photocopy of Goodhew's initial application, and the following pages were copies of training evaluations and exam results.

The originals would be held by HR, but it seemed that Marks had decided to keep his own complete set of records. Did this mean he did so for all the staff, or just Goodhew? She slid open the drawer again and checked the names on the first couple of files; no one she knew. There weren't enough files there for one per member of Marks' team, in any case.

She held her breath as she thumbed through the tabs. She checked each name and still recognized no one.

So there had to be some reason that Goodhew was the only one to be monitored this closely. Her heart resumed its thump-thump-thumping. She'd found nothing that proved Kincaide right, though. She knew she should leave now, come back when Marks was alone and unburden her suspicions. Risk looking stupid. Risk making serious allegations that could damage someone's career.

She knew someone could walk in at any moment. She also knew that she'd seen a file that she was not supposed to know existed. And it was there for a reason.

If she was going to get caught, it may as well be red-handed. She opened the file with a decisive flick that revealed the pages at random. It fell open at a section filled with sealed manila envelopes.

She rested the open file on the top of Marks' desk. Each envelope was stuck in the middle only. A tingle ran across her scalp and darted down her neck as she considered whether she should open it. She glanced towards the window. *It's the third floor, Sue. No one's watching*, she told herself.

Gary Goodhew hadn't taken his eyes off her.

She had pulled out a thick folder and begun to read an enclosed file.

Goodhew had squinted harder and managed to pick out the shape of a familiar name.

Goodhew.

As he watched her looking at his notes, he had caught a fleeting glimpse of his initial job application and personnel photograph. Gully frowned as she flicked further through the pages.

Goodhew didn't understand why Marks kept staff files in his office. In fact that puzzled Goodhew even more than seeing Gully having a sly read of his personal information. And, of course, he was curious to know what she was looking for. He kept his own illicit information-hunting exercises strictly crime-related, and the results had frequently been sent to Marks in the form of an anonymous tip-off sealed in a plain envelope. He couldn't think of any reason for her search – especially one linked to their current case – and he certainly hadn't expected to see anyone else follow his personal covert methods.

It was a weird thing for Gully to be doing, but he supposed she must have a reason. Good luck to her. He gave a wry smile, doubting that Marks would see it in quite the same indulgent light.

He checked his watch. Damn, she'd been in there nearly ten minutes already. Surely there should be a bit more urgency? Perhaps she knew where Marks was and felt safe.

Goodhew swung the telescope down towards the road leading to the car park, just in time to catch sight of what appeared to be the tail light configuration of Marks' dark-red Mazda 406 swing into view. It disappeared towards its parking slot, but not before Goodhew had picked out the first four digits of its plate and positively identified it.

He swung the telescope back up to Marks' office. Gully had returned to the filing cabinet and was flicking through more files. Then, instead of closing the drawer, she turned back to his folder.

'No,' he hissed. 'What are you doing? Shut the file, Sue.' She turned slowly towards the desk and broke open the file midway through. This wasn't the time for her to start reading anything new.

He swung the telescope on to the brightly lit stairs. Marks was trudging up them towards his office.

'Shut the fucking file and put it away,' he shouted.

But she'd taken out an envelope. And not any envelope but one of those he'd sent to Marks. He recognized the typeface and the white label positioned symmetrically on the front.

On several levels this was now not a good situation.

Goodhew grabbed his mobile and retrieved Gully's number from its memory. He heard it ring as he watched her, but she didn't move except to run her finger under the lip of the lightly sealed envelope. Shit. Her phone was off, or on silent. He kept it ringing, and willed her to pick it up. Suddenly she stirred, and pulled her mobile from her pocket. He watched her as she looked at the display. She saw his number, but clearly failed to recognize it. Then, finally, she answered.

He forced a relaxed tone into his voice. 'I was wondering whether you're back at the station yet?'

'Why?' she replied cautiously, but started to move at once, closing the envelope again and placing it back in the folder.

He tried to keep his voice casual. 'I'm after DI Marks, and he's heading back to his office right now.'

She turned back to the filing cabinet.

Goodhew paused long enough for Gully to stuff the file back into the drawer. She dithered for a second, glancing towards the door.

'So?' she said, moving away from the cabinet.

'The key,' breathed Goodhew.

'What?' she gasped and, like she'd received a kick from a mule, she shot back to lock it.

'The key thing is that I get hold of Marks,' Goodhew said smoothly.

'Oh, OK.' Gully gasped and stood behind the door like a frightened rabbit, not knowing whether to run for it or hide.

'Perhaps you could leave a note on his desk for me,' Goodhew added, and watched as Gully made it to the note block just in time to scribble a few words. Goodhew hung up even as the door opened behind her, and she turned round to face her boss.

Involuntary blushing had one advantage, Gully realized. If you did it often enough, no one noticed when it was the result of something suspicious. She was red and sweating when Marks discovered her, but he didn't seem overly surprised. 'I thought you were with Kimberly, Sue.'

'I'm sorry, but I really needed a break, and PC Wilkes said she'd sleep over. Goodhew just rang, asked me to leave a note for you.'

'That doesn't explain why you're here in the station.'

'Well, I came here to leave you a note, too, just to explain where I was.'

'Uh-huh,' Marks grunted and waited for her to add something.

Her mind went blank. Shit, she obviously needed to say the right thing. She tried to look relaxed but, as far as her acting skills went, that involved casually returning Marks' gaze with a fixed expression halfway between dazed and stupid.

He was staring at her hand. *Oh, shit . . . shit and fucking shit.* She hadn't put the key back in the desk. She watched as her own palm opened and she held it out to him, then spoke without any idea of what was about to come out of her mouth. 'Found it on the floor,' she said, feeling pleased that her subconscious had not for once entertained the concept of telling the truth.

Marks gave her a sharp stare, but luckily this was overtaken by another look that said he'd prefer to take her excuse at face value. 'Cleaners knocked it on the floor, I expect.'

He paused, and she didn't know whether she was supposed to stay or go. Don't gabble, that would make her look like an idiot – only crap liars gabble. So she waited until Marks spoke again. 'Kimberly Guyver will be making an appeal at a press conference first thing this morning. I'd like you to be there alongside her, of course.'

Gully nodded.

'You're coping OK, aren't you?'

'I don't feel as though I'm doing enough. I just sit and chat and keep her company, which isn't helping us find Stefan Golinski, or Riley. And the worst part is that I don't know what to say to her. It doesn't feel like there's much progress being made, but I can't say that to her, can I?'

'Firstly, Sue, it has been just over twenty-four hours –'

'It seems a long time,' she interrupted.

'Twenty-four hours since they went, less than that since they were reported missing, and it is relatively easy for anyone to hide out for a couple of days. It's after that, when they need provisions or get bored or complacent, that it becomes easier to find them. If Stefan Golinski is holed up with Riley, then he has to come out sometime.'

'What if they're dead?'

'Well, it is possible, you know that – we both do. But it's also possible that Riley is alive and at risk – and that's exactly why our focus is as it is. Come back here first thing in the morning, and you can relieve PC Wilkes after the early briefing. We'll need Kimberly

Guyver in a coherent state, so don't dwell in any way on the negative. Just concentrate on keeping her morale up, Sue.' He patted her on the arm, and she knew he meant it in a supportive way, not a patronizing one.

It encouraged her enough to speak out. 'There was a man in Kimberly Guyver's room last night.'

Marks' smile died on his lips. 'How do you know?'

'I saw him.'

'Why didn't you tell me sooner?'

'Because I think it was DC Goodhew.'

'You think?'

She took a deep breath and shook her head. 'I know it was. I saw him climbing over her garden wall.'

Marks laid his hand on her arm again, but this time he steered her towards the door. 'I will deal with that. You just stick to the job at hand.'

He closed the door behind her and she stood in the corridor, with shivers exploding like winter fireworks up her back.

His final words echoed in her ears: 'Say nothing whatsoever, and stay away from him.'

TWENTY-THREE

Half an hour later, Goodhew closed the street door of his building and headed back to Parkside. He had watched the exchange between Marks and Gully, wishing he had some degree of lip-reading ability, or alternatively a bug in Marks' office.

The threads of the investigation were inside his head and aggravating his every thought. Meanwhile, the additional tangle caused by Marks and Gully had obliterated any possibility of further sleep.

It was past 4 a.m. and he saw no one about; the moment was totally his own. He returned to his earlier thought that every square inch of his surroundings contributed towards the bigger Cambridge picture. A different question was where the city started and ended. Perhaps it started eight hundred years earlier, or as far back as the first Roman encampment; or maybe it started at the first houses that greeted travellers as they drove in on the A11 from London, and extended to the furthest reach of university land. It was all a matter of perspective and, while the team were mapping all the information they had in relation to Riley's disappearance, Goodhew was starting to question whether they had gone back far enough, or cast their net sufficiently wide.

He took a sheet of flip-chart paper and laid it flat on his desk. The timeline for Rachel's murder and Riley's disappearance was already documented, and he copied this information on to the sheet, using a fine-tipped marker. He started just about halfway down the sheet, and wrote each event on a separate line, spacing it out so that there was room to insert new details later.

At the top of the page he listed the rest, starting with Kimberly's and Rachel's trip to Spain. He plotted their arrival, and then Nick Lewton's disappearance. The dates they'd worked in the Rita Club, and when they'd returned to the Celeste. Riley's birth, and the discovery of Nick's body

There were gaps and questions, but there was also a clearer picture forming.

Jay's assault had occurred on 2 March 2007.

Nick's disappearance nine days later, on 11 March.

Riley's birth on 14 November 2007.

Nick's body was found on 4 June 2010.

The Golinski house burns down on 11 June.

'Good morning, Gary.' DI Marks was sitting there at the next desk, just like he'd teleported in from nowhere.

'Good morning, sir.'

'Talk me through it.'

'Something must have led up to Rachel Golinski's murder and the fire. Now, if Stefan Golinski is responsible, it's either down to a build-up of problems in their marriage or a sudden trigger. So, either way, looking into their background is going to matter.'

'And Riley?'

'There are plenty of killers who would baulk at the murder of a small child, but, once he's been abducted, Stefan's stuck with him. Riley would be able to identify him.'

'Unless it's not Stefan?'

'In which case, why would the killer not just dump Riley somewhere?'

Marks frowned. 'We know all this.'

'Yes, but we've been concentrating on the timeline of the last few days, simply because of the urgency of finding Riley. What if the trigger for all of this is much older? So I've gone back to include the time that Kimberly, Rachel and Stefan spent working for the Lewton family and living in Spain. And look what we get . . .'

Goodhew took Marks through the sequence of events. 'The attack on Jay and Nick's disappearance occurred within a fortnight of each other. And very close to the time that Riley was conceived. As both men had had a relationship with Kimberly Guyver, it would be one big fat coincidence if there was no connection whatsoever. Then, within days of the discovery of Nick Lewton's body, other people connected with Kimberly and the Lewton family start to die.'

'And you're thinking that it's more logical if it all fits together somehow?'

'Isn't it?'

'Yes and no. You're talking about two deaths and one assault taking place across a three-year period. One beaten, one possible RTA, and a suspected shooting – so no similarity in MO and no clue as to motive. If I could see some link that wasn't totally circumstantial, I think I'd be very interested.'

'You said "yes and no"?'

'Yes, I can see why it would make more sense if it was all connected. You arrived here at just after four, and have been piecing this together for the best part of two hours. You've merely added detail that, at most, will be useful. But it's still a 'no' because there's no proof. Nick Lewton's death could still turn out to be the result of an accident, and the Jay Andrews assault was just random drunken thuggery.'

Goodhew nodded. Having all the information from the start of an investigation was an impossibility; lab tests took time, companies could be slow at releasing records, and some vital witnesses were often still unaware that they'd seen anything of any importance. So the first few vital hours were overshadowed by data holes, black spots that caused resources to be misdirected and opportunities to be lost. Marks was right, it was all too easy to guess what those gaps in the picture might be.

Marks was meanwhile wearing an expression that said he was waiting for Goodhew to say something else, something specific.

'I'm still trying to locate the owner of that 'pay as you go' mobile . . .' Goodhew began, but immediately realized that he wasn't on track. Still, he carried on. 'I have a description, and I think I have his baseball cap. It's gone to the lab, so if we have his DNA, and if he's on the system, hopefully we can locate him that way.'

When Marks spoke again, his voice was quiet but with a cold and sarcastic edge. 'Well, I hope we find him first. Otherwise that's a lot of "ifs".'

Goodhew found himself glaring. 'I believe I *will* find him.'

'Is there anything else you would like to tell me?' Marks glared back, but with far more practice.

Goodhew shrugged. 'Like what?'

'If there'd been a rumour about your conduct?'

'No.'

'Or an accusation of inappropriate behaviour?'

Goodhew had never been susceptible to outbursts of temper, preferring to stay several emotional layers away from transparency. He now forced a couple of slow breaths through the rising anger. 'What inappropriate behaviour?'

'You were spotted in a witness's bedroom.'

'Who?'

'How many witnesses do you have to choose between?'

'No, I mean who saw me?'

'So you *were* there?' Marks' expression was impenetrable.

Goodhew hadn't been in her bedroom, just as far as the flat roof outside her window. He knew that choosing to home in on the most literal interpretation of the truth could cause trouble later. But, at this moment, later was convenient.

'No, I wasn't. I meant, who said that I was?' Goodhew looked across the room and his gaze fell on to Kincaide's desk. Had Kincaide followed him back to Kimberly's house? It was more likely, though, that Gully had seen him, and then Gully had told Marks after he'd caught her in his office. 'Actually, sir, it doesn't matter.'

Had she really thought there was anything 'inappropriate' going on between him and Kimberly? Had she really thought that there was some dark secret hidden in Marks' office?

Strangely his attention stayed fixed on Kincaide's empty chair, until Marks spoke again. 'You and I have both been awake for most of the night. I don't, therefore, want to make any decisions that are tainted by tiredness and over-emotion. But I do need some kind of response from you, before you've had too much chance to cook up something feasible.'

Marks leant back and waited for Goodhew's next move. Goodhew had no idea about playing chess, but he suspected that

Marks already had his game plan. Goodhew's own game was backgammon: he was used to throwing the dice and hoping for a decent roll.

'If I were you, sir, I'd consider whether the person involved in reporting this might have an ulterior motive. Or whether they've been led to false conclusions by a third party.' He stopped short of making any further denial about visiting Kimberly's bedroom; realizing that it was the same sort of fine line that separated smoking from inhaling.

Marks steepled his two index fingers together to form a point, then rested them against his lips. 'A diversion?' he murmured, eyes half-closed. 'Hmmm.'

Goodhew was just wondering whether he'd thrown a double six, when Mel opened the door. She was in early. He glanced at his watch and realized that the time had slipped beyond 7 a.m. and the night had moved on elsewhere without causing any further damage.

She addressed Marks. 'Dr Sykes is here. Can he come in?'

Marks straightened. 'Of course.'

She held the door for Anthony Sykes, waiting a few seconds longer than she needed, and using them to make eye contact with Goodhew.

He smiled. She smiled.

Who said the art of communication was dead?

He watched the door close behind her and realized he was still fixating on its scuffed paintwork as Marks reeled his attention back into the room.

'I worked through the night to finish this,' Sykes declared as he opened his briefcase. 'Thought I'd drop them off so you could see them as soon as you were in.' He placed a couple of sheets of paper on the desk, then continued to rummage through his briefcase, adding more pages as he found them. 'It's better that you're here, though, so I can talk you through them right away.' He closed the case, then looked at Marks, then Goodhew. For someone who had also been up all night, Sykes seemed unnaturally bright-eyed. 'If you two sit close together, I can show you both at the same time.'

He waited until Goodhew had finished moving his chair, then, with a flourish, produced the first photograph. 'Here we have a photograph showing the head as you first saw it, with that damage at the rear of the skull.'

He moved on to the second shot, which focused on the back of the head. 'The cavity measured eleven centimetres across and was situated just above the top cervical vertebra. I was initially looking at the possibility of a bullet, probably about nine millimetre calibre, having entered through the front of the face.'

He produced a close-up of the eye and nasal area. 'As you can see, the facial cavities have become enlarged in the heat of the fire. The eyeballs are soft, and obviously have a lower boiling point than other parts of the body, so they disappeared quite quickly.' He seemed to be holding on to that particular photo for a very prolonged period, and made a slightly theatrical show of pointing out the most likely entry point of the bullet.

'Chemical tests showed traces of lead, antimony and several arsenic compounds, but I ran a comparison test using tissue samples from elsewhere on the body and found similar levels.'

'Meaning what?' Goodhew asked.

'In a house that old, the traditional building and decorating materials would have contained plenty of toxins. Even in restored houses old varnishes are painted over and stripped wood still contains these old chemicals embedded deep within its fibre.'

Marks was massaging his right ear lobe and starting to fidget. 'So was it a gunshot or not?'

'Exactly my own thought,' beamed Sykes. The next photo was the stripped-down skull, with an assortment of bones and teeth all laid out against the background of a black cloth. 'By the time I'd finished the post-mortem the brain was extracted, in any case, so it was no problem to have a go at reassembling the pieces. Here's where it gets interesting.'

Sykes smiled, and Goodhew found the effect slightly sinister.

'Now, we've all seen the way the vertex of the skull is formed, haven't we? There is the soft spot, the third eye if you like, that allows for the skull to expand during growth, and the seams or sutures where the plates of bone have knitted together by adulthood. Now imagine a pressure cooker. High temperatures cause expansion, and expansion creates pressure, so it is along these seams that

136

I would expect to see the inevitable explosion. But not so in the case of another object, say a bullet, passing through the head and causing a hole, because the effect would be like opening a vent.'

His smile broadened. 'Which brings me to my final photograph.' He slapped it on to the desk in front of them, and didn't actually say *Ta-da!*, but it was close.

This one showed the back of the skull, post reassembly. The cracks ran outwards in a star-like pattern. Like the corner of a brick hitting a windscreen.

'As you can clearly see, the occipital bone has been fractured. This has been caused by blows to this area leaving a fracture pattern. In the fire, the heat would have created pressure which, in turn, would have produced the outwards explosion of soft brain tissue, and the resulting cavity. Easily mistaken for a gunshot injury until it's pieced together.'

Marks picked up the photograph and gazed at it for several seconds before he spoke. 'What's your opinion regarding the murder weapon?'

'Remember the missing teeth? I am still sure that those were dislodged as the result of a punch. Once lying on the floor, she suffered the remaining head injuries. If these were inflicted close to ground level, then, in my opinion, the murder weapon was a boot or shoe.'

'She was kicked to death?'

'Precisely so. I've ordered some enhanced prints of the injury site, and it's an outside chance we may be able to pick up some detail regarding the footwear involved. Not house slippers, that's for sure. And you may like to factor this into your considerations, since her neck and face or even the temples would have been easier targets . . .'

'Unless she was lying face-down?'

'No. No, that would have involved a downwards stamping action, and there would have been corresponding facial injuries. If he had been so concerned about avoiding facial damage, he would not have chosen to hit her in the jaw with the first blow, or mutilate her with fire.'

'That doesn't sound like the behaviour of someone committing an assault simply on impulse.'

'I'd call it a technique. Also I doubt he's a first timer.'

Marks passed Goodhew the photograph. It was one thing to plan it like this, but something else to follow it through, so there had to be either experience involved or intense motivation.

'She was definitely dead before the fire started?' Goodhew asked the question just to keep the conversation flowing, since he could tell that Marks thought they'd already heard enough.

'Absolutely. No damage to the back of the throat, trachea or lungs.'

'Would you expect injuries like that to be fatal?'

Goodhew sensed that Marks was now frowning.

Sykes frowned too. 'This attack definitely involved repeated blows or kicks. Had he stopped sooner, maybe she could have survived. Who knows?'

'Gary, are you now trying to argue that the killer didn't mean it?'

'No, I want to know what impact an attack like this would have entailed if the victim survived.'

'That would depend on a combination of timely and expert medical care. And luck, too, and plenty of it, if there was a chance the victim could make a full recovery. But some level of brain damage is also likely.'

Out of the corner of his eye, Goodhew saw a change in Marks' posture, so that now, instead of willing Goodhew to pipe down, he was also looking to Sykes for his next answer.

'What sort of brain damage?'

Sykes suddenly lost his authoritative tone and reverted to his standard cautious one. 'I'm probably not the best person –'

Goodhew cut in, 'What about Ventral Pontine Syndrome?'

'The medulla oblongata and pons Varolli are both situated in the brainstem, and therefore would be vulnerable to this kind of attack. And, yes, in most cases the condition is caused by a trauma to that area, specifically the pons Varolli.'

Marks waved his hand for them to stop. 'What the hell is Ventral Pontine Syndrome?'

'Cerebromedullospinal disconnection results from damage to the brainstem,' Sykes began.

Goodhew interrupted. 'It's called locked-in syndrome.' He pointed to his flip-chart. 'That means it's the link between Rachel Golinski's murder and the assault on Jay Andrews.'

TWENTY-FOUR

Mel often wondered why her life wasn't more simple. After all, it had the potential for simplicity: regular hours in a regular job, a long-term boyfriend, plus just one uncomplicated hobby. No debts, addictions or lavish tastes to complicate it.

She'd tried to figure it out on numerous occasions, and find an answer that didn't involve accepting the one glaring problem: her boyfriend Toby was a bastard.

Mel liked the idea of a straightforward life, one where accomplishments counted and success could be built upon. Mel also prided herself on her staying power, her ability to tackle the mundane and overcome the difficult. Maybe those were the reasons she stayed, and put up with Toby's petty jealousies and volatility. She knew men like that didn't change – every woman's magazine rammed it home – but she would have thought a toning-down might be possible.

Those mornings when she voluntarily arrived at work long before her 9 a.m. start were the ones that invariably followed a late-night row, disrupted sleep and a miserable walk in to the office. They were the days when she had plenty of time to wish for a life more ordinary.

DI Marks was already in the building, she knew, because his car was parked outside. She'd arrived at the same time as Dr Sykes, the pathologist, so she'd taken him up to find Marks. He'd been sitting in the Major Incident Room with DC Goodhew.

Gary Goodhew, who might have been able to offer her that life-more-ordinary if only she'd met him before her ill-fated fling with DC Kincaide.

She'd smiled at Gary; there was no need for any awkwardness now that he seemed to think it was way too late for anything to ever happen between them.

She returned to her desk and swivelled her chair in a slow clockwise twirl. How ironic it all was. It had been a row with Toby that had first led to her involvement with Kincaide, now another one that led to her exchanging today's smile with Goodhew. Toby was always there.

Who was she kidding? Toby was there because she kept him there. She didn't have the guts to leave because she doubted she had the strength to deal with his wrath and desperation and her own ensuing guilt.

She spotted Kincaide walking across the car park, and stopped swivelling her chair.

She still found him good-looking, and thought the old-fashioned terms like suave and manly suited him well. But what she'd once thought was confidence and charm, she'd since come to identify as arrogance and selfishness. And, despite his being almost ten years older than herself, she'd eventually decided that he possessed little more maturity than Toby.

He strolled through the nearest door and walked towards her.

'Morning, Mel.' It seemed like the first time he'd voluntarily chatted to her since their split.

'Hi.' She made sure her smile appeared steady and clear. She really didn't want any bad feeling to linger between them, especially when they would continue to see each other virtually every day here at work.

'You're in early. Everything OK?'

She shrugged and resisted the urge to start offloading her troubles. 'You know, same shit.'

'Saxophone going OK?'

'Yeah, yeah, I still do that jam night every Thursday. You could drop in sometime, if you fancied it.' Her words tailed off, as she hadn't even meant to say that. It had just popped into her head in a kind of check-out-the-gig type of way, but instead it had come out sounding like a proposition.

'I'll bear it in mind.'

She couldn't work out which version of the offer he'd responded to; he was either being polite or had delivered a pretty-bloody-insulting *If I need a shag, I'll put you on the shortlist.* And she couldn't work it out from his expression either, so she made sure her own gaze was bright and helpful but equally unreadable.

'Was that Anthony Sykes I saw driving out?'

'Yes, it was.' And she decided to volunteer nothing else.

'If he dropped something off, I could take it up.'

'No, that's fine, thanks.'

'So Marks already has it?'

'Yep, ages ago.'

'Any idea what he left?'

'No, Sykes met with them in person.'

'Who?'

'Marks and Gary. They were in well before me – obviously engrossed in some discussion when I took Sykes up.'

Kincaide left straight after that, no doubt hot-footing it up the stairs, desperate to find out what he'd missed. Although the exchange had given her a childish satisfaction, none of it seemed to penetrate Kincaide's thick skin. She guessed he would think she was being naturally obtuse rather than deliberately obstructive. He didn't expect women to be bright, but obviously thought they'd all become co-operative after a few flattering words.

It was still before nine and officially she wasn't even at work yet. So she took a slow walk to the coffee machine, and a slow walk back again, allowing herself time to ease into the new working day and to zip her problems into the pocket marked 'private'.

Back at her desk she found PC Sue Gully sitting jotting a note on a scrap of paper. They'd barely spoken since Gully had arrived at Parkside but, from what Mel had seen, the new PC had only two expressions: blush or scowl.

Gully looked up, scowled, and stopped writing. 'Marks wants everyone in the Major Incident Room straight away.'

'Me, too?'

'No.' Gully frowned. 'Sorry, that's not what I meant. He was just hoping you'd spot any stragglers coming into the building and hurry them up. I tried to ring –'

'I went for coffee.'

'OK.' Gully screwed up the paper and tossed it into the bin.

'DCs Young and Charles, right? Anyone else?'

'No, I don't think so.'

'They've been viewing some CCTV footage half the night . . .'

'They're not there now.'

'No, they went to the canteen for breakfast. I'll go get them.'

'It's OK, I can go,' Gully said, but didn't move.

It made Mel hesitate, not sure whether she was supposed to say something else. It occurred to her then that there probably wasn't more than a couple of years in age between them. Maybe not much in terms of looks or capabilities, either. The difference was that Gully's job required her to compete with the other detectives rather than provide admin support. Mel could imagine that would be enough to bring out anyone's surly side.

'I'll walk down there with you,' she said.

TWENTY-FIVE

Sue Gully had been the first to answer the 'room to let' ad. The house itself was a three-bed semi on Perne Avenue, and she'd liked it straight away. She'd been able to choose between the two available upstairs bedrooms and, with a quick calculation, had worked out that the front bedroom faced east. So she'd picked that one, liking the idea of warmth in the morning and shade in the evenings.

That had been three weeks ago and, as she now realized, everything had its flip side.

The window didn't face exactly due east, which meant she was spared the very first rays, but it wasn't long before the morning sunshine managed to stretch its way round the front of the house. So it was her choice of bedroom, on a sunny June morning at a northerly latitude, which meant she was destined to wake at 5.30 a.m., at least an hour before she needed to get up.

Like on every other sunny morning that week, she cursed her overly cheerful new curtains; their cascades of red and orange leaves had seemed like a good idea, but they were unlined and the room flooded with light too easily. The fabric had a sulphur-yellow background which washed over everything, from the plain white walls to her own half-awake features. On a bad morning it felt like someone had pissed on her.

She looked straight up at the toilet-bowl tinted ceiling, and promised herself that she'd swap them back to the older set of curtains on her next day off.

And that thought brought her working day into focus.

With it came that bad, empty, pit-of-the-stomach feeling. She knew it well, because it felt like guilt, but it came with the humiliation of mistakes made and the realization that she was the greatest threat to her own chances of success. She wanted to get this job right. More than anyone knew. More than she had words to express.

She tried not to think about Marks finding her in his office; only time would tell whether she'd done any long-term damage to their relationship. Instead, she wished she'd stayed with Kimberly; she could have spent the hours wasted both here and at Parkside by learning more about her.

Woulda-coulda-shoulda.

She kicked herself out of bed and ignored the ongoing urge to let her thoughts fester on any part of the previous day. As it turned out, she found it difficult to concentrate on any part of this new day except Kimberly's forthcoming press conference. Everything felt like a countdown until that moment when Kimberly would look into the camera and beg for the return of her little boy.

Gully's instincts told her that it would all kick off from there; that everything prior to it was just part of a holding pattern of resources, witnesses and anxious hours. And that everything that followed would be . . . She paused, the fingers of her left hand holding her hair in place, the fingers of her right hand poised with hairclip ready.

She wasn't sure what those next hours would hold, apart from the revelation of truths. A few truths, one truth, all the truths; she didn't know. She just had the feeling that today could be a big day.

She promised herself that today would be one for observing more and talking less and, with that resolution firmly in mind, she had been at work for about ten minutes before uttering her first words of the morning.

TWENTY-SIX

From first light, Anita McVey began to make regular checks from her upstairs windows. She checked her garden and each possible approach to her house, finding that her usual secure feeling of this being her sanctuary had deserted her. By 9 a.m. she was watching two robins bobbing back and forth between the lowest branches and her vegetable patch. As she drank her third coffee of the day, she tried to take comfort in remembering how Harvest Path had a history of being a forgotten spot.

It had been in 1955 when the 'Path' had been bisected by an access road for the post-war sprawl that developed on Cambridge's east side. The major part of the lane had been left as a cul-de-sac, so the final six houses were marooned on the other side of the new road, accessed via an unadopted track that alternated between hard-core bumps and muddy ruts, or alternatively by foot across the allotments.

Since 1955, four of the six had lain vacant after plans for the new road had earmarked them for demolition. Eventually they had crumbled and in a rare reversal of the progress of urbanization, the plots they stood on had disappeared under extra allotments.

The other two, both halves of a semi-detached pair, had at the time been occupied by the Boyle family. Cedric Boyle had managed to purchase both in the late forties and for the next thirty odd years his children and grandchildren had exercised a free hand in redesigning the house and its garden with a succession of 'projects' and 'finds'.

Trainee social worker Anita McVey had first visited in '82. The windows were open wide and 'A Town Called Malice' was rattling out from a large black and red portable stereo standing on the bathroom window ledge.

A mould-covered Vauxhall Viva stood in the far corner of the overgrown lawn. Two kids were perched on its roof. They both had wedge cuts, closely clipped from the back of the neck upwards and, even though their fringes were fairly long they both looked male. She knew from her notes that at least one of them was a girl; the Boyle children didn't have other kids round to play. They both wore bleached denim jeans, one wore a check shirt, the other a faded black T-shirt and a leather belt with chrome studs.

Check shirt turned out to be Darren, and chrome studs was Mandy. Anita was able to work this out herself, since Mandy's voice definitely sounded female as she yelled out. 'Who the fuck are you?'

Kelvin appeared at the bathroom window, aged seventeen and obviously quite happy to flash his naked body at anyone in sight. From there on, her Boyle experiences deteriorated, till her increasingly frequent trips into the mire of Harvest Path felt more and more like a one-way trip to the battlefront.

She had visited the family regularly for nine years, learning in gritty first-hand detail what had made the owners of the other four properties so happy to cash in at the first whiff of a compulsory purchase order.

Then in 1991, with the last of their children safely through their truancy years, and now happily unemployed or pregnant, the Boyle parents divorced, whereupon the pair of houses had remained abandoned for fourteen months. Despite feeling sure that she felt zero sentimentality for the whole mess, Anita found herself visiting first the empty property and then the half-empty sale room. The property market had been dead back in '92, so she made the only bid and found herself the proud but bewildered owner of a pair of cottages and the two lorry-loads and eleven skipfuls of crap that were finally cleared from every corner, inside and out.

There were still moments when she wondered about the eventual fate of Darren, Mandy and the five other Boyle siblings. In fact, she knew there always would be such moments and it was her inability to let the worst social cases leave her thoughts that prompted her to wonder what more she could do. Which led her to consider how else she could help, and finally led to her first foster child arriving at the newly painted, freshly decorated and renamed front door of Viva Cottage.

The arrival of the first, second and every subsequent child had cracked, dented and shattered all her chintz-filled fantasies about the whole escapade. There had been a huge gap between her original good intentions and the harsh realities of vandalism, police visits and foul-mouthed outbursts.

Two pints of cider on a Saturday night usually enabled her to smile at herself, but right now she felt nothing close to amusement. Throughout the countless times she'd heard 'Who the fuck are you?', she'd never once seen herself heading to this point.

Anita knew that she'd always swum in deep waters, murky in some places, fast-flowing in others, but she'd never seen the danger. That had emerged organically, as a series of developments that had rippled over one another and ultimately carried her too far out of her depth. She was no longer convinced that she could reach the shore, nor even had any idea whether the tide was in ebb or flow.

The knocked-together cottages allowed Anita a view of the approaches on each side of the building, and her new habit was to thoroughly check in all directions, then to sit with a drink near the upstairs window and watch to see if anyone should come up the pitted driveway.

As habits went she knew this wasn't healthy, and she also knew it couldn't continue for very much longer.

TWENTY-SEVEN

By 9 a.m. DI Marks was drawing his early-morning briefing to its conclusion.

'In light of the similarities between the attack on Jay Andrews and the attack on Rachel Golinski, we'll need another statement.' Marks paused and scanned the room. Gully thought this a slightly theatrical gesture since the only detective waiting to receive instruction was Gary Goodhew.

'Gary,' he continued, 'how's your Morse code?'

'Dash dash dash, dash dot dash, sir.'

Bloody smartarse, she thought. Then she realized that Marks was looking at her, and hoped she hadn't mouthed the words.

'Gully, I'd like you to go along with Goodhew.'

'I thought I was going back to Kimberly Guyver?'

'Change of plan.' There was an edge to his tone that made one or two of the other detectives look interested, Goodhew being one of them.

For a moment she thought Marks had made a mistake. 'But you said . . .' she began, then instantly realized how much worse she'd just made things. When would she learn that sometimes it was better to just nod and do what she was told.

She spent three of the final five minutes feeling like everyone in the room was thinking up some quip to deliver at her expense, then the last two asking herself whether she really was becoming too self-absorbed. No one cared about any job allocation except their own.

Marks then dismissed them. By the time Gully left the room,

Kincaide was already in the hallway, where he slipped alongside and tapped her on the elbow. 'Bad luck,' he whispered.

Gully stopped and turned towards him. 'It's OK,' she said. She watched him carefully, less than keen to accept anyone just at face value.

Kincaide seemed earnest and genuinely interested. 'Did you say something to upset him?'

'Who, Marks?'

'Yeah – why's he suddenly reallocated you?'

Gully concentrated on looking unconcerned. 'I have no idea. Obviously it wasn't going as well as I thought.'

'Really? Then maybe you should have a word with him.'

'No, I'll leave it. It's embarrassing enough already,' she said although she wasn't even the first shade of red.

'He's a decent bloke,' Kincaide persisted. 'You should talk to him, just tell him you don't want to be with Goodhew.'

She shook her head. Some people could just get too earnest and too interested. 'Are you winding me up?'

Kincaide raised his eyebrows. 'No, let me finish. Think about the resourcing situation. If you say you don't want to be with Goodhew, where else is he going to put you but back with Kimberly Guyver?'

'Thanks, but I'll stick with what I've been given.'

Kincaide's voice was gentle. 'Hey, I'm sorry.' He shrugged and raised his palms to the ceiling. She guessed this was a gesture designed to signify his divine acceptance of her will. Saint Kincaide: patron saint of hapless females. 'I was just trying to help.'

'Hey . . .' Gully paused long enough to note how much clarity could be gained from a few hours' decent sleep. 'Why do you blokes always say that when you want to manipulate? I'm starting to feel like a ping-pong ball being flipped back and forth between you and Goodhew.'

Saint Kincaide's palms got folded into his pockets. 'No, of course you're not. And that's quite insulting, actually. I've gone out of my way –'

'Oh, please!' She said it quietly but with a half-smile on her lips.

'I have, I'm trying to make sure you don't come unstuck. And all you do is lay into me.'

Goodhew was finally leaving the briefing room; he loitered in the doorway, having a final word with Marks. She lowered her voice further. 'You know that's not the case. I'll fight my own battles – which means I don't need you offering me direction any more than I need to get it from *him*.' She hooked her head towards Goodhew, just as Goodhew turned and moved towards them.

Kincaide flashed her his warmest smile. 'You'll be fine.' Then he reached out and squeezed her arm before she had the chance to move away. 'Have fun,' he added then left.

'For Pete's sake.' She rolled her eyes, then turned to Goodhew. He was wearing jeans and a short-sleeved, aqua-blue shirt. 'You look like a Tommy Bahama ad.'

'Not enough palm trees.'

'Yeah, but that colour still belongs on a beach.'

He started towards the main stairs and she followed. He set a brisk pace and her uniform already felt like she wore too many layers. By mid-afternoon it would feel like one of the hottest places in Cambridge. Maybe it was just the mood she was in, but she couldn't help wondering whether Goodhew's current choice of outfit included a small percentage of rubbing her nose in it.

They walked the length of the building and down two flights of stairs without another word. Gully felt little desire to break the silence, so it was no surprise that Goodhew spoke first. 'Kimberly's found you very supportive.'

They reached the car but she dallied over sorting out her car keys even though there were only two attached to the ring. 'She told you that, did she?'

'I've just been speaking to Marks and –'

'Oh, great.' She rammed the correct key into the lock, but still didn't turn it.

'What's wrong with that?' Goodhew tapped the roof of the car a couple of times, but she still didn't glance at him. 'I said, what's wrong with that?'

Her better side urged her to find some way of mustering a cool and dignified silence, but her mouthy side won through, after years of virtually undefeated practice. She glared at him. 'You're a DC, I'm a PC. You're new, I'm even newer. I understand that, but how would you feel if someone barely your senior was giving Marks feedback based on his cosy chats with a witness? Huh?'

Goodhew sighed. 'Unlock the car, Gully.'

'And why is it you don't drive yourself?' She turned the key and they simultaneously opened their doors and climbed in.

'I haven't slept enough. Wouldn't be safe.'

'Firstly, we're only going about a mile and a half across town and we'll be lucky to get out of first gear, so no real safety issue there. And, secondly, you never seem to drive anywhere.'

Goodhew didn't reply.

She turned left out of the car park, and left again across the front side of the police station heading towards the junction with East Road.

'Go straight on,' he advised.

'Quicker if I turn right, then left up Hills Road.'

'No, Mill Road, Devonshire Road, then join Hills Road up by the railway station. Nothing in it.'

His tone suggested it was now an instruction, not a discussion. She let it go and drove straight on. About two hundred yards after the lights, her mouth decided to have the last word after all. 'It's longer this way, but whatever you want.'

He said nothing but from the corner of her eye she could see his face turned in her direction. After a couple of minutes of this she couldn't stand the suspense and glanced across at him. 'What?'

'I think you should consider the priorities here.'

She didn't like his tone. Literally didn't. It had turned all serious and superior, and he'd only just started to speak. She wondered what was to come.

'Kimberly Guyver is traumatized,' he continued. 'Her best friend has been murdered and her son is missing. Yet you seem to be sulking because our DI has decided that the most appropriate use of your time is doing something that's not as high-profile or as important as you would like.'

'No, actually, I'm not sulking, and I'm not so stupid that I don't realize that this job involves plenty of mundane tasks.' She said *mundane* like it was a dirty word. She paused until he opened his mouth to reply, then spoke right over the top of him. 'I just think it's a pity that a fully fledged DC needs a chaperone.'

She checked his expression and was satisfied to note that he looked appropriately stung.

'Who gave you that idea?'

'What do you want me to say? Kincaide? I'm not giving you further ammunition for your petty war with him. I have eyes, and I have a brain. Out of the blue, you need someone to drive you, and the best you've got is you feel a bit tired? Please.'

They were inching past the first Mill Road shops, and Goodhew was now making a point of looking beyond her. He opened his mouth to say something, but looked too pissed off to form a sentence. He was obviously one of those blokes who gave up part-way through a row, then spent a couple of days brooding in a moody silence.

And he'd accused her of sulking.

In her opinion, an argument needed a clear start, a middle and an end. She was just considering goading him into round two when, without warning, his hand slapped down on the dashboard like it was a driving test. 'Stop!'

She hit the brake and he was out of the car and running through the traffic before the word 'What?' had even time to leave her lips.

Ahead of him a teenager had taken flight.

Gully pulled over to the kerb, then changed her mind. Instead, she switched on the siren and forced her car through the queue. Traffic ahead of her cleared a path with increasing efficiency, and by the time she'd crossed the first junction she could see she had a clear run.

What she couldn't now see was either Goodhew or his quarry.

She pulled over and let the siren die.

Goodhew had run off damned fast for someone feeling too tired to drive.

TWENTY-EIGHT

Goodhew wasn't finding his car trip with Gully much fun at all. He reminded himself that there were always two sides. Always two, and sometimes more. And Goodhew was stumbling across a lot of things on Gully's side that appeared to be symptoms of her choosing to believe the worst about him.

Marks had updated Kimberly Guyver and told her that Gully would be deployed elsewhere for the morning. Kimberly had immediately expressed her appreciation for the support Gully had already given her.

Marks could have told Gully that himself; maybe if he'd said it at the briefing, it would have diffused her embarrassment and left her in a happier place than her current one. Or maybe Marks had decided it was time Gully's skin thickened up a little.

The bottom line was that Marks had intended passing on the compliment via Goodhew, but Gully had leapt to the assumption that they were Goodhew's own words: a consolatory pat on the head delivered as a result of his 'inappropriate behaviour with the witness'.

The verbal exchanges between them were growing increasingly snappy. As far as Goodhew could work out, Gully's skin was more than thick enough already, and now she was accusing him of needing a chaperone.

Goodhew turned his attention to the other people on the pavements. Most were alone, most would be silent. Lucky them. He couldn't see one other person getting an earful.

It was strange how looking for one thing often led to spotting the thing it had previously been impossible to find. Like the teenager talking on the mobile, twenty yards ahead.

With hindsight, Goodhew would wonder why he hadn't just slipped up behind the lad and quietly taken him to one side. He concluded that it was probably childish to consider whether the irritating conversation in the car was directly proportional to the speed of his exiting the vehicle.

He had whacked the dashboard, and was out on the road before it was fully stationary.

The kid looked over his shoulder when he heard the door slamming. Goodhew dashed forward. 'Stop,' he yelled. It was all that Mobile Boy needed to galvanize him into a sprint.

Mobile's legs were long and the lollopy walk had morphed into the kind of strides that quickly swallowed the ground.

The kid had a good lead: twenty yards plus another ten that Goodhew had lost by crossing through the traffic.

Mobile was fast and darted away between the pedestrians. His reflexes were keen and he zigzagged easily round A-boards and waste bins.

Goodhew left the pavement, sprinting along the narrow gap between the kerb and the traffic. Mobile was still widening the distance.

Goodhew pushed himself faster. All he had to do was keep pace. Mobile was quick, but he couldn't go on running forever.

There was a right turn coming up, and Mobile glanced back. The approaching corner was busy with people and traffic. Goodhew couldn't risk losing sight of him if he made a turn first. Goodhew cut across, charging through the shoppers, following the most direct angle towards the corner.

Suddenly Mobile darted the other way, switching out into the flow of traffic, forcing Goodhew to brake before angling back towards the roadway. Goodhew's foot clipped a metal sandwich board, leaving its tubular frame clattering on the pavement. He stumbled briefly, but kept his balance and continued to run.

Mobile was now on the opposite pavement.

Goodhew ran towards him, then halfway over the road he changed his mind and sprinted along the white line until he'd made up ground again.

Ahead rose the carcass of the old Locomotive pub. Sudden instinct told Goodhew that Mobile would take the wide driveway running beside it, leading to Mill Road Cemetery.

Goodhew stayed in the centre of the road, since it would give him more space to make the turn, and he could see that Mobile was getting slower now.

Mobile looked back as he neared the alley, then darted left just as he reached the entrance. Then Goodhew accelerated, across the traffic and towards the same opening. He knew the driveway well: a long avenue of trees and thick shrubs, with no way out until further along.

Mobile was two-thirds of the way down, his strides becoming less regular, more weary. His flash trainers seemed to have downgraded themselves from running shoes to jogging weights.

By the short pathway leading into the graveyard, Goodhew got close enough to make a grab at the boy, and brought him down. They landed in a heavy heap amongst the long grass and thick nettles by the boundary wall.

Goodhew stood up and pulled Mobile back on to his feet.

'OK?' he asked.

Mobile scowled. 'I better not have any dog shit on me,' he panted.

He had a point, but the grass looked clear and they'd both escaped with nothing more than a few grass stains. 'You're fine. Might've been easier if you hadn't run away, eh?'

Mobile scowled. 'You ain't even panting.'

Goodhew fished a small notebook out of his back pocket and his phone from the front of his jeans. He showed his ID. 'What's your name?'

'Why?'

'There was a fire two nights ago in Gwydir Street. I've been trying to track down the person who made the 999 call. Fits your description.'

Mobile shifted his weight from foot to foot, and for a moment Goodhew wondered if they were about to have a rematch. But, as the boy was still puffing, Goodhew didn't feel too worried.

'Not me, mate.'

Goodhew nodded. 'Fair enough, I'll take your details and get them to cross you off the list.' He opened up his mobile. 'I'll phone my boss now.' He found the number and pressed 'call'. It took about three seconds for the phone in Mobile's hand to start playing a distorted version of some kind of techno-anthem.

Their eyes met and Goodhew knew that Mobile would have tried another runner if his legs hadn't been so far beyond co-operating. 'What's the problem?' he pressed.

Mobile shrugged. 'Didn't want to get involved.'

'Because . . .?'

Mobile pushed his hands into his pockets and shrugged again. And again he shifted his weight from foot to foot.

Goodhew pulled a face that said he was capable of patiently waiting through as many renditions of the fidgeting routine as it might take.

Mobile's attention span was pretty short, however, and it took less than ten seconds for him to start talking. 'I just know what it's like, right. You want to ask some questions. Did I see anything? No. Do I know anything? No. Then you want a statement, and I'll be down the cop shop for two or three hours telling you a-*gain* that I don't know nuthin'. Then I'll probably have to go to court, sit around for hours just so I can tell everyone a-gain that all I did was see the house on fire and ring 999 like anybody else would.'

'Witnesses have said you seemed to think there was someone inside the house?'

'No, I thought there might be.'

'You banged on the door and shouted, "Rachel".'

'Fucking didn't.'

'So you don't know the people that lived there?'

Mobile did a quick burst of shrug-and-shuffle. 'Right,' he said.

Goodhew drew a slow, deep breath. 'We'll start from the top then. Name first?'

Mobile sighed too. 'Mikey Slater.'

'Date of birth?'

'14 June '94.'

It was the first time Goodhew could remember being ten years older than anyone resembling an adult. Obviously, Mikey was still a kid but he could have passed for eighteen or nineteen, so it counted – kind of.

Goodhew ignored the urge to say 'Shouldn't you be in school?' or something equally lame. He took down Mikey's address and double-checked it via Parkside. Mikey lived with his mum in a flat on Devonshire Road, behind Raj's shop and in the direction of the railway station. Not closer to the town centre, as Raj had assumed. It was a minor inconsistency.

'So what brings you through here?'

'I cut through here for town, sometimes. If I go to the cinema, or in the Grafton Centre to meet my mates.'

'What about today?'

'What about it?'

It was Goodhew's turn to fidget. 'Is there some unwritten rule that says you need to make every single question as much work for me as possible?'

'Dunno what you mean.'

'There's a surprise. I'm actually trying to help locate the child that has been missing since that fire. You obviously possess some sense of responsibility, or you wouldn't have called the fire brigade in the first place, so please just start by explaining why you chose to come in here today?'

'All right, all right. I was just walking home from my mate's house when you started chasing me. That's the only reason. I thought I had a better chance of losing you.'

'And on the night of the fire?'

'I'd been in town.'

'With?'

Mikey reeled off a couple of names, no phone numbers, no addresses. He held eye contact much too long, so Goodhew was certain neither would check out. Goodhew didn't push it, however.

He glanced at his watch, realized time wasn't on his side. He wasn't keen to let Mikey just walk away, since there was always a chance that he'd just vanish. The small inconsistencies were the most telling; only the most accomplished liars had their answers ready for the minor questions. Mikey was a liar, but not much of one.

Goodhew was certain the boy was neither a killer nor a kidnapper, so he asked him a few more routine questions, then decided to let him go. 'But you'll need to make a statement.'

'Fair enough.' Mikey had his hands in his pockets and twisted his upper body in the direction of the main gate, ready to go as soon as Goodhew was ready to let him.

But Goodhew had one more question, which he'd kept back until the last moment; a final barometer reading to assess Mikey's honesty. 'Oh, and I meant to ask, what's your other reason for coming here?'

Goodhew's tone was deliberately casual, and when Mikey had first turned back towards him he clearly expected to need only an equally casual answer. One look at Goodhew told him otherwise, and for once in their brief relationship, Mikey didn't move. Hopefully he had sensed that this question was far more loaded than the previous ones.

He hesitated. 'What makes you think I do?'

Goodhew took a turn at shrugging, 'We recovered a cap here. DNA will confirm if it's yours, I guess. I wondered how you lost it?'

'Fucking unreal.'

Goodhew decided this was a compliment. 'Thanks,' he said.

'You ain't dumb, are you?' Mikey shook his head. 'I've gotta brother, five years older than me, he is. I heard he goes in there.' Mikey turned and pointed along the East Road side of the perimeter wall, then made his pointing gesture bigger and deeper. 'You know, right in there.'

Goodhew nodded.

'Mum's not well, and I thought he might want to know.'

'Did you find him?'

Mikey shook his head. 'Not yet – probably a waste of time. Haven't actually seen him since I was at junior school.'

'Thanks for your help.' Goodhew put the notebook back in his pocket, but Mikey kept talking.

'It's drugs, innit? He's addicted.' He was looking at Goodhew with new interest, as though he'd suddenly decided that Goodhew might have some answers.

Goodhew passed him his card. 'I'll be in touch to take a proper statement from you. If you think of anything else that might be important, ring me straight away, OK?'

Mikey looked disappointed but still nodded.

'Tell me about your brother then, and I'll see if there's anything we can do.'

'Appreciated.'

'Where are you going now?'

'Home. No chance of getting my hat back, is there?'

They made their way out through the same exit, walking in silence along the avenue of trees leading back to Mill Road. Mikey gradually lengthened his stride, till he put a gap of about ten feet between himself and Goodhew.

Gully was waiting in the patrol car, which was parked on double yellows at the end of the path. As Goodhew opened the passenger door, Mikey crossed the road ahead of their vehicle. He glanced at Goodhew, with little more than a casual movement, but Goodhew definitely detected a small nod of his head and sensed the word 'Cheers' grunted through unmoving lips.

Mikey Slater didn't stay on Mill Road for long. As soon as the patrol car was out of sight, he darted back into the cemetery and towards the exit on its opposite side.

He had things to do.

He'd finally realized something that should have smacked him in the face from day one; and that was the very reason he couldn't now phone ahead. At some point soon the police would know every number that he'd called; every number that had called him.

Clearly they didn't have the information yet, but how long would it be before they knocked on Kimberly's door?

Mikey felt the net closing, and he had no idea which way was out.

He broke into a run. Things to do . . . things to do.

Identifying the anonymous caller was one tick off Goodhew's 'to do' list. Running round Mill Road had been unplanned exercise, but it had allowed him enough distance from Gully to see that he needed to straighten things out with her before they went any further.

She glanced towards him and, even from the kind of distance that made her face resemble a few abstract smudges of light and shadow, he could tell that she was glowering. As he drew closer, she turned her head so she was looking away from him.

159

He refused to spend the remainder of the day fighting against her; it had to stop, now.

Goodhew opened the passenger door, and she started the engine. She looked like she was about to ask for the details, but he beat her to it.

'His name's Mikey Slater. He made the original call for help,' Goodhew informed her.

Gully pulled out into the traffic and, as they drove, he filled her in on his conversation with Mikey. He twisted around in his seat till his back faced the angle between his seat and the door. He watched her closely, but if she was interested in Mikey Slater she showed no sign of it. He guessed she was too busy dwelling on the wrong things to be able to focus her thoughts where they should be.

When he spoke again, his tone was far more matter-of-fact. 'Did you let the nursing home know we'd be late?'

'No.'

'Why not?'

Gully changed gear, she seemed to be concentrating on her driving but Goodhew spotted the red patches suddenly blossoming across her cheeks.

'Why not?' he pushed.

'I didn't think I needed to.'

'We made an appointment.'

'I know,' she said, her voice suddenly quiet.

'You didn't think we needed to because Jay Andrews is not going anywhere, right?'

She nodded and bit her bottom lip.

'He's fully aware of everything around him, though unable to move or ask questions, and you assumed that he didn't really need to be kept up to date, and didn't really need any common courtesy.' He kept his voice on one level, quiet and firm, free from any apparent anger. She looked over at him quickly and he could feel her embarrassment.

'I'm sorry,' she turned her eyes back to the road, 'I usually do better than that.'

'OK.'

'OK? You don't believe me?'

'I said OK.'

'No, you said it like you really meant 'If you say so' or 'In your dreams', or something.'

'Want to know what I actually think?'

'Not really.'

'Fair enough.'

There was a long pause then, and he hoped she was battling with the urge to have the final word. She stared at the road ahead just a bit too intently, her posture unnaturally correct and each mirror-signal-manoeuvre just too self-aware.

They'd travelled another half mile before she finally cracked. 'Go on, then. You obviously need to get it off your chest.'

The corner of his mouth twitched as he suppressed a smile, but luckily it went unnoticed.

'So, tell me, what do *you* think about Kimberly Guyver?'

Gully looked surprised. 'She's lying about something.'

'And what would that be?'

'If I knew, I think I would have already told Marks, don't you?'

'So you just have a feeling?'

'Yep.'

'Come on, it must be more than that. Get it out in the open, Sue.'

Gully gave a small smile.

He knew that if he kept pushing, he really was going to get it. So he kept pushing and as they turned into Cherry Hinton Road, the floodgates burst.

'Maybe she's not quite as cut up about Riley as some people seem to think. Maybe she has someone else to take her mind off it.' Gully laughed, but it was hard and humourless. 'I saw you leaving her bedroom, and I can't think of one legitimate reason you'd be up there. Did you think she needed a shoulder to cry on? That's an abuse of your position . . . such an abuse.' Her face screwed up into an expression that bordered on hatred. 'But maybe she's playing you. The fact is that at least one of you is making a fool out of the other. Either that or you're both cooking something up together.'

Goodhew said nothing, remaining silent for the length of Cherry Hinton Road, also the short drive along Hinton Avenue, and even while she manoeuvred the car into the last available space in the nursing-home car park. He waited until she'd cut the engine.

'Wait, don't get out just yet.'

'Why not?' Her face was an angry red, and she was beyond caring who else saw it. 'We're already late.'

'Another two minutes won't matter.'

'Fine.' She pressed her lips shut and waited with her hand on the door handle.

'I can see you have a dilemma, since you genuinely think I've behaved inappropriately, don't you?'

She levelled her gaze with his. 'Yes, I do.'

'And then it's compounded after you tell Marks, and he appears to do nothing as a result?'

'He told you?'

'No, I found out myself.'

She let go of the handle. 'And now you're trying to get me into your corner?'

'No, I'm trying to make sure that we can work together. I don't want either of us to miss anything important because we're too distracted by details that don't matter.'

'Of course they matter.'

'Not to Riley, they don't. Look, Marks will investigate me; he's a thorough man and fair, and he'd never just take my word for it. I wasn't following protocol, that's true, but my conversation with Kimberly Guyver was case-related, nothing more. It's the wrong time to drag her into anything else, so Marks will wait. I really am sorry that I seem to have put you in a difficult position.'

Goodhew didn't feel at all perturbed by the possibility of being investigated, and maybe that showed. For the first time, Gully's expression relaxed and became more thoughtful.

'What do you think of Michael Kincaide?' she asked.

Goodhew knew it wasn't the right time to be evasive, but a brutally honest answer wasn't going to promote his theory of working in harmony. 'Michael and I don't get on well, and it's partly a personal clash because –'

'Because you dumped Mel?'

The question was so abrupt that it caught Goodhew off-guard. And the information behind it was so wide of the mark that he didn't want to begin explaining how he'd never at any time gone out with Mel. And how, if he actually had, he could never imagine abandoning her.

He took a breath. 'Not exactly.' Then his mobile rang, ending the possibility of adding anything further.

TWENTY-NINE

The lobby of Hinton Avenue nursing home was light and airy, decorated with an assortment of artwork ranging from prints of traditional landscapes to hanging plates decorated by the residents.

Goodhew was studying a rather dark but striking abstract when the manager, Amanda Tebbutt, joined them. She must have followed Goodhew's gaze. 'Painted by a former patient.'

'He's good.'

'He died. Unfortunately that's how most of them become *former* patients.' She pointed towards another, less artistic, work, 'Our patients have a tough time physically, so for many holding a paint brush is a major achievement, which makes any small success worth a great deal.'

Maybe she also said that to those she interviewed about taking care of potential patients, but it still sounded totally genuine.

'How many residents do you have here?'

'Maximum of twelve, ten at the moment.'

'With similar needs to Jay Andrews?'

'Oh no, a few like him need twenty-four-hour attention, but the others have some movement and at least limited capacity for speech. Often, over time, we see small improvements, but in most cases their physical limitations stem from limitations in the brain's ability to function.'

She glanced at Goodhew to make sure he was still interested. 'What I mean is, there's a correlation. In most cases the physical signs are a reflection of how the patient also has a difficulty in understanding and thinking to full capacity. Jay's injury was

164

devastating, so it took us a long time to comprehend that he still possessed the same mental capacity as ever.'

'You mean locked-in syndrome wasn't diagnosed immediately?'

'No, no, what I'm saying is that there's a huge difference between being told that someone is trapped inside their body and actually breaking the automatic association between outward appearances and the way one should treat them. I had to constantly remind myself that I didn't need to speak to him slowly or simplistically; that he wants Radio 4 and the World Service, not just background music and daytime TV. He still has very clear recollection of all the things he used to be able to do. It really is the cruellest of conditions.' She finally drew a breath and, when she spoke again, she sounded apologetic. 'Just thought I'd explain, as it might help when you start to talk to him.'

'I'm sure it will.'

'Now, if you'd both like to follow me.'

Gully had become so quiet that Goodhew had almost forgotten she was with him. Amanda Tebbutt now led them through the patients' lounge into a ground-floor corridor that had two doorways along each side.

'I understand he communicates by Morse code? Why doesn't he have anything more sophisticated? I've read about equipment that responds to eye movement.'

'It took a while to assess him; then, when it was first offered, he refused. He couldn't bring himself to accept the idea until he'd accepted that his condition was permanent. Now that he wants it, it's –' she made the quotes sign and rolled her eyes, '– in the pipeline. Delivery next month is the latest promise. Ridiculous.'

'Do you know Kimberly Guyver?' he asked.

Amanda nodded. 'In my opinion she and the little boy have been wonderful. Family support is usually extremely good for morale.'

'Does she just sit and talk to him?'

Amanda Tebbutt stopped outside the second room to the right, and smiled knowingly. 'Now, you see what I mean – you can ask him yourself.' The door was already open, and they saw Jay Andrews propped up in a bed positioned to face them diagonally from the opposite corner. A thin blonde woman in her early thirties was waiting by the window.

'This is Anne, I've asked her to sit in, just in case Jay requires anything. If you need me again, I'll be in my office.'

Anne nodded and greeted them in a strong Irish accent.

Jay stared at them directly but with the slack-faced expression that Goodhew recognized from his previous experience of visiting geriatric wards. Jay had clearly once been handsome: his eyes were hazel with long dark lashes, and his skin was that shade of olive which still looked like it glowed from a recently acquired tan even in the middle of winter. Or in a hospital bed, under artificial light.

Goodhew wasn't sure of the exact etiquette required, but he crossed to the bed and briefly took Jay's right hand as though he were shaking it. It felt like the proper thing to do. 'Pleased to meet you.'

He then pulled up a chair, and Gully followed suit. She smiled at Jay then took her notebook and seemed to concentrate on an empty page as Goodhew finished their introductions.

'Kimberly's told me how you and she communicate using Morse code, which I can read, so I'll ask each question and PC Gully will make a note of both the questions I ask and what I tell her your answers are.'

No 'uh-huh' or even 'mmm' in reply. It felt odd.

'I forgot to ask Kimberly whether you have a shortcut for "yes" and "no". If you do, can you show me what "yes" is, please?'

Jay shut his right eye and held it closed for a full second.

'And "no"?'

Jay did the same with his left eye.

'Finally I should explain that this won't constitute a formal statement, so unfortunately, if we need one, it will be a repeat of this interview but on videotape, and with an independent witness to make sure you are fairly represented. All OK so far?'

Jay gave the *yes* signal and they began. It was a slow process but Gully was very thorough in her notes, so that when Goodhew reread the transcript later, he could hear it in his mind as though they'd been having a conventional conversation.

Goodhew asked him about Rachel, and how well they'd known each other.

'Pretty well,' Jay replied. 'It's sad.'

'Yes, it is. And you must be worried about Riley?'

'Dumb question.'

'Right, sorry. We're concerned because there's no trace of Stefan Golinski. His car's gone, but there have since been no sightings. Is there anything you know about him that might help?'

'Stefan's a bastard.'

'Violent?'

'Yes, irrational. A nut job.'

'Jealous?'

'Yes, totally.'

'Was he ever jealous of you?'

'No, why?'

'I'm trying to make a link.' Goodhew thought his next words through, keen to avoid an unnecessarily leading question. 'I'm looking for a link between your injury and Rachel's death.'

'There won't be one.'

'How do you know?'

'Mine was an accident.'

'How much can you remember?'

'Flashes. Pain and black patches. The sound of my head cracking.'

'Do you remember where you were?'

'Police said it was outside some bar I'd never heard of.'

'But you don't agree?'

'Don't know. I thought I was at her apartment.'

'Kimberly's?'

'Yes. But she said I'd left. It is possible.'

'And you trust her?'

'Another dumb question. When's the press conference?'

'They just phoned, and it's being delayed. The police psychologist is worried that such publicity will tip Stefan Golinski over the edge.'

'He's no good without Rache.'

'In what way?'

'She was his safety catch.'

'Her injuries were very similar to yours. Could Stefan have attacked you?'

'Don't know.'

'It's possible, though?'

'Yes.'

'And do you think he could have killed Rachel?'

'Absolutely. Like cutting off his own arm, but yes. His jealousy was out of control. I saw him throw a teenager down the stairs for just looking at her. He even hated Kimberly for being her friend. He only tolerated her because of Nick.'

'Her boyfriend, Nick Lewton?' Goodhew corrected himself. 'Her then boyfriend?'

'It's OK. There was some hero-worship shit going on there. Nick was the man, Stefan's mentor. Rachel and Kimberly's friendship had put Stefan up there with the bosses . . .'

Goodhew cut in, trying to be helpful. 'Nick Lewton and Craig Tennison?'

'And Tamsin, the sister.'

Goodhew asked several more questions but, without warning, Jay either couldn't or wouldn't reply. Goodhew glanced first at Gully then, as his concern grew, turned to Anne.

'He's fine,' she assured them. 'You just have to wait. Sometimes he needs to think or rest, just like any other person.'

So Goodhew sat back and waited; finally Jay's eyes started moving again. 'Going to Spain was Kimberly's only mistake. None of it is her fault.'

Goodhew leant closer. 'Is there something you'd like to tell me?'

'She's in too deep.'

'With what?'

'All of it. She's scared, but all she wants is Riley's safety. Promise her that and she'll talk to you.'

'How can I promise her something that I can't deliver?'

'She thinks you're OK. Tell her I said it's time to trust the police. If she won't talk, then come back here.'

THIRTY

As Goodhew left Hinton Avenue nursing home, he was hit by the impact of fresh air and the smell of newly mown grass. He guessed it had smelt like this on their way in, but he hadn't then been aware of it.

Gully was looking around her like she'd just been released from solitary.

'D'you think they ever take him outside?' she wondered.

The gardens weren't large but they were well tended and full of mature shrubs. In the corner was a sycamore which cast a frilled shadow on to the lawn. 'I'm sure they do. Small consolation, though, eh?'

She shook her head. 'What a shit life.'

'When we find Rachel's killer, it might help.'

'Maybe, but he can hardly move on, can he?' She stared into the middle distance, as though there might be a solution out there that the doctors had missed. He doubted she'd find one, but it demonstrated that maybe she really did possess a more compassionate side.

It felt like a good moment to clear the air.

She headed to the driver's side of the car and unlocked the door. The sun was shining into his eyes causing him to squint and making it difficult to see her clearly. He went ahead with his question in any case. 'Did you see me at Kimberly's house last night, then?'

'I make a couple of polite comments and then you think I'm a pushover?'

Goodhew sighed. 'No, I thought you might discuss it with me, that's all.'

'And how else do you think Marks would know you were there?'

'Dunno, Kincaide maybe?'

She made a sound like a pressure valve being released, yanked open the door and dropped into her seat. Goodhew followed suit, and was just in time to hear her mutter the word 'pathetic'.

'I didn't accuse Kincaide. I just knew that it had to be one or other of you. And I couldn't work out why *you* would have said it.'

'Because it was the truth?' Her eyes glinted angrily. 'I don't understand why it's such a heinous crime to blow the whistle on a colleague when they've been caught doing something blatantly wrong.'

'And what was I doing?'

'Leaving her room.'

'No, I accompanied her back to the window, but I was never inside her room. And how could you believe she'd be carrying on with anyone when her child is missing? The more I think about it, the more ridiculous that is.'

'I saw you both: you scampering away and her half undressed.'

'Well, lucky you.'

'Meaning what?'

'Oh, I don't know. It just came out.' Goodhew regretted starting the conversation. 'You did whatever you felt was appropriate.'

'So why wouldn't I go to Marks and tell him? You were taking advantage of a witness. You could jeopardize our entire investigation just to get your fingers in the cookie jar.'

'And if you're so right, why am I still at work?'

Gully glowered at him. She really did possess an impressive selection of angry expressions.

'Well, maybe,' Goodhew continued, 'maybe that's because Marks knows me well enough to spot a crock of shit when he hears one.'

'Yeah, and I'm so full of shit that he's asked me to spend the entire day holding your hand.' She started the engine. 'Maybe Marks simply knows that he can't prove anything yet. When this is over, I'm sure he'll suggest to Kimberly that she should make a complaint.' She made a clumsy attempt at finding reverse, and the gearbox made a chunking noise in protest. 'And you can keep your cracks about women drivers to yourself,' she snapped.

So much for clearing the air.

Goodhew picked up his mobile and phoned Marks.

THIRTY-ONE

DI Marks had started the day with a clear plan: first briefing, then press conference. At half-past ten he had met with Liz Bradley, the force's press officer. A petite woman in her early forties, she always dressed in suits which consisted of a hip length jacket and a skirt which stopped an inch above the knee. These suits seemed to be colour-coded to the information she would be imparting; paler shades for good news, like improved crime statistics; fawns and greys for public information announcements; anti-speeding campaigns and the like; then increasingly sombre shades for anything more serious. Today's code was very dark navy-blue.

Marks had worked with Liz for at least fifteen years, therefore knew she possessed a great capacity for public relations, made wonderful eye contact, had an authoritative voice and the kind of calmly logical brain that could make the most of any media opportunity. To back up her good points, she also had a fierce temper and a keen ability to sour the air if things didn't go her way.

She'd hurried into his office, as if propelled by the urgency of Riley Guyver's plight, holding a sheaf of papers which he knew would be press releases and several drafts of the statement that Kimberly Guyver would eventually read out loud.

Bradley was always highly efficient, even when working right in the middle of an ongoing police investigation, so he'd never known her to be thrown by an unexpected question, and guessed that part of this was due to the groundwork she always put in. So, frustratingly slow as it might be, he knew that his meeting with her now would ensure that the final versions of the documents she carried would become public only once they contained precisely the right messages.

Even so, he hadn't expected it to take them an hour.

When she'd caught him glancing at his watch, her expression became stern. 'The conference room at the Parkside Hotel is available. It's being set up even as we speak.'

'Is 1 p.m. still possible, then?'

'I'll schedule it for 12.45.'

'And they'll get here in time?'

'If they want the story, they'll have to, won't they,' she replied, her voice suddenly cooling by several degrees. 'I have already pre-warned them that it's likely to be early afternoon.'

He nodded slowly, reminding himself that he should have more faith in her organizational skills, having seen them in action often enough.

She mistakenly took his silence as a sign of hesitancy. 'Let me explain. When the time is fixed for quarter to the hour, the obvious sub-text is 'Every fifteen minutes matters', and as long as we're under way by one prompt, then there will be just enough time for the story to be posted in the *Cambridge News*'s final edition . . .'

'It's fine.'

'Let me finish.' She held up her hand. 'However, if you prefer we can shift the briefing to somewhere nearer three. It won't then make the evening papers, just the television and radio evening-news bulletins.'

'The sooner the better.' He passed some of her papers back across the desk. 'Make sure it's clear that Stefan Golinski could pose a threat to the public, then redraft what you've got and let me see it as soon as you can.'

She'd left the room before he risked sighing. He had the feeling it was going to be all uphill today.

At noon, Marks was standing in the function room of the Parkside Hotel, a small commercial establishment which lay within sight of the police station, just across the busiest edge of Parker's Piece.

A couple of uniformed officers were controlling access to the building, but apart from that they had the function room all to themselves.

A row of four meeting-room chairs stood behind two tubular-steel-legged tables butted together and draped in a twenty-foot length of navy-blue banqueting cloth. Behind the tables, the Cambridgeshire Constabulary's insignia was mounted on a free-standing, royal-blue display board, and in front were ranged seven rows of chairs.

Liz Bradley had just explained the seating arrangement to DI Marks. Kimberly and Liz herself would occupy the middle two chairs, with Liz sitting on Kimberly's right. Marks would sit on Kimberly's left.

Liz had redrafted everything in her usual succinct style, and behind her own name card she'd left a pile of half-a-dozen index cards with one key point written on each.

'Is Kimberly Guyver in the building yet?' she demanded.

Marks nodded. 'I wanted her here well before the press, so she's upstairs. PC Wilkes is with her.'

'Good, good. I'll go up just before it starts, for a ten-minute run-thorugh, then bring her down for 1 p.m. How does that sound?'

'Ten minutes is enough?'

Liz Bradley managed a smile that was evenly split between disbelief, amusement and mockery. 'If I spend too long over it, she'll get the jitters. I thought you'd have known that by now.'

'I wouldn't have thought it's the same in every case.'

'It's the procedure I follow, and I wasn't aware you had any issue with the way I conduct these events.'

'I don't.'

'So why are you so nervous about this one?'

'I'm not,' Marks replied, simultaneously wondering why he felt as though he needed to justify himself to her. 'I'm conscious that this briefing could be crucial, and therefore it needs to be right, and I know it will be.'

That seemed to placate her, or maybe she was nervous too, because, despite his denial, he was conscious of how very much rested on this single event, minutes that the media would cut and compress down to a few crucial soundbites.

Behind him he caught the sound of someone pushing open the door with a heavy thump on the wood panel. Liz looked past him and exhaled, and murmured involuntarily, 'Oh.'

Marks turned to see Bob Trent, behavioural psychologist, bearing down on them. His face was an unhealthy Merlot shade, and by comparison Liz Bradley suddenly seemed timid.

'This doesn't look good,' she muttered in Marks' ear.

The press was now gathered in the main conference room. One of the doors led to a cramped meeting room adjoining, spacious enough for two people to pore over a single document, but not so good with the addition of Bob Trent, specially now he'd broken into a heavy sweat.

A faulty thermostat had pushed the radiator up to maximum. Liz had tried opening the window but the road noise coupled with the risk that some over-eager reporter would find a handy spot in the flowerbed from which to eavesdrop had proved too much of a distraction.

So they'd convinced themselves that they'd put up with it; after all, how much longer could it take? Currently seventy-five minutes and counting.

Marks glanced at his watch again, and this time Liz didn't take it personally.

'How much longer will the press hang around?' he asked.

'I'll keep the refreshments coming. Meanwhile they'll sit it out. As time goes on, they're probably expecting an increasingly significant announcement.'

'This is significant.' Bob Trent's jaw jutted with determination.

Marks considered himself to be a tolerant man, but Call-Me-Bob Trent occupied a hefty and irritating spot right on the outer limits. The most annoying thing about him was his professional competence, since it made it hard for Marks to find an excuse for using anyone else.

Call-Me-Bob's job had been to give Kimberly's statement a final once-over, and so far that alone had taken him an hour and a quarter. Marks had worked with him since 2004 and, although Marks didn't like to own up to the idea that he jumped to conclusions based on looks alone, there was plenty about Call-Me-Bob that instantly got his back up. This included beige polyester trousers, bri-nylon shirt, a whiff of mothballs, slight hint of urinal, and short but greasy hair that hung with discs of dandruff like décor for head lice. Needless to say, Call-Me-Bob did plenty of work by phone, letter and email.

Marks knew that today's hold up was important, since Call-Me-Bob's insights had the potential to make a vital difference to the outcome. Whilst Call-Me-Bob was notoriously opinionated, he could be equally reluctant to pin his name to a decision and at that moment seemed in imminent danger of impaling himself on the fence.

'I'm not suggesting you abandon the appeal. As I keep saying, I'm only trying to ascertain whether you have fully considered Mr Golinski's state of mind.'

'And I was asking you to throw some light on what you mean by that. If he did kill Rachel, we already know that he must be in some kind of abnormal frame of mind. I want to know why it's now become such an issue that you're not even sure we should go ahead with this appeal.'

Liz stayed silent, but it didn't look as though she'd stay that way for too much longer. As Call-Me-Bob spoke, she pressed her lips shut and sealed them by pressing her knuckles against them. His voice was invariably whiney; it didn't matter if he was angry or serious or miserable, he still whined. 'You're not *listening*,' he protested. 'I only asked you whether you had considered the possibility that a briefing of this nature might, in fact, trigger further violence.'

'And I asked you to quantify that risk.'

'How could I do that without access to the subject himself?'

The heat of the room was bringing out the full smell of mothball.

'An estimate,' Marks snapped. 'Give me an estimate at least, anything to go on.'

Call-Me-Bob flared his nostrils as he considered. 'Eighty per cent.'

'Eighty per cent which way?'

'The wrong way.'

It was Liz's turn to scowl. 'That's far too high. How can a press conference pose such a level of risk?'

'It might not, and remember it's an estimate based only on the assumption that he will hear the broadcast. He might not. You *have* read my report, haven't you, Liz?'

'Yes,' she replied, but sounded a little more uncertain. 'Did I miss something?'

Call-Me-Bob flipped it open. 'Here, page eleven, paragraph three. 'Although Stefan Golinski is not directly related to Riley Guyver, it is reasonable to assume that the close relationship between Rachel Golinski and both Kimberly and Riley Guyver would lead Stefan Golinski to view all of these people as his family, or at least as his extended family. In the instance of a severe psychotic episode, it is members of the sufferer's family and extended family who are at greatest risk of violence.'

'Well, I read that part,' Liz replied.

'And, if you read on, you'll understand that Stefan Golinski and Riley Guyver are probably dead already.'

'But we're looking *forward*, focusing on the best chance of finding Riley alive.' Liz was now addressing Bob in a slower voice, clearly feeling, like Marks, that they'd reached stalemate without knowing why.

Call-Me-Bob looked equally pissed off. He placed his palms face-down, one on each knee, and stared at his hands, as if keeping an eye on them in case they decided to jump up and slap Marks and Liz for their blatant stupidity. 'And if you read on, you will also see that there is a large window during which one of these episodes can extend. It is a period which can lead up to a violent conclusion.'

Finally Marks was starting to see what Bob meant. Of course, he'd read the report, but it was littered with medical terms and footnotes referencing other cases. He didn't query them, because he had been certain he had understood the gist of it. Now it was dawning on him that he must have missed one vital point.

Call-Me-Bob continued, 'If the murder of his wife, Rachel, was not his ultimate intention, then it is likely that killing Riley Guyver is an aim that he is still working towards. Your assumption that he removed the lad from the scene because he wasn't expecting to find him there in the first place could be entirely misjudged. What if his plan is to exact some kind of revenge on Kimberly Guyver, and that could mean waiting until the eyes of the press are upon us all, then executing his plan in the most public and cruel way possible.'

'So,' Liz said, 'when you said "violent conclusion", you didn't mean Rachel's murder and the fire, but something that hasn't even yet happened?'

Bob clapped his hands together. 'Yes,' he crowed, with a *Eureka!* tone in his voice.

As much as Marks felt he didn't usually need things particularly spelt out, in this case he wished Call-Me-Bob had spoon-fed him this information an hour sooner.

He could feel himself wanting to climb right up on the fence along with Bob and his mothballs. If he cancelled, they'd lose the potential for a sighting, but if he went ahead he'd risk giving Golinski the green light for his endgame.

His mobile rang, and he glanced at the screen before answering. 'What is it, Goodhew?'

'Has the press conference started yet, sir?'

'Do you think I would be on the phone to you while I'm speaking on national TV?' he snapped.

Marks listened as Goodhew began to gave him a brief summary of his interview with Jay Andrews. He didn't even let him finish. 'No, you can't. She's right here, so I'll ask her myself.' Goodhew began to speak again, but Marks cut him off. 'If there's something I think you need to know, I'll be in touch.'

Marks shut his phone, then switched it off. 'No more interruptions. Everyone knows where I am.'

Liz looked at him questioningly. 'You said "she's right here", so was that message for me?'

Marks shook his head, 'No, it was DC Goodhew. He wants to interview Kimberly Guyver again, and I said "no". But if he thought she was anywhere else but in the room with me, he'd have done it anyway.'

'Something important?'

'No, Jay Andrews suggested we speak to her again.'

'About what?'

'Nothing. Just to have a chat, apparently.' Marks waved the subject away. 'We'll be debriefing her after the press conference. It can wait until then.'

'So we're going ahead?'

'Yes.' He jumped off the fence. 'We've already missed the window for the evening papers, so go out and tell them three o'clock. We'll use the extra time to tweak the wording. We must try our best to *engage* Stefan Golinski.'

Call-Me-Bob nodded but didn't look convinced.

THIRTY-TWO

The police had brought Kimberly to the Parkside Hotel with the expectation that the press conference would get under way almost immediately. She was impatient for it to begin, but initially not surprised that it had been held up by some hitch. She knew how officials were good at delays, having experienced them with everything from placing her with foster parents to the opening of the new central library.

She had various PCs, DCs and other acronyms trailing around with her, but PC Kelly Wilkes had been her constant companion since PC Gully had gone from her side.

The duty manager had shown them up to one of the second-floor guest suites. It had two double beds backing one wall, a dressing table on the opposite wall, and a table with chairs in the corner furthest from the door.

Kimberly sat amid the pillows on the bed nearest the window. It gave her a view and a bit of personal space, since Wilkes was hardly going to climb on the bed with her.

There'd been no sign of Goodhew either. When Kimberly mentioned the change in personnel, Wilkes merely looked vague and said she thought Goodhew and Gully had gone off to interview a witness 'or something'. She said she couldn't be sure because she'd stayed with Kimberly instead of attending the briefing.

Kimberly guessed that PC Wilkes did know, but just wasn't telling.

Her minder seemed keen to keep the conversation going, though, and she mentioned Goodhew three more times after that. 'He was promoted to DC in almost record time,' she explained, then, 'No one knows much about him,' followed after several minutes by, 'He's really fit, though.' Then Wilkes had grinned when she realized how it sounded. 'I don't mean like that,' she added hastily.

Oh, yes, you do, Kimberly thought.

'Like this morning he chased some kid through Mill Road. Gully radioed it in, said Goodhew had shot off like a rocket. She was still in the car, and couldn't catch him.'

Maybe it was just a coincidence, unconnected to the case, but Kimberly felt a tightening in her throat and the room closing in. Had Wilkes planted that line just to test Kimberly's response? Maybe it would seem unnatural to say nothing.

'And did they catch him?' she asked, hoping there was nothing in her voice but mild curiosity.

'No idea.' Wilkes smiled. 'Tea?'

'Please.'

Kimberly watched the kettle boil. It was very slow and seemed to take ages before the first wisps of steam condensed on the mirror behind it.

She wondered about the real reason for the delay in this press conference.

As the glass became moister, Kimberly felt like she was watching all the tears she'd ever cried appearing from nowhere and weeping on her behalf. This time they weren't for her, or Riley, Rachel or Jay – but for the new victim in all of this, Mikey.

She didn't need anyone to point out to her what it felt like to be fifteen and vulnerable. And, now being the cause of it made her guilty of one half of the same crime her mother had committed. But, unlike her mother, she wasn't going to shirk the responsibility.

It was 2.15 p.m. and she decided to give them until three o'clock to show progress with this press conference. If they were going to do it at all, then she was sure they'd want it on the afternoon news, and if they hadn't done it by then she'd call Anita, persuade her to call Mikey and check that he was OK.

Then she'd pull the plug on the whole thing.

She switched on the TV and put it on mute, with the Teletext displaying the time. It showed the seconds, too, and she couldn't believe how slowly they moved. She'd never been good at waiting, though she'd done enough of it in her time to qualify as a black belt.

Patience is a virtue.

Her mum had made her write it, over and over.

The lesson hadn't worked, and just the thought of those words brought back the unwanted sound of her mother's voice. The sickly-sweet tone when she wanted something, and the razor edge it acquired whenever she had to ask twice.

They'd had a clock in their front room. It was a fake carriage clock, with a glass dome and brass balls inside. It was quite heavy considering it was undoubtedly made of plastic. The balls were like the pendulum, twisting back and forth with the seconds.

It ticked with a relentless 'glop, glop, glop'.

Patience is a virtue.

Sometimes she'd been told to write it a hundred times.

Seventeen characters.

Twenty including spaces.

Eleven different letters.

All the vowels except *O*.

She'd spelt it out in her head, one character per second, three times per minute. Over and over, until she lost count.

And always that clock sounding more patient than she would ever be.

And eventually her mum would appear from wherever; the shop or the bedroom or the kitchen. Wherever. She'd take the sheet of paper, run a critical eye down the words, lines, making sure they'd been written enough times. But for everything Kimberly did correctly, she slipped up in some other way.

'Why are your letters tilting like that? It's really not good enough. Only disturbed people tilt their letters back like that.'

'Your handwriting's a mess. You need to take pride in your work. Anyone looking at this would think you were retarded.'

'Nasty people make tiny letters. Do you want people to think you're a piece of shit?'

Her mother would hold the pages up to the light and study them. 'Not good enough.' She would narrow her eyes and press her lips together in a critical line. 'Not good enough.' Kimberly would sit forever neat and straight and hopeful, feeling like the only time her mother paid her any attention was when she looked at those lines of writing. Kimberly wanted her to be pleased at the extra note she always added at the end: '*I love you mummy*' or something similar.

But, more than anything, she wanted her mother to set the sheet of paper to one side and just be glad to see her daughter. Sometimes there were golden moments when her mum would nod approvingly and declare the writing was 'getting better', or say 'you're getting quicker at last'.

More often that led to her asking for more lines the next time. Just enough to make her daughter fail in her task.

And the little girl Kimberly wrote on, trying to be patient, trying to be good enough and quick enough to deserve whatever it was that shone as the unspoken prize at the end of it all.

It took a long time for the little girl Kimberly to realize that, of all the men that had come and gone in their house over the years, the potential winners that had eventually revealed themselves as definite losers, there hadn't been a single one of them who had been considered less important than she was. No wonder that, by fifteen, Kimberly had been feeling pretty damn vengeful. Not at her mum particularly, but at her stupid, gullible, younger self.

Later she'd run away from Anita's, tanked up with Vodka Ice, and banged on her mother's door until it had been impossible for the woman to ignore it any more. It had opened by about three inches, and her mother's face appeared in the gap. She didn't make any attempt to remove the chain. 'What do you want?' she demanded.

'I came to see you.' Kimberly's voice didn't sound like her own.

'I worked that out, love. What do you *want*?'

Kimberly couldn't answer it. Not coherently. So she started swearing, shouting until she knew her throat would be left feeling raw. Her mother was a beautiful woman, but so much for looks when she was fucking ugly in every other way.

It was the utter frustration that had made Kimberly start to cry. She fished in her pocket and found a crumpled tissue. She used it to wipe her nose, then dried her eyes on the back of her hand.

One tissue didn't do it. She stood on the doorstep and asked for another.

There were dreams, not the sleeping kind but the timeless, longing kind, where her mother held her. Cried with her.

All Kimberly wanted was a tissue. She didn't even ask to come in. All her mother said was 'Fuck off' before slamming the door.

Kimberly waited to see whether the door would reopen. She still expected her mother to simmer down, grudgingly pass her a couple of Kleenex, and maybe say, 'Go on, have your fucking tissue', but in a slightly softer tone.

The door remained shut.

There was no room for denial, finally, and with terrible clarity she realized that the maternal bond was so nonexistent that it didn't run to a single tissue.

A tissue? Something you'd give a stranger without a second thought. Toilet paper would have done; a few squares of something that absolutely anyone could just take from a public toilet. Free. Gratis.

Her distress had zero value. She had zero value.

And how thick was she? All those years of being told she wasn't good enough, and she'd only just grasped the message.

From that moment she despised her young and stupid self.

First she kicked at the front door but when that held firm, she pushed her way through the side gate and attacked the rear. She found a brick and bashed the crap out of one patio door.

She ignored her mum's screams of abuse.

Little bitch.

Fuck-up.

Stupid ugly cow.

None of it was new.

Instead she went in and took the clock, still counting out the seconds with that smug 'glop, glop, glop', and smashed it on the hearth.

The glass case cracked but it still ticked.

Her mother grabbed at Kimberly's sleeve. She shook her away, seeing nothing but the clock. She kicked and stamped on the fucking thing until its mechanism was reduced to shards of broken plastic.

Then she kicked it some more.

Her mother stood back, arms crossed, face set in a mask of sour disdain. Kimberly knew she never wanted to see her again.

It took her a long time to walk home to Anita, and by the time she arrived she understood that her childhood had been unfair and unkind. Although she knew how wrong her mother had been, she never quite shook off the feeling that she wasn't good enough, and began to fear what kind of parent she could ever be.

It didn't matter whether it was genes or upbringing that counted; either way she knew she should never risk motherhood.

THIRTY-THREE

Jay Andrews had lost more than his life. He frequently thought he'd be better off dead, which made what he had left a minus life.

He didn't even have the ability to scratch an itch or look around a room. However the nurses propped him dictated what he could see, which was why his bed was positioned to jut out from the corner, rather than the conventional way with the bedhead against the wall. In theory no one could approach him without being seen, unless they chose a weird route, like sliding under the bed. What might be lurking under the bed had bugged him for some time. Then there had been other days when not seeing the ceiling had disturbed him. A few times, in the early days, he'd been left in a position where he couldn't even see his own hands. He had feeling in his whole body but, without being able to make any movement, he'd started to torment himself with the idea that they were just phantom sensations, that his arms and legs had gone.

He tried philosophy and meditation but had come to the conclusion that there was no hell like being locked away with only yourself for company.

No wonder they called it Monte Cristo Syndrome. Except, unlike the Count, Jay knew he'd never have the luxury of hearing his own voice, of speaking thoughtlessly or being chided for a tone that was too flippant or sarcastic.

Eventually he accepted that he needed to trust what he couldn't see.

Each time Kimberly left his bedside, he believed she would return.

From time to time she played him a video they'd once made on a trip to London. They'd spent the weekend in a cheap hotel on the

Euston Road, and filmed each other on the upper deck of an open-topped sight-seeing bus.

He didn't have the heart to tell her that his recorded voice didn't sound the way he remembered it. He guessed she knew. She knew many things without being told.

He shut his eyes. In his condition it represented the peak of activity.

She wasn't the only one; he himself knew things without having to be told. He knew that Kimberly loved him, less than she loved Riley but more than she loved just about anybody else. He knew she would help him die if he ever wanted it. He corrected himself: *if he ever asked her*. He frequently wished it, but was held back by the suspicion that he still had a purpose, and to thwart that purpose would tip the order of things in a way that produced more repercussions than he could foresee.

He knew that Kimberly blamed herself.

But that wasn't why she visited; their friendship was genuine, and he chose not to think of her with other men. In his more analytical moments he knew the pair of them had no conventional future, and he hoped there would be someone else for her one day. But if he let his thoughts run too freely he'd find himself imagining the moment when she'd break the news to him. The thought of it filled him with dread.

Fear was his constant enemy. When it flared, it sucked him into dark places, leaving him to roam in the maze of tunnels running through the coldest recesses of his mind. He would lie awake for hours, pinioned by night terrors and loneliness. It would continue for several nights, or sometimes several weeks, a relentless 24/7 torture.

Somewhere in his brain lay an abyss he'd been close to, but not across. He guessed insanity lay on the other side. One day he thought he might tip into it, but that hadn't happened yet. That's when he most wanted someone to slip into his room and drive something brutal through his failed body.

But he was starting to learn that the panic was eventually washed away by mental exhaustion, and that the sleep following such an episode of terror was as peaceful as any he'd ever experienced.

When he woke from it, he often felt relaxed enough to conjure up clear and perfect memories. He chose the ones where he and Kimberly made love. Not a fantasy in any way, but a specific time and place being replayed exactly. There were many to choose between, and he never blurred one into another.

Today they were lying in bed. Viva Cottage stood empty apart from them, but still they hid under the covers. Fresh sheets, line-dried and unsoftened, were pulled over their heads. They talked and laughed in whispers. They had made love and were naked still.

He lay on his back and she on her side, her left leg lying across him and her inner thigh pressed soft and warm against his groin. Her skin was smooth and downy, lightly sprinkled with a few pale freckles. He traced his fingertips over her breasts and on to her belly. She never moved, content for him to explore just because she was confident in him, never because she possessed any real understanding of her own beauty.

Her mouth, close to his ear, whispered, 'I want to do it again.' Then her lips found his and she began to kiss him, teasing with her tongue, working harder than she needed to in order to seduce him.

She never seemed to realize that each time they made love he marvelled at his own amazing luck. She took nothing for granted, never once understood the extent of her talent and inner strength, and while he loved that about her it made him feel sorry for her too. And protective.

If he could have smiled, he would.

The memory vanished.

Jay fixed his gaze on a patch of sky in the top right corner of his window, and then forced himself to think about the baby.

That was something he never usually did. It seemed too much like poking a finger into a yellow flame; one second didn't hurt, but a moment too long and it became really painful.

He hadn't known how to react when she gave him the news. She was crying, which didn't help. He'd said 'shit' several times, which hadn't helped either. It had made her cry even more, and then run.

She'd never done that to him before. They were soulmates: he was the one she'd run to, never from. He went looking for her later and apologized.

187

She'd said she wanted an abortion. Said she couldn't have a baby, but wouldn't tell him why.

She didn't need to. He already knew.

It was all about her bloody mother.

She didn't rush out to do it though and, as the weeks passed, he'd begun to hope she'd changed her mind; even then he had an aversion to playing with fate. In the tenth week of her pregnancy, she left Viva Cottage one morning without a word. He later found her sitting at a child's grave in Mill Road Cemetery, and sobbing because she'd miscarried.

They both then cried together, holding on to each other like the bond between them was back to being unbreakable. She told him she'd been terrified that she wouldn't be able to love a child. That had been her overriding fear until the moment her body had rejected the baby, and she'd finally understood how mistaken she'd been.

She wondered whether she'd pushed the baby away with such thoughts alone. She held on to the guilty thought and let Jay go too.

Then she ran and ran, all the way to Spain, blowing a hole the size of a cannonball right through the centre of his life.

Anita had helped him through it, and he hoped that he'd helped Anita, too. Of all the children she'd fostered, he knew that he and Kimberly were closest to being the son and daughter she'd never had.

Occasionally Anita would update him either a passing 'She called, she's fine' or 'She seems different, I'm worried about her.' Then, one Saturday morning, he caught Anita gazing at him with an expression halfway between preoccupation and duty.

'She sent me a letter.'

'And?'

'She's with someone else now.'

He didn't know how he was supposed to respond, so he just said, 'Oh.'

'I thought you should know.'

He nodded, trying to keep his feelings private. 'Thanks.' He had known it was over, so what did he expect? Except it had never been over for *him*. He'd continued just about functioning, not really living, treading water all that time, and waiting for her to come back.

Anita watched him closely, and it was only then that he spotted the battered white envelope that refused to sit still in her hands.

'What's that?' he asked.

'There's a photograph.'

'Of Kimberly?'

'Kimberly and Rachel, and some others.'

'And you want me to look?'

'I've had it a few days. There's something about it that's been bothering me.'

He stared at the envelope. 'Is *he* in the picture?' He knew it was cowardly, but wasn't sure he could face seeing her with someone else.

'No, it's just a group of girls. His name's Nick, by the way.' Typical Anita; her life philosophy was face up to the truth, then get on with it.

Despite his apprehension, Jay reached for the envelope. The photo inside was a six-by-four snap taken in a bar. All seven girls were dressed to party: micro-minis and heels, midriff tops and bare legs, skin that was uniformly brown and glowing in the heat. A couple of them were holding drinks; all were smiling at the camera.

Seven go wild.

'They're the staff,' Anita added.

He then understood precisely why she'd needed to share this photo: to anyone else Kimberly would have just looked like one of the girls, but she'd never before been part of any crowd. Her smile was dazzling, but they could both see it was fake. *Her eyes looked empty.* It could have been down to drink or drugs, but they both knew it was neither. This was the same Kimberly that had first found her way to Anita's door. Heading for oblivion, and content to self-destruct.

Jay handed the photo back to Anita. 'Maybe this boyfriend, Nick, will be good for her.' There was nothing Jay could do. She'd moved on.

That was when he had told Anita that he didn't want to know anything else, and from then the months slipped by with eerie slowness. He had thought he was almost over it, until the day Rachel phoned from Spain and told him that Nick had beaten Kimberly unconscious.

He had arrived to find her in Rachel's apartment. Her face was swollen but they'd kissed, and then it was like all the months in-between were nothing. It had taken until then for her to stop punishing herself about their baby. They'd made love, staying in bed for two full days, then she'd told him to go home.

'I'm not going to run away from here,' she declared. 'I'm going to leave.'

She promised to follow in a few days.

There was nothing he remembered from that moment . . . until the realization hit him that Kimberly was back, but all the possibilities had gone.

He didn't blame her, because it wasn't her fault, but that didn't mean he didn't wish some things could be different.

Top of the list, Jay wished that he really was Riley's father.

THIRTY-FOUR

Stefan Golinski had partial movement in his body and about the same in his brain. Neither would do what he wanted and, although he knew his arms should have had the strength to break free, they only flapped and jerked at his command.

He knew he'd been drugged, of course. His brain wasn't *that* incapacitated. He was well aware of the other signs, too, but he couldn't work out what he'd been given, or when.

He tried to think of something to take his mind off his current situation, and ended up thinking about Jay Andrews.

Was this what it felt like to be Jay?

Stefan could speak, though, and could also move. The last time the door had opened he'd tried both but to no effect. Perhaps Jay also thought he could still do both.

The pen is mightier than the sword. He'd never recognized the truth in that until the last day or so. He hadn't known a single person that would have been able to take him in a fight, yet here he was immobilized by someone smaller and weaker.

And he was fucked.

The ceiling was white but looked grey. In fact the whole room looked dull, especially around the edges of his vision . . . it made him wonder if the air was bad. Tough shit, there was nothing he could do about that; he needed to breathe.

The television was still switched on, stuck on a channel broadcasting an endless stream of US imports. He hadn't seen the news appear again: didn't know the latest on Rachel, didn't know for sure that she really was dead. He knew he was still angry with her, but somehow couldn't feel it any more. Didn't even feel anything for Kimberly or Riley, or the recriminations they deserved for screwing up his life. It was as if he was letting them go.

Facing death did that.

THIRTY-FIVE

They'd barely left the Hinton Avenue nursing home car park before Goodhew's mobile rang. It came so soon after his conversation with Marks that he hoped to see his boss's name on the display, and to hear Marks telling him that he'd be able to interview Kimberly Guyver after all. But it was Bryn, and Goodhew felt a pang of guilt as he remembered how Bryn had already left one voicemail asking him to call.

'Can you stop by?' Bryn asked.

'It's a bit tricky right now.'

'I need to talk to you.'

'About last night?'

'Yeah.'

'Is it important?'

'Maybe, maybe not.'

'OK, give us five minutes.' He hung up.

Goodhew realized how his end of the conversation would have sounded to Gully, and smiled. 'I need you to drive down Mill Road, on the way.'

This time she made that hissing noise and shook her head at the same time; advanced manoeuvres. 'I thought we were going straight to the station. We've been out of the loop for long enough.'

'Marks doesn't need us right now. In any case, how do you know we're not still in the loop? *Someone*'s going to make a breakthrough; and it could be us.'

'Yeah, I'm sure that whatever it is we learn "about last night" will really help the case along.' Gully continued driving with a frustrating level of accuracy, keeping the car within the speed limit, changing gears and indicating like she was doing her driving test.

It was 1.45 p.m. when they pulled up outside O'Brien and Sons. Gully scanned the front of the building. Bryn had his back to them as he leant into the engine bay of a fifteen-year-old Vauxhall Vectra.

'What are we doing here?' Gully asked.

'Semi-social occasion. I was at school with him. Coming?'

'Why?' Her face clouded with the kind of deep irritation she'd been demonstrating off and on for the entire day. Somehow he didn't think she'd be impressed to find out that he'd enlisted a mate to help with unofficial surveillance.

'Just to say hi? You don't have to. I'll only be a minute or two.'

She looked doubtful. 'I can't tell if that's reverse psychology to get me out of the car, or a double-reverse to keep me in it.'

'Why go for a single when the double's handy?'

'Nah, too confusing.' She reached for the door handle then changed her mind. 'Two minutes, right?'

'Absolutely.'

Bryn still didn't move. His elbows rested on the front wing and his hands were oily but empty – not a spanner in sight.

'Are you OK?' Goodhew asked him, as he approached.

Bryn finally turned. It was as if in slow motion, and maintaining contact with the vehicle seemed pretty crucial. He settled with his back against the car and one elbow resting on the roof. 'I'm beyond knackered today, thanks to you.'

'Because . . .?'

'Because you sent me snooping at the Celeste, and thanks to you I've had an hour's sleep, and rehydrated soup for breakfast.'

Goodhew glanced back at Gully, but the car windows were closed and he was sure she was out of earshot. 'I have to be quick, so just give me the potted version, anything that might be relevant to the case.'

'You realize that's not much of a bedside manner, right?'

'So, you went into the Celeste, and then?'

'OK, OK. I went up, and your girl was nowhere, so I hung around the bar. Didn't really think that there was any point in it, but I decided to stay for a while longer. I thought I'd just buy a drink and keep my eyes open for a bit. She had to leave sometime, right?'

'I saw her come out.'

'Good, because I sort of lost track of the time. I mean, I saw her leave but by then I was chatting to Star ... she's this Aussie girl works behind the bar. She's been there since Easter, so she knows Stefan. When she saw Kimberly, she said, "That's Stefan's wife's mate," so I asked her what Kimberly was like, and she said she didn't know. Said her instinct was not to like her just because she's "built like a stripper".'

'That's not fair.' The protest was involuntary.

Bryn raised an eyebrow. 'That's *not* an insult. She just meant that women are usually suspicious of really beautiful women.'

'Maybe. Go on.'

In the end she started to wonder why I was asking so many questions. I told her how I'd seen the murder investigation on the news. I said I was a big CSI fan.'

'Great.'

'It was, too. She loves the programme and asked if I was watching the latest series.'

'Bryn, get to the point.'

'I am. It was because she watches CSI that she took me back to hers and started telling me her theories. I don't even watch the show, but she had most of it on DVD. One dismembered torso later and she's on top of me, acting like she hasn't had a bloke for a year. She's still breathing her ideas into my ear, mostly the same stuff that's been in the papers, when she comes out with the one thing I hadn't heard anywhere else.' Bryn slid a packet of Wrigley's Juicy Fruit from his top pocket, and offered it to Goodhew.

'No, thanks. What did she say?'

'I couldn't tell her why I needed to phone you, so I slipped into her bathroom.' He unwrapped the gum, folding it in thirds before putting it in his mouth. 'You heard my message, right? "Hi, it's me. I won't be back tonight. Ring me tomorrow." Star heard it too, made up her mind I was phoning my wife or something. I came out of the bathroom, and she's standing there in just her underwear. Hands on her hips and livid. Totally fucking livid. Wouldn't have helped to tell her the truth, would it – "It's OK, I was on the phone to my detective mate, thanks for the info." You screwed up my getting screwed, Gary.'

'Well, I really appreciate your sacrifice. In fact I'll appreciate it even more when you finish the story.'

'Mule's gay.'

'That's it?'

'Yes. But think about it. Star's been there just a few weeks, and she's known that practically since day one. It's not information that this Mule guy volunteers openly, but all the staff know. It's an in-joke that all the best-looking women go after him but all the best-looking men end up with him.'

'Maybe he's bisexual?'

'Absolutely not. So Stefan must have known . . .'

'Yeah, I get it. Rachel wouldn't have been sleeping with him.'

'Exactly.'

'So he punched Mule for another reason entirely.'

'Wow, Gary, you should do this professionally.'

THIRTY-SIX

They tracked Mule down to a lock-up garage behind a house in Victoria Avenue. It was larger than average, and one of several with a pitched roof over properly constructed walls built from mottled Cambridge brick.

But where the others had their fascias and down pipes conventionally painted either grey or black, Mule's garage was trimmed in red and cream.

Mule opened the door from the inside, probably using his elbow since both hands were loaded with a pile of six shoeboxes.

He wore boardies and a baggy sleeveless T-shirt. The facial swelling had now subsided and his hair flopped forward over the bruising evident across his right cheekbone.

'I guess you're not here for the delivery,' he smiled warmly at them, looking like the perfect ad for cosmetic dentistry or the New Zealand Tourist Board. 'Come on in, then.'

Goodhew glanced at Gully and caught her staring at the back of Mule's torso with a slightly titillated look in her eye. When he waggled his finger at her jokingly, she tried to look exasperated but didn't quite succeed.

The inside of the garage was a revelation: the unplastered walls had been whitewashed, the floor covered with a stark black-and-white striped lino. A six-foot by eight-foot work table stood in the centre, its surface empty apart from the pile of boxes that Mule had just dumped in the middle.

Instead of legs, the underneath was a solid block of drawers and cupboards. The rear end section of the garage had been fitted out exactly like the interior of a VW campervan, with red and cream seating, a two-ring hob and a miniature sink. A ladder rested against a roof truss, and Goodhew could see that the low triangle of loft housed a mattress.

'You live here?'

'Stay over, sometimes.'

'We don't have another address for you.'

'Either I'm between places, then, or I'm trying to give you an answer that won't get me evicted.'

'Fair enough. We're here to ask a few more questions about the assault.'

'Shoot.'

'You led us to believe that when Stefan attacked you, it was because he suspected you of having a relationship with his wife. Is that correct?'

'Yeah. Pretty much.'

'But you didn't tell us you that you're homosexual.'

'Yeah, I'm gay. I just don't feel the need to announce it every time I'm introduced to anyone.'

'Except it's very relevant in this case.'

'No, not really. I mean, Stefan's the sort of bloke who'll get an idea in his head, and that'll be it. You can't tell him he's wrong. No point in trying.'

'Does he know you're gay?'

'I guess. Everyone at the Celeste seems to have worked it out.'

'But you've never had a relationship with Stefan?'

'No way. Sometimes I've suggested he's too homophobic to be totally straight, but it would take a lot more than that to make him my type. He races dirt bikes for a start.'

'Did he mention Rachel when he attacked you?'

'Yeah . . . or maybe not by name.' Mule's eyes half closed as he thought back. 'No, not by name. It was one of those alpha-male *Get your hands off my woman* outbursts, something like *Don't touch what ain't yours* plus expletives, of course.'

Gully spoke next. 'You'd have known Rachel since she started work at the Celeste?'

'Yeah – and Stefan and Kimberly, of course.'

'And could you notice any recent difference in Rachel's relationship with Stefan?'

'They were always volatile, but Rachel always insisted that no one knew him like she did. He had a "really sweet side", or so she said, but Kim was worried. She herself had been through all kinds of shit with that Nick, reckoned it was only a matter of time before Stefan and Rachel would implode too.'

'So you know Kimberly well?'

'She's bloody reserved, even for a Pom, but we'd talk sometimes. You know we share the same stall at the craft market, right? We do alternate Sundays, because it gives her more time with Riley that way. Means we don't see much of each other, but we get to chat every week.'

'What do you paint?'

'Heels, uppers, whatever – but I design the whole thing, too.' To demonstrate, Mule flipped open the nearest box and lifted out a gold shoe with a Perspex wedge heel. A series of tiny Mardi Gras masks had been painted in a ribbon that curved from the toe and around to the back of the heel. 'Primarily, my customers are drag or burlesque acts.'

'You design shoes?' Gully asked, as though seeing the opened box hadn't been evidence enough for her.

'That's why they call me Mule.'

'Oh,' Gully mumbled, with just the hint of a smirk in her eye.

THIRTY-SEVEN

Marks wasn't the only person at the Parkside Hotel who was keeping a close watch on the time, for amongst the gathering press pack stood the robust figure of Bev Dransfield. Aged forty-three, with twenty-one years' reporting experience under her ever expanding belt. She liked to think her coverage of news was efficient, but her specialty was sport. She felt passionate about everything from football and cricket to Formula One and the annual boat race, but her specialty was horse racing.

Throughout the year the racing fixtures gave her enough stories to fill a whole edition of the *Daily Star*, and she'd carved out her niche so distinctly that it was rare for her to be expected to cover anything appearing in the front two-thirds of the newspaper.

Rare and, to her, unwelcome.

She'd been hammering up the M11 towards the Newmarket race meet when details of the press conference had come in, and therefore she'd landed it for no other reason than her editor noticing she was already in the area and deciding that a female take on the story would work better. And where was a serious-minded, non-pregnant co-worker when needed? She soon discovered there was no one available for her to dump this on. And why the editor, Barry, had thrown it at her rather than one of those family-minded 'new men' in the department was anyone's guess.

Barry was taking the piss, that was for sure. Bev never had kids, never would, so she was sure that Kimberly Guyver's take on being female would have been shaped by radically different experiences to her own.

Her first job as junior reporter had landed her with the nickname 'Geezer Girl', more recently shortened to Geez. She had seen first hand that some people had doors opened in their path, while others got them slammed in their faces. Through her own career she'd had to earn every success.

Bev had felt the injustice of being judged every time she'd been hit by the door handle of bigotry, but in this case it was a dead cert that no one had ever pinned the dyke badge on Kimberly Guyver, or complained that she didn't project the 'right image for the company'.

Once it became clear that the conference was delayed, Bev slipped outside to phone her editor. The call was routed straight to his mailbox. 'It's been delayed until three,' she informed him. 'My entire bloody day's down the pan thanks to this.' She ended the call, and was about to phone back into the newsroom and get swapped to another assignment, when she happened to spot her Peugeot. She'd taken one of the parking spaces closest to the hotel, and her car was now trapped behind two other rows of vehicles. If Anglia TV's outside broadcast unit had got any closer it would have looked indecent.

There wasn't even room to open her car's doors. In fact the only open doors available were inviting her back into the hotel. So what if this was the 'hot' story of the week, or even the month, she really didn't give a shit. The fact was she'd been stuck here since noon, and would now be unlikely to get back out again before the end of the rush hour.

'Fuck.'

She opened a new pack of Benson & Hedges. The passenger window of the OB unit had been left open by an inch and she pushed the empty cellophane wrapper through it, then crossed to the perimeter wall and sat with her feet on someone else's front bumper and her back to the sun. She smoked two cigarettes in quick succession, aware that, even if she was going back into the press conference, she still had almost an hour to kill. She tried to buoy herself up with the thought that this delay might signal a major development, but even that prospect failed to ignite any of her dampened journalistic curiosity.

She lit cigarette number three, then tuned in to the radio via her mobile phone. Any sport would do but, just as she found the tennis, her mobile rang.

She was tempted to ignore it but pressed the *OK* button instead. 'Hi, Barry.'

'Have you left yet?'

'No chance. I'm blocked in by a sodding TV crew. Bastards.'

'Good. Listen, here's something to chase.'

'What now?'

'Jeez, Geez,' – he loved saying that – 'get your arse off of whatever you're slouched on, and listen. I've had a call – seems that a nurse at Hinton Avenue nursing home has a theory. She reckons the kid shown in the picture's not the same one that comes in to see Jay Andrews.'

Bev scowled. 'Whose kid does the mother take in there, then?'

'No, wrong way round. The kid she takes in *is* the one that's missing. It's the photo that's wrong.'

Bev dropped the rest of the cigarette and left it smouldering in the dust. 'Is the nurse sure?'

'The kid is only three, so looks like a thousand other kids unless you know him. No one else questioned it, so the woman's doubting it herself. Partly why she had a quiet word with us before embarrassing herself with the police. Our good luck, then, so don't waste it.'

Bev hung up. It took a lot to make her discard a perfectly good cigarette. Usually only a major sporting upset could achieve that.

And to her this now felt like a kind of sport.

THIRTY-EIGHT

On the way back to the station, Gully asked him if he would now try to find Marks. But in Goodhew's opinion there was little new to tell their DI, and certainly not enough to drag him away from a press conference. The only reason Goodhew might want to be over there was to talk to Kimberly but, as long as Marks was staying cheek-to-jowl with her, he didn't see what could be gained.

'I'll type up some reports until Marks comes back,' he said.

Goodhew and Gully parted wordlessly at the station entrance. She headed straight for the canteen which reminded Goodhew that he hadn't eaten since breakfast. He followed, saw her take a tray and order a hot meal, while he himself grabbed a sandwich to go. She was still being served as he turned to leave. Gully glanced at him, then looked away, but he saw a pink glow rising in her cheeks. He'd already worked out that she blushed a lot. Anything and everything seemed to set it off, but once or twice there had been no such reaction at moments when he might have expected one, so he guessed it was triggered at those times when she felt most self-conscious.

Gully's eyes were dark-brown and framed by long dark lashes and, although her build was far from slight, her face had a doll-like quality, a little like Clara Bow or one of her silent-movie contemporaries. It gave the impression that she might be vulnerable and uncertain.

But he was now sure that, once she settled in properly at Parkside Police Station, that was the last thing she'd be. She'd been quick to judge him, and seemed determined to keep up a cold wall of suspicion between them, yet between the bricks he'd seen flashes of both compassion and humour. Despite her accusations, he couldn't help liking her.

He switched his attention to the sandwich he'd chosen, turkey and cranberry sauce. It seemed a weird thing for the canteen to be serving in June. Egg mayo appealed to him more, but the salt and vinegar crisps were sold out, and in his opinion egg mayo without salt and vinegar crisps just didn't work.

He broke open the packaging and started munching the first sandwich as he headed up the stairs. He hadn't been lying to Gully about typing up some reports, but, as he debated where to start, and how to explain discovering that Mule was gay without involving Bryn, he ran through the mechanics of the case. He had no sense of progress being made, more like an ever-increasing number of loose strands that seemed to be spinning into a stagnant cocoon.

The need to ensure Riley's safety was, of course, everything, and Goodhew tried hard not to dwell on any outcome but a positive one. He was also aware that in the corner of his mind's eye there constantly lay an image of Riley's small and unmoving body. Each time his thoughts had taken him close enough to it, he'd felt his skin prickle with cold sweat and his stomach lurch with fear.

And, each time, he would push those thoughts away again, knowing he needed to work with facts and logic alone.

And there were plenty of facts, no doubt with some lies hidden between, but they all seemed too disparate and he doubted that enough of relevance had yet emerged for logic to make any impact.

He reminded himself that Marks had the big picture, and that he himself saw only the précis. Maybe they already had all they needed, or maybe they weren't looking at the information from the right angle.

He hesitated at the second-floor landing and closed his eyes for a moment. As he reopened them, his grandfather sprang into his memory. Goodhew turned to take the next flight up to the third, and top, floor.

There was a quiet corner up there, five-feet square and useless in everyone else's eyes. It contained nothing but an old desk with a broken printer, and a couple of defunct desktop computers stowed beneath it.

The narrow side of the desk faced the window, so he sat with his back to the wall and his feet flat on the desktop, and clasped his hands around his knees. He was facing Parker's Piece, an expanse of grass interrupted by two footpaths which crossed it diagonally, meeting in the centre at a spot marked by an old lamppost known locally as Reality Checkpoint. To the left lay the Parkside Hotel and the swimming pool, but he looked only in the opposite direction and stared across at the building that housed his flat.

That's where he'd just remembered his grandfather, in the same pose as Goodhew himself was now sitting. Goodhew tried to remember how old the man had been but couldn't be sure. His grandfather had died shortly before Goodhew's twelfth birthday, and this mental picture came from sometime before that. So he guessed it might have been fifteen years ago.

His grandparents had owned the whole building then, a huge four-storey town house with a basement. It was still huge, of course, but Goodhew himself only occupied the small flat at the top, and never understood why they had needed so much space.

He'd often gone to visit his grandfather on the way home from school; it kept him away from his parents' daily fights for the longest possible time. On this particular day he had encountered his grandmother first. She stood on the front step like she was waiting for him. She held an empty mug by its handle, supporting it underneath with her other hand, as though she hadn't even noticed she'd drunk it all. Her eyes were sad and she pressed her lips tight, like she didn't have words to express how she felt.

He ran up the steps and instinctively buried his face in her shoulder, whereupon she planted a gentle kiss in his hair. This was a gesture he usually felt too grown-up for in public but, at that moment, comforting her seemed to be all that mattered.

'Is Granddad OK?' he had asked anxiously.

'He's fine.' She sat down beside him on the step, and gave him a reassuring hug. 'Sorry, I didn't mean to scare you, but he's fine. Someone broke into the house and they've made a mess. It was a bit of a shock, but we're both fine, and that's all that matters, isn't it?'

And, naïvely he had nodded, because when you're a kid you

believe that's the truth of it. 'Did the police come?' he asked, after a moment.

'They've finished.'

'They did fingerprints?'

'Yes, I'm sorry you missed that part.'

'Me too.'

She then nudged him off the step. 'Go and find Granddad. I'll be in soon.'

He ran into the house, then stopped in his tracks. This was no minor break-in, he saw. Pictures lay smashed on the hall floor, and the plum-coloured carpet had been savagely hacked at, leaving two great rips running down its entire length. He went as far as the open doorway of the drawing room and halted on the threshold, transfixed by the destruction beyond. Nothing had been left intact: ornaments had been smashed, curtains ripped down, the family photos gouged. Someone had even pissed on the sofa. He turned away in shock, feeling that it would have been better to have stolen everything and left the place empty.

He had mounted the stairs, guessing he'd find his grandfather up on the second floor where he kept all his books and papers. The same devastation could be seen through each doorway he passed, and even his grandfather's library hadn't escaped. He examined it first through the gap that ran between the hinges, and gasped in disbelief. Scattered across the floor were thousands of pages, each torn from one of the many first editions that now lay in a broken pile beneath the smashed doors of the largest bookcase.

His grandfather sat on the floor with his back to the wall and his head buried in his hands. For a moment Goodhew thought the man was crying, so stayed where he was and didn't move. This was private, and he had no right to be there, but the boy found he couldn't look away either.

Finally his grandfather drew a breath and gazed straight through the gap between the door and its frame. 'It's OK, Gary, you can come in.'

Goodhew was carrying his schoolbag and felt like he didn't dare put it down, just in the same way he wouldn't do so in an unfamiliar or over-tidy house, so he sat down cross-legged on the floor with it still on his lap. He didn't know what to say: this was too far beyond his experience. He looked to his grandfather for a cue, and for the first time registered that the man's face showed no visible sign of distress.

They probably stayed silent like that for a while, or that's how it seemed then.

'Who would do this, Granddad?' he began eventually.

'No idea.'

'You must be really, really mad with them.'

When his grandfather spoke, there was no anger in his voice. 'Of course, I'm upset, Gary, and I don't want you to think that this doesn't matter to me, but I'm trying to concentrate on the solution. Do you know why?'

Goodhew shook his head.'

'Because the solution is usually more important than the problem.'

'That doesn't make sense. Everything's broken.'

'And I can't unbreak it, can I?'

'No, but I don't get it: how do you find a solution to this? And why did they have to do it?'

'I don't know, Gary. But all we can ever do is go forwards – do you see that?'

'You mean we can't go back in time? Of course, I understand.'

'If I'd been here, it might not have happened, but I have to accept that I wasn't here, or if I had been here it might have been worse.' Goodhew's grandfather's explanation was patient. 'None of those thoughts will clear up this mess or stop it happening again.'

Goodhew listened carefully, somehow understanding that he was being given words of wisdom that would serve him well at some other time.

'You will have times in your life when you don't know what to do next, when the problem seems so large or complex that it fills your entire head, and there's no room left for a solution. Do you know what I do then?'

Goodhew shook his head but didn't speak.

'I find somewhere quiet and I sit there alone, just like I was when you came in, and wait until the problem thinks I've gone away, then . . .' He clapped his hands in front of Goodhew's face, making him jump. 'Then I creep up behind it with the solution.' He grinned and his eyes sparkled with devilry.

'And that works?'

'More often than you'd think, Gary.'

'This time, too?'

'Absolutely. It will take more than a burglary to ruin this home, you watch.'

And he was right.

Looking back, he knew that his grandparents must have been hit severely by the usual feelings of loss, violation and fear, but neither of them ever spoke of those things. Despite the changed locks, the wrecked carpets and the irreplaceable books, Goodhew's grandfather made sure the most important lesson learnt came in those minutes the two of them shared ankle-deep in debris.

A deep-seated longing pressed against Goodhew's chest as he now sat by the window all those years later. He still understood that he couldn't go back in time, but even now that understanding left a lump in his throat. All it seemed right to do now was to follow his grandfather's advice, so Goodhew leant his head back against the wall and half-closed his eyes.

He ate the second half of the sandwich while, beneath him, Parker's Piece bustled on just as it had every day of his life. People outside appeared the size of ants, as some wound their way in purposeful trails to and from the city centre, while others played or lounged on the grass. From this distance it all looked so simple.

His gaze drifted to the car park outside the Parkside Hotel, which was still full of vehicles and looked more congested than anywhere else in sight. He wondered how Kimberly was coping, but didn't regret staying away. He was still nudged by an instinct that told him she was holding back.

Gully had called it 'lying'. But *lying* was a strong word.

He let his brain turn it over several times, just to hear how it sounded. So much for his grandfather's theory, however. Now the problem seemed bigger, and the solution more distant.

A familiar voice broke the silence. 'I guessed I'd find you up here.'

Goodhew turned and greeted Sergeant Sheen, who was carrying a half-inch-thick sheaf of papers. He lifted them closer to his chest as he saw Goodhew try to identify the unfamiliar logo on the top sheet.

'Don't worry, you'll get to read it soon enough.' Sheen spoke leisurely, his Suffolk accent rolling slowly over the words. 'This is the latest from our Spanish counterparts, concerning their ongoing investigation into the murder of young Nick Lewton.'

'Oh, good.' Goodhew reached out hopefully, but Sheen wasn't ready to hand anything over just yet.

'Now, I wanted to put this straight into the hands of DI Marks but, since he's up to his neck over there, I thought I'd trust you to deliver it to him. However, I can also see that leaves you with a minor dilemma.' Sheen pointed to the pile of papers. 'I have more downstairs to drop off with you lot, so you'd be best to walk with me while I explain.'

Goodhew slid his feet from the desk and followed Sheen back into the corridor.

'I know your reputation, son, and I can see that you might not want to hand this stuff straight on to Marks without having a read-through on your own . . .'

Goodhew shook his head. 'That's not really –'

'Gary?' Sheen shook his head, too. 'Don't bother denying it. My job's local intelligence, remember? You ferret for facts, you do – see, I've got your number already. What I was going to say is that you might not have time to read the whole thing, but luckily for you they faxed it. And the fax came through slow enough for me to scan through it page by page, as I was waiting. I couldn't take in all the detail but there's an autopsy report and some witness statements. They're sending the hard copy by express courier.'

Sheen stopped at the door of Marks' office. 'You sit in here and wait for Marks, and you can say I told you that he was on his way back. That way you can read it right now.'

'Why encourage me to get ahead of DI Marks?'

'Simply because that'll be the quickest way for the most important details to get through to him. I could take them over myself, and find they get put to one side amongst all that press chaos.' Sheen held out the pages but, before releasing them, added, 'You might disagree, but if it says what I think it says, I know you'll put it straight in his hand. You'll find pages three and four the most helpful.'

Goodhew sat in Marks' chair and fanned the pages out on the empty desk. There were too many to read quickly, so he took Sheen's advice and jumped to page three. The Spanish pathologist had enlisted the help of a forensic anthropologist, and the pages that had been faxed over were a summary of their combined findings.

The autopsy report was written in English, a translation he guessed since some of the sentences seemed rather stilted. Nevertheless, it was still all clear enough.

Nick Lewton's body was severely decomposed, consistent with a corpse that had been submerged in water over a long period. The pathologist had been reluctant to attach any firm dates to this, but estimated that the minimum length of time the body had been down there would be four to five months, and that the earliest date possible should be taken as the night of Nick Lewton's disappearance.

The vehicle's windscreen had been destroyed on impact with the water, allowing access for marine scavengers to pick at the corpse. The warmth of the water had then encouraged rapid decomposition, till both the skull and the hands had become separated from the rest of the corpse.

Lewton's body, fully clothed, was still in the driver's seat when the car was recovered, and the clothing had helped to keep the general body structure intact. That meant the larger bones remained in more or less the expected position, and still retained some of their tendons and ligaments.

The left hand had been discovered still inside the vehicle, whilst an extensive search of the seabed had eventually led to recovery of the skull. There was no indication, however, that the body had been dismembered in any way and therefore, the report concluded, it would be reasonable to surmise that the missing right hand had either been washed away by the current or carried off by a larger type of predator.

The bulk of the subsequent findings related to skeletal evidence.

The report came complete with photographs whose originals were undoubtedly clear and in full colour, but these were compressed into grainy black-and-white by the faxing process. The clearest one was a shot of the skull, reduced to bare bone apart from a few patches of scalp that clung to it, which looked like they were still sprouting unnaturally clean-looking clumps of hair.

The pathologist and the anthropologist were clearly men with a sense of drama as, rather than working through the body's bones in any methodical sequence, they'd chosen to list the injuries in ascending order of severity. Goodhew had reached the top of page four and still resisted the urge to skip to the conclusion. Instead, he wriggled into a more comfortable position in his chair, and read on.

Some minor post-mortem damage was visible on the bones, mainly as surface scratches. These were attributed to the scavenging of the overlying flesh by crabs.

There were several observations made about older injuries: Lewton had previously suffered cracked ribs, repeated nasal fractures, and a single fracture to the zygomatic – Goodhew paused to Google that one . . . the cheekbone.

They'd spotted some pitting in the sinuses, and had run chemical analysis on samples of his hair. The results had proved Lewton to be a regular and long-term cocaine user.

Drugs *and* violence, what a charmer.

Their report finally turned to the most recent injuries. Nick Lewton had received a single stab wound to the chest, inflicted with a thin, serrated blade with a pointed tip. The tip of the knife had snapped during entry, so the triangle of metal had become lodged in the lower ribcage.

From this they'd been able to identify that the knife was of the same make and design as the steak knives used at the Matt Adore restaurant, two doors down from the Rita Club.

The skeleton also revealed signs of a struggle, with a small notch evident in the bone at the base of Lewton's remaining index finger.

Goodhew could not help wondering what injuries the other hand might have sustained.

The main stab wound would have caused extensive bleeding, but had not been deep enough to hit any major organ. If left untreated it would, theoretically, have been a life-threatening wound but, in this case, death had been caused by a separate set of injuries.

A long paragraph followed, peppered with technical phrases like 'delamination of the outer table' and 'inward bevelling of the bones'. It concluded with the cause of death as 'a transverse compression fracture of the occipital protuberance'. Goodhew had perused enough details in the previous few days to translate this phrase without the need of a medical dictionary, or even Google. Just like Rachel Golinski and Jay Andrews, Nick Lewton had had his head kicked in.

Goodhew stared at the page for a long minute, then checked his watch: ten to three.

Sheen had been right, this was vital information for Marks, and while Goodhew wasn't sure whether it warranted causing further delay to the press conference, he was equally convinced that any decision had to rest with his superior.

Goodhew tapped the papers back into a neat pile, and only looked back into Marks' office as he pulled the door shut after him. That was the moment he noticed the key in the lock of the filing cabinet, and he hesitated.

He gave the office door a gentle push and it swung wide open again, then he glanced along the corridor, already knowing he would find it deserted but double-checking because that was his way.

The key turned silently, he gave the drawer a tug and it slid out on its runners. The files inside were organized almost exactly as they had appeared when he'd been watching Gully through his telescope. The only difference now was the crucial one: his file had disappeared. To make sure, he checked under the other files, then in each of the other three drawers.

He was lost in thought as he relocked the filing cabinet, then stood facing it for a minute and only stirred as he realized he was no longer alone. He spun round to find Mel with her arms crossed and leaning against the door frame. Her pose suggested she'd been standing there for hours but, while he knew that couldn't be the case, it was obvious she realized he was doing something he shouldn't.

212

'I won't tell Marks,' she began.

'I wouldn't ever ask you not to.'

'Fair enough, but I still won't. What *were* you looking for?' She stepped closer.

'Honestly? I believe there's a file with my name on it, and I wanted to see what was in it.'

'Ah,' she said, and gave a small but knowing smile. 'I think that's a Kincaide myth.'

'You know about it?'

'Kincaide always likes to paint you in a bad light, makes out you're just one step from career suicide. He told PC Kelly Wilkes that it contains reports on your misconduct, told me that you take bribes, and doubtless Kincaide probably invented something else for Sue Gully's benefit.' Her tone was dismissive. 'He says it's all here in "The File".'

'What if it exists? I'd want to check it.'

'You're no rule-breaker, Gary Goodhew.' She grinned, gave his arm a reassuring rub and he felt his pulse quicken. 'I can guarantee it doesn't exist, so you're worrying about absolutely nothing.'

He smiled back at her. 'You're misguided, then.'

Without warning, she reached up and her fingers touched his face. 'I don't think so,' she replied softly. Her touch was firm. She leant closer and her lips brushed his cheek. Maybe he was reading too much into the gesture. Then, again, maybe he wasn't. He inhaled, drawing in the scent of her hair, and took the hit of heady intoxication that followed. He had no idea why it surprised him, but he pulled away.

'No,' he muttered, 'nothing's ever going to happen between us.' Then he snatched up Nick Lewton's notes and hurried away from Marks' office.

It was several minutes after he'd left before Mel realized that her hands were shaking. She guessed she was as surprised by what she'd done as he was. It was completely unplanned and spontaneous but, then, so was his response, and it spoke volumes about what he really felt.

She watched from the window as Goodhew crossed Parker's Piece, and only then felt comfortable to return to her own desk. She slumped in her chair, with more work coming in than there were hours in the day, but instead of making a start on it she found herself reorganizing the stationery cupboard, where no one ever bothered her.

Typically, within fifteen minutes, someone did.

'Hi.' It was PC Gully. 'Have you seen DC Goodhew?' She held up an envelope.

'Why would I?'

Gully ignored her question. 'Are you all right?'

Mel nodded.

'You look like you've been crying.'

'I'm fine.'

'Sure?' Gully persisted.

'It's just hay fever.'

'Oh.' Gully let the excuse settle for a minute. 'So, do you know where he went?'

'Parkside Hotel.'

Gully thanked her, then left. Mel closed the door and sank silently on to one of the boxes of photocopier paper. Sometimes it was good to cry, she reminded herself and, later still, tried to tell herself that it was for the best. She failed to feel convinced until it finally dawned on her that the one thing she'd always possessed were choices. That wasn't an entirely new revelation, but this time it came with a conviction that she could carry it through.

THIRTY-NINE

As Goodhew stepped outside, he noticed that the day was cooler, a persistent breeze pushed through Parker's Piece and heavy grey clouds limped across the sky. People seemed to have rapidly swapped their sandals and T-shirts for trainers and pullovers, and the chill slipped through the thin fabric of his short-sleeved shirt.

He shivered, then quite deliberately turned his attention back to reading the Spanish report. It wasn't logical to expend energy or emotion anywhere else, and he wanted to deliver it to Marks with some understanding of the remainder of the contents. He began scanning the rest of the paperwork as he walked towards the Parkside Hotel. On page eleven he slowed his reading to fully digest the background of the Spaniards' investigation.

Whilst Nick Lewton lived in Spain there had been several unproven accusations of assault against him, and police in Cartagena had drawn pretty much the same conclusions as Sergeant Sheen had formed during Nick Lewton's years in Cambridge.

From time to time, investigations had probed the Rita Club, trying to confirm suspicions of drug dealing, money laundering and even tax fraud. In each case, however, they had drawn a blank.

But those same avenues had provided initial lines of enquiry after Nick Lewton's disappearance, and had led the police to formulate two broad theories. Either Lewton had been murdered because of his criminal activities or he had done a runner for exactly the same reason.

Goodhew stopped reading long enough to cross East Road in safety. He'd be at the hotel in less than a minute, so reverted to skimming the remaining pages. As he shouldered open the door into the foyer, he flipped to the penultimate sheet. Nothing jumped off the page like a long row of zeros.

On performing an initial audit, the Rita Club's finances had seemed in order but a more detailed review had discovered large quantities of alcohol which had been purchased off the books, and therefore a sizeable discrepancy between the revenue reported and the actual bar takings.

A conservative estimate suggested that over three hundred thousand euros was adrift from the Rita Club's accounts. It hadn't gone with Nick, so where was it?

Goodhew shuffled the papers back into a neat pile and went on the hunt for his boss.

Bev Dransfield knew nothing about either the layout of the hotel or what the protocol might be for dealing with the kid's mother, Kimberly Guyver. Maybe she was just a cynic but to Bev a public appeal for information usually involved wheeling out the prime suspect, shining bright lights in their eyes, and hoping they'd crack.

She had no doubt that Guyver was already somewhere in the building, and the consensus amongst the press pack seemed to be that she was currently being briefed in an office adjoining the main conference room. Bev dismissed this, as the atmosphere amongst the reporters had become increasingly fraught. Tedious waits and last-second delays were part of their job, but so were the vocally aggressive protests that met each explanatory announcement. Sitting within earshot of their complaints would have rattled all but the most arrogant and media-savvy parent.

And, even if the police had been that insensitive, there was no way of reaching Guyver, so Bev had to assume that she needed to look elsewhere inside the building.

The hotel didn't look like it had more than twenty-five bedrooms, thirty at most, and all appeared to be located on the opposite side to the public areas and meeting rooms. Using one of these bedrooms would seem to be a logical choice.

Bev approached the reception desk, where the only member of staff was smartly dressed, with the name *Stella* pinned to her lapel.

The counter top was bare apart from a small and well-polished sign announcing *SORRY, NO VACANCIES*. 'It's running late.' Bev jerked her head in the direction of the press scrum. 'If it goes on much longer, I'll need to stay in Cambridge tonight.'

The receptionist looked sympathetic but shook her head, while she pointed to the sign. 'I'm afraid we have nothing available.'

'That's right, but Detective Inspector Marks suggested I should have a word with you. He's using one of the rooms today, and he thought I could take it for tonight.'

'Oh, I see, let me look.' Her fingers flashed through a routine that required hammering a rapid succession of function keys. 'Yes, yes, it is booked until this evening but, as long as he's finished by then, it's a possibility. The room will be already paid for, so he could just hand you the key.'

'I don't think that would be approved – too much red tape, you know.' Bev rolled her eyes.

'God, yes . . .'

'That's fine, though. I'll come back and book it once DI Marks gives me the nod. Thanks for your help.'

Stella smiled. Another customer satisfied.

Bev turned away, then back again with what she hoped would sound like a casual afterthought. 'It's not on the ground, is it? I can't get to sleep on the ground floor.'

Stella was still smiling. 'No, the second,' she replied.

'Great,' Bev grinned and, a couple of minutes later, when she was sure no one was looking, she headed towards the stairs.

The press were gathered in the main conference room, some working on laptops, others busy with their mobiles. No matter what occupied them, it seemed they were tuned in to any new arrival, and therefore, as one, eyed Goodhew with renewed interest. Aware of a hunger in the air, he gripped the paperwork a little tighter, just in case they sniffed the possibility that it contained anything offering reason for further delay, and angrily shredded it on the spot.

'DI Marks?' he inquired of the nearest journalist, and she pointed him towards a small anteroom.

He found Marks inside, along with Liz Bradley and Bob Trent.

Marks greeted Goodhew warmly, Liz barely glanced over at him, and Bob Trent totally ignored his arrival. Liz Bradley and Trent sat facing each other across a narrow desk, while Marks stood at one end, giving Goodhew the impression that Marks had been acting as referee. For a behavioural psychologist, Trent seemed strangely oblivious to the expression on Liz's face, which to Goodhew read as: *If you don't back off, I'm going to leap across this table and rip your stupid head from your sweaty body.*

No wonder Marks seemed pleased to see him.

'Can I have a word please, sir?'

Marks nodded and said, 'Walk with me.' He led Goodhew across the lobby towards the bedroom accommodation. 'I'd better go and explain the delays to Kimberly Guyver in person, as I would think she's becoming quite anxious by now. What have you got there, anyway?'

Goodhew offered his boss the paperwork.

Marks shook his head at the amount of it. 'You've read this?'

'Not thoroughly. It needs to be gone through in detail, but there are a couple of points worth explaining. Nick Lewton's injuries are consistent with both Jay Andrews' and Rachel Golinski's, involving significant damage to the base of the skull.'

'The same killer? That's interesting. What else?'

'Police suspect that an amount of money in the region of three hundred thousand euros disappeared from the Rita Club in the months leading up to Lewton's murder.'

Marks had taken them to the second floor, which contained fourteen rooms, seven along each side of a straight corridor. He knocked softly on the door of number 37. PC Kelly Wilkes opened it immediately.

Goodhew's focus was drawn beyond her to the bright rectangle of light created by a large window at the far end. Kimberly stood almost in silhouette against it and, as she spoke, her voice sounded distant.

'What's happened?' she asked.

'I'm very sorry that we've been so delayed, but this isn't unusual,' Marks assured her. 'We have to assess any risks that may be created in making a public announcement of this nature, and our behavioural psychologist has expressed some concerns.'

'Such as?'

'He fears that a public announcement could push Stefan Golinski towards a violent outcome.'

Kimberly finally took a few steps towards them. Goodhew thought she looked thinner, like the stress was deflating her from the inside. 'If he killed Rachel, he's already dangerous.' She stared down at the stretch of floor between them. Even her voice sounded more frail but the fear in it was still palpable.

'We've received information from the Spanish police relating to Nick Lewton's death.'

Marks paused, and Kimberly waited. Just the fingers of one hand moved, and they curled into a loose fist that she drew close to her stomach.

'The post-mortem shows that he died from a severe head injury.'

She raised her head and shot a startled glance at each of them in turn. 'In the crash?'

'When the car was dumped, he was already dead. We believe he was kicked to death before that.'

There was a long pause then, and Goodhew realized that they had not even stepped into the room, and Kimberly had not yet come anywhere close to the door. It was an image that would stay with him, a depiction of her isolation and their inability to save her from it. She stepped back towards the window, and dissolved into her own silhouette.

Although no question had yet been asked of her, they all seemed to be waiting for her to reply.

'You want my blessing, don't you?'

'Not blessing, exactly. But I feel that abandoning this press conference will not help us find Stefan Golinski, and until we find him we may not know the whereabouts of your son.'

'This appeal for information,' her voice had suddenly regained its strength, 'it must go ahead. It's imperative.'

Marks gave a small nod, 'Thank you.' He turned to address PC Wilkes. 'I'll send someone up to fetch you both' – he glanced at his watch – 'assume twenty past.'

* * *

219

PC Sue Gully waited in the foyer of the Parkside Hotel and tried to remain patient.

The envelope in her hands contained records of the calls and texts made from the mobile phone owned by Mikey Slater.

Marks had been waiting for these since the night of the fire, and she failed to understand why communications companies involved had taken so long to hand them over. Despite having the rules regarding privacy explained to her on more than one occasion, it still baffled her why there were so many bureaucratic hoops to jump through just to see details that any member of their staff, however unreliable, could probably access instantly.

The pages had arrived by courier and, since all the other officers working on the investigation were occupied outside the station somewhere, she herself had signed for the envelope. She tried to deliver it to Goodhew but even he had gone, leaving a tearful Mel in his wake.

She'd decided that taking an initial peep was nothing more than showing initiative.

She emptied it out on a desk top, and smiled as she ran her finger down the list of dates and times. This was a document that deserved to go into a time capsule as a record of the social habits of the British teenager circa early twenty-first century. A ratio of at least ten texts for each phone call made, few before ten in the morning and most sent after eight in the evening.

Her gaze had run down the various numbers, all to other mobiles or local Cambridge calls, her finger stopping at '999'. The detail read 'CALL CONNECTED – EMERGENCY SERVICES.'

That should have been the only familiar number except, as she'd glimpsed the line below, she could see it wasn't. Her eyes widened as they picked it out again and again. It was Kimberly Guyver's home telephone number.

Gully pulled out her notebook and checked Kimberly's mobile number. It, too, was on the list, and even more frequently than the home number.

She looked back to the minutes after the 999 call and saw it there too, along with a third number. This was a Cambridge landline, and the final four digits were a memorable '0101'. She returned to the pages of her notebook. She had definitely heard it before.

Nothing in the notebook.

In the end she dialled it.

On the fifth ring it was answered. 'Hello?'

It was Anita McVey's voice and she sounded nervous.

'I'm so sorry, wrong number.' Gully replaced the handset and realized that her own voice had trembled too.

Yes, she'd sensed there was something about Kimberly Guyver, but her foster mother too?

The idea unsettled her.

She had failed to reach Marks by radio, so she'd hurried from her desk and driven the short distance to the hotel, with the blue light flashing. As she saw the TV vans and the cram of parked vehicles, she felt her conviction weaken. If she was about to make a fool of herself it would be hard to find a larger or more embarrassing audience. Perhaps she'd overlooked something, misread the detail in some way, and now Marks would dismiss her findings as a waste of his time.

She brushed these reservations away. This *was* a vital lead.

And if Marks was too busy to see her, she'd find Goodhew and ask him to take it to their DI. Gut feeling told her that he would oblige.

She found only Kincaide.

'I'm looking for Goodhew.'

'He's here somewhere. I saw him go off with DI Marks.'

'But you don't know where?'

'Nope, but considering the stress level in there . . .' Kincaide jerked his thumb towards the main conference room, 'I wouldn't bother Marks unless it's really urgent.' His hungry gaze fell on the envelope. 'Do you want me to take that in for them?'

Gully shook her head and replied 'No' a little too sharply. 'This is mine. I just needed a word with him.'

Kincaide shrugged unhelpfully. 'Don't say I didn't warn you.'

Now she waited in the foyer, clutching the inconspicuous business envelope that potentially held so much. She would deliver it personally either to Marks or Goodhew, but no one else. It had to be passed into safe hands.

The realization sank in.

Despite his secrets and despite her doubts about Goodhew, she suddenly knew that he wouldn't let her down.

Anita McVey had locked all the external doors and double-checked the window locks, at teatime the previous day. Mikey had dropped off two bags of groceries but, apart from opening it enough for him to pass them inside the house, the front door had remained firmly sealed.

Anita was now thankful she'd spent extra on the security, imagining at the time that the worst she'd have to repel would be undesirable teenagers. And, of course, they would have been bad enough.

She'd gone to bed early the night before, but watched television into the small hours, scanning the Teletext and all the local channels, penduluming between searching for the latest news and seeking any kind of diversion. When the TV schedules had dwindled to a choice between phone-in competitions, world news headlines or reruns of murder dramas, she switched it off. Then she lay in the dark staring into the speckled blackness, wondering why she hadn't called a halt to it when Kimberly had begged her to. Dawn had broken sometime around 5 a.m. and Anita was sure she'd had no sleep. The skin around her eyes felt bruised and her mouth tasted sour, but, most of all, the sleeplessness was adding to her rising sense of panic.

She switched on the TV in her bedroom, keeping the volume just loud enough so she could still hear it, and stop to listen if the local news team began to report anything relevant. She tried to tidy up the room but after an hour was sure she'd made no progress.

She wanted to call the police but instead decided to stay upstairs and as isolated from the real world as possible.

The landing at Viva Cottage was nearly wide enough to warrant boxing it off at one end and calling it a study. Anita preferred it as it stood though: an airy space with a large picture window overlooking the front garden. It was there that she always chose to do the ironing, and now sorted a basket of her most crumpled clothes and set up the board facing the only item of furniture on the landing.

That was Kimberly's favourite seat, an early Victorian rosewood nursing chair, or at least that's what the label in the Antiques Barn had said. She wouldn't have guessed so in a million years. It sat low to the ground, with a high back, a deep seat and no arms, and she couldn't help thinking how plenty of new mums must have slid off it to either side, and found themselves an exhausted heap on the floor.

Anita herself had stripped and varnished the wood, then had it reupholstered in a buttermilk damask, before putting it into the landing corner to stand there on its fat little scroll legs as a robust piece of art. Something about it had attracted Kimberly so that, when she couldn't sleep, she'd drag her duvet from her bedroom and sit in that chair to watch the night sky.

Anita wished Kimberly was here. Perhaps she'd feel calmer if she were able to discuss it. She stared at the chair, then asked herself whether it really mattered if she didn't get a reply, maybe the talking alone would help her clear her mind. She switched on the iron and, while she waited for it to heat up, tried a couple of tentative sentences. Her voice sounded unnatural, hollow and self-conscious.

She never left the iron unattended whilst it was reaching temperature, but even that seemed oddly slow today. She began turning the smaller items of clothing the right way out, smoothing them and straightening the sleeves. By the time she'd finished preparing the second shirt, her attention had strayed to the window.

It looked like rain but, aside from that, nothing seemed to have changed. 'So, what's different?' she murmured. At the start of this she'd been adamant that her plan was the safest. Where was that resolve now?

She tried to run through her logic once more but, now that the initial eureka moment had faded, she could see too many unmapped steps along the path. She turned back to the chair and, instead, pictured Kimberly sitting in it. She tried again. 'Nothing's changed. The plan is fine. It *is* fine.'

The iron's thermostat clicked and almost simultaneously the telephone rang. She picked up the hands-free from the windowsill, but it only gave a double beep and died. Shit, it had been beside her bed all night, when it should have been put on charge again.

She knew the iron was still visible from the bottom of the stairs, so ran down and snatched up the handset there on the fourth or fifth ring.

'Hello?'

There was a pause at the other end. Anita heard a sharp breath, then a woman's voice apologized for dialling the wrong number. When the caller hung up, Anita dialled 1471 and was told 'We do not have the number'.

She walked back up to start on her pile of laundry.

The voice had belonged to a young woman and Anita thought it sounded familiar, but she couldn't dismiss the possibility that it was just her rising paranoia that led her to suspect that.

She ironed the first T-shirt, then pressed too hard on the second and felt the hot metal of the iron begin to singe the soft jersey fabric.

Identifying voices had never been a talent of hers. She wondered if it had been Tamsin who'd just phoned? And what would it mean if she had? A stray jet of steam blew out and stung Anita's fingers. She pulled the iron's plug out of the wall, deciding this wasn't a good day for her to be in charge of a hot and heavy electrical implement.

She took the laundry basket and set it in front of the rosewood chair, smoothing and folding each item while she talked to an imaginary Kimberly.

'I admit it, I didn't have a plan to get us out at the end of it, but I'm not concerned about that. The first thing we need to do is get to the end. That's still the plan, right? Hold firm and get to the end.'

Kimberly made no argument.

'Once we get that far, I could own up and say it was all my doing. I wouldn't care as long as you're both OK. Hang on, though.' Anita raised her hand as if for silence, and a news reporter's voice reached her ear. *Still delayed?* She wasn't sure what that implied, or even whether it lay in the ballpark of good or bad.

Her stomach gave a queasy shift, as if offering her the answer. She leant towards the banister stairs and looked over, wondering whether she'd heard something from downstairs too.

Her pulse quickened, but downstairs nothing moved.

'It's OK,' she whispered at last. 'It's just us two.' That didn't stop her from creeping to each upstairs window in turn, and checking the ground outside. The skyline of Cambridge city centre stood in the middle distance, and she paused to study it, trying to pick out familiar rooftops and work out exactly in which direction Kimberly might be now.

Anita had been cooped up indoors for too long – they both had – but it wasn't fair to ask Mikey to help them any more. She turned back to the nursing chair, but this time stopped pretending it was Kimberly who was actually sitting there.

'I love you.'

Riley looked up and held out his empty plate. 'Gone.'

'Good boy. D'you want some yogurt now?'

He nodded. 'Where's Mummy?'

Anita tried to sound cheerful: 'We'll see her soon.' She lifted Riley on to her hip, holding him close. He had perfectly functioning little legs, so she was aware that the cuddle was more for her own benefit than for his. She carried him into her bedroom. 'Let's turn off the television.'

'Riley do it,' he told her.

She swung him in the direction of the 'off' button. At the last moment, his pointing finger changed course and waved at the screen in excitement. 'Look!'

The photograph that Kimberly had given the police flashed on to the screen. The voiceover announced 'growing concern for the safety of two-year-old Riley Guyver'.

Riley beamed up at her. 'Daddy.'

'That's right, sweetheart. You love that photo, don't you?' Anita smiled back at Riley, and the bleakest edges of her anxiety softened. As long as they were looking for a child resembling a two-year-old Jay Andrews, Riley would remain hidden. And as long as Kimberly stayed with the police, they'd all be safe.

As soon as Jay's photo disappeared from the screen, Riley happily turned off the set. Anita tickled him in the tummy and he giggled.

'We should play in the garden. Would you like that?'

Riley nodded and wrapped his arms around her neck, gripping her tightly as they descended the stairs.

The second floor corridor was relatively short with the lift and stairs at one end and a fire exit at the other. Bev Dransfield had made it around the corner and into the alcove housing the fire-door with no time to spare.

Despite the close proximity of the bedrooms, the building's acoustics killed sound very efficiently, and by the time DI Marks and his sidekick left again Bev had discovered just two facts: Kimberly Guyver was in room 37, and there were only fifteen minutes available for her to nail the story.

Bev pulled a small Dictaphone from her inside pocket. Sometimes just two facts were plenty.

Kimberly had always hated magicians: those satanically charming men whose relationship with the audience consisted of controlling their thoughts and receiving their adulation.

And that same flock of people who were inexplicably happy to buy into the concept of a world where subjects could vanish and the mysterious appearance of the odd garish trinket warranted amazement.

Magicians took their bows, facing the audience with a smug flourish and a superior glint in the eye. They were nothing more than tricksters, liars essentially, rewarded for practising trickery until it was flawless. Kimberly was well aware that magic was a myth.

Maybe there was another way of looking at it, but if so she'd never worked out what it might be, and she had never understood the fun in being deceived.

In her young imagination, she'd played out a fantasy where she'd found the courage to speak up right before the climactic *ta-da*. But even then she'd been smart enough to realize that she would be vilified for spoiling the fun, so instead she'd imagined an unassuming stranger, a man who stepped from the shadows and was content that the only public appreciation he received for unmasking the con should come from her.

DI Marks had just revealed himself to be that man. But she'd been too stunned to even thank him.

The door closed behind him and DC Goodhew, and Kimberly sank on to the end of the bed.

Hope was an unfamiliar luxury, but here it was springing up in front of her and begging her to chase it. She knew she needed time to absorb all the implications, but time was one thing she didn't have. The situation had already developed too far.

She drew a deep and calming breath. In fifteen minutes she'd be escorted down to that conference room, and she knew she had to act before then. She just had no idea where to start.

Kimberly sat just feet from the dressing table, and it was an automatic reaction to stare at her own reflection. She was wearing a small amount of foundation, with brown mascara and neutral lipstick. None of these were items of make-up she would have chosen, but they were what she'd been advised to wear, 'in order to gain sympathy with viewers'. She had found that laughable: did it mean that Riley's life was worth less if she didn't tick all the boxes of responsibility, modesty and respectability?

Clearly it did, for the next thing had been the arrival of a choice of two outfits, both her own, but from that forgotten section of the wardrobe reserved for interviews and funerals. She hadn't objected when she realized that someone had searched through her home; she guessed they must have asked her and she'd OK'd it, but she was beyond remembering. Neither did she protest at the idea that she needed a make-over before she was fit to be seen.

She wondered whether everyone else spent their lives dancing to someone else's tune.

Enough was enough.

A pack of cleansing wipes lay in front of the mirror. She pulled two out and started removing her make-up.

Maybe PC Wilkes had been watching her all along, for she reacted instantly. 'Don't do that. We'll be going down in a minute.'

Kimberly shook her head. 'This isn't right. I'm not going to be dressed up like some puppet.' She scooped up the jeans and blouse that she'd removed earlier. 'This is what I'm wearing. I'm good enough to be Riley's mum without needing to change my clothes.' She bit her lip and tears pricked her eyes, because it was the first time she'd ever thought that. 'I'll be five minutes, OK?'

PC Wilkes nodded. 'I do understand. Be quick, though.'

Kimberly grabbed her things and darted into the bathroom. She locked the door behind her and sank to the floor with her back resting against it. She pulled her mobile phone from the inside pocket of her jeans and had begun to dial when she heard a loud banging on the outer door. She stopped short of pressing that 'call' button and tilted her head so she could listen.

PC Wilkes was smart enough to keep the door shut. 'Yes?'

'I'd like a word with Kimberly Guyver.'

'Who are you?'

'Can I speak to Miss Guyver, please?'

'She's not available. I'm a police officer. Please identify yourself.'

'My name is Beverley Dransfield. I'm a reporter and I need to ask Miss Guyver a couple of questions.'

'Please return to the press area.'

'Why has Kimberly Guyver released the wrong photograph of her son?'

Kimberly froze.

'Please return to the press area,' Wilkes repeated.

'What's she hiding? Has she kidnapped her own child?'

'I'm calling security now.'

Kimberly finally pressed the green button and, as the call connected, she whispered, 'I need your help. I've got to get out of here.'

Outside, the reporter was still shouting. 'Did you stage the whole thing, Kimberly? Come on, answer me. Have you killed your son? What is your true relationship with Stefan Golinski?'

'You can help, I know you can,' Kimberly breathed into the phone. 'I never killed Nick. Stefan did it.'

'Kimberly,' the reporter shouted, 'I can ask you the same downstairs in front of the cameras.'

PC Wilkes had stopped trying to negotiate by now, and was using her radio to call for assistance. 'Ms Dransfield, officers are on their way. Get away from the door.'

Kimberly felt the first beads of sweat breaking out on her forehead. She whispered into her phone, 'Meet me – Blossom Street entrance to the cemetery.'

FORTY

Neither Marks nor Goodhew said a word as they returned to the ground floor. There could have been many things occupying Marks' thoughts, but it was just a single moment that filled Goodhew's. When Kimberly had asked how Nick Lewton's fatal head injury had occurred, her exact question had been '*In the crash?*' Her tone hadn't been one of curiosity, but a stronger emotion than that. Shock? Disbelief? It was reasonable for her to feel both those things, but somehow he knew he'd heard the wrong kind of shock in her voice.

He slowed his step, replaying the words and trying to replicate the precise intonation Kimberly had used.

Marks glanced back at him. 'All right, Gary?'

'Fine. I'll catch you up.'

Marks gave a quick nod, and was gone. And so, too, for that moment at least, was any chance of pinning down the real emotion Kimberly had expressed.

His grandmother was always convinced that nothing was ever forgotten, but merely filed in an inaccessible corner of the memory. He had never been sure what the difference was between forgetting and being unable to remember, but he decided to place his trust in her wisdom and left it to percolate in his subconscious.

Goodhew hurried on down the stairs and into the foyer. Gully was standing at the far end. She was heading towards Marks, then stopped when she spotted Goodhew.

DI Marks paused as if to speak to her, but she just shook her head and pointed in Goodhew's direction.

She carried an envelope, holding it upright between her hands as if they were two brackets displaying an important landscape painting. He noticed she also looked pretty chuffed with herself.

Goodhew found it impossible not to smile. 'What have you got there?'

She passed him the envelope. 'Have a look.' She bit her bottom lip like it was a struggle not to blurt out the exciting part. He immediately recognized that the contents was a phone bill but, before he'd had a chance to spot who it belonged to, she grabbed it back again. She turned it to him face-on, then pointed to the number at the head of the sheet. 'Mikey Slater's mobile, right?'

'OK?'

'Look who he phoned straight after his 999 call.' She tapped the listing: 'Kimberly Guyver – he rang her home number *and* her mobile. That means he already knew her.'

'But why didn't . . .?'

'Yeah, why not just come clean, eh?' Gully realized her voice was rising, and she continued in a whisper, 'I *said* there was something she was holding back.'

'I need to speak to her.'

'Wait.'

'I've still got time now, before the press conference.'

'No, I mean there's more.'

Goodhew tried to pull the sheet from her, but she held it tight. 'Look, he knows Anita McVey, too. In fact he phones her as much as he calls Kimberly.'

'Let me see.'

She finally released her grip on the pages, and he double-checked everything she'd told him. As he glanced towards the stairs, his instincts shied away from confronting Kimberly with this. It would result in more delay and therefore a greater threat to Riley.

Through the window he could see the first dashes of fresh rain starting to make their hatching pattern on the glass. It seemed to him that everything within the confines of the hotel was under control. The greater prospects, however, lay outside.

And as though Gully had read his thoughts, she said, 'Anita's at home, if you want to see her.'

'How do you know?'

'I rang her to check if that was her number?'

'Oh.'

'I said I'd misdialled, so she'd never know it was me.'

'Maybe,' he said slowly. 'Seeing Mikey Slater might be a better bet.'

Goodhew took the list across to the receptionist and asked for a photocopy to be made, then sealed the original back in its envelope. He turned to Gully. 'Would you give this to Marks or Kincaide for me?'

She frowned. 'Why?'

'I don't want to get stuck in there.'

She snapped the envelope from his hands and straightened up irritably. 'I see.'

'And we still have this.' He held up the duplicate.

'We?'

'What are you supposed to be doing right now?'

Her frown faded, and she shrugged. 'Paperwork?'

'Right. Same as me.'

'And I have the car.'

'I'll wait here, then?'

One corner of her mouth curled up into a wonky grin. 'Thanks.'

She disappeared towards the conference room and returned in less than a minute. 'Kincaide's now got it.'

'You told him what it was?'

'Yeah, and he said he'd pass it to Marks. And I told him I thought it was important.'

'He probably won't look at it, then.'

Gully led them out to the patrol car, shaking her head. 'You two are so childish.'

'I know,' Goodhew shrugged, 'but he started it.' Gully pulled out of the car park, and he turned his thoughts back to the case. 'Let's just worry about Mikey.'

'First thoughts?'

'Just how he knows Anita McVey and Kimberly Guyver, and why he held back on that information, might make a few things clearer.'

'I can't see the three of them being behind Rachel Golinski's murder, somehow.'

231

'No, Nick Lewton was most likely killed by the same person, and Mikey would then have been about twelve. And, as far as we know, Anita would have been in the wrong country at the time.'

'Leaving only Kimberly.'

Goodhew shook his head. 'There's something up, but not that.'

'What if Mikey Slater's not at his home address? Do we phone him?'

'No, we try Anita.'

'We could head there first?'

'No, we'll be at the Slater house in a couple of minutes, then we'll decide.'

Gully's driving was swift and efficient. She seemed to know the Cambridge streets as well as Goodhew himself, and guided the car to a halt outside a large house in Devonshire Road. It had been converted into flats, and next to the front door there was a panel with nine doorbells grouped in three rows of three.

The house looked dusty, both the paintwork and window-panes coated in the thin layer of sootiness that came from being located so close to the road. The only thing that shone was a thick chrome handrail bolted to the wall. It ran alongside the two chunky steps rising to the front entrance, and seemed like a very recent addition.

Goodhew pressed the bell labelled 'Flat A'.

No one replied until they buzzed Flat D, then the intercom crackled and a male voice with a thick Scottish accent growled, 'Willya be ringing ev'ry flamin' letter of the alphabet till ye get someone?'

Gully was first to reply. 'We're looking for Ms Slater and her son Mikey.'

'Well, in this arse-about-face building, H is on the ground floor so I'd try that one, if I was you.'

Gully thanked him and stabbed the 'Flat H' button just as the front door swung open. The woman that faced them looked as though she was still in her thirties, but her face was gaunt and her frail frame leant heavily on a walking cane. 'I'm Collette Slater, Miss. I'd have opened the door sooner but I was having words with Mikey.'

Goodhew stepped forward. 'May we come in?'

'Go through, first on the left.'

Goodhew wondered whether Mikey would have bolted already, but they found him sitting quietly on the settee.

Mikey nodded to Goodhew. 'I wasn't being lazy,' he sounded genuinely apologetic. 'Mum insisted on going to the door.'

Goodhew brushed his apology away. 'It's time to get serious. We need to know how you come to know both Anita McVey and Kimberly Guyver.'

'Anita looks after me sometimes. It's a kind of fostering. When my mum gets too ill and needs a break or goes in for treatment, then I go to her house. That's how I met Kim, too.'

'So why keep that from us?'

'Dunno.'

'Mikey!' Collette cut in sharply.

For a moment he looked mutinous, but his resistance crumbled almost immediately. 'I just phoned and said it was on fire. All I was thinking was *get hold of Kim, quick.* Then, when I spoke to Kimberly and Anita, they both said the same thing, told me to keep my mouth shut . . . that it wasn't safe. That's all.'

Collette banged her cane once on the floor, but she looked like her frustration was born more of concern than of anger. 'That's not all. There's more to it, but he won't tell me.'

'That is everything I know, Mum. I swear it is.'

'No.' She sounded weary. 'You probably think you're trying to help them, but now's not the time, Mikey. Think of Riley, son.'

He shook his head. 'Please, Mum, I know what I'm doing.'

Goodhew shook his head, too. 'I'm very sorry, Miss Slater, but I'm going to need to take Mikey to Parkside Police Station to make a statement. Will you be able to accompany him?'

It was Mikey who replied. 'All that waiting 'round down the cop shop would be too much for my mum, physically I mean. There's nothing for me to say anyhow, so can't you just get one of those social-worker people to sit in, instead.'

Whatever else Mikey was, he was certainly a pragmatist. He saw no reason to argue about his inevitable trip to the station, and equally saw no reason to inconvenience his mother.

They loaded Mikey into the back of the patrol car and, until they pulled away, Collette stood at the window with an expression set in a fixed but watery smile.

Once they were out of sight of Devonshire Road, Goodhew twisted round in his seat to check that Mikey was OK. He caught a moment's uncertainty in the boy's expression and realized that behind Mikey's swagger was a teenager who seemed to care deeply about the people in his life.

Goodhew suspected that Mikey was lying for no other reason than a misplaced sense of loyalty. That didn't diminish the problem; blind devotion could be a very dangerous thing.

Kincaide knocked on the door of room 37 and waited. 'C'mon, c'mon,' he muttered, then rapped harder and called out, 'Make-up time's over, ladies.'

No doubt Kimberly was being zipped into something impossibly staid, right this moment, but then again he doubted she could wear a hospital gown without giving the impression that she'd slipped it on over lingerie from Agent Provocateur. He leant back against the opposite wall and waited, feeling impatient for more than just professional reasons.

It took a few more seconds before his ears picked out the sound of running water and, beyond that, the sound that it was all but drowning out: a muffled '*mmm mmm mmm*'.

He rattled the handle, then threw his shoulder at the door, but it held solid. 'Hang on,' he shouted, looking up and down the corridor for anything that could substitute for a crowbar. 'Wait there. I'll get help.'

There were plenty of officers already in the building, so he radioed down to them, then sprinted towards the stairs. He waited on the landing, holding the door leading to the stairs open, but still keeping room 37 within sight. He kept cursing the valuable seconds that he felt he'd already wasted.

DC Charles appeared first, taking the stairs three at a time, and dashing past Kincaide. Other footsteps followed.

Kincaide released the intervening door and ran after him. 'We need the key,' he shouted.

'Got the master,' Charles panted, as he reached number 37. He pushed the card in and out of the lock, and the little light obediently turned to green at the first attempt. Charles pushed down the handle and used his fingertips to push the door open.

As it swung wide, the first thing Kincaide noticed was steam pouring from the bathroom, and the sound of the shower. He pushed his way past Charles, and rushed forward. He found PC Kelly Wilkes sitting on the tiled floor, handcuffed to the bath's handrail and gagged with a pair of tights. Water sprayed from the shower hose, and she was drenched but appeared otherwise unharmed.

He leant forward and tugged the gag out of her mouth and over her head.

'Kimberly's gone,' were her first words.

'Are you hurt?'

Behind him, he heard DC Charles urgently contacting dispatch.

'I'm fine,' she replied. 'The key's sitting on the basin. Where's DI Marks?'

'I'm here.'

Kincaide glanced over his shoulder. There were now other officers in the room, but standing aside in order to let Marks through. Kincaide quickly found the key and released Wilkes.

Marks reached forward and pulled her to her feet. 'What happened?'

Wilkes' face looked washed-out and her voice trembled. 'A reporter, Beverley Dransfield, came to the door, wanting to ask questions. I called for assistance, but then she left, so I cancelled it.'

'And then?'

'Before that, Kimberly Guyver was fine.' Wilkes spoke so quickly she was in danger of falling over her words. 'Straight after that she turned. I'm so sorry . . . she was so fast, and stronger than I would have guessed.'

'Did she threaten you?'

'No. Just caught me by surprise. It was like she was angry, but not with me. We need to find that reporter. She shouted a load of questions through the door. Like accusing Kimberly Guyver of having a relationship with Stefan Golinski . . . things the tabloids have been hinting at all week. The only other thing she said was that it was the wrong photo of Riley.'

Marks scowled. 'In what way?'

'She never said.'

'Why didn't you radio this down to me?'

Wilkes paled further. 'I never had the chance.'

Marks shook his head slowly. The room was silent apart from the crackling of DC Charles's radio, which reached them from further down the corridor. 'Make an announcement to the journalists waiting downstairs. We need urgent help in identifying Beverley Dransfield.'

Suddenly Marks straightened and took a few steps towards the window, his focus then seeming to fall on the faded print of an insipid watercolour that hung over the bed.

He turned sharply and pinned his attention on Kincaide. 'Did anyone verify that the photo given to us by Kimberly Guyver was an accurate likeness?'

Kincaide felt all eyes in the room swivel in his direction. He was trying to recall which officer had taken the photograph from Kimberly, and who else had seen it. He knew Jay Andrews hadn't. He had no idea about Anita McVey. The kid didn't go to playgroup or nursery, so who else was there, apart from them, able to verify it?

He knew Marks wasn't blaming him personally but he willed himself to find an answer that would make him sound well-informed and confident. The silence stretched out until he ended it with a dismal, 'Don't know, sir.'

FORTY-ONE

Most things could be cut several ways and Cambridge was no exception. There was the famous side: the colleges, the history and the universal acclaim. Then there was Kimberly's side: anonymous streets, daily grind and unremarkable people. She knew the score on her side of the city, trusted the honesty of it. Thank God, that was where the Parkside Hotel lay.

She'd slipped down the fire-exit escape stairs until she'd reached the ground floor, then climbed out of an open window just in case the external door was alarmed.

Then, like Brer Rabbit into the briar patch, she'd scuttled through the warren of back alleys and short cuts that would keep her out of sight as she made for her rendezvous in Blossom Street.

Her heart had already been pounding when she left the hotel room. It didn't let up and she ran with it thumping like a war drum, pushing her on. Her breathing imposed its own rhythm over the top, so the two sounds played together to block out every other noise. She didn't listen out for sirens; they'd come soon enough but she needed to be gone before that.

The grubby passages gave way to deserted side roads. She broke cover to cross Mill Road, then disappeared into the alleyways on the other side, finally scrambling over a wall into the graveyard. She sprinted the length of the cemetery, through the main body of the guitar and up into its neck. She never even glanced at her own home, nor at the dead eyes of Rachel's house. She watched for nothing but the Blossom Street gate, and for the flash of familiar dark-green paintwork that would signal his arrival.

She had twenty yards still to run when a Transit van swung into view, its passenger door flying open just feet beyond the gate. She ran through the exit and bundled herself inside the vehicle, pulling the door behind her as it pulled away from the kerb again.

She slid down low in the seat and pressed her left hand against the side of her face, shielding it from the view of any pedestrians they might pass.

She tried hard to speak, but her lungs were still in overdrive, clawing back the oxygen deficit.

He swung the Transit out into the traffic, heading away from the city centre.

'Just catch your breath,' he said. 'Put your head between your knees.' He reached over and gave her hand a quick squeeze.

She nodded, grateful for the calmness in his voice, and bent forward. It only made her feel queasy, so she slumped back again.

He reached down beside his seat, steering with his knees while he retrieved a bottle of water. He gave the lid a sharp twist, and the seal clicked open: 'Just in case you're feeling too weak to open it yourself.'

'Thanks,' she still puffed though her heartbeat had steadied, 'but I'm not quite that feeble yet.'

She swigged from the bottle, glad it was chilled.

He shot her an inquisitive glance. 'On the phone, you said Stefan killed Nick?'

'Shit, he's killed Rachel, too. And beat up Jay, for all I know.'

'You have proof?'

'I can prove it wasn't me, and that's all that will matter to Dougie. I don't have to hide from him now.'

'It might not be that easy.'

'Why not? Nick died from a huge head injury, because he was kicked to death. I never did that.'

'What if Dougie doesn't believe you?'

'It's not physically possible. I just don't have the brute strength to shatter a skull that way.' Kimberly slammed her hand on to the van's dashboard. 'I haven't come this far just for you to tell me it's too risky. For the last three years I've been waiting for Nick's body to be found, thinking that it would prove I killed him, and that Dougie would then come after me. Now I just want to square things with him.'

'And two days ago you were begging me to get Tamsin off your back?'

'Don't you see, finding out the truth about Nick has changed everything. Did you call him or not?'

Craig shrugged. 'Yeah, of course, and he wants to meet you. You and Riley.'

Kimberly calmed immediately. 'He knows that Riley's Nick's son?' She wasn't as surprised as she might have been; it seemed somehow fitting that Craig should have told him.

'I'll take you to him right now.'

'Riley's with Anita.'

'I know.' He smiled. 'And I've been watching her place to make sure he stayed safe.' Just then he turned right, and she knew they were heading for Viva Cottage.

A wave of contentment washed over her at just the thought of holding Riley again. 'We need to be quick. They'll already know I've gone.'

'I was worried that you would tell the police everything.'

Kimberly felt the van accelerate. She didn't bother to reply. She didn't need to explain to Craig how the police were another species to her, or how much she feared being branded unfit and then watching Riley being sucked into the care system. Dougie was far from perfect, but he knew how to get problems sorted and, now she was no longer one of those problems, she was sure that things would be different.

Craig's Transit bounced along the track to the allotments, and towards the rear garden of Viva Cottage, coasting to a standstill.

When Kimberly trusted, she trusted absolutely, and to her Craig was the proverbial rough diamond. Heart of gold.

Or so she thought until he reached across and tied her to her seat. She merely smiled because she still felt so calm and contented. She slumped forward and the bottle of water tipped over and trickled on to her leg.

Spiked water. Supposedly sealed bottle.

Damn him. Damn her. She thought she knew better than that.

He reclined her seat just a little, and tilted her head back until she appeared to be dozing. Then, through her half-open eyes, she watched him striding towards Viva Cottage.

He disappeared around the side of the house and she then knew she'd failed them all. Her eyes drooped further and heavy tears fell on to her cheeks.

Anita held out her hand, palm upwards, to check for the first spots of rain. She was grateful for the cooler weather; it saved the worry of reapplying sunblock and trying to keep a hat on Riley's head. The garden needed the rain, too.

'I've started thinking just like my mother. It's a bad sign, Riley.'

She'd unwrapped an ice lolly and held it out for him. He was a sturdy little boy, quiet in the house, non-stop when he played in the long front garden. He kicked his football away and ran over to her. His expressions were always open and unguarded, the sight of the ice lolly filled him with delight.

'What do you say?'

'Thank you.' He grinned, and she released her grip on the stick.

'Good boy.'

She settled on the front step and watched him battle with his orange rocket, he was doing his best to catch every drip, although it soon seemed his T-shirt was better at that than he was.

'I think it's going to rain.' She pointed up to the sky. 'Look at those clouds.'

He turned and pointed along the side of the house. 'Rai.'

'That's right, rain.'

'Rai,' he repeated and ran to the corner of the house and out of sight.

'Hang on, Riley.' She jumped to her feet and hurried the few steps to the corner. Craig squatted there, speaking quietly in Riley's ear. Riley giggled.

Her first response was to smile. Craig had always played the part of the quiet uncle, sending them the occasional toy, dropping by once or twice with sweets. Anita had once wondered if he had a soft spot for Kimberly, later hoping it had been for herself.

'Did Kimberly send you?' she asked.

He looked up at her and her smile faded.

Sue Gully loved to drive and, while she couldn't fathom Goodhew's apparent lack of interest in getting behind the wheel, it suited her far more than being the one in the passenger seat.

The first spots of fresh rain to strike the windscreen had fallen with no rhythm, hitting the glass randomly and giving the illusion they might be just spillage from the overloaded clouds. But half a mile later and the skies unleashed their earlier threat of a downpour, hurling the raindrops at them like a volley of tiny bullets.

She turned the wipers to full speed, and pedestrians vanished from the pavements like she'd swished them away with the first two or three sweeps of the blades. Simultaneously, the traffic slowed to a crawl.

If anyone inside the patrol car had been trying to speak, they would have needed to raise their voice over the sound of the water hammering on to the car roof. She reached towards the volume control on the radio, just as Goodhew did the same. They both mumbled an unnecessary apology, then only caught a fragment of the dispatcher's message: '... Kimberly Guyver, suspicion of assault ...'

In the back of the car, Mikey swore.

'Did you catch all of that?' Goodhew asked.

The radio was broadcasting non-stop, the voice strangely matter-of-fact.

'No, all I got was something about Kimberly and an assault. You need to speak to Marks.'

'OK, OK.' Goodhew's phone was already in his hand, but he gave up again after a few seconds. 'It went straight to voicemail,' he explained.

'Contact him with the radio,' she suggested.

He gave a small shake of the head, and she guessed he was thinking it was better to speak to their DI without being overheard by Mikey. 'I'll keep trying.'

She checked in the rear-view mirror: Mikey's head was lowered but she could still see his face. His eyes were roaming from side to side and whatever thoughts were running through his mind were making his lips twitch with the suggestion of speech.

Suddenly he looked up, alert to the latest update coming from the radio. *Riley Guyver still missing. Age correct. Await description.*

Gully had stared at the radio, too, then back at Mikey. He'd looked away, into the rain, with no trace of surprise in his expression.

Await description?

'Meaning what exactly?' she murmured in Goodhew's general direction.

'We disregard the photo, that's what.' For a fleeting moment she thought she'd noticed despondency in his tone, but by the next sentence it was either gone or had just been her imagination. 'She gave us the wrong picture' he added.

'Why would she . . .?' She raised her voice for Mikey's benefit. 'Tell us, Mikey, why would she do that?'

He said nothing, but one unpalatable answer had already jumped to the tip of her tongue. Perhaps Riley was dead. 'What's she done to him?'

That made Mikey's head turn. 'Nuthin,' he sneered.

'She must've done something or she wouldn't have lied to us.'

She rephrased and repeated it as a question. She ignored Goodhew whispering for her to stop. She couldn't now, even though she knew he was right, and that she should wait until they arrived at Parkside before pushing this further. 'And you, Mikey, you know what it is, don't you?' she pressed.

Mikey punched the seat impatiently, leant forward and hissed, 'She hasn't hurt him.'

Goodhew twisted around in his seat so sharply that Mikey shrank back in surprise. 'Right, you just said "hasn't", which means you know.'

'No, it don't.'

'Kimberly *knows* where Riley is.' There was a new intensity to Goodhew's tone that she hadn't noticed before. 'You both know where he is, because it doesn't make any sense otherwise.' Goodhew pointed his finger at Mikey as though trying to pin down an elusive thought. After several seconds, he stabbed the air with it and turned to Gully. 'Are we slow or what?'

She shrugged.

'Anita,' he was close to shouting, 'Anita McVey. *She* knows it was the wrong photograph.'

Gully switched on the blue light and spun the car around in the road, shooting puddle water up on to the pavements, and pushed on through the driving rain towards Viva Cottage.

FORTY-TWO

Anita McVey's eyes were open, but beyond seeing anything through the thickening blood and dirt that was swallowing up each of her senses. She felt it warm and wet on her cheek, then being drawn up into her nostrils by her laboured breath. The blood smelt like rust and filled the back of her throat, coating the back of her tongue like treacle.

Her hearing survived the longest, sending delayed messages to her brain, echoing back the sounds of being kicked, telling it that her skull was broken, that her eye socket was cracked.

Then finally informing it that somewhere in the distance was a siren.

For the last few minutes of the journey, Goodhew was overcome with a feeling of urgency, which had temporarily washed away every other concern about the present case. Visibility was poor, and he knew that Gully was pushing through the downpour as quickly as possible, but every sense told him that it still wasn't fast enough.

The patrol car skidded to a halt and Goodhew threw open his door, leaping from the vehicle and dashing towards Viva Cottage. As soon as he had a clear view of the front door he spotted the body. She lay on her back, her face tilted skywards but half hidden by tattered curls of her dark hair. Her clothes were sodden, and clung to her like strips of papier mâché. She didn't move.

Behind him he heard the car doors slam. 'Call an ambulance,' he shouted.

It was only the rainwater, splashing down on her, washing the blood across the garden path in heavy purple trails, that showed there had ever been life within this pile of rags. He knelt beside her and began pushing the hair aside from her face. Her lips were parted, but her features seemed to have caved inwards.

Facial fractures.

For the first time he caught a gurgling noise, a rasp of air dragging through a broken airway.

'Anita, can you hear me?'

He slid his fingers into her mouth, probing for an obstruction.

'Call an ambulance,' he yelled again.

'It's coming,' Gully's voice responded, from somewhere close beside him.

He heard Mikey there, too, sobbing. 'Is she dead? Help her, please help her.'

Goodhew shut them both out.

Anita's breathing stopped with the next trickling intake of air. He put his ear to her mouth. Silence. His hands were cupping her face at the temples, and instinctively he slid them down her jawline, until his thumbs were on her chin and his first two fingers were positioned on each side, at the angle of the jaw.

Keeping his grip as firm and steady as possible, he hinged the lower section of her face up until he was sure that her airways had sufficient space to open. He watched the blood around her nose and mouth, tried to blot out Mikey's screams and the deafening rain. Instead he willed Anita to breathe, willed her to make any sound that would reach him.

'I need help here,' he shouted.

'Tell me what to do.' It was Mikey.

'Hold the jaw just the way I am now. I need to give her mouth-to-mouth.'

'It's impossible,' Mikey mumbled. But, without hesitating, his hands reached down to try to replace Goodhew's, then suddenly retracted. He exclaimed, 'Look.'

A bubble of blood and saliva had formed and now burst on her tongue.

'She's breathing,' Mikey gasped.

'Anita, listen to me. There's help coming.' Goodhew watched her chest rise and fall for the next few seconds. 'Hang on. Just hang on.'

Goodhew snatched a look over his shoulder. Their patrol car still stood alone out in the lane. Where was that damned ambulance?

He turned back to Mikey, as though he might provide the answer. Then Goodhew heard the uneasiness in his own voice as he shouted, over the rain, 'Where's PC Gully?'

'She went round the side.'

'Why?'

'Dunno. She just walked off.'

'Shit. Hold Anita's head, just like I'm doing. Watch her breathe, shout for me if she starts struggling at all.'

Mikey took over from him.

'Got it?' Goodhew snapped impatiently.

Mikey nodded dumbly. He looked terrified but his hands were steady.

Goodhew dashed to the corner of Viva Cottage, grabbing the downpipe to swing himself through the turn, and then went running down the side of the house. He pulled up short before he drew level with the rear corner.

Gully's radio lay on the ground, still crackling. Above it the wall was smeared with an arc of blood and closer still to the furthest corner, there was a single palm print – too small for a grown man's, but too big for a child's.

FORTY-THREE

Sue Gully lay on her side, her cheek resting against a tight roll of rough carpet, and her chin pressed at an awkward angle to the floor. They were in the back of a van, with one grubby window high in the back door. No other light but it was something.

She felt a breath on her face, not like the movement of the air against her skin, but the heavy fug of tepid second-hand oxygen that smelt of decaying food, and which meant that someone else's mouth was quite close to her own.

She was too close to see him clearly, but as her eyes adjusted to the light she picked out a close-up of open pores and greasy skin, unwashed hair and a glimpse of his half-open left eye. It was enough to recognize him as the man in the enlargement pinned up in the incident room.

She tried to speak, but it came out only as a gasp for air. She tried to move, hoping to heave herself more upright. Her left hand lifted a few inches, succeeded in making only a twitch, then flopped back to her side again.

She scowled in frustration and put all her efforts into speech. 'Stefan,' she rasped, 'say something.'

'Uhhh,' emerged from his throat, but nothing more.

She managed to move her head just enough to see her own hand. The fingers were swollen and caked with blood. They looked painful but she felt nothing, and although her body throbbed gently, enticing any movement from it seemed beyond her.

She closed her eyes and concentrated on the noise of the engine, which sounded as though they were travelling at about fifty. Worn brakes, manual gearbox, she decided. The van bounced on a slightly uneven surface, so she guessed they were on a fast country road. The clear patch in the window revealed only open sky and flashes of passing foliage.

The van gradually slowed, till the driver applied the brake harder and it slid to a standstill. Gully's whole body lurched, ramming her face harder into the curl of carpet. Stefan cannoned against her, his upper body rolling heavily on to her chest. 'Stefan,' she moaned, 'get off me.'

This time something registered in his face and he managed to move his mouth. A tidemark of dried saliva rimmed his bottom lip. A name slipped out with his exhalation. 'Craig.'

It took her a moment to place the name. 'Your boss?'

Stefan gave a small grunt, and she thought he was beyond speech until he managed two final sentences: 'He killed her. Us next.'

They continued to drive, picking up speed again, and at the first right-hand bend he lifted his head just enough for the sway of the van to tip him away from Gully and on to his back. Thank God for that. She took a deep breath and, as she exhaled, realized for the first time that blood was trickling through her hair, and seeping down into the neck of her shirt.

Maybe that was why her body didn't hurt so much. Maybe that was why her limbs felt too heavy. She looked up towards the window and saw streaks of cloud flitting past. Seen through her eyes, the sky was becoming anaemic, washing out to a shade of sepia. Or else it was tinted glass. The van was warm and she shut her eyes to block out the rumble of the road.

Just for a few minutes . . .

To let herself drift away.

More officers from Parkside arrived, with the ambulance on their tail. The medics were fast but efficient, attaching a drip and loading Anita on to a stretcher within a matter of minutes.

'Let me go with her,' Mikey whispered. Goodhew nodded.

The ambulance switched on its siren and accelerated away from him into the wet afternoon.

Goodhew hurried to the nearest patrol car, just as Marks was patched through to him. 'Goodhew, are you sure that Riley's with them?'

'According to Mikey, Riley has been here at Viva Cottage the whole time. Where else would he be?'

'OK, fair assumption. What about Gully?'

'I didn't see anything, sir. I just looked round and she'd gone.'

'The helicopter's up, but nothing seen yet.'

'You know what you're looking for?'

'Estate car or larger.'

'Great,' Goodhew replied flatly. He sped away from Viva Cottage, desperate to be doing something, but filled with the fear that there was nothing worthwhile within his grasp.

The Transit lurched around a tight right-hand bend, quickly followed by a sharp left. Gully saw the tops of a series of lamp posts pass the window. Then nothing.

The back of the van was filled with the earthy smell of young crops, and she realized they were heading deeper into flat fenlands. She thought of the low horizon: perhaps, in the distance, the cathedral at Ely, or windmills and isolated farms. She knew the landscape well, and closed her eyes to imagine large fields planted in neat corduroy-striped rows, and others black-soiled and left fallow.

She began to feel dizzy again.

Then she imagined the double-engined freight train passing Newmarket, lumbering at a steady forty mph. Pulling its rolling stock of sixty open bucket trucks. Unchallenged by inclines. Plugging on with nothing to consider but its eventual destination at the rail depot at Queen Adelaide, on the outskirts of Ely. The driver would apply the brakes two miles before, dissipating the momentum of the load, coaxing it to a crawl, then a final halt on the track. Trains couldn't afford to make sudden moves.

She opened her eyes again, and saw streaks of cloud.

But she now couldn't visualize sudden moves. In her confused mind everything involved big movements, bold strokes of colour and action, huge skies, vast farms and direct journeys.

Her eyes closed again.

She listened hard for the rhythm of the train. Two miles to go, two miles to go.

'Get up.' The words were spoken slowly the first time, repeated more quickly the second. By the third time she was trying to obey, and by the fourth she finally realized that the voice was her own. By then she'd somehow manoeuvred herself on to her hands and knees, and began crawling towards the back of the van, each sway of the vehicle almost toppling her over. The back doors lay in deep shadow, so she felt along their meeting point. The door mechanism was enclosed, and she immediately realized that it would be impossible to open them from inside.

Both doors had once possessed a window, but now only one of them remained, the other space blocked with a welded panel. Gully gripped the rough inner edge of one door and with her swollen left hand reached up to the grimy glass.

What was it with kids and communication? Gillian Reynolds had pondered the same question many times, and on this particular occasion she had a full range of examples here in the car with her: three-year-old Ben who could talk but preferred to shout, eight-year-old Amy who only seemed capable of engaging in anything complicated when paired with another eight-year-old, and Kirsty.

Kirsty, fifteen years old, permanently texting but only seemingly capable of communicating with her mum via a full dictionary's worth of silent verbs, adjectives and pronouns. The fact that her choice of GCSE subjects included three languages hadn't in any way aided her ability to speak.

Kirsty pressed *send* on her latest text.

Gillian sighed in irritation, she realized it sounded slightly theatrical, but then again if that was the only communication they were going to have, she might as well get it off her chest.

'What the . . .?' Kirsty muttered.

'The traffic's terrible,' Gillian lied, and glanced at her daughter expecting the usual accusatory stare in return. But neither Kirsty's gaze nor her comment was aimed in Gillian's direction, but straight in front. Kirsty's expression revealed a mix of confusion and something not so easy to identify. Revulsion perhaps?

'No, look,' Kirsty gasped, pointing to a tatty Transit van driving about twenty feet ahead of them.

Gillian ran her gaze over it but failed to see what Kirsty obviously could. 'What?' she demanded, a little too crossly.

'There was a hand at the window.'

'A hand?'

Kirsty nodded, her face now ashen. 'Covered in blood.'

Gillian's foot lifted off the accelerator, and the gap between them and the van ahead expanded to about forty feet. 'Don't be . . .'

'Ridiculous? No, just get closer. There's blood on the glass.'

There was something in her daughter's tone that made Gillian do what she was told. She edged her car forwards until she, too, could see smears on the pane. 'I don't think it's blood. It's just dirt.'

'That's the marks on the outside. We're not close enough yet.'

'Any closer and I'll be on his bumper.'

'Signal, make it look like you want to overtake – then you can get up his arse and he'll think you're just a crap driver.'

Gillian bit back the urge to reprimand her daughter for her language, but instead signalled to overtake, and then pulled closer to both the white line and the van's rear bumper. She tilted her head to the right, as if peering along the side of the van for oncoming vehicles, but all the time kept her gaze on the small square of glass in one back door. She was within a car's length when she spotted the marks on the window. For all she wanted to deny that it was blood, she knew she couldn't. 'It's writing,' she breathed.

Kirsty squinted up at it. 'It says "So".'

Gillian nodded. 'Phone the police,' she said quietly. She dropped back a bit and memorized the van's registration number. What lay behind those closed back doors? She wondered why the hand hadn't reappeared during the minutes she'd been in pursuit. And why it had not attempted to complete its message with a final 'S'.

Goodhew slowed to take a left back towards Parkside Station, just as the radio crackled into life. *Ford Transit, Victor 3-0-6 Echo, Yankee, Alpha. Location Bravo 1102 travelling between Lode and Swaffham Bulbeck. Reported possible injured passenger in rear of vehicle.*

Goodhew instantly activated the lights and the siren, swinging the patrol car to the right, into the bus lane which ran along the edge of Newmarket Road. He floored the accelerator and the vehicle responded, leaping rapidly to sixty as he kept it on the red tarmac that lay between the kerb and the main flow of stagnant traffic.

He guessed it was still about two miles to the end of the road, two miles equalling two minutes at this speed. And it just wasn't fast enough.

The speedo nudged seventy as he approached the humpbacked bridge that spanned the railway line. At the peak of the hump the patrol car rose in a shallow arc, lifting away from the red stone parapet.

He gripped the wheel tighter and, as the tyres hit the ground again, drove hard through the sweeping curve that cut through the inter-war housing sprawl on the other side.

At the end of the bus lane, he veered into a gap between two trucks, over-steering while skidding towards an oncoming learner driver.

He hauled the steering wheel to the left, and the car responded, first listing then straightening itself in the middle of the road, gobbling up the dirty white line beneath its front valance.

A crash barrier sprang up, dividing the carriageways a few feet ahead. Goodhew again yanked the wheel to pull to the left of it, and continue the approach to the Quy roundabout. The front wing clipped the barrier and the bumper's end cap sprang off, bouncing off the car's body before flying backwards into the road.

The roundabout itself was a half mile in circumference. Aluminium railings, steel-grey tarmac, then he took the second exit: *Burwell and Fordham.*

He shouted into the radio. 'Have they caught it yet?'

'No, still searching. What's your location?'

'Quy roundabout. Who's in pursuit?'

'DC Kincaide, one marked car and the helicopter. There are others on the way but you're still ahead of them.'

'And no other sightings?'

'Nothing yet. Member of public lost sight of the van during the bends at Swaffham Bulbeck.'

*   *   *

Craig knew there would be police chasing him, and perhaps a helicopter too, but for anyone who knew the landscape of the Fens it was easy enough. Springtime made the trees flourish, the hedges thick and the countryside more accessible to the public. By early summer it was easy to hide there, if you knew enough about the concealed entrances and derelict grain stores.

The Transit simply reversed into a farm track and used a thick screen of horse-chestnut and hawthorn trees to let its pursuers rush by. A heap of four rusting cars stood under the overhang of branches, three of them stacked in a precarious pyramid with an old Fiat Strada at the top, decorated with bird droppings and the remnants of dead leaves. The Transit now slipped into the gap between the cars and the nearby tree trunks.

A minute later the police helicopter passed high above, too busy catching up with and overtaking the police vehicles to notice.

The car standing on its own was an old-style model Renault Megane. Craig quickly unlocked it and opened all four doors. Transferring Kimberly was relatively easy, as the threat of anything happening to dear little Riley rendered her as good as useless, and she took her place in the passenger seat without any argument.

He next carried the policewoman, who was now partly conscious. The small amount of resistance she made helped him propel her into the rear seat, directly behind Kimberly. Stefan was the most awkward, flopping around like he had jelly for a spine; ironic that he was the one passenger who would have to change seats yet again.

Last to be moved was Riley, not destined to sit in the car with the others, but gently placed in the boot like the precious cargo he now was. The look of openness and trust had disappeared from his little face, but he didn't struggle or cry, just shook his head and said, 'I don't like it,' as the boot lid slammed shut. Craig figured there were a lot of things in life that weren't to be liked, but that didn't mean they weren't necessary.

He started the engine, and checked his watch before he pulled out on to the road, continuing in the same direction as before. As he changed up through the gears, crunching into second and again into third, he shook his head and indulged in a little smirk. He was entitled to suffer from some nerves, after all, and as much as this part of it was risky, it was also the climax of his plan. Nerves were good: they kept the mind in focus and the adrenaline pumping – and never had his mind been more focused. This, finally, was his endgame, and the prize was almost within his grasp.

Kincaide passed Burwell and reached the outskirts of Fordham, with the marked car in tow and a helicopter overhead. The Transit van seemed to have vanished into thin air, and the worry that it was somewhere behind them was beginning to niggle at the back of Kincaide's mind.

He pressed on, desperately hoping that he'd round the next bend to find the van had crashed, involving only a minor RTA and a humiliating arrest. There would be good coverage from that, his friends in the press would want pictures and then, as far as the police shots went, it would be him.

He approached a T-junction but there was still nothing in sight. Left or right?

Where the fuck was that van?

Better look decisive. He turned left.

Kincaide considered the report of the blood on the wall at Viva Cottage. He hoped it wasn't Kimberly's, since rescuing a dead mother wouldn't have the same impact.

But then, again, he'd get the credit for apprehending a killer.

He uttered one word aloud, 'Cool.'

The following police car was approaching tight in his rear-view mirror, so he squeezed the steering wheel and leant forward, trying to see further up the road. He was definitely the man of the moment.

Another hundred yards and the radio crackled.

'*All units. Renault Megane involved in suspicious behaviour on the level crossing between Burwell and Fordham. Please respond.*'

Perhaps there was no connection? 'Shit.' Of course there was a connection.

The railway line was about half a mile behind him.

He slammed on the brakes and immediately swung across the road and into a wide driveway on his right, mounting the pavement in order to make the turn. As he suspected, PC Rimes, driving the other car, knew the area less well. Rimes now shot past him, fumbling through a turn further up the road.

The chopper banked sideways and would have the crossing in sight almost instantly.

Kincaide screeched back up the same road. It wouldn't do for anyone else to reach the vehicle first.

No. No. No.

He turned right, back on to the Burwell road. The level crossing was ahead, the gates open, traffic flowing freely.

'They're not here,' he yelled as he drove across it.

Marks replied, 'There's another crossing. Can you see it?'

Kincaide looked, and immediately spotted it to his right.

'It's about half a mile.'

The next right-hand turn led to nothing much except the railway itself and the adjacent but unoccupied crossing keeper's cottage.

The helicopter hovered above, and straddling the tracks was a dark-blue Renault.

Marks spoke again. 'If they are in the car, get them out. There's a train due in three minutes, and we can't seem to make contact with it.'

Kincaide pulled up at the side of the road, and leapt from his vehicle at a run. He scrambled to the top of a grassy mound rising ten yards back from the track. The car had three occupants: Stefan Golinski in the driver's seat, Kimberly Guyver sitting next to him, and PC Sue Gully in the back.

'There's a train coming. Move the car,' he shouted. 'Move the fucking car.' Kimberly turned her head in his direction, but no one else moved.

Kincaide looked along the track in both directions. There was nothing in sight. But he'd heard of trains gliding silently into groups of railway workers and he stayed put.

He didn't yell again, just stared down into the car. Stefan stared at the middle of the steering wheel, content to wait. At peace with the decision that they all should die.

But Kimberly never looked away from him, her eyes pleading with him, begging him to help.

Gully lay in the back of the car, but it was hard to see her clearly.

He could pick out the blue of her uniform, and the white of her upturned palm. And the rust-red smears that soiled it.

He saw her fingers move, folding in as if to grip another imaginary hand.

He looked up and down the track once more. There was still nothing to see. But, even so, he knew the helping hand wouldn't be his. His feet had become rooted, and the pounding of his heart had overtaken his ability to act.

He looked away again. The field next to him was part of a nursery growing ornamental trees that were trained up bamboo canes. In one row were slender shrubs with weeping pink leaves. They looked like stick men draped with occasional chunks of flesh.

He felt sweat squeezing out on to his forehead and he hoped he wouldn't throw up.

FORTY-FOUR

It was one continuous road to Burwell, and Goodhew knew it well.
A few twists through village streets then the open countryside:
centuries old farmland with small communities gathered every few
miles along the old highway.

The road zigzagged through ninety-degree bends in Swaffham
Bulbeck, and on past the white sails of the windmills at Swaffham
Prior.

Then fields. Immense flat fields that stretched out towards the
distant low horizon.

The rain had stopped at the outskirts of Cambridge. Here there
was mellowing sunlight, and the dome of the sky was skimmed with
grey cloud combed into parallel lines, like ribs.

In the far distance, the sky seemed to exaggerate the earth's curve.
pushing it downwards.

Pylons strode from right to left, like giants disappearing into the
distance, vanishing as mere specks twenty miles away.

Goodhew noticed another speck, this one ahead of him, just a dot
moving through the air.

The police helicopter.

As he reached the edge of Burwell, he didn't slow, but raced
through the place at double the speed limit. He willed that no one
would step off a pavement. He willed that the housing would soon
finish. The village was only two miles from end to end, but each one
of them felt like ten.

He finally broke out on to the open road, and now he could see
the dot of the helicopter again, but this time it was hovering.

Telegraph poles followed the road, running alongside his car. They marked the way ahead, flitting past him with increasing frequency. The hedgerow dropped back, and in the distance he could see the level crossing.

He heard Marks: 'We can't stop the train.'

The crossing was still a mile away, but he was closing in at sixty. He saw the red warning lights start to flash and the barriers begin to fall.

Goodhew yelled to Marks, 'There's no one there!'

But, as he said it, his eyes were drawn to where the helicopter hovered half a mile to his left.

'The other crossing,' Marks shouted. 'To your left, over to your left.'

Goodhew skidded into Cockpen Road, saw the freight train rumbling through the first crossing even as he made the turn.

The second crossing was two hundred yards straight ahead of him.

Cars littered the side of the road. People stood with their doors open, staring at the Renault Megane stationary on the track.

Goodhew held his line, furiously hitting his horn and leaving them to find their own way clear.

He heard the frantic warning of the locomotive's horn, the squeal of the brakes the driver was now applying one and a half miles too late.

A moment before the impact Goodhew prayed.

Prayed he was fast enough to miss the train. And slow enough not to kill them all.

He broke through the crossing barrier, a crack and splinter which had barely begun to register before being swallowed up by the impact of metal on metal, as he slammed into the rear of the Megane.

His airbag launched itself, his eyes closed, and he flopped into its bulging arms.

He didn't know where he'd ended up, or whether his car lay in the path of the train.

He kept his eyes shut, and waited for one long second. He prayed everyone else was clear.

And not dead.

The train's brakes still screamed as it roared past, rocking the patrol car on the remains of its suspension.

Then there was silence, and he opened his eyes, saw the grey clouds. They weren't shaped like ribs at all but train tracks. The blue sky faded, the sunlight fingering it the colour of gone-off milk.

He spoke into the radio's earpiece. 'Get an ambulance.'

But the device was dead; he pulled it off and threw it to one side.

Someone opened his door, told him not to move.

He looked down at his legs, and knew for certain that they still worked. He hauled himself out then, stumbling towards the wreckage of the other car.

It had smashed through a picket fence into the derelict garden of the crossing keeper's cottage, so that only the driver's-side rear corner hadn't ended up in the rubbish-filled enclosure. Its indicator blinked at half speed.

The car's front end had joined two abandoned VW Campervans and a wrecked towing caravan.

Most of the damage was to the back. The boot was crushed into the rear passenger area, the rear windscreen was gone, staved in by the weight of Goodhew's car. The rear seat had doubled over, leaning against the back of the front seats.

Four or five onlookers had already gathered around. They had pulled the front doors open and they were leaning inside. No one was checking the back, or even trying to open the rear doors.

He pulled a man aside and peered into the front. He saw Stefan first, slumped forward, with eyes gaping. Next to him was Kimberly. Blood was running from her forehead, and PC Rimes was holding her hand.

'Riley,' Kimberly kept repeating.

'Where is he?' Goodhew had to ask it twice before his question filtered though to her.

She shook her head. 'I don't know.'

Rimes spoke calmly. 'Help's coming.'

Goodhew grabbed at the back door; it wouldn't open, twisted too far out of shape to ever again separate from the body shell. He reached through the broken side window and twisted the seat back into a more upright position – revealing Gully's face.

Her eyes were half-closed, her pupils immobile. A dark pool, still shiny, coated the seat. Streaks of blood had dried like earth stains on her cheek.

'Sue,' he whispered. Then louder, 'Sue.' He heard the desperate tone in his voice and tears pricked his eyes. 'Sue,' he said again.

He put the back of his hand to her nostrils and felt her breath tickle his skin.

He stretched his arm in further, reaching for her hand, squeezing it in his.

'Sue, talk to me.'

Her eyes didn't move but she spoke, barely moving her swollen mouth. 'What?'

'Talk to me.'

'It hurts.'

'I'm sorry.' Tears rolled on to his cheeks.

'Help me.'

'We'll get you out in a minute. Just hold on. Talk to me. It was the only thing I could do. I never meant to hurt you.' He wiped his eyes with his cuff.

'Riley?' she muttered.

'Do you know anything, Sue?'

'He's in the boot.'

'No!'

'He is,' she insisted. 'I saw him being put there.'

A coldness passed through Goodhew, knowing he had rammed the back end of the car hard enough to compress it by at least two feet. He'd pushed the upright section of the back seat out of the way in order to reach Gully, but from the first he could only remember watching for some movement from her. He'd never checked behind the seat. 'Sue, I need to fold the seat down on you again. Will you be all right with that?'

'Why?'

'It's just for a second. I need to look in the boot.'

'OK.'

He let go of her hand and reached across to the nearer rear-seat headrest and gave it a sharp tug forwards.

* * *

260

Gully drifted up through the fog of sleep, near the surface but not quite breaking through it. She heard Goodhew's voice, muffled and faint, like he was speaking in another room.

She was talking to him in that other room, too, letting words slip out without her brain's say-so.

He was doing something with the seat now, trying to fold her up in it, or something. She heard him draw a sudden breath, then say, 'Thank God, thank God,' over and over.

He took her hand. 'Which car is Riley in?'

'Not this one.'

'I know, Sue, but did you see him in the boot of another vehicle?'

Her voice became quieter, until he seemed to be finding it as hard as she was to distinguish the poorly formed words.

'Sue, say that again.'

'Can't remember. It was red. Small saloon.'

'And Craig drove it?'

'No, he drove us . . . then moved Stefan from back here to the driver's seat. You wouldn't know that if we were dead, like we're supposed to be.'

He pulled away from her for just a second and she heard him shouting, 'Over here, quick.' He squeezed her hand again. 'Help's coming, Sue.'

'Can you stay?' She hoped she hadn't blushed. 'Stefan's dead, isn't he?'

'Yes.'

'Anita?'

'Not sure. Listen to me. You need to stay awake, Sue . . . Sue.'

She thought she *was* awake, but he repeated her name several more times before she muttered a response. 'Why do people play games?' she asked.

'I don't know,' Goodhew replied.

'Do you?' she persisted.

'I try not to.' He added, 'When I crashed into you, I never wanted to see you hurt.'

'Hmm,' she replied.

She wondered why she was still talking, she felt so tired. Too many questions, too much effort . . . God, she wanted to sleep.

Why did he keep bugging her?

His voice kept on though, chipping away at her, dragging her back. Making her think about words. And he sounded so strange. She listened more closely; he sounded sort of choked.

'I didn't have a choice . . . the train would have hit this car. It was the only thing I could think to do.'

Gully listened, wondering what he had to cry about. She squeezed his hand and concentrated on opening her eyes. She managed to get him into an intermittent fuzzy focus. He looked a mess – perhaps he was in shock and just needed to talk. 'No wonder you don't drive,' she said, making an effort.

'Why?'

'Well, you're crap at it, aren't you?'

'Absolutely.' He still sounded distracted. He let go of her hand and she heard him shouting something about an ambulance. She didn't want him to go.

He stroked her cheek. 'How are you feeling?' He smiled at her.

'I won't smile back at you in case I dribble,' she whispered.

Behind him she saw the vague shape of a torso appear, dressed in paramedic green.

'You'll be OK,' Goodhew told her, and gave her hand a squeeze before finally letting it go.

FORTY-FIVE

The paramedics all wore the same closed expression, the one that allowed them to view the scene whilst avoiding any personal interaction that might scar them later. Kimberly had concussion, blood loss and showed signs that she was under the influence of some kind of sedative. Meanwhile, Sue Gully had also suffered a head injury and they were struggling to keep her conscious. They would talk to her, calling her by name, but all the time thinking of her in terms of vital signs and body trauma, concentrating on the medical know-how that would deliver her safely from the scene of the accident to the handover at A and E.

Goodhew turned away and found himself face-to-face with DI Marks.

'How are they?' Marks asked.

Goodhew muttered a one-word reply, 'Alive,' and continued to walk away from the wreckage.

Marks followed him. 'They were facing certain death.'

Goodhew stopped in his tracks. 'I know, that's the logical way to see it, but that doesn't change the fact that their injuries were caused by me driving straight into them.'

'Not Stefan's most likely though. Kincaide said he seemed totally unresponsive before impact. It'll be interesting to see his post-mortem results.'

Goodhew changed subjects. 'Craig Tennison abducted all of them, he wanted it to look like Stefan had cracked and gone on a murderous death spree.'

'And if that locomotive *had* hit them, it could have been a very different story.'

Marks didn't need to elaborate: Goodhew was more than capable of picturing the carnage that would have resulted. He'd seen cars disappear under lorries, leaving nothing larger than a bonnet badge to identify the vehicle's make or model. He could still see the train bearing down on them, and now, in his mind's eye, it sliced through the helpless car, devouring its occupants. They remained mute, however, while his head filled with the scream of those futile brakes. Goodhew recognized it as a sound that would now stay with him for a lifetime.

'Gully's certain she saw Riley being put into the boot of a small red saloon. The rest of them were transferred into that Renault, which Craig Tennison then drove on to the track. I guess he must have dumped the van then.'

Marks nodded. 'I have the chopper searching for the van right now, within a two mile radius initially, then widening gradually.'

Goodhew frowned. 'That's over twelve square miles, but reduce the radius to a mile, and there's only three and a half square miles to cover. We have the best odds of finding it within that distance unless, of course, he's still driving it.'

'That would be too risky. He knows we're looking for it, and anyway he had the option of this other car.'

Goodhew studied his boss for a moment, then looked away, his gaze falling on the spray of sparks sent flying by the cutting equipment, as the firemen fought to dismantle the Renault.

IV bags hung alongside, their diminishing fluids glinted in the watery sunshine. Every person in his field of vision was working with purpose; he could see the medics trying to keep Gully and Kimberly stable while the fire crew worked towards releasing the two injured women and the body of Stefan Golinski. The scene was being recorded by police photographers, while other officers were collecting evidence and further back was a camera crew belonging to a news syndicate. He scanned the scene again, in every case each person's motivation was clear and drove each task they undertook.

For the first time, Goodhew began seeing a more complete picture of Craig Tennison. Nick Lewton, Rachel Golinski and Jay Andrews had all fallen victim to the same signature attack. Anita McVey, too, except that in her case he'd been too rushed or too distracted, and the fatal kick had been delivered inaccurately. None of these people had been strangers to him, but his method required the use of force without hesitation. No doubt, also, Jay and Nick had been far from the first.

Tennison was smart never to have been caught. Brute force alone was rarely the only skill involved when such crimes had gone undetected for so long, and yet he still appeared to be working for the Lewton family rather than breaking out on his own.

Goodhew began speaking before his thoughts had finished forming, but he felt sure they were making sense. 'If Tennison wanted to kill Riley, he would have left him in the car with the others. He's ruthless enough to do it. So now he's got a child on his hands, yet this isn't a random little boy but one belonging to his employer's family, so whatever he stands to gain by this is personal.'

'He's taking a huge risk, though. If he's caught with Riley, the game will be up.'

'Here's a better question, why put Riley in the boot? Even if he were strapped in a car seat in a state of distress, no one would have taken much notice of him because that photo most people have seen is one of Jay Andrews as a toddler, not Riley himself.'

Marks eyes narrowed. 'So what are you thinking?'

'By hiding Riley in the boot, there's no possibility whatsoever that we are likely to pinpoint where or when he was handed over.'

'OK,' Marks said slowly, 'now explain a little more because, right now, I haven't a clue what you're getting at.'

Goodhew nodded in the direction of the level crossing, 'Tennison's plan was for them all to die – I guess to make it seem as though Stefan had committed suicide and decided on taking Kimberly with him. Tennison would then be able to pretend he knew nothing, as long as he couldn't be placed anywhere near the Transit or its occupants. He could say that Stefan handed over Riley to him as the last decent act of a desperate man.'

'For that to work, Tennison needed to know for sure that both Stefan Golinski and Kimberly Guyver were dead.' Marks turned to survey a full 360-degree scan of the countryside. 'To be convincing, he would have called us at the earliest opportunity. He couldn't hang on to Riley a moment longer than necessary, so I wouldn't be surprised if he was parked somewhere nearby, watching for the collision. That means you scuppered his plan.'

'And now he doesn't know what to do with Riley?' Goodhew felt suddenly restless and took a couple of involuntary steps in the direction of the nearest patrol car. 'He must know we're on to him.'

'And he'll be panicking, but he doesn't yet know whether Gully or Kimberly will be in a fit state to be interviewed. Maybe that gives us an opportunity.'

Goodhew bit his lip thoughtfully. 'How up-to-date is the press?'

'They simply know there was an incident at the level crossing, with one fatality.'

'Why not announce that the others are seriously injured, and that the police are still waiting to interview them.'

Marks shook his head but didn't actually refuse. 'Or, better still, that there were no survivors.'

Goodhew was surprised to see that his boss was giving his idea serious consideration. This wasn't the kind of misinformation that could be smudged or glossed over later.

Marks' phone rang before he reached his final verdict. 'DI Marks,' he answered. 'Who?' then 'Really?'

Goodhew watched Marks' expression intently, wishing he could hear what the caller was saying, especially as whoever it was seemed to be speaking twenty words for each short phrase grunted by Marks in response.

'Where are they?'

Marks' eyes met Goodhew's, and his expression had brightened. 'What about . . .?' A half-smile flickered. 'Good . . . Excellent.'

Goodhew dug his hands into his pockets and did his best not to fidget.

Marks snapped his phone shut. 'Riley's safe.'

FORTY-SIX

As far as police activity was concerned, Parkside Station was as quiet as it could be. Most spaces in the car park were empty and the corridors were deserted. An ambulance had pulled into the closest available bay, its lights on and the doors open, but without a paramedic in sight.

Goodhew followed Marks to the farthest and most spacious of the interview rooms. It was kitted out with the usual Government-issue furniture but had also been equipped with a junior-sized table with matching chairs, two beanbags and a box of random toddler toys.

DC Charles was waiting just inside the door and, aside from him, there were five people in the room. A man in his late forties, who Goodhew recognized as Dr Gregor, was kneeling in front of a little boy who stood next to one of the children's chairs. Behind him a female paramedic was sitting on the floor. The boy had been crying and looked up at Goodhew and Marks as they entered the room. Then his face fell again.

Goodhew smiled, for beyond any shadow of a doubt this was Riley Guyver. Riley had only a vague physical likeness to his mother but his expression, as he glowered at the doctor, was totally Kimberly's.

Marks addressed Charles. 'Is he all right?'

Charles nodded. 'The doctor's checking him over, but no sign of any problems for the moment.'

'How about her?' The second paramedic sat alongside Tamsin Lewton at the full-sized table, and the resemblance between her and Riley was startling. She took no notice of any of the officers, but

267

continued talking quietly to the paramedic, with her gaze firmly fixed on her little nephew.

'Sir, I'm sorry if I've done the wrong thing, but I wasn't quite sure how to handle this. I thought maybe they should be held separately, but I wanted to keep Riley as calm as possible.'

Marks waved this concern aside. 'Least of our worries. What can she tell us?'

'Not much, I fear. Tennison borrowed her car earlier then returned it about an hour ago. Just after that she had a call from him, telling her to look in the boot. That's when she found Riley.'

'Where is Tennison now?'

'She says she doesn't know, but I didn't question her for long. I was more concerned with getting the little boy checked over.'

'Do we have a Child Welfare officer on the way?'

'Yes, sir.'

'Good. Find out how long until he or she arrives, also get me the latest update on the mother's condition. If she's conscious, she should be told that her son is safe, but no more than that. Oh, and is Miss Lewton a key holder for the Celeste?'

'No. That's in hand, though. I'm expecting a call back from one of the security staff at any minute.'

'Well, let me know as soon as.' Marks turned his attention to Goodhew. 'I need to speak to Dr Gregor and while I'm doing that, I want you to start questioning Tamsin Lewton. She can stay in here for now, but get shot of that ambulance crew.'

Tamsin wore jeans and a chunky sweater, and even in winter she should have found the room uncomfortably warm, but her shoulders were hunched as if freezing and, beneath her tan, the blood had drained from her face.

While the paramedics were leaving, Goodhew visited the drinks machine and returned with two teas. He slid into the chair opposite her, and she reached for the plastic cup before he even had a chance to set it down.

'I can't stop shivering.'

'It's shock.'

'I know.' She scowled at him. 'Of course I know that, but it doesn't make me any warmer, does it?'

'That's what the tea's for.'

She blew steam from her cup and took a couple of sips. 'Riley doesn't even know who I am.'

'He looks like you, though, doesn't he?'

'He looks like Nick. And Nick never even knew she was pregnant.' She shivered. 'I opened the boot and he was just lying there. What if I hadn't checked? He could have died in there, couldn't he?'

'Maybe.'

'What was Craig trying to do? He must have flipped or something.'

'How did he seem?'

'I don't know.' She shook her head. 'He posted the keys through the letterbox, but I heard them drop so I went to the door. He was already walking away, I called to him and he spun round, seemed agitated, said nothing until he was almost on top of me. He came right up close,' she raised the flat of her hand to her face, 'uncomfortably close like he was really angry. For a moment I felt threatened, but then he just thanked me for the use of the car, and he walked away.'

Tamsin stared beyond Goodhew, as though she was still watching Craig Tennison stride into the distance. She then swung her attention back to him, a small sad smile playing on her lips. 'He phoned a few minutes later and told me to look in the boot. I asked him why, but he just hung up.'

'It's vital we find him as quickly as possible.'

Marks was standing within earshot. He'd hovered in the same position for the last couple of minutes, facing Dr Gregor and Riley, but it was obvious that Goodhew's boss was currently tuned into Tamsin.

'I don't know where Craig went, I'm sorry. If I knew I'd say so, but I don't.' She ran her fingers through her hair, as if smoothing out a non-existent tangle. 'I don't understand any of this, and I've known Craig since I was just a kid. All I can think is that he's cracked up, and was getting his revenge on Stefan for Nick and Rachel . . .' Her voice trailed off.

Marks raised one eyebrow and gave Goodhew a small nod before

269

turning his back on them. It meant an OK to follow the conversation wherever it led.

'Tamsin,' Goodhew lowered his voice, which alone was enough to focus her attention, 'Craig Tennison is our main suspect for both those murders.'

She stiffened, and he thought he discerned a slight hardening in her expression. She said nothing, however, just spent what seemed like several minutes staring directly into his face. It felt like she was trying to read something deeper into his words, maybe to find a hidden truth lurking behind them or decide whether he was bluffing. Then she turned to look at Riley again and, without warning, her eyes welled with tears. 'I don't know anything about children,' she said finally. 'I thought two-year-olds were still babies. I'm sure they are in many ways, but when I first saw Riley he seemed terrified. Craig did that too.'

Riley was holding two Mega Bloks, one in each hand, but wasn't attempting to construct anything, just gripping them like two batons. Goodhew knew nothing about children either, but understood that this was a small but symbolic marking of territory.

She shook her head. 'This is going to stay with him always, even if he doesn't remember what happened. He's learnt more than he should know at his age, hasn't he?'

'Probably,' Goodhew conceded. He had no idea what children might learn in the years before they could articulate properly or reason fully, nevertheless he held the belief that some babies were born with character traits and knowledge already hard-wired into their brains. And, whatever else had happened, Riley was still Kimberly's son. Then he added, 'but I believe he'll be OK, especially once he's reunited with his mum.'

Tamsin pressed the back of an index finger to each eye, pushing back the tears. Her voice sounded thick with emotion: 'I can see that.'

'Tell me how you feel about Kimberly.'

'In what way?'

'She was your brother's girlfriend right up to the time of his disappearance, so it would have been natural for you to stay in touch with her once she returned to England, wouldn't it?'

270

The threat of tears vanished so fast that he wondered if there had been any genuine emotion behind them. The hard edge now returned to her voice. 'Nick's girlfriends were *his* business, some I liked, some I didn't. Kimberly lasted longer than most and, yes, we rubbed along well enough for a while. When she and Rachel first started work at the Rita Club, they both attracted plenty of attention, but they kept their work and partying quite separate. I assumed she'd be just another of Nick's one-week wonders, but it wasn't that long before she moved in with him. I doubt he'd suddenly discovered monogamy, but she hadn't either.'

'Meaning?'

'There was something about her that made me always suspect she was seeing other men.'

'Based on what?'

Tamsin grunted. 'You're a man, so you won't get it.'

'Try me.'

'She looks like that in the way she moves,' Tamsin curled up her nose, 'in her body language.'

'Because she's very attractive?'

'Right.' Tamsin waved away this observation. 'Put it this way, I wouldn't ever trust her around any boyfriend of mine.'

'I see, but apart from that suspicion you don't actually know that she was unfaithful to your brother?'

'She screwed her ex, isn't that enough?'

'Nick told you?'

'No, I could see what was going on, and I told him.'

'And how did he react?'

'Thrilled, how do you think? Probably would've beaten the crap out of her if he hadn't disappeared first. And I, for one, wouldn't have blamed him.'

'Wow, that's a really enlightened attitude to relationships.'

'It's *my* attitude, full stop. Why the fuck would I treat other people's relationships differently?'

Goodhew leant back in his chair.

He ran his finger tips along the plastic trim running round the edge of the table. Something flat and sharp had been used to gouge it, leaving it feeling gnawed. A little further to his right the moulding had been broken off, leaving a two-inch gap that exposed the chip-board cross-section of the table top. He would have guessed that, under its bland grey veneer, there was nothing more substantial in its construction than the compressed wood shavings, just as he would have assumed the missing piece of moulding had been identical to the surviving section.

Maybe it had been once, but another maybe was that it was so chewed and damaged by the time it broke away that it had been barely recognizable.

'So,' he said, 'you've known Craig since you were very young?'

She nodded.

'Has he always worked for your father?'

'For as long as I can remember, and he also moved out to Spain when we did.'

'What reason did he give you for borrowing your car?'

She shrugged. 'Said he needed it urgently. It's hired through the Celeste's business account, so there's no reason he shouldn't use it, I guess.'

'And you trusted him?'

Again she nodded.

'Until when?'

She looked puzzled. 'I'm sorry, I don't . . .'

Goodhew rewound. 'You didn't keep in touch with Kimberly when she left Spain? You didn't know she was pregnant, never mind giving birth, right?'

'Yes.'

'So learning that Nick has a son – that you therefore have a nephew – comes as a shock to you?'

'Of course.'

'But the family resemblance is unmissable, and as soon as you took a good look at Riley you would have known. And then you would have realized that Craig would have known too.'

She leant back in her chair then, mirroring his posture. She, however, didn't fiddle with the edge of the table; instead she steepled her fingers and seemed to be using their apex as a gunsight. Her expression suggested she was capable of doing damage with a single shot.

'Tamsin,' he kept his tone even, using the words alone to prod her along, 'for over two years he's been keeping that knowledge from you, denying you information that could have helped your family at the time they were dealing with the loss of their only son.'

She didn't react.

'He was harbouring a grudge for that entire time.'

'Not possible.'

'What if it is, though? What's his motive, then?'

Her gaze fell on to the desktop and seemed to settle on the cluster of mug stains just in front of her left elbow. She seemed as absorbed by them as he'd been by the damage on his side of the table.

He waited.

Her thoughts stretched out until he knew she was no longer even in the room. He waited some more, wondering where they had taken her, wondering whether she had a more vulnerable side to her nature, and whether she was prepared to visit it even on behalf of her brother.

Then, with nothing more than a quick double blink, she was back with him in the room. She mumbled something he didn't catch, the word or words blocked by her hands in front of her face. When he didn't reply, she slapped her hands, palms down, on to the table. 'I said "Money". Craig's been loyal to my dad but there's always been money involved too. And money's behind everything – it always is. After Nick went missing, we found a gaping hole in the accounts.'

'I read that in our notes, about three hundred thousand euros.'

'At least, but could be much more. If Nick had done a runner, he would have taken some cash. That was a possibility, he loved our family but not the responsibility of the club, and he'd taken off for a month or two in the past. But when his car was recovered and there was no sign of the money, it made me wonder . . .'

'What exactly?'

'Nick was sharp, and that much money would have taken months to siphon out of the club, so there wasn't much chance that he didn't know about it. I thought maybe he'd blown it on something, feeding a gambling habit – or drugs, maybe. He'd dabbled with both. But, even when we found out he'd been murdered, I never considered it was about that money.'

273

'And now?'

'I don't understand, why would Craig hurt Stefan and Rachel? And Nick was supposed to be his friend. But if I had to think of one motivation, I can see that money might be it.'

Her voice trailed off and was overtaken by the dour three-note ring tone sounding from Marks' mobile. A few seconds later he called Goodhew over.

'We've now found a key holder for the Celeste. I've asked Charles to come and take the statement from Tamsin Lewton. I want you to come with me.'

FORTY-SEVEN

It took just five minutes to reach the Celeste. Marks parked on the pavement nearest the club, then he and Goodhew walked side by side down Market Passage. The doors were unlocked but the building was quiet. A lone bouncer came to the top of the stairs as they were halfway up. Goodhew recognized him as one of the body-pierced doormen he'd seen on his previous visit.

'You the police then?' he demanded.

'Cambridge CID. We're looking for Craig Tennison.'

'Rob,' he introduced himself, shaking hands with both of them. 'Not in yet. Ironic' – he said it as if 'I' and 'ronic' were two separate words, 'I-ronic, the one day he's late is the day you lot decide you need to come in. I wasn't due here for another couple of hours.'

So Rob clearly hadn't been anywhere near a TV or radio for the last few hours.

'When would you be expecting him?' Marks asked.

'Any minute – he's usually in by now. Is there anything I can help with? And if Craig don't show up, the boss'll be here in a bit.'

Goodhew blinked. 'Dougie Lewton?'

'Yeah, coming from Spain, flight landing in about two hours. Obviously it'll take him a bit of time to get through Customs . . .' his voice trailed off, like he'd already said enough and couldn't be bothered to reach the end of the sentence.

Marks adopted his formal voice. 'Mr Tennison is wanted for questioning in relation to the murder of Rachel Golinski, as well as several other serious offences. We're currently searching his home

275

address, but do you know of any other locations that might be of interest to us?'

'Nope, don't know a thing about him outside work – except that he spends most of his time here. My missus would kill me if I clocked up the hours he does.'

'Can you find me Dougie Lewton's contact details?'

'I guess.' He turned back.

'We won't be opening tonight, will we?'

Marks shook his head. 'We have a team coming who will make a thorough search of the building, but right now we'd like to take a look at your CCTV footage for the last twenty-four hours.'

The doorman raised one studded eyebrow. 'Yeah, sure. It's in Craig's office. I'll take you through.' He paused, then added, 'I've worked here three years, so if there's anything else you want to know . . .'

'Thanks,' Goodhew replied, guessing that Rob was quietly thrilled to be swept up in the drama of a murder investigation.

Like most nightclubs Goodhew had ever visited out of hours, it looked run-down and grubby without the distraction of lights and noise and punters. They followed Rob up to Craig's key-coded door, where he punched in five digits and waited for the click of the locks releasing. There was no sound, however, but he pushed at the door in any case, before trying the same number two more times. 'That's a bit odd,' he muttered, and ran his eyes around the door frame, as though he expected to find the answer there.

'Can it be overridden?' Marks asked.

Rob shrugged. 'I guess. You want me to try?'

'As quickly as possible, please.'

Rob shrugged again, stepped back, then with a single kick sent a foot-sized panel of the door flying through into the office on the other side. He reached through the hole and released the lock. 'That's called manual override,' he grinned. His expression transformed as the door swung open. 'Holy shit,' he breathed.

Craig Tennison's body hung from one of the air-con pipes by an extension cable. A chair lay on its back, near his feet. The ceiling had never been high enough to guarantee an instant death, and in his last moment he had fought against the cable, the first two fingers of his left hand still trapped between the knot and the skin of his neck.

His trousers were urine-soaked and dripping on to the hard floor.

Goodhew stepped forward and checked him for any slim chance of life.

Nothing.

Rob remained silent, his feet anchored but his body swaying ever so slightly. Goodhew persuaded him to go out of the room and sit down somewhere. Rob made it through the doorway, then slid on to the carpet, slumping heavily against the nearest wall. He glanced back in the direction of Tennison's office, turned pale and tucked his head between his knees.

A folded note lay on the nearest upright chair. It was handwritten, using a black marker pen, so the ink had bled through to the reverse. Neither of them touched it, but deciphered what they could through the back of the page.

It's all gone wrong. There's nothing left.

There was more, folded out of sight.

'Suicide?' Goodhew pondered aloud.

'Maybe. But I'm not convinced.'

Marks and Goodhew stood side by side, staring silently at the body. Goodhew had no idea what Marks was thinking, but then he rarely did. For his own part, he realized how little they knew about Craig Tennison. He had no criminal record and, apart from that, they knew nothing of his private life. Maybe Rob the doorman was right, and there wasn't much for him aside from the Celeste. Tennison was wearing a club T-shirt at the time he died, having chosen a fit that stretched slightly across his chest and his biceps. Now that his body had slackened, he just looked overweight and middle-aged, but Goodhew knew this man had possessed the strength and bulk to kick the life out of several victims.

And developing a lethal technique like that hadn't come overnight. Who knew how many others had fallen victim to his violence in the years preceding his assault on Jay Andrews? Keeping himself out of suspicion all that time had undoubtedly required ingenuity too.

Marks began making phone calls and Goodhew turned towards the computer. 'I'd still like to check the security footage.'

Marks scanned the desk. 'Go ahead.'

The PC was on stand-by, and burst back into life almost immediately. The software controlling the cameras had been left open on the screen, with a separate window for each of the six devices employed, currently displaying a live feed of key locations around the building. Goodhew clicked on the one labelled *Back Door*, which showed the rear of the Celeste Club and a small yard with sufficient parking space for two cars.

'This one's not recording.' He tried one of the other CCTV feeds. 'In fact they're all off.'

Marks leant closer. 'Since when?'

'Nothing for the last forty-eight hours.'

Goodhew checked for the obvious, calling up lists of files deleted in the last two days, and searching for any others created or modified during that time too. He found nothing.

'We shouldn't be surprised,' Marks remarked. 'He didn't remain free all these years by leaving a trail of evidence.'

'Or by getting grassed up.' Goodhew stared down at the keyboard, and found himself thinking about something Tamsin had said. In fact it was just about the last thing she'd said to him, but definitely the most useful: *Why would he hurt Stefan and Rachel?*

FORTY-EIGHT

Kimberly lay on her back, her body straight with her ankles touching and her hands resting at her sides. She realized, as she regained consciousness, that she was in a hospital bed. She'd arrived there by stretcher and had barely moved a muscle since. Her sleep had been heavy, so she had no idea how much time had passed. She remembered she'd been drugged and her body still felt reluctant, tempting her to drift off again, but at least nothing seemed to hurt.

She thought of Riley, then. Had someone really told her that he was safe – or had that only been a dream too?

She wondered whether she'd now open her eyes and discover that she'd missed days rather than hours. The thought scared her for reasons she didn't totally understand, but it made it illogical to hide herself away in sleep any longer.

There were three other spaces on the ward but none were occupied and even the area around her own bed was devoid of any personal effects – no clothes draped over the nearby chair, the bedside locker empty and no flowers or get well messages on top of it. She hoped the absence of the latter items meant she was still a new arrival. Someone had left a jug of water and a half-filled clear plastic tumbler next to her bed. She took a sip but the water tasted stale and nowhere near as refreshing as the business card she suddenly spotted protruding from under the jug.

A phone rang at the nurses' station. The voice that picked up and answered was warm but firm. 'Miss Guyver? No, not yet.'

'I'm awake,' Kimberly called out. 'Hello?'

'Hold on.' The nurse brought the handset into the room, but hesitated before handing it over. 'I can just give them a message if you like?'

'No, no,' Kimberly began struggling up on to one elbow.

'Careful, you've had quite a knock and some nasty bruising.'

Kimberly smiled ruefully. 'I'm just finding that out.' She made it as far as a half-sitting position, and waited while the nurse jammed an extra pillow behind her spine. 'OK,' she nodded, and held her hand out for the phone. 'Who is it?' she mouthed to the nurse first.

The nurse beamed. 'Your boyfriend, Jay.'

There was a certain look that appeared on Goodhew's face when his thoughts were interlacing and combining and percolating. Marks had seen it before on only a couple of occasions, but recognized that the end product would be worth waiting for.

The first officers were arriving, so he turned away to deal with them. When he looked back across the interview room Goodhew had gone.

PC Bell came over. 'Are you looking for Goodhew? He was at the top of the stairs when we arrived, talking on the phone and pacing around. But he said to tell you two things.' Bell held up two fingers and bent each back in turn. 'Firstly he reckons there's no chance that this is suicide and, secondly, he was going to the cemetery. Then he shot off like a rocket . . . you know, like he does.'

Marks pursed his lips together and chose to say nothing. Even the next moment, when he received a call to say that Kimberly Guyver had absconded from her hospital bed, he had nothing else to add.

Of course it hadn't been Jay on the phone but the call still gave Kimberly the incentive to find a quiet moment in which to slip in and out of the adjoining ward, successfully raiding it for clothes, cash and a mobile phone. She felt no guilt although she hated any kind of debt. But it was the need to clear a greater debt that played on her conscience, and now made her leave the building. She guessed she could have met him on the ward, but she didn't want nurses telling her when she was allowed a conversation, and for how long. And she didn't think they would have been happy to let her out of her bed to make her way along to the patients' lounge.

She'd had her fill of official authority over the last few days. She was grateful for it, too, but it would be better when she could leave this chapter of her life behind.

It was 1 a.m. but she felt like she was finally stepping into the daylight. Her whole body ached and she was forced to walk slowly as she left Addenbrooke's Hospital main building and crossed to the taxi rank. She wore only the clothes she'd snatched – just jeans and a jumper, with nothing else underneath. The night air tickled her bare skin and made her shiver.

She sat in the front, next to the driver, and asked him if he minded turning up the heater. The hot air poured out immediately, leaving her feeling no better, so she put it down to exhaustion. Then, a few minutes later, she began to wonder whether it was due to shock or her injuries. Her head began to pound, she touched her scalp and winced as, for the first time, she realized the skin was held by a thick welt of stitches.

She was still shivering as they turned into Mill Road, and by then she realized that she was scared. She assured herself that she had nothing to fear any more, that she was there with her olive branch, and only paving the way to a better future.

She wished she could have arranged to meet somewhere else, but where else wasn't deserted at this time? In any case, the cemetery had never scared her before. Hadn't it always felt like her home ground?

She slid her hand into her front pocket to pull out a stolen twenty-pound note. Her fingers found the business card first, then she delved deeper and retrieved the money at the same time.

The card was a standard size, and blank apart from the mobile number scribbled across it in biro. She couldn't remember how it came to be on her bedside table or if he'd given it to her, or even if she'd seen him write it, but she'd instantly known that it came from DC Goodhew. She guessed he'd now be asleep, or too far away to come, but, for the first time since leaving Addenbrooke's, the shivering stopped.

He answered almost instantly, and she told him where to find her and hung up before he tried to ask her what she was doing there.

Now she was inside the graveyard, and waiting at the grave of 3192 Shoeing Smith T. Smith of the Suffolk Yeomanry. The grave was white marble and lay just a few feet from the circular footpath at the very centre of the cemetery. On any clear night it glowed like the moon, making it easy to find. She knew, without reading the inscription, that he'd died on 30th November 1914 at the age of 37.

In the past she had felt sadder for him than for the younger casualties, figuring that he'd been old enough to understand what he had to lose. Now she realized it wasn't just about age, but how much value you put on your life. The voice in her head that kept her reckless was unexpectedly still.

She tried to remind herself that there was nothing to fear, and told herself to rehearse what she needed to say. Then, behind her, she heard the heavy tread of a man approaching.

She felt her legs turn leaden and the shivering return. The last thing she would remember was the night becoming blacker and the warm trickle of blood as it spread across her scalp.

Goodhew took Marks' car and sped away, though he doubted he could make it there in under five minutes. He radioed in immediately but the station was close to Mill Road and he doubted there was anyone else who could get there faster.

He tried the mobile Kimberly had used to ring him, but she still didn't reply.

When she'd first rung he'd imagined her still on a ward at Addenbrooke's, connected up to a gadget or two, and groggy maybe from sedation. He'd listened to a few seconds of her apologizing for bothering him, *I know I'm wasting your time* and *I know I'm safe now, but* . . . then she told him where she was going. She had a head injury, it wasn't even safe for her to be out of bed. He wished he could have shouted at her the moment she said she'd left the hospital; instead she hung up, never giving him enough time to tell her he knew who she was meeting and how much danger she was in.

He drove up Mill Road and as close as possible to the cemetery entrance, then jumped out of the vehicle and ran in through the gates. He could just pick out the line of the footpath, but stayed on the grass next to it and moved silently towards the centre circle.

There were trees and shrubs to skirt, and he was edging round what surely must be the last clump when he heard an abrupt movement. He crept to one side of the nearest tree and bent down to get a view beyond its low-hanging branches. No one was visible from that angle, but he could pick out a small rustling sound, so he inched towards it. He was only a couple of yards from the clearing, when it stopped. The stillness triggered him to action: he ducked under the final branches and into the open.

A fox stared back at him, its muzzle bloodied, a dead rabbit at its feet.

Goodhew realized then that there was still another clump of trees between him and where he needed to be. And from the other side came a voice, a flash of torchlight, and the first half of a rapidly smothered scream.

Goodhew ran.

Kimberly regained consciousness. She wasn't in the hospital now but somewhere cold and damp. The cemetery. She remembered the blood too and winced as she touched her scalp. A clump of her hair was missing around the stitches and they were coming apart, but that didn't bother her as much as she thought it might. It would be OK, and it would heal.

She guessed she'd passed out and wondered whether she'd missed him. She thought he'd wait for her, then she thought DC Goodhew would have come too, but there was now no sign of either of them. The nearest headstone felt solid enough, so she gripped it and pulled herself upright. She picked out the shape of a nearby grave; Father Daniel lay there, buried in 1921. There was an empty space on his headstone as though he hadn't expected to remain alone. Kimberly knew this grave and that was when she realized she'd wandered away from the centre.

A moment later she spotted him, standing about thirty feet away. He wore jeans and white trainers, and he stood still for several seconds before he turned through 180 degrees, then did the same in the opposite direction. He called out her name, his voice soft, with no anger in it. Perhaps he already knew the truth, so perhaps there would be no awkward moment before she told him. Simply the embrace of forgiveness.

'Kim,' he repeated.

'Over here,' she responded.

He moved in her general direction. 'Where are you?'

'Here.' She raised one hand, still gripping the headstone with the other.

He still hadn't picked out her exact location, and stopped, his white trainers planted squarely. Suddenly his tone changed. 'Are you fucking with me, Kimberly?'

She released her grip and slid down on to the grass. It wasn't because of the swear word he used, since he swore all the time, like other people would use a noun or a verb. It was the use of her full name that rattled her, something she'd picked up on just weeks after they'd met. He continually used nicknames or abbreviations when he spoke to you and that was fine, but when he was talking to you and started using your full name, it meant you were in the shit.

Deep fucking shit.

Dougie Lewton only used full names before sackings or when dishing out beatings. He used them when he was angered beyond reason, and when his mind was set on wiping out anyone who dared oppose him.

And, of all the graves in the cemetery, she was hiding behind one of the smallest. She kept totally still with her face and hands concealed behind the stone. The rest of her clothes were dark but she knew it was just a matter of time before he found her.

Think.

Think.

Think!

'I never killed Nick,' she yelled. 'Craig did it, but I didn't know until yesterday.'

A torch flashed close to her, illuminating Father Daniel's stone first, then swinging towards the one next to hers. The beam seemed to intensify even as it closed in. Then he was on her, and she tried to shout out, but the scream was knocked from her lungs.

He pinned her down, his sheer bulk preventing even her hands from moving. 'You thought you'd stabbed him to death, though, didn't you?'

She nodded silently.

'And Stefan and Rachel helped you dump his body. Then you didn't even know whose kid you were pregnant with. And you had Nick's baby, and kept Riley from us.' He pushed his face close to hers, his breath hot and damp as he hissed her name. 'Kimberly, you should have died under that train.'

He glanced over his shoulder, and she instantly knew what he was planning.

'You'll get caught,' she gasped.

He shook his head and a moment later hauled her to her feet, then almost immediately threw her to the ground at the foot of a tall, weathered headstone. He pressed his foot on to her chest and began to rock the stone. She knew it wouldn't take long for him to topple it. Fragments of stone started peppering her face, confirming the trajectory the whole monument would follow.

'I will, you see, because I have a fucking alibi,' he announced, as the tombstone began to visibly sway.

The next moment was a blur. The dust was stinging her eyes, making her blink. It seemed like a dark shadow had passed over her, springing from nowhere and flying in a low arc, finally demolishing the grave and taking Dougie Lewton down too.

There was a terrible silence, then she wiped her eyes clear. And saw DC Goodhew now quietly cuffing her winded attacker.

'Fucking useless alibi, Douglas,' she muttered as she watched Goodhew read him his rights.

The single-engined plane touched down on a private airstrip in Norfolk. It taxied to the end of the runway but waited only ten minutes. The pilot knew by then that the plan to swap places was done for. And, without an alibi to put him in the air over another country, Dougie Lewton was done for too. The pilot knew when it was best to keep a distance, so he took off again and set a course for Europe.

EPILOGUE

One Month Later

The email had started tentatively, and ended with a jokey comment followed by a couple of exclamation marks. But ultimately it was only the sentence in the middle that counted for much.

I've handed in my notice and I wanted you to hear it from me first.

He had found it in his in-box the morning after Dougie's arrest, and now, four weeks and two days later, it was time for a final round of after-work drinks.

Mickey Flynn's American Pool Hall stood halfway down Mill Road, in a modern, purpose-built club that looked like a sports hall from the outside. Beyond the exertion of a walk to the bar and back, there wasn't much about the interior that hinted at any connection with physical fitness. Activity was split between a cluster of poker tables and an L-shaped arrangement of pool tables running alongside two adjoining walls.

Their party of eleven included three detectives and two PCs. It was an unusual place to have leaving drinks and, judging by the looks of recognition that greeted them, a number of the regulars agreed. But, after the first round, they grouped themselves round a couple of the pool tables, and forgot about everyone else.

Bryn and Goodhew's grandmother were playing doubles against Mel and Aaron Young, while Goodhew himself pulled up a chair next to Sue Gully. She was wearing a baggy T-shirt over a pair of belted men's jeans, claiming that any tighter garments were still uncomfortable. Her right arm remained in a plaster cast and sling.

'Not playing then?' he asked her.

'Not funny.' She raised her plaster cast a couple of inches. 'Mind you, once this thing's off, you'd better watch out.' She nodded towards Bryn and Goodhew's grandmother. 'How come Mel invited them?'

'She met my Gran at some gigs, and they just hit it off. And Bryn's just being nosy, said he wanted to meet Mel before she left Cambridge.'

Gully rolled her eyes in mock exasperation. 'I suppose he's into redheads today?'

Goodhew screwed up his nose. 'Every day, I expect, but I think Mel's safe.' They fell into an easy silence, just as they had on the several occasions when Goodhew had visited Gully in hospital. Now he used the moment to reflect how quickly their friendship had grown during that time, and how easy it was to chat to her openly about everything – from the crash on the level crossing to his letting go of his feelings towards Mel.

Sue gave him a quick jab in the side. 'Pack it in.'

'What?'

'You're doing that reflective thing again.'

'I was not.'

'Bloody were, I can see it in your face. I never thought I'd be telling a bloke to lose touch with his feminine side.'

'You're a pain in the arse, Sue Gully.'

'Just go over and talk to her.'

Goodhew shook his head. 'I already did and it's all fine.'

'What did she say?'

He gave a small smile and shrugged. 'Trust me, it's all fine.'

Gully smiled too. 'She knocked it on the head with boyfriend Toby *and* Kincaide, right?'

He didn't plan on being drawn further. 'Whatever you say.'

'D'you happen to know why we were all invited *here*?'

Goodhew shook his head. 'I never asked.'

'Mel told me how she used to wait in for Toby to return home, and quite often he'd come back drunk, angry and skint after a night

287

out. Apparently this was his favourite drinking hole, but he started a fight in here a couple of weeks back and he's been barred. Mel likes being able to come here when he can't.' Gully paused to sip her drink. 'As for Kincaide, she told him she's looking forward to concentrating on her music degree without the distraction of a relationship. His response was to ask her if she was a lesbian.'

'That figures.'

'So was it the same sort of conversation she had with you?'

'Yes and no, you tell it with a bit more drama, and she's definitely very excited about going to uni.'

He hoped leaving Cambridge would put enough miles between Mel and Toby to help keep their split permanent. He glanced at his watch, decided it was time he went, and began looking towards the exit.

'She's coming over now.' For no apparent reason, Gully blushed. 'You always treated her with respect and she appreciates that.'

Mel wrapped her arms around his neck and hugged him. 'You're off then?'

'I seem to be easy to read today.'

'No, Bryn told me you had to go. I hope you weren't leaving without a proper goodbye.'

He squeezed her tighter for a moment. ''Course not.'

They let go at the same instant. She studied his face for a few seconds, then grinned. 'I'm glad we got through whatever never happened without any bad feeling.'

'Me, too. Let me know how it goes.'

She nodded. 'You, too.' She gestured to the furthest pool table, where Bryn and Goodhew's grandmother were now playing singles. 'You'd better not leave without saying goodnight to them either but, be warned, your grandmother took loads of photos of classic cars when she was out in Cuba. That's all they're talking about now. I mean, what the hell is an Edsel?'

He checked his watch again, decided there was time to spare. He didn't know a Fairlaine from a Bel-Air either, but he picked up a cue and joined the pair of them at their table.

Leaving Mickey Flynn's reminded Goodhew of being a kid and leaving the cinema after a teatime film. With no windows and no noise penetrating from outside, it was easy to lose track of the passage of time. The day had moved from the end of a hot afternoon to the approach of nightfall. The streets were still full but everyone seemed to have shifted down a gear. He turned into Gwydir Street and headed along to the Cambridge Blue. The pub was busy but he queued for two glasses of Coke, and was served almost immediately. He carried on through, to find Kimberly waiting for him in the beer garden.

She took her glass and placed it straight on to the table. 'Come with me,' she said, and he followed her to the rear of the garden and over the wall into Mill Road Cemetery. She picked her way through the long grass until she reached the path, then proceeded up the neck of the guitar until they were approximately halfway between her house and what was left of Rachel's. She chose a large toppled headstone and sat at one end of it, facing her own back wall. A light glowed in the bedroom window.

He sat down next to her.

'How's Anita?'

'We're much the same, bruised and battered but glad to be alive.' The words seemed to come a little too easily, and Kimberly looked away, as if giving them some more thought. 'Her facial scars will be very noticeable, I think.' Her voice was quiet, and sounded less guarded now. 'She'll need to have cosmetic surgery. She's renting out Viva Cottage for now, and moving in with me. We're sticking very close, at least for the time being.' She tipped her head in the direction of her house. 'She's upstairs there now, keeping an eye out for me, probably.'

'And Riley?'

'He's great, but he witnessed Anita being attacked and he's now having some help from a psychotherapist who specialises in dealing with child trauma.'

'And you're OK with that?'

'God, I've learnt so much these last few weeks, and if Riley needs something, I'm not going to let my stupid hang-ups stand in the way. Well, not all of them, anyway. I'm not prepared for him to have contact with the Lewton clan.'

'See how you feel after the trial?'

'Maybe. Nick's mum maybe, but Tamsin . . .'

Goodhew couldn't help but agree. 'Oh.' He suddenly remembered the piece of paper in his back pocket. 'I have something here for Mikey.' He unfolded it slowly. 'Mikey's been looking for his brother . . .'

'You found him?'

'Not exactly, but he was cautioned by the police a couple of months ago,' he handed her the notepaper, 'and that's his last known address. It's a hostel in London, and it's OK to leave a message for him there, just in case he comes back.'

'Thanks.' Kimberly refolded the page into a neat rectangle, then turned it over a couple of times. 'Life's full of unknowns, Gary, and you and I . . . you're dependable, careful and . . . more . . . everything I thought I'd never admire in someone.' She reached towards his face and pressed the flat of her palm against his cheek.

Sure, looks weren't everything, but he now swore he was gazing at the most stunning woman he'd ever encountered. He drew a breath, wanting to tell her how nothing could happen for them but equally not believing for a moment that she had any interest.

But she spoke first. 'It wouldn't work between us, would it?'

He shook his head. 'No.'

'I love Jay – always will – and I need him, not the other way around. Well, maybe he *does* need me, but it's him that keeps me steady. I guess I will have other relationships, but it would have to be something special, and even then I will never give up on him. Never.'

'That's good.'

'That's the only thing I know about the future. I never look too far forward, because it scares me.' She gazed at him hard. 'You don't live just for today, do you?'

Goodhew heard himself start to disagree.

'Gary, you never want to make mistakes, so you hold back. Do you even have a girlfriend?'

'Not right now, no.'

'Is there anyone that interests you?'

He hesitated.

'Shouldn't I ask that?'

'No, actually, it's fine.' Goodhew stared into his hands for a minute or two, then back at Kimberly. 'I had a girlfriend, called Claire . . . we split up after uni and I didn't think I'd see her again. But now she's here in Cambridge, working at an architect's office.'

'Have you talked to her?'

'No, but I followed her once and I've driven past her office window a couple of times. I don't now if it's wrong to try to go back.' As he spoke, he realized the poignancy of his words.

'Personally, I'd love the chance.'

'Sorry.'

'Look, I'm no advert for making good decisions, but being too much like you is no better than being too much like me. You drove straight into the path of a train, for God's sake, so how hard can it be to ask her out, if that's what you really want to do?'

He didn't have an answer for that one.

'OK,' she said finally, 'but I have something for you. Follow me.' She led him towards the back wall of her garden.

'So why were you asking me all that personal stuff?'

She kept moving but spun round, so she was now walking backwards. Her eyes were dancing with mischief. 'Because I want you to kiss me, Gary Goodhew. Just once, and just for the hell of it.'

He returned her smile and shook his head.

There was something lying on the flat roof at the rear of the house. She scrambled up on to the garden wall, then jumped across the narrow gap onto the roof to pick it up. It was a rectangular package which measured about three feet by four, and was wrapped in brown paper.

'It's that picture,' she explained.

'The girl on the punt?'

'Yep, just a print, though. I'd have given you the original, but Mule sold it. Sorry.'

Whether he ever saw her again or not, Goodhew realized this would always be the moment he'd remember most clearly: beautiful Kimberly, brave but vulnerable, proud but wild, talented and loyal and giving.

He made the leap across to the flat roof, landing almost next to her. Her lips were soft against his. They wrapped their arms around each other, and clung together until the rest of Cambridge dissolved into the fading light.

Marks had been working late into the evening and was still seated at his desk as he spotted Goodhew crossing Parker's Piece. Observing Goodhew had become a little bit of an obsession lately, and now he was seeing him from more or less the same height and angle as when he'd watched him swimming.

But, since then, his perspective had changed and he'd learnt a great deal more about his youngest detective. For one thing, to be more careful about what he did with his filing-cabinet key . . .

Marks slid a couple of newly typed sheets of A4 into the file marked GOODHEW, and returned it to his desk drawer. Just like Goodhew himself, those pages held a whole lot more than anyone might have expected.

Marks watched Goodhew climb the steps to the front door, and could not help wondering where it was all going to end.

Goodhew walked home alone, with the picture tucked under one arm. After their embrace was over, he and Kimberly hadn't spoken another word. She'd disappeared through her bedroom window and he'd slipped back over the garden wall, both knowing that their moment on the roof had been the start and the end of it.

Once home, he switched on the jukebox and let it randomly choose what to play. *The Girl on the Punt* had caught his attention from the very first moment he'd noticed it.

Pre-Bryn, pre-Kimberly, pre-Mel even.

He slid the package under the settee, without unwrapping it, then sat on the floor with his back against the speaker grille, and gazed up at the print's original hanging on the opposite wall.

THE SOUNDTRACK FOR
THE SIREN

When I write a book I find there are songs that 'keep me company' at various points. By the time I finish I have a playlist that belongs to that book alone. Maybe the concept of a book having a soundtrack seems a little odd, but that's how it works for me.

Hey Girl – Hot Boogie Chillun

I Drove All Night – Roy Orbison

Ice Cold – Restless

In the Still of the Night – The Five Satins

Nobody But You, Babe – Hot Boogie Chillun

Rampage – The Planet Rockers

Send Me Away – Jacen Bruce

The Sun Refuses to Shine – Richard Hawley

The Thrill of Your Touch – Elvis

The Whole of the Moon – The Waterboys

Tonight the Streets Are Ours – Richard Hawley

Valentine – Richard Hawley

For more information please visit www.alisonbruce.com